John L Hewitt

Inspiration and Other Discourses

John L Hewitt

Inspiration and Other Discourses

ISBN/EAN: 9783337182540

Printed in Europe, USA, Canada, Australia, Japan

Cover: Foto ©Andreas Hilbeck / pixelio.de

More available books at **www.hansebooks.com**

AND OTHER

DISCOURSES,

BY

REV. JOHN. L. HEWITT, A. M.,

OF THE

WISCONSIN CONFERENCE.

PASTOR OF

FIRST M. E. CHURCH,

BEAVER DAM.

————————

JANESVILLE, WISCONSIN:

RECORDER PRINTING COMPANY, PRINTERS.

1883.

TO

MY FRIEND

AND SPIRITUAL FATHER,

UNDER WHOSE FAITHFUL MINISTRY

I BECAME A CHRISTIAN,

AND A MINISTER,

REV. P. S. BENNETT, A. M.,

THIS

HUMBLE BOOK

IS

AFFECTIONATELY DEDICATED.

PREFACE.

Having been frequently invited, by different persons, in various places, to give some of my pulpit thought to the press, I at length, with unaffected diffidence, yield to their persuasions and present this volume of sermonic literature, hoping that, as some of the thought herein embodied did when spoken accomplish good, so in book form, it will, at least, do no harm.

It is possible that some of those three thousand people, or more, who have composed my congregations during the last seventeen years, will read and recognize these discourses; nothing could add more to my happiness than to know that they recognize them as old friends, whose love was sincere, and whose utterances were intended for good, though imperfect. The author is not blind to their imperfections, and he earnestly requests his friends to quicken these old embers with the breath of prayer.

> " The vows
> Of God are on me, and I may not stop
> To play with shadows, or pluck earthly flowers,
> Till I my work have done, and rendered up
> Account."

JOHN L. HEWITT.

TABLE OF CONTENTS.

Mount of Inspiration - - - - - - - 1
Groans and Glory, - - - - - - - 15
Gospel Remedy for a Troubled Heart, - - - - 27
The Lord's Witnesses, - - - - - - - 43
Christian Example, - - - - - - - - 57
The Buried Talent, - - - - - - - 69
Parable of the Leaven, - - - - - - - 85
The Irreproachable Gospel, - - - - - - 103
The Pillars of Our Faith, - - - - - - - 119
The Standard of Right, - - - - - - - 140
Profit of Godliness, - - - - - - - 156
Strength, - - - - - - - - - 173
The Wonderful Works of God, - - - - 190
Short Beds and Narrow Coverlets, - - - - 209
The Bread of Life, - - - - - - - 230
The Christless World, - - - - - - - 248
The Mouth of the Wicked, - - - - - - 268
The Resurrection Body, - - - - - - 283

THE MOUNT OF INSPIRATION.

See, saith he, *that* thou make all things according to the pattern shewed to thee in the mount.—*Heb.* 8. 5.

The historic parts of the Holy Scriptures might be said to be a record of remarkable events; but profane history is as mysterious as sacred; the present is as strange as was the past: history repeats itself: marvels of Providence are perpetually recurring. The Aztec civilization is wonderful to us, and certainly ours as now it is would be strange to them could they behold it. Washington and Franklin, were they to become "Rip Van Winkles", could scarcely believe their own eyes, so great have been the changes of a century. Only the present is real, the past and the future are mythical, "distance lends enchantment to the view."

The Hebrew exodus from Egyptian bondage, and the settlement of an empire of slaves under a government of their own, free from the shakles of the bondman, is more than equaled by a similar emancipation of a far greater number of serfs and slaves during the last forty years.

The supply of "manna" that fell from Heaven around the tents of Israel, finds its antitype in the present age; to-day, food does not descend the sky, nor is it carried to us on downy wing, yet, the hungry are fed, the supply is always at hand, the plenty of to-day covers the needs of to-morrow, and it does not seem to us that the supply is miraculous. As those old Hebrews were more inquisitive to know what kind of stuff that "manna" was, than whence it came, so we investigate the nature of things, far more earnestly than we do the source from whence they come.

If those Jews had seen steamships ploughing the sea, and long trains of cars drawn by iron horses over the desests, the valleys and the mountains; if each were burdened with bread; or, had they heard the click of the telegraph telling them that the world were rushing to the rescue; then had they seen their warehouses bursting with abundance, the result of Christian sympathy; it would have been as wonderful to them as the manna that fell every night from the cloud. Whether, therefore, fallen from Heaven, or conjured and manipulated by science, or flowing from plethoric granaries, God is in it, it is one of the methods by which Providence interposes himself.

One of the most singular histories recorded in Scripture is that of the sacred Mount Sinai; those strange phenomena that appear to many incredible, and were fearfully awful to the Israelites are repeated to-day. That burning mountain has its model in modern history; its quaking, rocking, smoking, thundering can be accounted for by natural causes; it stands amid dessolate surroundings, many a terrific convulsion must there have taken place; possibly on the recurrence of one of these the law was given. That burning mountain may not be more significant than other shuddering volcanoes; there is a moral law in each of them, equally so as between Vesuvius, Pompeii and the nineteenth century, as between Horeb, the Hebrew and the modern Gentile; smoking Sinai is at least not any more strange and suggestive than a burning world, a sun seen, even in our day, to consume away in the Heavens. Indeed, if each of us were a Moses some glorious inspiration would come to us, both out of the peace and out of the storm.

There is a Sinai in life for each to ascend; there are bounds in individual history that are too sacred for the multitude to touch; God is near though his pavilion be a cloud; consider therefore

I. THE MOUNT OF INSPIRATION.

" A French writer, it is said, passed an entire night in the cathedral of Notre Dame, for the purpose of inspiration. The confessor moved down the aisle, the lingering incense at length vanished on fragrant wing; evening shadows lengthened, darkness lent its subduing power; the moon shone through the stained windows; shadows softly crept up the altar stairs, touched the dreamer and passed away, as though they were spirits that had slipped from the vaults beneath; before the dreamer's fancy an emperor was crowned, bridle robes rustled by the railing, a funeral procession bearing bier and pall moved slowly forward, and, when the midnight bells were ringing, groined arches, stately columns, and the long nave and transept throwing back the echo, it seemed as though the dumb dead had found a voice and filled the cathedral with upbraidings and blessings;"—a strange wierd solitude in a grand old sanctuary simply to inspire a fiction. But so each one of us must be alone sometimes, each must ascend the Mount of Inspiration; and, according to our purpose, according to the nature and peculiar impressiveness of our minds, we shall secure the inspiration that we seek.

To the skeptical spirit of the age inspiration is superstition; the world of humanity is an opaque body and in all the universe there is not a ray divine to fall upon or be reflected from it, it gropes in the dust and moves eternally in the same rut. Nor can it be expected that one who persuades himself that he has no soul, that he is nothing but a roll of organic mud, kneaded by an evolution of circumstances into a brief intellectual self-hood. and destined soon to be dissolved into the inorganic—that he will be able to discover truth or beauty in the thought of inspiration.

To the unprejudiced observer however, the man who is not overwhelmed by some pet opinion of his own, even matter is seen to be under the influence of some subtle inspiration. The very rocks and stones are in an unconscious struggle to rise from their graves into the light of day; inert bodies rush into chemical wedlock, and unskilled atoms crystalize into beautiful forms, the very plant springs upward from the soil, and the flower aspires to pursue the sun in its celestial flight; an uplifting life has breathed power into all things.

Scientists confronting mystery, as when " the undulating wave is transmuted into a sensation of sound", or a molecular motion is metamorphosed into a feeling of pain, or sorrow, or joy, are not only astonished, but stand on the very verge of the realm, the unknown, which is to them a perpetual inspiration. Tyndal says, " the translation of the shock of the etherial wave into consciousness eludes the analysis of my science", yet he aspires to analize it. " I never expect to know anything," says Mr. Huxley, "concerning the steps by which a molecular movement passes into a state of consciousness," yet he is in endeavor to make the discovery; the unknown is a mount of inspiration to the scientist.

That which leads the scientist on to discovery and opens to him the everlasting gates of Truth, is the angel of inspiration; or the bow of promise with which God has crowned the future and without which all progression would cease.　It touched the alchemist and brought the human mind into the magic and marvelous realm of modern chemistry.　It touched the astrologer and lifted him into the universe of order and beauty where the astronomer counts worlds by millions, and watches them in their majestic march.　Indeed, the materialist might declare, as the Greeks did of the symbolic Psyche " my soul has wings", I am furnished for a loftier world and a nobler destiny.

Nor can it be doubted that inspiration more or less full, at least occasionally, is the experience and privilege of all men.　When Newton beheld, in the purple depths of the starry concave the splendors of the Almighty; when Kant heard the divine voice within him; when Plato felt an assimilation to the Eternal; when the self-hood of the Pantheist is for a moment lost in the infinite grandeur about him; when the seaman is overwhelmed with a thought of vastness, and the mountain shepherd with a grateful conception of peace and lovliness; when the Feegian fears the thunder and the lightning, or the African fancies that a supernatural being is enshrined in a fetich; yea, when the soul in any sense communes with God, or thought rises into a realm supernal, it is under the spell of a spiritual inspiration, it is up in the mountain, above the earth, and the sapphire pavement is not far away.

All religious beliefs are rooted in the supernatural; Fetichism, Tanism, Buddhism, Mohamedanism, The Vedas, The Shasters, The Sybilines and the Koran are each inspired; each is a revelation, though perhaps because of the imperfection of the human mind and language, mixed, more or less, with error.　But to the faith that grasped it, to the mind that recognized it, to the soul that fed upon it, to the age and the people that cherished it, each was divine.

On this broad thought, let me postulate my belief,

namely: that *all* men are necessarily honest in their peculiar religious convictions; they ought and they must be respected.   Indeed, all religious belief must have a seeming of truth to the mind and the heart that appropriate them. Nay, there is in each an element of truth and at least a blush of inspiration; there is something worth saving, something that will advance into the evermore; and, as between the votaries of the various religions there ought not to be any ungentle antagonism, but rather those who occupy the loftiest places should invite those who are beneath to broader views, to more perfect forms of truth and higher aspirations.

There is then a mount of inspiration, nor need we go to Arabia to find it.   It is where the soul builds its refuge, where it thinks its best thought, where it grasps its grandest ideals and makes its best resolves.   It is the greatest altitude the soul can reach at this hour, the place where we form our supreme convictions; here our differing experiences are discovered and our individualities are bounded.   We ought all pause long enough, in life's noise and hurry, to forget, each day, our surroundings, to ascend the mount of our inspiration, to meditate on the truths and commune with the inteligence above us.   Let us consider.

II.   THE REVELATIONS THAT ARE MADE IN THE MOUNT.

If inspiration is a fact, important revelations will be expected; indeed revelations are numerous as inspiration is general; there are fresh unfoldments every hour.   Something has been disclosed to-day which hitherto was unknown, at least by the individual upon whose mind the vision dawned.   By inspiration the soul is quickened to receive truth, and by revelation truth is communicated to the soul.   It were strange, in a world where these two forces are in constant play, if occasionally the cloud did not break and disclose some truth golden beyond.   What though the notions of men are often crude; what if many theories have fallen to naught; what though much of ideality is fiction; yet, "the universal feeling after truth, the universal belief in truth, and the universal consciousness of the need of truth" are indications that truth is working in the human heart, and some day will break full-orbed upon it.

Whence come those invisible influences that lift up and enlarge men? The race being animal born how is it that it has now been civilized and christianized? I say, these things result from the inspiring, quickening forces of the divine spirit revealing to man the depths of his own soul, also the possibilities of his self-hood, adding to him all the sublime things of the universe of God, and calling out his innate powers just as the coaxing sunbeam calls out the wondrous nature of the seed; without this man would petrify where he stands.

Thus each new thought becomes a new revelation. What a wonderful phenomenon is a thought? Born in the hidden depths of your brain, made audible in words, vibraing on the etherial wave, striking the drum of my ear, quivering along my nerve, pouring a subtle influence on the very center of my mind, discovering the throne of my invisible spirit, and metamorphosing thought into feeling, and sensations into ideas—how wonderful is the miracle of a thought! How strange that your unseen thought, without disappearing from the sanctum of your mind appears also in mine, and perhaps, in a thousand others, making in each a various train of ideas, and, it may be quickening empires and ages into action.

One can scarcely think, so the philosophers suggest, of so common a thing as an apple, or an orange, without also thinking of it "as something contradistinguished from nothing, as possessed of attributes, as being similar to something else, as belonging to a certain class, as being the

effect of a cause, as occupying space, as the product of time,"
and with many other inductions and inferences.

But if a thing so common is the fruitful source of so
many ideals, what shall be said of those uncommon
thoughts, those great conceptions of the brain which, like
Newton's thought of universal law, or Watt's thought of
imprisoned power, or Darwin's thought of the descent of
man, sweep down upon the world, affecting its philosophy,
its mechanics, and its science?

Yes, there is nothing more impressive or comprehensive, or suggestive, or potent, or enduring than a thought;
each thought is a revelation in itself: each time I capture
the soul of a new idea I not only secure what I never had
before, but have discovered the gates of a new realm which
I possess and control, "turning into shapes the forms of
things unknown."

The thoughts of scientific thinkers must be accorded
the honorable place that belongs to them. Science has
climbed far up the peaks of inspiration. The savants lead
the way and we follow; from the higher altitudes of their
thought remarkable revelations have been made to the
world. The Hindoo Manu, whoever he was felt an earthquake shock, or saw a bursting volcano, or watched a river
overflow its banks, and from these conceived a geological
age, which, carried forward by a Cuvier or a Dana resulted
in a revelation of the structure of the earth, and the methods by which its materials have been arranged.

The soul of Franklin reveled in the storm-cloud and
carried away the spirit of the lightning, others profited by
his inspirations, and now the magic empire of electricity
flashes before us.

The Chaldeans conceived the idea of measuring time by
the motions of the heavenly bodies; Ptolemy climbed the

mountain a little higher and pointed out the center of the planetary system; Tycho Brahe still higher and by an elipse explained the motion of Mars; Newton still higher and on his mind dawned the thought of the power that holds the planets in their orbits; LaGrange and LaPlace higher still and thought out the laws on which the starry system depends: and now as the result of scientific inspiration, a universe of worlds and suns divulges its secrets, and the first astronomer of the day becomes our Moses, who leads the Aarons and the Joshuas up into the mountain, receives the law from hands divine, and bids them declare to us what are the patterns of celestial things.

Revelations in science are not all. Science is only one peak of the mountain range of inspiration; The moral reaches higher than the material; conceding the importance of one, we must concede still greater importance to the other; a perfect theism, and a divine moralism, would if revealed, transcend all other revelations; the Supreme God, and the supreme good are two eternal suns having a common spiritual center of gravity.

Men's morals are affected by their conception of God; Venus was Goddess of passion therefore prostitutes were consecrated to her worship. In the days of Polytheism Varro collected all the opinions he could on the great question, "What is the supreme good?" and counted not less than three hundred and twenty different answers. As compared with eternal right how small is the formation of a crystal, the unfolding of a flower, the construction of a magnetic coil, or the oscillations of a star. Indeed, it must be allowed that a revelation of God, a proclamation of moral law, would be the most important office of inspiration.

Admitting that all men may be more or less inspired that all are climbing the mountain, some to one altitude, some to another, and allowing as we must, that sometimes

whole empires are moved as by a divine impulse; it is still
an important question, where can the highest moral inspiration and revelation be found? that which will the
clearest reveal God and principle to me?

Not with Thales, Pythagoras, or Zenophanes for the
heart feels that there is something higher than nature.
Not with Socrates, Aristotle, or Plato, for the mind longs
for something greater than itself. Not with Zoroaster,
Buddha, or Confucius, for there is something more potent
than fire, more wonderful than thought, even the power
that quickens it. Nor does the whole world desire to go
back to those old masters; they were superior to the people
of their age; they lifted the world upward but not to the
loftiest places.

But where is now the highest table-land that inspired
thought has reached? Where are the fullest revealments
of God? Where is the most perfect code of moral law?
The broadest scolarship and the profoundest wisdom of this
age, point to the old Testament and the New and say
there it is.

Possibly, inspirations more intense than these. revelations more wonderful than these *may* come in the future;
but man need not get nervous for their coming; it is from
the high places of these, that he shall discover the golden
summit of the loftiest mountains of some terra incognita still
farther away; here are all the theism and moralism that
man can master at present.

The world may have its side-issues, orthodoxy its conflicts, the Church its quarrels, dogma its heresies, and science its flings at religion, yet, the Diety that the Bible reveals, and the morality that it requires are, a platform on
which all can stand, a religion that all can adopt; when
men shall have become " perfect, even as the Father which

is in Heaven is perfect," then they may *perhaps*, look for further revelations.

The Bible is a whole mountain range of inspiration. It is the history of the gradual revealment of God, and of the unfoldment of His righteousness. It contains the best thoughts of the best thinkers of the ages that preceded this. Its later are much in advance of its earlier utterances, not contradicting but perfecting them; and. the world of modern thought has moved so far beyond the orbit of the ancients that, were God to be judged of by the peculiar methods and symbols that were employed in the infancy of the race, w should have very erroneous, not to say grotesque notions of Diety.

The world to-day does not need a fiery Sinai to demonstrate the powerlessness of idols; nor consecrated altars, ceremonious priests, and unblemished offerings to teach that God is holy and that his children should be pure. It is not necessary to slaughter a lamb or an ox to convince *us* that sin deserves punishment. Those antiquated forms, ceremonies and symbols awakened in the mind emotions of awe and reverence, made Jehovah to stand forth crowned with the dignity of absolute holiness; and taught, not that Diety is propitiated by blood. and by blood only, but that a sinning soul is deserving of death; and that God in the greatness of His love, and the fulness of His wisdom would provide a means of redemption.

The Levitical law was the world's spiritual "schoolmaster;" through it has come our purest Theism. Those ancient sacrifices were the pictures in the primary books of human ethics; and should men ever know more about God than they do, those obsolete old symbols would still be the A B C of its knowledge, and not of its knowledge only but also of its morality.

When the revelation of Diety was complete: when every essential moral truth had been grasped; when an empire for the world's sake had learned the important lesson that God is propitious, then the Mosaic symbols melted away; and the Eternal All Wise, stood forth, a pure spiritual conception in the human mind: the intellectual scaffolding fell from the infinite idea that inspired thought had built, and universal Love and Intelligence appeared in everlasting fullness unobscured by any earthly splendor.

Christ is the most perfect revelation of God ; but that revelation is not fully understood : Christ crucified will always be a stumbling block until the whole world shall recognize Deity in him.   Christ was not a creature appointed by the the Creator to suffering and Death, in order that man should love the divinity who made the appointment; in such case we should pity the victim and hate the Deity. But Christ is Jehovah himself, in self-sacrifice and suffering, manifesting eternal love in an omnipotent attempt to reconcile the world unto himself.   He is the Lord stooping to our need and lifting us up; he is "the branch" let down from the tree of life, by which the trailing downtrodden vine of humanity, might twine its tendrils of faith and affection about him, and thus rise again to the bosom of the Father.

If there can be found anywhere an exhibition of love more complete, a revelation more sublime, and made by methods more simple and successful, the church, nay the whole world, by every deeper longing of poor appealing humanity demands that it shall be pointed out.   Atheism cannot do it, skepticism cannot, nor all the rude jokes and gibes of sneering infidelity; but in the presence of this truth, *God in Christ,* each heart can feelingly exclaim "O ! the depth of the riches, both of the Wisdom and Knowledge of God."

In conclusion, are we under no obligation to conform to the patterns that have been revealed? If there are moments of illumination and of clearer spiritual vision, the thoughts that are then awakened must be the major premises of man's supreme convictions: we are all superstitious enough to regard them with sacredness: every man feels disposed to preserve his best thoughts and to give serious heed to those convictions that come to the soul in its purest moods, for, we know not to what heavenly proportions they may expand, or what potent influences may be folded up in them.

They think best who think amid the universe of moral truths that are engermed in the Bible; they climb highest who step first on this rock; they are most perfect who make all things conform to this pattern. The erection of a Tabernacle was an important work, it was a type of the Temple and of Heaven, it could not have been made without a pattern; but we are builders of Temples that will continue when every material beauty has passed away; our moral characters must stand eternally; shall we attempt to build without a pattern? but the model is found nowhere save on the summit of this spiritual Sinai; are we willing to climb the Mount and secure it?

Do you want a theology? and you do, for every heart wants God, here is the pattern, in the scripture is revealed humanity's best concept of God; the world therefore owes it to the integrity of its own intelligence to worship Him.

Do you want Salvation? and you do, every soul that is conscious of sin inquires what must I do to be saved? In the Bible is the only plan the world ever knew, carefully unfolded and earnestly recommended; how absurd then to quarrel with it, rather should our scheme conform to the divine plan.

Do you want hope? and you do, then, you can never

be satisfied until your hope has measured up to the fulness of the pattern revealed in the mount, it is a hope bright with joy and big with eternal life.

There are those who accept the Bible as a history, as a book of instruction, and even as the greatest inspiration of the ages, but who, in their hearts, reject the Christ whom the Bible reveals—believe me—Christ and the Scripture stand or fall together: like that celebrated shield of old, which was so made that the name of the artist could not be moved without destroying the shield. So we cannot accept the Bible and reject Christ, nor accept Christ and reject the Bible, they are one, and accord with the pattern revealed in the mount, we must make our choice to correspond.

By the purest impulses of our hearts, by the loftiest convictions of our reason, by whatever is lovely on earth and perfect in Heaven, we are led to search these Scriptures, for the ideal character they contain, for the salvation which they assure, and for the eternal life that they promise.

If ever man was inspired, if ever he had a noble thought or a holy inspiration, if ever he was restful in trouble or uncomplaining in affliction, if ever he was hopeful in darkness, if ever to him Death seemed to be but the pearly gateway to everlasting glory, it was when his spirit communed with the spirit of revelation, and according as he climbed to the brow of this God-touched Sinai. Well might Sir Walter Scott declare—

> " Within this ample volume lies
> The mystery of mysteries;
> Happiest they of all the human race,
> To whom their God has given grace,
> To read, to fear, to hope, to pray,
> To lift the latch, to force the way;
> And better had they ne'er been born,
> That read to doubt, or read to scorn."

GROANS AND GLORY.

For we that are in *this* tabernacle do groan, being burdened: not for that we would be unclothed, but clothed upon, that mortality might be swallowed up of life.
Now he that hath wrought us for the selfsame thing *is* God.
—*II Cor.* 5. 4-5.

Compared with that which is unseen that which is seen is small: You do not at present see Milwaukee, nor the States that surround Wisconsin, nor those on the Atlantic coast, nor those on the Pacific slope; you do not see the oceans that impinge on our shores, nor the great continents beyond the seas, nor the icebergs of the Arctic circles, nor the luxuriant vegetation of the tropics; you simply believe that they are. We do not see the stars, do not know that we shall see them when the sun goes down to-night; we do not know that we ever saw a star, the most that can be said is that the effects of a few quivering beams of light have perhaps been seen; it may be that the worlds from which those light-beams flashed sunk in the sea of oblivion a hundred years ago, yet we believe in the stars and believe also in light. Man has never seen a soul, a mind, a thought, an emotion, or the essence of the commonest atom that exists. I never yet saw myself, or any other person; I have been the recipient of many impressions, but I am doubtful whether I ever saw anything or not; I never saw Life, or Death, or what is beyond the grave; I never saw God; in fact my blindness and my ignorance utterly confound me; I am overwhelmed with the thought that the unseen is greater, more important, potent and real than the seen.

Man waits to investigate and compass that which is invisible; life is made up of progressions from the seen to the unseen; such is the case in education, in business, in agriculture. The unseen or the unknown does not dampen human courage, nor dishearten man's intrepidity; man stands on the threshhold of every terra incognita and demands that it shall give up its secrets; at his mandate the bowels of the earth rush out, the sea unlocks its hidden treasuries, the atmosphere divulges its mysteries, and unseen empires disclose their wonders. He interrogates death and requires to know whence it came and what its mission. He is ready to extort the secrets of the grave; he knocks at the gates of the empire of spirits and waits for a revelation; and to a God unseen he cries, in the anxious words of Moses, "I beseech thee show me thy glory."

That man thus searches for the invisbile is prophetic, it suggests that there must be something existing beyond the bounds of the seen. There is not a word or an instinct among the lower orders for which Nature has not made a provision, thus, hunger is prophetic of food, thirst is prophetic of water, weariness is suggestive of rest, and inquisitiveness of knowledge; so, too, the heart-nature of man is the exponent of love and friendship. If, then, humanity, by some inherent impulse, by some innate inspiration, is seeking for that which is unseen, eager for that which things visible cannot afford him then, he is to himself a prophecy of coming benedictions; he is greater than he seems to be, greater than his earthly surroundings are, greater than his present knowledge, greater than time, great and glorious as the pregnant possibilities of eternity.

If the little birds which in summer fill our woods with song, are impelled by their inborn instincts, when the autumn leaves are falling, to seek and find some sunny southland where frosts never come and flowers bloom perennial so. methinks, my hopes and longings shall not mock and disappoint me; sure as there is sunshine and summer-time, for the birds there is a Heaven for my soul; I may not see it now, but when comes the frost of Death I shall unfold my wing and soar away; the unseen will by and by become visible; what is now a dream will soon be a reality; every inborn want is a prophecy of supply; "what thou knowest not now, thou shalt know hereafter."

In the unseen man discovers his supreme ideals; in short, it is the finding of the highest reason that in the unseen is God. But if a God, he must have a purpose, everything must have a meaning; Omnipotence, Wisdom, Love, Justice mean something; nothing has been ordered in vain; each world has a history and a mission; each living thing is pregnant with eternal significance; there is not a leaf trembling on its parent stem but works out the purpose of its being; all things work together to consummate the designs of a Father's love; the trials I endure, the tears I shed, the sorrows I feel, the pains I suffer, each has its meaning and its benevolent ministry.

What may be the purposes of God in regard to the atoms and molecules of matter we may not know, but it is declared that the *good* of those who love God, entered into the eternal councils of his love, and that "*all* things work together for good to them that love God." Now, therefore,

bearing in mind the fact of the unseen, the thought that
God is in the universe, and that God is working with reference to a purpose, let us try to evolve the thought and suggestion of the text, and notice

I.   THE TRANSITORY NATURE OF OUR EARTHLY LIFE.

It is suggested that we are in a "tabernacle". The
apostle alludes to the human body, it is regarded as a tent, a
booth, or a tabernacle, that is, a place for temporary residence. The idea may have been suggested to Paul by his
own profession, that of a tent-maker; or possibly he bor-
rowed a figure from the ancient Jewish Tabernacle; or we
might say that such imagery was common to the Hebrew
mode of expression; thus, a veil was called "the house of
the face", a glove was a house for the hand, a shoe was the
house of the foot; we use the same figure when speaking of
clothing as a habit; but the idea is that of a temporary purpose; we are in a tabernacle; this body is a house that will
soon wear out, a tent that must shortly be taken down. a
booth that the storms of time will in a little while render
useless; our bodies must dissolve, like worn-out clothing they
will be cast aside, like old gloves they will be slipped off and
thrown away, like old shoes they will be discarded.

Such being the case, what is the object of life? Why
have a body at all if it must be cast off so soon? The allotted three score years and ten pass away "like a tale that
is told", or "as a dream when one awaketh": there is not a
day or an hour when our earthly existence may be said to be
secure; the question "is life worth living?" may well be
asked; can it be that God has a benevolent design with regard to a life that blossoms to-day and perishes to-morrow?
I am nothing but a worthless ephemeron. what does God
care for me?

We do not know all, perhaps we *know* none of the

reasons why it is necessary that man should mingle with matter; but of one fact we are certain, namely, that matter is the base on which human life is built. It is said that Enoch passed to Heaven, but did not go down into the grave, and that Elijah ascended but not by the way of Death. Yet Enoch and Elijah each possessed a material body, and it is suggested that even God himself could not assume our manhood without assuming our flesh.

It seems therefore necessary, for some reason, perhaps unknown to us, that we should be born into a material world, be possessed of matter for a time, be nourished by those material elements in the midst of which we are placed; that creation should combine its forces for our development; that the process of building up should be begun though it continue only a little while; three score years, or two score, or one decade, or one year, or one brief day, the length of time is nothing, the essential thing is that we inhabit this tabernacle, that we should be " in this body pent."

As the seed takes to itself a life from the soil, appropriates something of the essence of the rain-drop and the dew, the darkness, the tempest and the sunbeam, then, rooted and grounded in the earth, it lifts up a stem, puts forth a bud, a leaf, a flower full of fragrance, " a thing of beauty, a joy forever," so from the mass of matter in which we are rooted we may derive some life, some power, some beauty or quality germane to our individuality, essential to the possibility of our nobler being.

When this has been accomplished, whether it require a hundred days or a hundred years, what use have we of a body more? Considering, therefore, the brevity of an earthly existence, do you ask is life worth living? I answer yes, it is the very base of immortal being, it is the source whence comes the essence of self-hood, it is the bud that will develop into the flower, without it there could not be the bloom and beauty everlasting.

If matter is heavy and grievous it is not long that it must be carried; if the body is racked with pain and corrupt with disease, its shuffling off is not far away; if this earthly house should be storm-beaten and time-worn, not long and we shall pass from the old house into the new; in a little while we shall strike tents and move to more inviting scenes, and there may after all be a joyful note in the fact that "our hearts, like muffled drums, are beating funeral marches to the grave."

The philosophy of Christianity suggests that the body is not the man, he only lives in it, it is a tabernacle, man is superior to the house in which he lives, while his temporary residence is decaying an enduring palace is being built for him, that palace will be complete when this cabin has served its time, until that is ready we must abide in this. The earthly tabernacle may require a good deal of patching up, so do all the residences of earth, the sills may rot, the rafters break, it may become defaced and disfigured, it may be smitten with the lightning, or scorched with fires, it may be swept from its foundations or sent to roll and tumble in the flood, but when it shall have served its purpose, the resident will have stepped out, the soul will have reached a shore where fire, flood and decay cannot come. I cannot see, therefore, that the divine management is at fault, God is among the atoms making them work for our good. Notice

II. THE BURDENS THAT OPPRESS US IN THE PRESENT.

"We who are in this tabernacle do groan, being burdened." We have been perplexed on account of the transitoriness of our earthly existence; but conflict, sorrow and pain utterly confound us, they have made us wish that we had never been born; and men under the pressure of their burdens have declared " there is no God". And who shall solve for us the enigma of suffering? The very thought of the fearful struggle that is always going on strikes us with terror.

"The whole creation travaileth together in pain;" all life is a battle, the strong trample down the weak, atoms dash against each other, the oak wrestles with the tempest, the flower is in conflict with the weed, the air swarms with hostile multitudes, the very rocks are sepulchres, the soils are the ashes of heroes that fell in battle, the sea also is a grave vast and deep; and man, since first he stepped on the earth, has waged a perpetual warfare, his struggles and sacrifices, his pains and sorrows have marked the progress of knowledge and the advance of civilization; and to-day, as ever, he shoulders his burden and goes forth to the fight.

Even innocent little children have their burdens; we have seen them languishing in sickness, we have heard them cry out with pain; "we are born unto trouble;" it pursues us even to old age. The stress and strain of life are real, terrible sometimes, bleaching the hair, wrinkling the brow, softening the brain. When we realize it, it seems that a wail of woe is going up from the crushed heart of humanity and sounding in the ear of God. The picture as the apostle drew it is *dreadful*, "the whole creation groaneth and travaileth together in pain until now."

Why all this? It seems sometimes that if the world ever knew a Providence it is now withdrawn; if on this earth the hand divine ever moved it must now be paralized; if ever there was an overruling Deity now he has ceased to reign. The atheist haunts us with the question "where is thy God?" Why all this?

It would seem that with life so brief, and burdens so numerous, an earthly existence is not worth having; nor is it, if there is no God; cast him out then indeed evil outweighs the good, and the condition of man is the most unhappy that can be conceived; but grant that God is in this empire of pain, that he steps softly amid our woes, that an unseen presence is behind the shadows, that beside human weakness is omnipotence, that under the watchful eye of infinite love all this is permitted for our discipline, for our good; then a ray of light shines upon our gloom; then we see that it is possible after all that these afflictions may " work out for us a far more exceeding and eternal weight of glory".

Such a plan is analagous with the plan unfolded by nature.   In that wonderful realm one force or element is made to balance another.   The sea and the atmosphere, the air and the earth, the animal and the vegetable, the vegetable and the mineral, the cold and the heat, the opposite poles of the magnet, the centrifugal and centripital forces of the heavens, seem to be related to and mutually balance each other; such is the constitution of things that the law of compensation prevails.

Paul recognized a similar plan in the unfoldments of Providence, in the kingdom of God's moral rule; he saw spiritual experiences in pairs or opposites, one experience compensated by another, so he speaks of being troubled but not distressed, perplexed but not in despair, persecuted but not forsaken, cast down but not destroyed, delivered unto death yet living, afflicted and yet glorified.   Then again, the apostle balances one thing with another, things seen with things unseen, things temporal with things eternal, things dissolvable with things perpetual, houses made by human hands with houses made by divine power, and things on earth with things in Heaven.   So in the text, by the side of dying groans he places immortal glory; he intimates that these earthly things, these temporalities precede, predict, and are to be sublimated into eternal things.

Thus, if in nature, one law, or force, or element is made to balance another, why not in Grace? As the mineral is prophetic of the vegetable, and the vegetable of the animal, so we expect that the natural will foreshadow the spiritual. Is not sin a silent testimony in favor of holiness? Is not suffering a prophecy of rejoicing? And so Death itself, must in the reason of the case be a testimony in favor of immortality.

God has put us into contact with matter that we may subdue it, he leads us into the realm of suffering that we may triumph over it; had I never borne a burden or felt the sting of pain, I should never have known the possibilities of my own being; every sorrowful experience convinces me that I am not a rock but a *life*, and that I am a creature of the most delicate susceptibilities, it makes me tender, sympathetic, brotherly, loving: and having triumphed in the kingdom of groans and burdens, God leads me onward through the gates of Death, into the empire of spirits. and bids me win immortal laurels there; so that we may learn some day that every pain produced a pearl for our crowning. Consider

III. THE ATTITUDE OF MANKIND WITH REGARD TO THEIR BURDENS.

Do they crush all the manhood out of us? Is it true that the race generally is ready to declare that its condition is the worst possible? Should we advocate the doctrine of universal suicide? The Apostle Paul did not so think; he stated the case just as it is; he conceded that " we who are in this tabernacle do groan being burdened," but denies that there is any feverish anxiety to "shuffle off this mortal coil", he says " not that we would be unclothed."

Nor is there in the present age. any more than there was in the apostolic age, any general nervousness to pull down the tabernacle and be gone. One man in ten thousand may be a suicide, but there are nine thousand, nine hundred and ninety-nine in every ten thousand who are ready to believe that the suicide for the time-being must have been insane. We read of Tay bridge disasters, Winter Palace explosions, Nihilistic murders, famines, pestilences, conflagrations and all such catastrophies that sweep men into the grave by the score, and the hundreds, not with rejoicing but with horror; the world would avoid these things if it could; men submit to the inevitable, die in horrid accidents, still they prefer life; we say to-day as Paul said "not that we would be unclothed".

On the contrary there is an eagerness to live; we shrink from the shock of mortal dissolution. The deepest, the most earnest want of the human soul is for a continuance of existence; life may be brief but it is precious; it may be only a bubble but we believe that the bubble contains a pearl; such an inspiration is man's desire for life that all the pessimistic philosophy on earth does not discourage him; with undesparing fortitude the race lives on; with utter contempt of trouble men press onward in life's highway; with sublime heroism they enlist in the fight for existence; though the foot-prints of the generations have been stained with blood; though their backs broke beneath the crushing weight of burdens; though human hearts may have been pierced through with many sorrows; though the fathers halted and went down to death, yet nothing daunted their sons press onward in the same path, with similar burdens and experiences to a similar destiny: there is in humanity no indication of a desire to be unrobed of life, to pass out of being, but there is a longing to be clothed upon, to find existence constantly intensifying, to see as the apostle expresses it " mortally swallowed up of life."

Whence comes this sublime arrousement? Not from our pain, not from our sorrow, not from death, nor even from our existence in itself considered, but from without us, evidently it is the arrousement produced by a living God in humanity. He has ordained that we should sometimes groan in this tabernacle, that toiling hands shall be burdened, and weary hearts heavily laden, in order that our thought and hope may be lifted Heavenward, that we may be able to look toward the unseen and the eternal, and earnestly desire to be clothed with our house which is from above.

It is then, in accordance with the divine plan that we shall never reach our ideals here, never see in this world hope brighten into full fruition, never compass our possibilities; we are being ever led onward, the rainbow is always ahead of us, if it arches the hills to-day it will encircle the mountains or even the heavens to-morrow. Life is ever advancing, Love always reaches outwardly, Faith looks ahead; and because there is a divine power behind us, a divine thought within us, and a Father's love before us, we bravely lift our burdens and press into the evermore.

Because God is with us, we touch matter and subdue it, pain touches us and we triumph over it, Death encompases us and we conquer it and soon we shall enter the realm of spirits and reign over it; God has so created us that we can anchor nowhere but in Heaven—so "we walk by faith not by sight," and "he that hath wrought us for the self-same thing is God."

The conclusion therefore is, though life is built on a material base it is all right; though the scaffolding fall suddenly or gradually it is all right; though we who are in this tabernacle do groan being burdened, it is all right; though the grave is before us it is all right; God's management is wise, under the direction of his love all things are working together for our good, eternal glory must be the outcome; "He that hath wrought us for the self-same thing is God."

You are troubled about the unseen, you ask yourself a thousand perplexing questions, dear soul your faith in God meets your interrogatories and solves your doubts; and the Gospel touches all the mysteries of earth with a heavenly radiance.

Have you sorrow? then let me invite you to the fountain of healing, in its waters life never grows old: the love of God heals your heart wound; immortality makes you master of your sorrows; live in the light of the Gospel and the world, and time, and pain, and death, shall be under your feet at last.

THE GOSPEL REMEDY FOR A TROUBLED HEART.

Let not your heart be troubled; ye believe in God, believe also in me.

In my Father's house are many mansions: if *it were* not *so*, I would have told you. I go to prepare a place for you.

And if I go and prepare a place for you, I will come again, and receive you unto myself; that where I am, *there* ye may be also —*John* 14 1-3.

Ever since that fatal day when in Eden, man ignored the divine plan and "became a law unto himself" there has been an abundance of trouble in the world. The earth, the domestic hearth, the religious altar, the elements, society, the shepherd's tent, the palace, the municipality, and law itself became a reason for disturbance, the *cause* though not the *seat* of trouble.

There was trouble in the bosoms of the patriarchs; there was trouble in the breasts of prophets; there was trouble in the hearts of kings; there was trouble among apostles; Christ himself was "troubled in spirit." Trouble seems to be the birth-right of humanity; "Man is born unto trouble as the sparks fly upward;" it is the legacy of nations; I have a troubled heart, you have a troubled heart. Whatever disturbs the tranquility of our emotions, our feelings, that is trouble.

Where is the seat of trouble? "It cometh not forth of the dust," "it springeth not out of the ground." It is not in the howling wind, nor in the beating storm; it is not in the thunder, or the the lightning or the flood, or the flame; it is not in toil or poverty, or disease, or pain, or bereavement, or death. Sweep the material universe through, and through, and you shall not find trouble; yet mankind is born unto it; if man were not, trouble were not; it has no empire, no throne, no sway anywhere save in the human heart.

Trouble is disturbance in the hidden recesses of self-hood. The lower orders suffer pain but they are not troubled. Man is susceptible of trouble because he has a heart-nature, a soul. If there is no life beyond our troubles must die with us; if there is a remedy for trouble it cannot be produced by a transformation of the Cosmos; the cure must come by the application of some sovereign balm to each individual heart.

Now if trouble is enthroned within, man must look to himself as the cause. Why then am I in trouble? Why have you a troubled heart? Is it not because affairs are not regulated according to our preconceived plans and notions? because the universe moves on, and law operates, and man thinks and talks and acts despite my agitated feelings, and contrary to my will and my wish? If it were possible to bring my heart-nature into harmony with all things universal and human, should I be disturbed? should I have trouble?

The cause therefore is inadequate confidence; I fear that the laws of nature will somehow work me harm; I fear that the contradictions of men will produce injury to me;

I fancy,if I could only manage all things myself I should
be in absolute repose; but this is impossible; must I then,
without respite, carry through life, my crushing burden of
sorrow?

Many remedies have been proposed. The modern Pessimist advises the immediate and general suicide of the race.
The old Stoics recommended cold, grim, stony endurance.
The ancient Persians advised submission, they declared that
to pass between the mill-stones is necessary, it is impossible
to avoid it, the only way for us to do is to march straight
into the hopper, with the hope that perhaps the mill-stones
will burst some day. Others have prescribed medicine for
a disturbed heart, and the Epicureans said, " Let us eat
drink and be merry for to-morrow we die."

Need I say that each of the proposed remedies has
been tried and has failed? With suicidal intent men have
stood, weapon in hand, ready to annihilate self and trouble
at once, and something has suggested that perhaps leaping
out of present troubles, we " fly to others that we know
not." Men have stood defiant as rocks to breast the
storms of life, and while no complaint fell from their lips,
the disturbance within arose and raged like the restless
sea. The race has been passing between the upper and
nether mill-stones, lo these long centuries, still the
crushing goes on, and there is no promise of respite. Men
have drugged and doctored but trouble does not cease; they
have eaten and drunken but sorrow has multiplied. Thus
each prescription has failed, indeed the proposed remedy
has been worse than the disease.

But there is one, just one remedy that has not failed,
that proposed and provided by the Lord Jesus Christ. "Let
not your heart be troubled; ye believe in God; believe also
in me; in my Father's house are many mansions; if

it were not so, I would have told you, I go to prepare a place for you, and if I go and prepare a place for you, I will come again, and receive you unto myself, that where I am, there ye may be also."

Let us then consider this Gospel remedy for a troubled heart. What are its elements?

I. SELF–CONTROL. "*LET* NOT YOUR HEART *BE* TROUBLED."

Men have entertained very strange opinions in regard to the Gospel and those principles that represent it. "That Church," said one, "is not worth a chew of Tobacco." My friend there may be some portions of the peculiar creed of that Church, that you may feel called upon to criticise, but if you are an honest man, you cannot censure the moral character it requires. "Is that the Methodist Church?" said a wag, as he pointed to a rude building for a derrick that had been erected over an artesian well. The question was meant sarcastically. I said *yes*, for there flows from the Methodist Church, as from an artesian well, streams of refreshing and cleansing for the people and the nations.

It is also objected that the Church does very well for women and children; that the Gospel it teaches may touch the more tender emotions of the human heart. but to awaken the more manly and noble qualities of the race it is useless. Surely such innuendoes are the results of ignorance; prejudice or malice aforethought, for the Gospel not only crowns woman with a complete womanhood, but it has planned for man a perfect manhood. Of those influences that shaped the character of a Miriam, a Ruth, an Esther and a Mary, no thoughtful person need be ashamed; and a large souled Abraham. a meek but manly Moses, a glorious Joshua, an unearthly Elijah, and a stirring and resolute Paul are equally worthy of admiration. Indeed it cannot be questioned that Scripture, Christianity, and the Christ, seek to secure for the world, a holy, a well balanced and a thoroughly rounded manhood.

One essential element of manliness is self-control; recognizing individuality, personal responsibility, and ability, the Gospel puts each man on his own base, and says, "he that ruleth his own spirit is better than he that taketh a city". While it provides the opportunity for salvation, it says "work out your own," "take heed unto thyself," "keep the body under," attain "unto the stature of a perfect man," and even Christ, though he accomplished so much for the world, did not presume on the passivity of the race, but recognized the worth of determined self-hood; therefore when the Disciples were in trouble, he did not say go and weep over your misfortunes, and give vent to your feelings, but " *let* not your heart *be* troubled", that is, whatever be your disappointments hold self in control, keep your feelings and passions down, rise above disturbance with a sublime all-conquering manhood, let not trouble master you but master trouble, resolve to be brave, do not trample on your heart-nature, but " keep the heart with all diligence", let your heart be *not* that of a child but a man; "*let* not your heart *be* troubled neither *let* it *be* afraid."

There is some comfort to one who can control himself in trouble. The engineer must be conscious of a thrill of inspiration when, with his hand on the lever, he knows that the great powerful locomotive is simply the servant of his will. Is there not pleasure also for the man who controls himself? Every man knows by experience that, when in the battles of life, he has conquered himself, the victory is more than half won; Christ knew this also, therefore he said " let not your heart be troubled."

Thus the prime element in the Gospel remedy for a troubled heart is self-control. It is not proposed to do away

with a single disturbance provoking cause; nor to provide
immunity from law; nor to make the poor rich, the illiterate
learned, the sick well, nor to restore the physically dead to
life; but the remedy promises that the soul may harmlessly
tide itself over its own troubles, if the heart is only prepared to meet them. It does not teach courage *once* and
done with it, but that the battle for self-mastery must be
continued, the heart must never allow itself to be overpow-
ered, a sublime purpose of victory must characterize all
men, everywhere and always.

This, then, is the basic element in the remedy, there
is of course much more to follow, but this makes practical
what is to come. The Gospel cannot build up a character
on nothing: it must find in humanity a sterling something
for a foundation; it must ally itself with whatsoever is
greatest and grandest in the human soul; the fabric will expand as these foundation elements are strengthened; you cannot make a man of faith out of one who is changeable as
the wind and fickle as the sea. Therefore as a prerequisite
to the sublime overpowering *faith* to which Christ directed
his Disciples, he said, "*let* not your heart *be* troubled."

II.   FAITH IN GOD.   "YE BELIEVE IN GOD."

Faith is an universal element in human experience; it is
what we *live* by; everybody has faith; brutes live by what
they see, hear, smell, taste, feel; *man* lives by what he
thinks. There are men who desire to make brutes of themselves and to live simply by what the senses can bring to
them; in short, they say, we believe or live by *only* what we
know. Strictly speaking we know but little, we do not know
ourselves, nor each other, nor the things that are about us;
we see superficially, know only in part, we simply *believe* or
form an opinion in regard to them. We believe in places
we never saw, in histories that were made before we were
born; we believe that the moon is 240,000 miles away from

the earth; we believe in business and it is a belief that
quickens our pulses and stirs our activities; we risk fortunes
on our faith.   Our faith is a mighty impulse pushing us
forward steadily as if we actually *knew*.   Indeed, we often
say "I know", when we do not know, we believe.   We
could not be rational and have no faith; wherever is intelligence there is belief.

It is the privilege of these heart-natures of ours to believe in God.   Faith in God is as universal as faith itself.
God is a necessity of our thought.   If I reason him away
I must invent something to take his place.   You cannot
find in the whole world a man whose heart-nature is atheistic; we would be unwilling to venture such an assertion in
regard to his head.   Your belief may not be exactly the
same as mine; and all faiths may differ in some particulars,
but all of us from the ignorant savage to the most cultured
philosopher believe in God.   In every consciousness lies the
belief that there is authority and supremacy somewhere.

What if there were no God! if the heart were doomed
to drop its faith and cease its trust, who could draw the melancholy picture?   Not only would the great world be orphaned; not only would confusion reign, but the very
foundation on which we stand would be dropped out;
trouble would deepen into blank and utter despair; existence
would be a fearful plunge into a hell of darkness and
eternal woe.

It is a great privilege to believe.   Better believe in an
universal force, an all pervading law than believe in nothing.   Better have the faith of a Pagan than no faith.   Better be a Deist than an Atheist.   Our troubled hearts fasten
to this idea of God and are comforted.   The disciples believed in God and it was a balm for their troubles.   The
old Jews believed in God and they were comforted; to believe as *they* did is a cordial for *our* fears.   They believed

that the world was built and is governed by God; " that in him we live, and move, and have our being;" that in him are Fatherhood and Providence; that he is inffnitely good, wise and powerful; that he brings forth the seasons in their order, spreads the stars in their glory, commands the destinies of men and nations, and that " he is a rewarder of all who diligently seek him"; this gave them comfort and consolation, it made them sing "the Lord is my Shepherd, I shall not want".

When I can take in this thought in all its fullness, how it inspires me with hope. I believe in God, he is greater than I, therefore he can help me in my perplexity. He has a strong arm, I may lean upon it. He made the world, it serves my interest, therefore he is my friend. He sees further than I, perhaps then beyond present disturbance he sees rest, it may be better after all that I should fight and overcome; if I love him perhaps it will be all right in the end. If only I shall love him so well as to be in harmony with all his laws and plans and providences, if my thought shall sink into his, and my will melt into his, then "all things shall work together for my good," and my anxious, troubled heart shall rest.

This is a wonderful comfort; with an unwavering confidence in God as my friend, my King, my Father, I can say, burn out ye suns, fall ye worlds, howl ye winds, strike ye lightnings, fade ye fields, perish ye flocks and herds, fill up ye graves and crumble poor body of clay. " yet will I rejoice in God, I will joy in the God of my salvation;" nothing can hurt or injure me if God is my friend; the larger, the more perfect our faith in God, the stronger becomes our assurance, we rest as we believe.

III.   BELIEF IN CHRIST.   "BELIEVE ALSO IN ME."

Belief in God is fundamental; with this faith the soul

finds a sure foundation; finding God it finds an explanation of, and an author for, the universe; it finds also a father for the spirit, and the very wisdom, love and leadership that the heart-nature needs. Now, Jews and Deists stop right here, but Christianity goes a step farther, and seeks a deeper and more perfect manifestation of God; it reaches beyond Paganism, beyond Philosophy, beyond Judaism, beyond the revealments of natural Religion, and requires belief in Christ also, who was "God manifest in the flesh."

This utterance, "believe also in me," is the whole Gospel in four words; if this requirement is not imperative then the Gospel is not necessary: by these words Christ put himself side by side with God; if these words are true he is divine, if they are false he was a demon. He directed the faith of mankind toward himself as he recognized that faith going out toward God; he said be not troubled because I die, death cannot prevent my work, by death I conquer death, therefore "believe also in me."

Christ did not say believe in the sermon on the mount, believe in what I tell you about the Father, believe in the doctrines that my disciples shall preach, or in those that uninspired men may proclaim, and that shall be sufficient for your faith; but he said "believe also in me;" believe in me as a person, in me as a life, in me as a power, in me as the embodiment of truth; do not cast God *out* of you faith by any means, but take me *in*, your faith in God is incomplete if you leave me out; I represent a phase of diety that Natural Religion does not reveal, that Theism does not apprehend, that Judaism only faintly foreshadowed; beyond Creatorship, Legislation, Providence, there is Love, Pardon, Reconciliation, Salvation, Sanctification. I am the manifestation of God in the forgivness of sin, in the work of reconciliation, in redemption, and in regeneration, for "there are diversities of operations, but it is the same God which worketh all in all," therefore while you believe in God in the old Jewish sense, believe also in God as the author and finisher of human redemption, or what is the same "believe also in me."

But can we believe in Christ? His contemporaries may have believed him, but can we who are separated by a great gulf of centuries? I answer yes.

We can believe in the history of Christ, for the records are here, those records are true or false, if false they could have been contradicted, when first written they were not contradicted and all modern attempts at contradiction, have been failures, we can therefore believe in the historic Christ.

We can also believe in Christ as a supernatural man, that is, one whose life is above the plane of ordinary experiences. To the Barbarian civilization is supernatural; to the plodding, unlearned rustic, the measurement of the celestial angles is well nigh supernatural; to the scientific savant each new development suggests something beyond the plane of common experience; worlds they say have been born of vapor, moons have leaped out of the bosoms of planets, chaos has moved into cosmos, frogs have metamorphosed into birds, and birds into apes; if there has been a supernatural ape, why may there not have been a supernatural man?

I can therefore believe in Christ, the supernatural, the sole man whose life was above the plane of ordinary human experience.

We can also believe in Christ the divine man; not merely one whose lofty mind arose, and enthroned itself above the realm of humanity; but one more truly inspired, more deeply touched with the spirit divine.

Believing in God, one can believe that God would choose the truest heart and fill it with his fullness; what we know of the nature of God, what we know of our own need suggests that this might be expected: if God is a father he would seek his children; he would make himself known to them; he would commune with their loftiest thought; he would condescend to the lowest plane, he would thrust himself into the midst of their struggles; he would woo them away from sin; he would by example teach them how to overcome the world; but how could this be done, what better plan could be suggested than that taught in the Gospel? "Verily he took not on himself the form of angels, but the seed of Abraham." But this was Christ! the divine man; "in him dwelleth all the fullness of the God-head bodily." Thus we can believe in the Christ of history, we can believe in the supernatural Christ, we can believe in the Christ divine.

Such a faith is a balm for trouble; it brings God in the person of Christ very near to the human heart. It shows that my Heavenly Father's hand is open to bless me, in a sweeter sense than nature ever revealed; it teaches that God has even condescended to suffer for me; that he comes down to my "slough of despond," lifts me out, and points me upward; believing this and accepting the proffered hand I shall enjoy a better, a broader life. If my belief in God as a pure spirit, as the Creater of the universe, as the all-provident, was healing to the hurt of my soul, much more must be my faith in Christ.

But is this the full measure of faith? Is Christ nothing more than an examplar, a teacher, a supernatural man, one stooping from heaven to reveal the Father, to instruct in spiritual things, and by living and dying to show men how to live and how to die? then why "make his soul an offering for sin?" why should "it please the Lord to bruise

him?" His death on the cross was an expenditure greater,
infinitely greater, than teacher, or examplar, or martyr was
ever called upon to make. The expen liture was imperative or it would not have been made. His death must have
been designed to meet some awful necessity of law, some
deep demand of moral being; faith therefore accepts Christ
as an absolute necessity.

Christ fills a deep need of our nature. We need deliverance, redemption, and to be reconciled with God; but
there is no pardon or pity in all the realm of nature; the
laws of the universe are inexorable; the heavens, the earth,
the sea have no Savior; but Christ comes and says, "believe
me." I can supply your need; I come with law and authority in my hand on purpose to provide a great salvation; I
am your redemption; trust me and your most essential
moral need shall be satisfied. "Let not your heart be
troubled, neither let it be afraid."

We all like sheep have gone astray; like planets that
have leaped their orbits and are rushing away from the sun
we are wandering away from God; sin hath separated; we
rush one against another; is there no power that can reduce our moral confusion to order and bring us back to
God? No! unless the sun, God himself, shall come where
we are. This is just what God has done, he came in the
person of Christ, and soon men began to move about the
Sun, God, and so Christ declared, "and if I be lifted up, will
draw all men unto me." True, the act was above nature,
it was a necessity and infinite wisdom was sufficient to accomplish it.

Such a belief in Christ is a cordial for our fears, a remedy for our troubles. If Christ was indeed God incarnate,
if the Heavenly Father has thus come down and touched
the heart-nature of his children, if Diety has thus come into
complete unity and sympathy with men, made himself one

with us, made our interests his own. taught us how to live, suffered for us, became reconciled unto us, it must be because he loves us.

We can confide in such a friend: we can rest in his goodness; we know he will manage things wisely and lovingly; we can commit our eternal interest into his hands; we need not be troubled or fearful; for the heart that trusts him there is peace and joy. With qualities that are strong to triumph over foes without and passions within, with a divine friend who lives above and controls all natural law, with an almighty Savior speaking peace to my soul and inviting me to cast all my burdens on him. there is no reason why any earthly disturbance, any thought of my heart in respect to my relations with God should cause me trouble; I believe, I live by my faith, and therefore I rest.

III. A CHRISTIAN'S CONFIDENCE IN A FUTURE LIFE.

We are strange beings, our very needs frighten and inspire us, we want life. we do not want death. Oh! if I might but know that by dying I shall conquer death, I should not be afraid to die. If he who breathed moral life on the world could impart life eternal, if the hand that swept away my earthly troubles would sweep away from the grave its mists; if the love that provided home and plenty for us here would engage to make all necessary provisions for another world, then I should not only be tided over trouble, but I should be happy, forgiven. redeemed, immortal, nothing could do me harm.

Well. here it is, here is all a deathless soul can ask: God, in the person of Christ, has come down and told us that all these deep and awful longings shall be satisfied: God, through Jesus Christ. declares to each child of his that there is triumph, there is life forevermore, and that in the Father's house there are many mansions.

You have lived in one of those mansions many years, a grand one too, 8,000 miles broad, 25,000 miles in circumference; what wealth is stored in its cellars; what variety of beauty is spread upon its floors; what splendors crowd its ceilings; but there are many more, unnumbered, they shine in everlasting glory; they crowd the infinite distances of space; they make the Father's house; his providence reaches each one of them; they become more magnificent as they spread outwardly toward the throne; the city of the throne is 375 miles broad, 375 miles long, "and the length, and the breadth of it are equal". Be not troubled therefore dear soul, if saved and redeemed there is in one of those mansions a place for you. Without this belief a black pall would fall on the heart.

Yes, you say, I have looked out upon yonder worlds; I have seen Venus in her beauty, Jupiter in his banded strength, Saturn in his rings of gold, Sirius in burning glory, and all the flaming host that sweep the sky; aye, I have thought of things more beautiful than those, more vast and enduring, of a life where sin cannot trouble, death cannot come, night cannot enter; I have dreamed of a city out of sight, with walls of jasper, gates of pearl, and streets of gold, of nations saved, of songs sweeter than ear ever heard, and of joys purer than any that have yet filled the human spirit. But you say perhaps all this was nothing but a dream. Christ said, "if it were not so I would have told you." He came to confirm your dearest hopes, if they were false he would have corrected them; if there is no Heaven he would have told you. Go on then fostering this blessed belief, it will extract the sting of death, it will spoil the grave of its victory.

I have sometimes wished that he who came to breathe courage into human hearts, to quicken confidence in God,

to command faith in himself, and to assure that man's longings for a deathless existence are not in vain; I have sometimes wished that he had remained here on the earth: then we
might fly to him with our doubts, our fears, our fancies, with
our sorrows, our sins, our heart-wounds, and consult him.
Each would have ten thousand questions to propose to the
Master; we should each know that the truth had been told us
But he anticipated my wish; he said "what thou knowest
not now thou shalt know hereafter;" "it is expedient for
you that I go away;" "I go to prepare a place for you."
Oh, this is the sweetest utterance I ever heard. He who
strewed the earth with flowers and spangled the skies with
stars, has become my servant; I may have been a poor sinner, little and unknown, cast out, forsaken, and forgotten
among men, but he who made the worlds promised to prepare a place for me. He knows my needs; if prepared for
me it will suit me; it will be ready when I am ready for it.
I can rest in this assurance for "I know in whom I have
believed;" I need not multiply questions, I shall be satisfied.

There is something in a Christian's confidence in a
future life that somehow appeals to the most responsive
part of our being. It is not the result of cold metaphysics;
it does not say matter is imperishable, therefore probably
man shall not die; it is God speaking to man and saying, "I
am the All-Father, you are my children; because I live you
live, you shall be where I am, I will receive you unto myself, I will come to you, I will conduct you safely through
the dark death-valley, and fold you in my everlasting arms
at last." It appeals to the heart as well as to the intellect;
it makes immortality a part of my inheritance, not by a
frigid syllogysm, but by "Christ formed within me the hope
of glory."

Thus the Gospel is a panacea for a troubled heart. It
bids me subdue myself and promises the peace that comes

of such a victory.   It invites me to look above men and
above matter to that Omnipotent Being who overrules all
things for my good.   It points me to Calvary and the great
scheme of Redemption, and thus lifts from my troubled
conscience a dreadful burden.   It opens up the evermore,
and promises that all things are mine: "life. death. things
present, things to come, all are mine."   Indeed, the Gospel
is a finality, it solves all doubts, answers all questions and
satisfies the deepest longings of the deathless soul; with
such a sovereign remedy provided for all, there need not be
a troubled heart on earth.

This world, with the Gospel working in it would be
Heaven were it not for our unbelief.   Unbelief makes sin,
and sin is the mother of all misery.   Correct the confidences
of the human heart and trouble can trouble us no more.
We do have some faith, and in so far we rest: but when the
world shall be in harmony with itself; when man's confidence in his brother man shall be unshaken; when the
world's faith in God shall be complete; when the belief of
humanity shall comprehend Jesus Christ, and when faith
shall be crowned with the Christian's assurance of Heaven
and eternal life, then trouble will die and joy will reign.

THE LORD'S WITNESSES.

Ye *are* my witnesses, saith the Lord, and my servant whom I
have chosen; that ye may know and believe me, and understand that I *am* he; before me there was no God formed, neither
shall there be after me.—*Isaiah* 43, 10.

We receive moral complexion from our surroundings; the influence of association is marked: impressions
received at home are indelible; when individuals mingle or
nations flow together one is influenced by the other; the
character that each assumes is indicative of the atmosphere
in which he has lived; go into the garden and you carry
away with you the scent of the flowers; visit the barnyard or
the kitchen and you will be odorous of the cattle and the
kettles.

Association made the Hebrews idolatrous; idolatry became their besetting sin, commencing with their earliest
history it pursued them for more than a thousand years.
Contrary to the divine command, they sought heathenish
and unhealthy associations, and golden calves, corruption,
demoralization, expressed their groveling desires and carnal
purposes. Their mission was to annihilate every vestige of
idolatrous seperstition, which, if they had accomplished,

would have resulted in the prevention of much national trouble and moral obliquity, but instead, they mingled promiscuously with the heathen and reaped the baneful consequences.

The heathen claimed strange things for their deities; thus, the Egytians believed that their gods sometimes transformed themselves into animals, hence the ibis, the ape, the cat, the dog, the bull, the crocodile and the beetle, were reverenced as divine. The Carthagenians declared that Urania could control the clouds and speed or withhold the rain, and that Saturn could command all possible calamities, and even perform the remarkable feat of swallowing his own children. Other deities, it was claimed, held fortune, the crops, and life or death in their hands. The Greecian divinities, it was said, incited to war, nerved the arm of the warrior, assumed the forms of men, fought on the battle-field, and contended with, wounded and slew each other. But there was no history, there was nothing but myth to substantiate such claims.

On the contrary, the Hebrew people, if they saw not the person of God, felt his power, The manna that fell from Heaven, by which the hungry multitude were fed for forty years, was no trick of legerdemain. The thunderings and legislations of Sinai were more dreadful and glorious than any magnificence that can attach to an earthly tribunal. Then that Holy Temple and Sacred Altar, those heavenly communings, those frequent shouts of spiritual triumph, that covenant and oracle, that promise of Messiah, how strengthening and inspiring! Neither Egyptian, nor Median, nor Philistine, nor Tyrian could boast a history like this. The God of the Hebrew was not the idol Apolos bound to the altar with a chain of gold, but

"The God that rules on high,
That all the earth surveys."

Israel, though perverse and apostate, was pursued and environed by the active love of an unforgetful Providence; perhaps no more than other peoples, but they more than others, learned at last to recognize it. Should we stop and consider, it would appear to the worst of us that God has not been far away. The divine spirit woos us as individuals, as nations, along the line we ought to go. In the lapse of years we look back and see where the doings of Providence were kindly intended for our good, and would have accomplished good had we yielded to our supreme convictions. So after ten centuries of experience in apostacy and penitence, unbelief and service, Israel retrospected the past, compared their history as sinners with their history as believers, and their experiences as idolaters with their experiences as worshippers of Jehovah, and confessed that the Lord had been good. It was in the subduing atmosphere of such a review that Isaiah addressed Israel in the language of the text, "Ye are my witnesses, saith the Lord, and my servant whom I have chosen, that ye may know and believe me, and understand that I am he; before me there was no God formed, neither shall there be after me."

God's people, in whatever clime or age they live, are witnesses. If the Jew could testify of the divine character and power. much more can the Christian, for he stands as it were on the shoulders of all who have preceded him; the past as well as the present is his. Messiah has come—salvation is an actual experience. But modern unbelief would dethrone God both in the moral and material universe. That which can destroy the unfaith of the times is testimony. God's people have proved the truth of the Gospel in their experiences, therefore "Ye are my witnesses saith the Lord, and my servant whom I have chosen." It will be practical therefore to inquire

I. WHAT ARE THE QUALIFICATIONS OF A CHRISTIAN WIT-
NESS?

II. WHAT IS THE BURDEN OF THE CHRISTIAN'S TESTIMONY?

Numerous learned volumes have been written on the
" Evidences;" they are as good in the sphere of theology,
as other text-books are in the sphere of geology, botany,
chemistry. or astronomy; there is Butler's Analogy, for
instance, the author of which shows clearly that Nature
and Christianity proceeded from the same source; other
books that prove the harmony of nature and revelation;
others that scientifically demonstrate the integrity and authenticity of the Sacred Records; books which, if the wise-
acres of infidelity would diligently and faihfully read,
would destroy some of their conceit and vanity.

Great and complete as are the written evidences of
Christianity, we must not make the fatal mistake of sup-
posing that they are pre-eminent; there is a silent testimony
far more convincing, the testimony of a perfect Christian
character, such is a living epistle known and read of all
men.

In answering the question what are the qualifications
of a Christian witness? we might answer

1. *Correctness.* Presumptive or untrustworthy evidence will not do. In law there is such a thing as legal presumption. Show that a man has not been heard from for
seven years and the law will presume that he is dead. Prove
that a certain person has held peaceful possession of a piece of
land for twenty years and the law will presume that he
must be the rightful owner; or prove that a child is under
seven years of age and the law will presume that he is without discretion. Such evidence may do for the law. but it
will not do for Christianity. One cannot declare the "Old
Adam" has been harmless for seven years therefore he is

crucified with Christ; nor that he has been a professor of religion for two decades therefore he must be a Christian; nor that he has been testifying for Christ for seven years and therefore his testimony is true, for it is plain the Old Adam asleep, is not the Old Adam dead; profession is not possession; what a man says is not necessarilly true; correctness means more than presumption, it means "truth in the inward parts".

A witness must present "the truth, the whole truth, and nothing but the truth"; no mere theory of his own can be received. So a Christian must testify as to what Religion is to him, it were insufficient to declare what it has done for others, or to expatiate on the indwelling powers, or even the sublimities of the Gospel, except so far as they touch and morally quicken his own soul.

The world cannot be convinced of the power and blessedness of Christian truth by witnesses who know nothing about it. To witness a good profession it must be put on the ground of experience. The people are convinced of the healthful properties of certain water, not so much by the analysis as by experience; invalids drank, were cured and confessed it. So God asks for witnesses who have tasted and seen that he is good; witnesses who have washed in the fountain opened for sin and uncleanness and have been healed of their moral maladies; men cannot long resist the honest testimony of experienced men.

Correctness implies a well-intended, unremitting effort to obtain a perfect experience. It is true that everything has its weight; what is seen in the momentary flash of the lightning, what is felt in the sudden and violent movement of a spiritual spasm, it may be better to have loved a little and lost it than never to have loved at all, that man who is awakened to-day and backslides to-morrow may know something of the Christian life; but it is he who has started and goes on, he who climbs despite every obstacle, he who goes through summer heat and winter cold, he whose experience widens and deepens and intensifies day by day, he who has become "rooted, grounded and fixed", and not he who had an experience once, but has none to-day, who may expect to convince the world by his testimony.

Perhaps you have heard of the old colored man who, when he was asked his age, said, "Well, sah; I doesn't know how old I is, but I knows how old I is as de Lord's chile; I was born again" he said "jest afore Christmas a long time ago, and every time dat Christmas came I jest drop a pebble into dis here bottle; now, massa, if you jes count dem pebbles you'll see how old I is as de Lord's chile." The pebbles were counted and fifty-one told the story of his Christian life. That old negro had an experience. So we need an experience that counts one every year, an experience of constant service, growing love, and increasing faith.

2. *Information.* Intelligence in any possible position in life is better than ignorance; a full head is always preferable to an empty one, unless it is full of nonsense. The merchant must have brain as well as push; the farmer, to succeed, must have mind as well as muscle; the mechanic must have good sense as well as good tools, and the minister who deals in words rather than in thought would, in this educated age, very soon play out.

Christianity cannot afford to put a premium on ignorance; it would be contrary to its own genius, for it turns darkness into light and barren brains into productive brains. It is wonderfully connected with universal knowledge, and to the inspiration that is necessary to its pursuit. Having found a Divine Father, the soul seeks to know the universe he has made. Science is the natural result of devotion, a devout man beholds the earth and regards its vales, hills, mountains, rivers, lakes, seas, its flora and fauna, its laws and its wonders, and loves to study its clouds and storms, its blue skies and beaming stars, because he loves God. "An undevout astronomer is mad."

A child of God has an inborn right to know every good thing and to be able to distinguish what is bad that he may shun it. The more a man knows the more perfect will be his testimony for God and Christianity; he may even open the gates and let in the flood of the world's thought. Why make him a hermit locked up in the cell of his own opinions? Thoroughly educated in the wisdom of the Word of God, there is nothing in Vedas, or Shasters, or Koran, or Philosphy, or Infidelity that can injure him. The testimony of a Christian cannot possibly suffer on account of being able to offset the excellencies of other religions by the greater excellencies of his own, and certainly a sound Christian should be able to point out the defects cf opposing systems. It is not intelligence but ignorance that kills, "the people perish for lack of knowledge."

Let us sustain the public schools, support and endow colleges of the highest order, encourage those who devote their lives to the profession of a teacher, give the boys and girls the most liberal education, seek to sanctify knowledge with the spirit of the Gospel; let us determine to devote at least one hour in every twenty-four to the reading of good books, let us think for ourselves, let us encourage thought in our Sunday Schools, our class-meetings, our prayer-meetings, then there will be less religion of a treadmill character, and less cant, and with an undoubted Christian experience which is of the first importance, we shall be able to witness a good profession before God and man.

3. *Individuality.* Variety prevails, "one star differeth

from another star in glory." Earth is diversified, mountains swell, valleys sink, rivers roll, lakelets dance; there are trees of all kinds, sizes and forms; there are flowers of every hue and tint and shape, and no two blades of grass are exactly alike. One thing cannot metamorphose itself into another; it is well that it cannot. A like variety exists in the human body. Paul alludes to it, the foot, the hand, the ear, the eye; one cannot say to the other "I have no need of thee;" it is the variety of members in one body that makes the perfect man. Similar differences exist in a building, the parts are numerous, the material is not all alike, it is in different forms and places, and because each part and piece serves its particular purpose the building stands forth in all its finished beauty, all its elaboration of convenience and comfort. Should the foundations and cornices undertake to exchange offices, confusion and destruction would reign.

God has planned dissimilarity in the church among his witnesses; one is a mountain and can never make a sea of himself, another is a flower and cannot become a star, another is a hand and cannot change himself into a foot, an eye, or an ear, while still another is a girt and cannot become a sill or a rafter.

The Gospel has probably done for us each a different work; it has conquered this man's appetite, subdued this man's passion, and chastened the thoughts and strengthened the love of these, so that under Grace we need not be ashamed of our individualities; it is better to be what we are; whether, therefore, we be corner stones or shingles in the Temple of God, let us be thankful and do our best in whatever position Providence may place us. Even shingles can tell of pattering rains and smiling sunbeams; iron girts can tell of form and strength acquired in glowing heat and by anvil ringing. and the hard, cold, marble can tell of polished veins and nobler destiny secured under chisel, and mallet, and revolving irons.

Yes. positive characters are few, a majority of men are willing to become the shadows of somebody else, at least transparent bodies through which the sunbeams of other men's minds pass without absorption; you can look through their transparency and see whom they imitate; thus they throw up their own individuality. they step out of the sphere for which they were intended and forego their own personal influence and all the good that might possibly come of it. Some Goliath takes a sling and pebble and makes a child of himself, or some David puts on a giant's armor which crushes him with its weight.

The Gospel influences man in the depths of his own self-hood, it makes the best kind of a man by sanctifying his peculiarities, and sends him forth complete in himself to testify to its saving truth and power; there will be phazes of difference in the individual testimony. but in its general effects it will blend like the moving bits of a kaleidoscope, or like the varied forms and tints of a landscape. As witnesses for God, therefore, let us endeavor to be correct in our spiritual presentation, let us witness an intelligent profession. and let us stamp our testimony with the seal of our redeemed individuality. Let us inquire.

II. WHAT IS THE BURDEN OF A CHRISTIAN'S TESTIMONY?

1. It is the burden of the Christian's testimony to demonstrate the possibility of salvation. There are many truths in which the world is interested. There are many questions started even by the Word of God, that really deserve consideration. and yet are secondary in importance. In the early Church it was a lawful question—What is to become of the rites and ceremonies of Judaism? What is

the position of the Church with regard to holy days? What is to be done with endless Jewish genealogies? But there was one thought paramount to every other thought, the thought, nay, the historic fact that "Jesus Christ came into the world to save sinners."

So there are many things to which Christians may testify, if they are able, and many opinions that may be discussed: they may talk about inspiration, the authority of Scripture, the Trinity, the procession of the Spirit, the philosphy of the Atonement, the geology of Genesis, the science of Darwin, the speculations of Heckel, but the fact most worthy of thought and testimony is the salvation of sinners. The Israelites may have been idolaters, Butler's analogy is a great book, knowledge is important, individuality must not be forgotten, the M. E. Church has a million and a half of members, Arminianism is better than Calvinism, but *this* is the faithful saying, *this* is worthy of *all* acceptation, *this* is the burden of the Christian's testimony, "Christ Jesus came into the world to save sinners."

The problem of salvation to the sinner is strange and enigmatical; he may see its beauty but fails to see its application; he does not even, by nature, understand his own moral danger, therefore God sends the quickening spirit and requires each Christian to present the convincing testimony. Build a church, open the Bible, present the glorious scheme of salvation by faith to large and listening audiences, yet if there were none to whom the arm of the Lord had been revealed, who would believe your report? Missionaries often preach and labor in new fields many years before a soul is is converted, but one faithful native Christian having been secured, then, under the influence of personal testimony they press on to win. Give a few who know the way and walk in it, who have found the light and keep it shining, and are willing to let the world know what the Lord hath done for their souls, and the conviction is complete, the victory is sure: an honest man's testimony cannot long be resisted; thus the evidence of the possibility of salvation rests upon the Christian; argument is unavailing without the clinched nail of personal testimony.

2. It is a burden of Christian testimony to show that the Gospel universalizes sympathy. The Church, during its history, has at times given poor testimony to the power of the Gospel to make men broad and sympathetic. Nay, those who called themselves followers of Christ were often mere pretenders; men have been recreant to their sacred trusts and false to the principles proclaimed by the Master.

"I will tell the Church," says Ingersol, "why I hate it: You have imprisoned the human mind; you have been the enemy of liberty; you have burned *us* at the stake, roasted *us* before slow fires, torn *our* flesh with irons; you have covered *us* with chains, treated us as outcasts; you have filled the world with fear; you have taken our wives and children from our arms; you have confiscated our property; you have denied us the right to testify in courts of justice; you have branded us with infamy; you have torn out our tongues; you have refused us burial. In the name of your religion you have robbed us of *every* right, and after having inflicted upon us every evil that can be inflicted in this world, you have fallen upon your knees, and with clasped hands implored your God to finish the holy work in hell."

To charge such things on the Christian people of the present age, were impossible except to the slanderous daring of infidelity. Yet, to this terrible arraignment, there was once a party in the body of the Church who might have pleaded guilty; it would be foolish for us to deny the fact or attempt to palliate the wrong; zeal fired by ignorance, bigotry inspired by fanaticism have been a consuming flame of cruelty, as ready to dart out from the heterodox as from the orthodox. The enthusiastic theories of men have been accepted as the revelations of God, the glosses of un-principled disputants have been uttered as inspirations. Hypatias have been given to death, a Galileo and a Coperni-cus to the inquisition, and dissenters to the flames; and prayers have been offered that the blue fires of hell might penetrate the souls of the martyrs.

The present is not responsible; the past has been as marked with gentleness and sweetness as with persecution. Infidelity forgets or ignores this fact. We can only lament that ever men have been narrow and cruel, and regret that they have so much lacked the spirit of the Gospel, and hope that the sharp, scathing sword of educated criticism may be always and everywhere used against whatever may corrupt or cripple the faith as it is in Christ.

Wherever the Gospel is permitted to work unhindered in the human heart it strengthens the bonds of brother-hood, and widens and deepens the sympathies of men. The fruits of the spirit are not "bigotry, superstition, hatred, wrath, murder;" but "love, joy, peace, long-suffering, gen-tleness, goodness, faith, meekness, temperance." Christi-anity broke in upon a blood-thirsty age and softened it with love. Christ came and suggested, and accomplished a plan by which the world might be lifted out of superstition, dessolation and woe. If Christian law is in certain cases more rigid than the Mosaic, it is always more benign. It breaks into the harem and stricking the shackles from the hand of woman, it makes her the partner and the equal of man. Pagan nations slaughter their children; the Romans exposed their little ones to death; infanticide has prevailed in India and China, but Jesus took little children in his arms and blessed them. As for the present, we see that, while custom degrades this man and honors the other, while the rich regard the poor as an inferior race, while the capitalist puts his foot on the neck of the laborer, and the plebeian is arrayed against the patrician, the Gospel would destroy all caste, bitterness, and strife, and fold the race, without respect of person, in the arms of a blessed and universal brotherhood; it is a voice that whispers "little children love one another," for love is of God; "he who loveth not his brother whom he hath seen how shall he love God whom he hath not seen."

Do you ask then for the proof that Christianity is of God? Then your attention might be aroused by argument; the person of Jesus would crown your reason with heavenly reality; but when I show you a living example of the Gospel power, a man who has broken away from the narrow environments of selfishness, a soul moving seraph-like in the broad field of universal fraternity, his sympathy sweeping onward like moving light, his love reaching this man in his joy and that one in his sorrow; a sanctified spirit doing by proxy the work of Jesus Christ, you will be convinced beyond a doubt or a question.

The greater the love-work the Church shall accomplish, the more willingly and generally it shall rise to the sublimity of unselfish sacrifice, the more overpowering will be the evidence that Christ, Christianity and the Church are divine. If Christians therefore would render their testimony complete, let them, by deeds of love perpetually repeating, manifest the spirit of Christ, and prove that the Gospel enters into whatever can lift up, make better, or bless the race.

" Ye are my witnesses saith the Lord:" but brothers, have you entered into the rich experiences of regeneration? Are you seeking information in regard to the things of the Kingdom? Are you working in that particular sphere,

and with those peculiar talents with which God designed
you should?   Are you trying to pursuade the world that
Christ Jesus saved sinners?   Do you feel yourself bound by
a chain of Christian love to all mankind?   Then continue
the voice of your testimony, for soon it must be hushed.
While we are on the witness-stand, and so many are await-
ing for our testimony, let the burden of our testimony be
on the side of Christ and his truth.

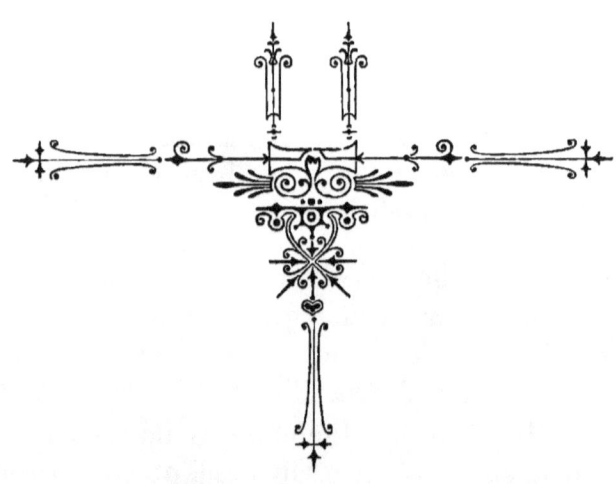

CHRISTIAN EXAMPLE.

"In all things shewing thyself a pattern of good works."—
Titus, 2:7.

Titus was a Greek gentile converted to Christianity.
Paul was his spiritual father. It is not known where he
lived, but probably somewhere in Asia Minor; nor is it
known at what time he was converted, save that it was
previous to the fourteenth year after the conversion of Saul.
He was for some time the traveling companion of the great
apostle, who seemed to repose perfect confidence in him, en-
trusting him with letters to carry to Corinth, appointing
him to heal the divisions of that Church, and sending him
to Crete to ordain elders in every city. The tradition is that
Titus soon left Crete, but returned and preached the Gospel
there, and in the neighboring islands, dying in the ninety-
fourth year of his age.

Crete is an island in the Mediterranean Sea, 250 miles
long and 50 miles broad. It is supposed to have been settled
originally by a people from the coast of Palestine, who were
called Crethi or Cretans. The island was once infested with
pirates; it gave eighty vessels to the Trojan war; it

furnished Lycurgus a model for his code; it was celebrated for its hundred cities; during the time of Christ and the apostle the Cretans were in a greatly degenerated state; the population of the island was composed largely of rough seamen; Paul describes them as being "liars, evil beasts and slow bellies," or gluttons.

Titus was a young man when the apostle appointed him to that large circuit, therefore, soon after his arrival in Crete Paul wrote and sent to him a letter of advice, counselling that he exhort the aged men to be "sober, grave, temperate, sound in faith, charitable and patient," that the aged women be "in behavior as becometh holiness, not false accusers, not given to much wine, and teachers of good things;" that "*they* should teach the young women to be sober, to love their husbands, to love their children to be discreet, chaste, keepers at home, good, obedient to their own husbands;" and to exhort "the young men to be soberminded;" but especially impressing that young minister that in all things he should "show himself to be a pattern of good works."

> " Some parsons are like finger posts,
>   I've often heard them say
> They never go to Heaven themselves,
>   But only point the way."

But it was not so with Titus, he was to win by pure precept and proper example; he was to exert on those semi-barbarous Cretans a transforming influence, first by his preaching, but secondly and more effectually by his Christian example.

What is true of the ministry is true of the church; in a sense we are all " priests unto God", so that the counsel of the text is profitable for the pew as well as the pulpit; and when Paul said to Titus " in all things show thyself a pattern of good works," he spoke to the laymen as well as to the minister.

There are three points presented in this text that are worthy of consideration.

I.   THAT CHRISTIANS ARE PATTERNS.

II.   THAT CHRISTIANS ARE PATTERNS IN ALL GOOD THINGS.

III.   THAT CHRISTIANS ARE TO *SHOW* THEIR PATTERNS.

There are several anglicized words having nearly the same significance; for instance there is the word *model*, from modus, which means a measure, or standard. or copy, hence a copy of a statue, a bust, a machine or a structure of any kind, on a reduced scale. In this sense a Christian is a model of Christ, and Christianity is measured by the character of the Christian. Men judge of the Gospel by the moral life of its adherents. There is nothing in Christ which is not in Christian character if the Christian is *true*. The difference is one of capacity, not of quality; a Christian is a model of Christ.

There is also the word example from the Latin eximere, to take out, meaning literally that which is taken out of a larger quantity, as a piece, a sample; thus the Christian is morally speaking a piece of Christ; "ye are ensamples to all that believe." What a privilege, what a responsibility, to be in moral fibre, and texture, and in all those elements that enter into character just like Christ. We cannot be ensamples without first having undergone a new creation.

Finally, there is the word pattern. which is something to be copied or imitated. The command is " in all things shew thyself a pattern," that is, one who can say " follow me," for I follow Christ; make your life after mine, for mine is made after Christ; imitate me for in mind and spirit I imitate the Lord Jesus. It will not do to eulogize the beauty of Christian precept; if we would win men to high spiritual attainment, we shall succeed best by the power of a good example. The injunction, " do as I tell you, not as I do," kills and quickens not. The Christian parent must be able to say to his children, " I am your spiritual pattern;" the teacher to his scholars, "copy after me"; the minister to his congregation " follow me:" the Church to the world, " live by me." We as Christians are to manifest the due proportion, the grace, the perfection of true character. We are in all things to be patterns—but if patterns, how important that we should be correct.

A pattern must first pass through the experienced hand, under the trained eye and the unerring rule of the pattern-maker. So a Christian character must first be fashioned by the hand of Christ. No inexperienced hand can be a pattern-maker, for the work requires exactness. There is only one artisan who can make a model of Christ, only one who can transform souls into patterns, Christ himself. Only when we have passed under his hand can we say "follow me." Ministers boast of *their* converts, but it is an idle boast. God made the mind and he must renew it: he created the soul and only he can convert it: a man is transformed from sinfulness into holiness by the perfect law of God.

Yet the Church has its work, and each individual Christian in the Church has his work; the particular work of the Christian Church is to aid, instrumentally, in lifting this world into a higher life; but it cannot be done unless the individual Christian has attained to that higher life himself. To cut a garment according to an imperfect pattern is to spoil the garment; to pour melted metal into a mould formed from a defective pattern is to make the machinery defective; to introduce false figures into the solution of a problem is to carry them on and multiply them throughout the whole process. So to attempt to give shape and character to human souls by an imperfect or defective example is to mould them into moral deformity. The sinner compares himself to the Christian, if that Christian is a better man than the sinner, that sinner in thought at least is won to Christ; but if he is no better, if he sinks below the moral level of the sinner, that sinner is driven farther away from the Cross.

To be exemplary, Christians must be decided. A hybrid religion, a mixture of worldliness and the Gospel is poor stuff out of which to make a pattern. The man who stands on both sides of the line is really nowhere, he must get to one side or the other before he can find *himself*; neutrality makes a sandwich of a man; then to be a pattern is impossible because he imitates neither Christ or Belial.

Professions, however loud or long-continued, amount to nothing unless backed up by the power of a good example. There is a pointed story told about some workmen who, when strong drink was more commonly used than it is to-day, believed that one of their company visited the brandy bottle more often than the law allowed, so blackened its mouth on purpose to detect him. Soon there was a cry made, "somebody has been at the bottle." The drinker, though the black mark was on his lips, loudly protested that he was as "innocent as a child unborn." So a profession of religion is of poor effect when the black ring of hypocrisy is on the lips.

Even to proclaim and teach the precepts of the Gospel without the flame of a holy life, will fail to promote the moral interest of the race: precept and example must blend into one beautiful character as they did in Titus; they are distinct, yet they are vitally united: they are like the Siamese twins, to separate them were to destroy them.

Precepts are nails, they serve an excellent purpose, the

world cannot get along without them, they have been provided by the Master of Assemblies; but a good example is
the hammer that drives the nail into the sure place; without
the hammer the nails are useless. How ludicrous to see a
minister carry into Church his keg of nails twice each Sabbath, fifty-two Sabbaths each year, and year after year—
nails that have been wrought on the anvils of logic, eight-
pennys, tens, twentys, finishing nails, nails with silver tips,
nails with golden heads, and never bring in one exemplary
hammer.

The world is cumbered with precepts or nails, the pulpit is full of them, they have been scattered through the
pews, the people have carried them away, they are piled up
in our houses, Methodist nails, Presbyterian nails, Baptist
nails, Temperance nails, Philosophic nails, and now the
world is demanding a few more exemplary hammers to relieve the monotony, tack-hammers, sledge-hammers, hammers of sterling character, hammers consecrated to good
works, hammers with the ring of the right metal in them,
hammers that can break, or mend, or build, hammers that
will hammer away until worn out, or until the Gospel Temple shall be completed.

II   CHRISTIANS ARE PATTERNS IN ALL GOOD THINGS.

"All good things" embrace not only those things that
pertain to church membership, but also those things that
pertain to good citizenship.

Of course a Christian will be devout, an undevout
Christian is a burlesque. He must study his Bible, if he
does not love his Bible he does not love his religion; he duly
appreciates the various means of Grace, for there he enjoys
communion with saints; he will go to church on Sunday—
"he who walks six miles to church preaches a sermon six

miles long, for he preaches, by his example, to all the residents on the road as he passes." He is as religious at home as at church, if he has not an altar in his own house he is a hypocrite; he gives liberally of his substance to support the Gospel, else he has a religion that costs him nothing, and a religion that is not worth a sacrifice is not worth having. He is also engaged earnestly in the great work of saving souls, for he who is not interested in the salvation of another has no interest in his own. These things are so evident that a *Christian* without these qualifications is inconceivable.

A model Christian will aspire to make the Church of which he is a member a model society. The Church is the exponent of Christian civilization, and should not be a whit behind it; indeed it ought to be a little in advance of that which has become respectable through its all-polishing influence. Yet in some localities the Church has receded from its true position; the water that clothed the wilderness with beauty has become stagnant and, possibly, unwholesome; its own members being unprogressive have handed it over to inferiority, and made it the laughing stock of the world. A model Christian will not be satisfied with such social degradation; he will not limit his religion by his devotions; he will not be content "to dwell in a house of cedars while the ark of the covenant of the Lord remaineth under curtains"; if he cannot have elegance he will insist on neatness, he will work that his Church shall exert the greatest possible influence, that it shall cultivate the best society, and secure the best schools and the best teachers. True, locally, this cannot always be the case, but a model Christian will certainly wish for, and earnestly seek for, the *best* of all good things that the circumstances can afford. Wealth may not be at command, but a church may be strong despite its poverty, if a pattern of wise zeal and of good works.

A model Christian is a pattern in *all* good things; not only is his heart aflame with heavenly devotion, and his church-home the very cream of good taste and sociability, but in all places, under all circumstances, he aspires to be the highest type of a man, and he has the elements right within his reach by which that loftiness of moral manhood can be secured. He will not be effeminate if the spirit of Jesus controls thought, passion and purpose. He will not be cowardly if devoting his life to his principles. There will be no sourness about him if his heart is filled with divine love as it ought to be. There can be no cold exclusiveness about him who lives for his race as the God-man did; and there is no complaining on the lips of him whose faith "like the cammomile-plant", develops the more rapidly for having been crushed. The model Christian therefore is the best man everywhere and every time, in all things a pattern.

If a Christian is in *all things* a pattern, then he must be actively interested in whatever belongs to the well-being of men. If it were better for mankind that all the barriers of caste should be broken down, the model Christian would be the first to step out of his cell and move, seraph-like, among his fellows in order to promote their fraternity. If it is better to be happy than miserable, the model Christian, having filled himself with joy by drinking at its fountain, will move among men, not in solemn sombreness, but bright and smiling as a sunbeam. If it is better to be benevolent than selfish, that Christian who is a pattern in all good things will wisely consecrate his substance on the altar of human need, knowing that "he that giveth to the poor lendeth to the Lord". If intemperance is a curse, corrupting the bodies, blasting the brains and blighting the eternal hopes of men, the Christian will be a leader in all honest endeavor to banish it from the world. If the Gospel contains those truths and moral forces by which mankind can be lifted up to its God-intended place, if it can render the race happier, wiser and better, if it can sweep the shadow from the face of death, and the mist from the gates of eternal life, the pattern of Christianity will be indomitable in . his sublime purpose of giving the Gospel to the world. Thus there is a completeness in the Christian life, it makes its possessor a pattern in *all good* things.

III. CHRISTIANS *SHOW* THEIR PATTERNS.

There is a class of professed Christians who seem to think that they should live in a perpetual eclipse; they are harmlessly good; they are silently righteous; they have an experience but never refer to it; they engage in good works but the world does not know it; the only prominence they enjoy is a prominence of obscurity.

But thus " the children of light are not as wise as the children of darkness"; for the merchant, for instance, makes a success of his merchandize by a judicious display of his goods; the inventor blesses his brother-man by telling the world of the benefits of his invention. By a similar display and comparison international expositions stimulate progress in commerce, science and art. The world would become insipid and stale if it were to hold every good thought and thing in obscurity.

Of course it would be wrong for a Christian to work simply for notoriety, to pray just to be seen of men, to give alms simply for the sake of applause and prominence; if such were the motive to an action better not act, better " not let the left hand know what the right hand is doing";

but a Christian, one whose eye is single to the glory of God, need not blow out his light lest the world should see and praise it, nor put it under a bushel lest the heart should become vainglorious.

It were a great pity to deprive the world of the light that comes of a holy life and a good confession. It is something to know that goodness is not all dead. When angel fingers touch the chords of a human soul, the world, if possible, should hear the melody.

The Gospel is not in need of silent adherents. For the love of Christ rocks would speak if men did not; Christ likens character to "a city set on a hill that cannot be hid", to "a light that is on a table and not under a bushel"; and the Great Apostle requires that we "*show*" ourselves to be patterns in all good things.

But this is an individual matter. The command *show* thyself a pattern is meant for you and me as much as it was meant for Titus. We are so constituted that we *must* "show our faith by our works". No work means no faith. When love is in the soul it will display itself, like the life in the rose it *must* burst out and scatter its sweetness. " Every man is to look to the things of others;" "to take upon himself, Christ-like, the form of a servant, to *work* out his own salvation, Every knee is to bow, every tongue to confess; the sons of God are to hold forth the word of life. In the midst of a crooked and perverse nation we are to *shine* as so many lights in the world."

God expects me to contribute something. I am to hold forth what light I can, starry rays if possible, a tallow dip if I have nothing better. In every thing that can edify the Church, or elevate the race, or promote a good cause, I am to have an equal interest and a proportionate share. Each man's contribution too will be counted; if tears are all that can be given I know that "they that sow in tears shall reap in joy": or if a prayer is all that can be offered, I am sure that that will not be forgotten; for John tells me "that the golden vials full of odors, in the hands of the four and twenty elders, are the prayers of saints." I am not to stand back from the fire that is to warm this frozen world into summer beauty, because I can add only a straw to the fuel; nor on the other hand may I reap any of its direct benefits unless my little straw has been contributed.

The idea is, do something. There is something in which the poorest. the most unworthy may excel. God has not left even the least of us without a mission. If nothing is done it is our own fault; it is perhaps because we are ashamed to show ourselves " faithful in what is least"; we are attempting great things that are beyond our reach, or dreaming of chances that may never flit across the field of our vision. Oh, let us take the little chances, the world is full of them, so full that no generous soul need wait a day without reaping a harvest of benedictions. Let us show ourselves to be patterns of good things in the opportunities that we have, and perhaps our example may encourage some other soul to go and do likewise.

I have heard that one day a little boy went home from a mission school with his face washed clean, his mother saw the improvement and washed her face; coming home from his work at night, the father, by the force of example, was induced to wash his face; they then washed the faces of all their children. and all the neighbors that lived in the alley went to work and washed their faces; and thus the people that had so long lived in filth became an amusing instance of a good example. So let us wash the thunder from our brows, the melancholy from our long-drawn countenances, and the glue from our finger-tips; let what good nature we have flow freely out. embodying itself in good works, and, perhaps, men who are dead and buried spiritually may be resurrected by our example.

Others may hide their light under a bushel, let us be exemplary. Others may pursue schemes of self-aggrandizement, let us seek a moral up-building. Others, sluggard like, may fold their hands and be at rest, let us be patterns of good works, looking not for the perishable reward a worthless world can give, but to the "exceeding and eternal weight of glory" which God has promised to bestow.

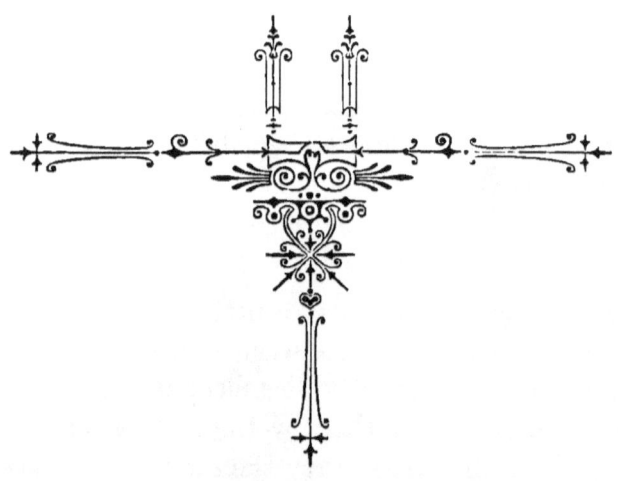

THE BURIED TALENT.

And I was afraid, and went and hid thy talent in the earth: lo, *there* thou has *that is* thine.—*Mat.* 25, 25.

This chapter contains two parables; that of the Virgins, the design of which is to teach that the heart, the inner life which is represented as being a lamp, must be kept supplied with the oil of Grace, and burning with the flame of love, so that character shall shine forth in its moral purity. Also that of the Talents, which beautifully sets forth the truth that the outward life and activities of the Christian, must receive due attention and be properly regulated.

The plot of the parable of the Talents is admirably conceived. The idea is that in church-life there are certain phases resembling certain features that are common in the business world. "The Kingdom of Heaven," says Christ, " is like unto a man traveling into a far country, who called his own servants and delivered unto them his goods." Of course being servants they were in the service of their master voluntarily. So church-membership and the responsibility of the Christian profession, though beneficial and necessary, are not compulsory, they are freely and voluntarily assumed.

It was customary in olden times for a master to leave his business in the hands of his servants or agents; they took his land and paid him a portion of the produce, or they took his money and loaned it for him, paying him a stipulated part of the interest.

The traveler spoken of in the parable is represented as being a money-lender. On the eve of starting on a journey he calls three of his servants and "delivers to them his goods," to each according to his ability. To the first he delivered five talents, or about $7,500.00: to the second two talents, or $3,000.00, and to the third one talent, or $1,500.00, and then undertook his journey to a far country.

Straightway the agents began their work. The first advertises that he has money to lend on good securities, and soon a flourishing business is on hand. The second does likewise, and although his capital is smaller he succeeds, proportionately just as well as the other. But the third, either stupidly misapprehended the nature of the contract he had made or was guilty of supineness and indifference, so instead of advertising money to let "he went and digged in the earth and hid his lord's money."

After a long time the master returned and inquired into the condition of his business. The servant who had received five talents opened his books and demonstrated that the principal had doubled; with great satisfaction he announced, "behold, I have gained". The servant who had received two talents also displayed his accounts and he was glad to be able to report "behold, I have gained two more". But the servant with one talent had no such a happy settlement; he accomplished no good for himself, he had not used his talent to benefit others, nor had he been of any

use to his master; he had gained nothing, had not even
tried to do anything, he could not say, "behold. I have
gained", and was too cowardly to confess, "I have lost!"
but, as delinquents often do, he began to upbraid his master and to excuse himself. "You are a hard man. You
exact conditions that your agents cannot meet. You have
made me afraid; I have not embezzled your talent, nor mis-.
spent it, nor lost it, but I have buried it in the earth; 'lo!
there thou has that is thine.'"

What think you of such a servant as this? Was he
worthy to enter into the joy of his Lord? When the re-
ception shall be given, when the banquet is spread, when
the song swells upward, will he be worthy to participate in
the festivities? Nay, rather, he should be dismissed the
service, he should not be permitted to sit in the joyous light
within; he deserves to be thrust into the darkness without.
What if thou art the man?

My subject is The Buried Talent, to this I invite attention by considering

I. THE VARIOUS ENDOWMENTS OF THE CHURCH.

Althouh the talent stands for a certain amount of
money, yet the money represents what is far more valuable, even the intellectual and spiritual endowments of an
individual or an aggregation of individuals. When Christ
left his disciples, he left them duly endowed, equipped and
qualified for the work that they had to do. Similar endowments, with perhaps two or three exceptions, charaterize
the Church of to-day. Those exceptions are the gift of
miracles, the gift of tongues, and possibly the gift of
prophecy; they were the blushes of Pentecost, and were
not to be perpetuated any more than the rosy hues of
morning are to continue until noon; they were to melt and

fade into the better, intenser, more practical work-a-day of Christian life and character.

The Church is endowed with a variety of *natural* gifts. Not that these obtain in larger measure among Christians, but that they have a generous share of them. Take the organizing talent, that which groups social forces and quickens them into service, and whose plans exceed those of such men as Wesley. Take the faculty of discernment, who can take the palm from such men as Bacon? Take the teaching talent, none excel the instructors that Christianity has produced. Take the gift of wisdom; surely "the Seven Wise Men of Greece" would fade in the presence of such metaphysicians as Hamilton, such observers as Newton, such scholars as Dr. Adam Clarke. Take the talent of eloquence and who in point of success ever swept beyond the magic of a Chalmers?

Or, if you please, take the several aesthetic talents, that skill which embodies ideals in picture or in marble; or that wonderful genius by which ideals are created, or that heavenly art by which discordant sounds are swept into pleasing harmonies, and where can such talent be found in greater measure than in the Christian Church? Christianity has built thought, feeling and devotion into its temples; it has swept the vicious spirit from sculpture and painting; it has put soul into poetry and Heaven into song. Where is better verse than Cowper's or Milton's? Where are sublimer harmonies than those of Mozart or Beethoven? As one contemplates such magnificent endowments of genius, two questions occur: How grand must be the possibilities and how fearful the responsibilities of the Christian Church?

Besides natural gifts, the Church is spiritually endowed. Among those spiritual gifts I would, though doubtfully, place prophecy, the power of foreseeing the future; for it seems to me that the human mind is a far-reaching faculty, touched by the finger of God it may detect some coming calamity, or some approaching benediction; when a thoughtful man gets hold of one of God's unchanging laws, he can predict its results, with sublime confidence he can utter a prophecy. Then what is love if it is not a spiritual endowment? John truly said "love is of God;" at this perennial fountain the Church professes to be drinking; can there be an endowment more glorious than this? Add to these "the Baptism of the Holy Ghost", which is a divine presence in the world, helping those who call upon him; this spirit is claimed by the Church; he is said to "help the infirmities" of God's people and to "lead them into all truth"; baptized with such a spirit the Church is indeed endowed with power from on high.

In addition to these natural and spiritual endowments, certain talents belong to the Church in consequence of the fact of her existence. I call them accidental. Thus the Church has had time. Who knows the value of time? Some men make much of "three score years and ten"; with a few thirty years have been pregnant with astonishing results, but the Christian Church has had two thousand years. Time has given prestige to the Church; she has lived while a hundred generations have arisen and perished. She has survived the revolutions of history. She has grown reverend while philosophy has assumed a thousand shapes and faded a thousand times, so that her words have weight, her prestige gives her authority, wealth, learning, wisdom.

With such endowments as those I have mentioned, the Church should be well-nigh omnipotent in the world, its heart full of the life of God, the remotest corners of the earth should feel the vitalizing warmth of its influence, and the centers of society should glow with celestial fire; it should not merely impress but *sway* empires; in short, with such endowments and opportunities each Christian should be able to adopt the language of the apostle and say " now, thanks be unto God, which always causeth us to triumph in Christ, and maketh manifest the savor of his knowledge by us in every place." But the question arises, is the Church of Jesus Christ as potent a factor in the formation and control of the great moral forces that enter into the lives of individuals and communities as it ought to be. This brings us to considder

II.   THE BURIED TALENTS OF THE CHURCH.

Speaking of the Church I use the term in its broad, not in its restricted sense. I do not mean the company of God's elect children, nor the community of true believers who live as they believe; but I mean the sum of the various Christian denominations that have been or are now in the world. Of many of these I fearlessly declare that they are not so important a power in the world for the uplifting, swaying, evangelizing and blessing of humanity as they ought to be, they are like the man who went and hid his lord's money in the earth.

Nor do I mean to say that Christianity has not been, and is not now, a gloriously aggressive force in the universe; it has won its saving way wherever the heart has been open to its influence. Christ proclaimed it, and the common people gave it their sympathy, though Pharisees and Saducees opposed; at Pentecost it was victorious. When persecution prevailed its triumph continued. When scholars like Lucian, Celsus, Porphry, Hierocles, attacked it, it lost none of its power. It marched upon the barbaric tribes of northern Europe and morally subdued them; when ignorance and immorality prevailed, when the organic

Church itself was corrupt, and all Europe held her priests, her doctrines, her ordinances in contempt, pure Christianity sprang to the front and led humanity forward to morality and victory. Denominations have fought, but the principles of Jesus have triumphed. In the eighteenth century the Gospel was undermined, but in the beginning of the nineteenth century a powerful reaction set in in favor of Christ and his truth. The infidel philosophy and opposing science of our day are but strengthening the scholarship and broadening the culture of Christianity.

I make, therefore, a distinction between Christianity and the Church; the former is a divine life-force that is destined to conquer, the latter may for all I know, in some of its existing forms, vanish away.

To a large extent the Church has buried its talents, and whether Protestant or Catholic, in so far as its God-given energies are dormant, it is to-day, as Dr. Ewer said, " only a miserable raft, its fragments floating apart, like the flying rack of the Heavens." The present Church may go under, but the Gospel will win.

It is true that certain individuals in the Church are faithful in that whereunto they are called; the servant with two talents has gained two, and he with five has gained other five. It is true that the number of these faithful followers has reached large proportions. In every denomination there are earnest, loving, devoted souls. In each Church there are believing, praying, zealous, efficient spirits. The salt and leaven of Christianity are at work everywhere. " There are a few names even in Sardis who have not defiled their garments;" yet there are many in the so-called Christian Church who " have a name to live and are dead."

Take the Church in this community as an example, it

will stand for the Church in many other localities: it is represented by fourteen sanctuaries, about the same number of priests and ministers, a Christian college and hundreds of adherents; it has intelligence. education, culture, wealth, genius, prestige; it has experience, superior facilities and thorough organization. There is no active opposition, no organized enmity has as yet risen into sufficient prominence to be worthy of notice; yet the Church is not perceptibly beating back the flood of sin. Saloons open their doors, profanity progresses, immorality thrives and souls go down to hell, while professed Christians stand and look on with stolid indifference; and it seems sometimes that a dead wall of adamant, impenetrable and insurmountable, has been built around the unsusceptible hearts of the children of men.

Nor can my own congregation plead that it is not guilty of having buried its talents. True, a revival wave has occasionally swept over this people, and there are many who will forever thank God for the fervent zeal of the Methodist Church; but alas! how few are ever heard pleading with and praying for the ungodly. Most of the young people of the congregation are still unconverted. Methodist children have forsaken the altars of their fathers because there was not religious and social power enough to hold them. The Church has won because a few have been faithful, but it has lost all it would have had if the eighty had been as true as the twenty have been.

Why then are the ungodly unconvinced of sin? Why are they not induced to become Christians? Is it because the Moral Law has lost its power? I think not, for atheism has but a small and negative influence; idolatry is unpopular, profanity is generally acknowledged to be wrong. The Sabbath is recognized as being a wise. good and useful provision; filial love is universally applauded; murder is frowned upon, adultery quickens general disgust, stealing is regarded as a crime against society, perjury is punishable by law, and covetousness dare not come to the front, for the spirit of the covetous man is regarded as low and mean. Neighborly love is extoled, and love of God, it is allowed, may deepen and intensify the love of humanity. Granting. therefore, that the Church is weak and futile, it is not because the Moral Law has lost its power on the consciences of men.

Do men refuse to become Christians because Christian character has lost its charm? I think not. Character is capital the world over, and the true Christian maintains a complete character. No one is willing to confess that he holds Christian virtue at a discount. The world may be wicked, yet, while it hates hypocrisy, and despises the spirit of whining sanctimoniousness, it admires the man who would die rather than cause principle to blush; it honors the man who will not lie, who is not for sale, whose virtues are sterling, and whose very impulses are formed under the scrutiny of "the all seeing eye". If the Church is feeble, therefore, it is not because Christian character has lost its charm in the world.

Nor is the Church inefficient because the Bible is untrue. Deism has assailed it, but it has failed to prove it false, or even to any considerable extent to shake the faith which the world has reposed in it. Gibbon, Paine, Voltaire, are dead, but the Bible still advises men of "Teperance, Righteousness and a Judgment to come." Naturalism indeed objects to the supernatural that is in the Scriptures; but the reason that would lift the hand divine from the Bible must restrain it in the universe. it insists that all the phenomena of nature are produced by blind force acting necessarily; yet despite naturalism, "the Heavens declare the glory of God and the Book even more sweetly than do the stars. Spiritualism tries to shift inspiration from the Bible, and to place it in the inward consciousness of humanity, nor can it be denied that man is inspired sometimes, but the spirit of Scripture feeds and satisfies the loftiest aspirations of the human soul. Rationalism has indeed overthrown a few of the darling theories of men, and has attempted to deprive the Word of its authoritative character, but according to its own confession, "the ideal, the spirit still survives, and this *must* shine in its own moral splendor." It cannot be claimed therefore that the moral impotency of the Church is the result of the falseness of its Scriptures.

If then, neither the impotency of the Moral Law, nor the unloveliness of Christian character, nor the untruthfulness of Scripture can account for the spiritual indifference of the unsaved world—what is the cause? Why is the Church in many localities so unsuccessful? I answer, the denominations by frequent abuses of Christianity, by a spirit of sectarian intolerance, by the inconsistency of professed Christians, and especially by the inertia and spiritual lassitude of its own members has impeded its own progress. This spiritual indolence is an obstacle in the way of the progress of the Gospel far greater than any philosophy or infidelity that ever assailed it. The buried or misdirected talents of the Church is the principal cause of its past and its present failures.

There are several reasons why the Church thus buries its talents; for example some Christians are inactive because they misapprehend the nature of God. Even good people have indulged the thought that he is "a hard master, reaping where he hath not strown", and requiring duties that cannot be done; therefore, however faithful in other things they are neglectful of spiritual responsibilities; but God is not such a master. He knows all the burdens that we carry, he entrusts those with five talents, those with two, and this with one talent. "Every man according to his several ability."

Others imagine that the little they can do is not worth doing. So, perhaps, thought the servant with one talent, who went and hid his lord's money; yet if he had used it it would have doubled in exactly the same time that it took to double the two or the five. Much is lost because we are afraid and conceal or withhold the little ability we have. If the men and the women in the Church who have only one talent would all arouse themselves there would be a grand movement in the "Valley of Dry Bones". The great dead-weight that is pulling down the cause of Christ is the thousands, perhaps millions of one-talented people who withdraw from active service under the plea that they can cultivate a solitary piety.

But what is more damaging to the cause of Christ even than indolence; is a certain tendency among people of good endowments to turn the Church into a board of trade and sell their talents to the highest bidder. There are members of the Christian Church who, like that automaton bird which an ingenious French mechanic put on exhibition at Vienna, have sweet voices, beaming eyes, and brilliant plumage, and they can sing the praises of God in the sanctuary with spirit and with power, but their song is awakened by no inward soul-life, they never indulged in an outbreak of gratitude to God for his goodness, and to start their music you must wind them up with a golden key. There is a superabundance of talent in the Church of God, its natural gifts consecrated and sanctified are sufficient to make it the Kingdom of Heaven indeed. What a pity so many talents should be buried and hid out of sight, because selfish souls demand pay, in dollars and cents, before they will serve God.

The result of inaction is forfeiture of ability. No matter what may be the cause, indolence, indifference, disaffection, apostacy, selfishness; once cease to work and soon you will forget how to work; neglect to take up your cross, and soon you will have neither disposition or strength to to touch it. Muscles unused lose their power, so ability unemployed will soon become disability. And that is one difficulty with the Church to-day; hundreds of its members are useless because they are out of practice. When indisposition prevails the Church is like a great Corliss engine, endowed with wonderful capacity but silent and inactive, because there is no steam in the chest and no fire in ths furnace. Give us the motive power of Love and we can move the world. This brings us to consider

III.   THE RESPONSIBILITY OF THE CHURCH IN THE PREMISES.

Christ declares that "the Kingdom of Heaven", that is the Church, or the people over whom Christ reigns may be compared to a number of servants, to each of whom has been entrusted certain important duties, which, during the temporary absence of the king must be faithfully performed, and in such a manner as shall promote the best interests of the servant, the glory of the kingdom and the honor of the king, and that "after a long time the Lord will come and reckon with them."

That reckoning is to be with each individual, not with the whole Church at once: each Christian, the successful and the unsuccessful, will be called to account. God will not say well done good and faithful Church, you have accomplished a great work, the redemption of this lost world "enter thou into the joy of thy Lord," but each servant, the faithful and the slothful, the good and the wicked, must appear personally before the Lord, at the reckoning that is coming there will be no opportunity for the servant who has done nothing, to slip in under cover of one who has been faithful unto death. Each must answer for himself.

That day of reckoning will be a joyful day for every true soul; it will bring the joy of satisfaction, the joy that comes to him who has done the best he could; it will be golden with the joy of approbation when the Master will say "well done"; it is no weakness to desire to be approved for our fidelity; it will be memorable with the joy of promotion, having been faithful "over a few things". how, inspiring to be made "ruler over many things"; besides that day will be full of the joy of reward, rewards so rich that "eye hath not seen, heart hath not conceived." Oh! think of entering into the joy of the Lord, and sitting down on his throne.

That day will be a sad day for the fearful and the unfaithful; in the presence of an assembled universe, what terror will strike the soul, when the Lord shall say "thou wicked and slothful, good for nothing and unprofitable servant, enter into outer darkness," and be divested of what few endowments you have. It is an awful thought that, because we have abused, or have not used for the glory of God the talents that here we possessed, we shall loose them all yonder. Perhaps this will be the punishment of the unfaithful; each exalted genius who ungenerously hid his talent in the earth, or selfishly endeavored to barter it for gold, will in the life to come be doomed to see that talent waste away. When our best gifts shall thus fall to naught there will be bondage, darkness, "weeping and angry gnashing of teeth."

In conclusion, we may observe that the practical points of this parable cannot be intended for Church members only; no greater moral obligations rest on them than rest on other people; it is as much the duty of the sinner to be in allegiance to the Kingdom of God as for the Christian. One distinguishing feature between the Church member and the outsider is that he who is within recognizes his moral responsibility, but he who is without ignores or evades it; neglect is equally as culpable in one case as the other.

The fact is, every creature is a "servant", and God has commissioned each servant to perform a certain work "according to his ability", and endowed him for his work, therefore if you, my unconverted friend, have concealed your talent in the earth, you cannot escape the judgment of the last day any more than will the delinquent Church member.

Standing before your Judge, what plea would you make? Would you accuse God of being "a hard master"? Every star that shines, every flower that unfolds its beauty, every joyous note of singing bird, every diadem of intelligence, every human soul, so precious that a world could not equal its worth would rebuke you for your folly. God, your Master, is Love.

Would you accuse him of "reaping where he has not sown"? Such a plea would be as absurd as the other; look at yourself, God has given you a heart-nature, a thinking mind, a life-time full of golden opportunities, a spirit capable of communion with the Father of Spirits, and a field for infinite, intellectual and spiritual development; from such a sowing God has a right to expect a harvest of improvement.

Would you in excuse of your neglect plead that you

were "afraid"? Afraid of what? Of some dear friend who has entrusted you with his property? This is what your divine Lord has done. Afraid of your fellow-men? You fearlessly do business among them every day. Afraid of yourself? How strange! You would trust yourself always where you would not dare to trust another. You have not feared to do wrong, but you have been afraid to do right; thus you are self-condemned, the plea of fear condemns you; there must be something radically wrong in that man who is afraid to be true.

Before that Judge who knows all would a sinner in his sober senses presume to make the plea that his talent, which for a long time has been unused and concealed in the gross things of earth, is pure and perfect as when first bestowed? Try such an experiment in other things, neglect your farm for a quarter of a century. or your business for a decade of years, or refuse to exercise your power of thought for six months. or sit down and do nothing, not even use a muscle of your body for a whole week and see, when you have made the experiment, whether your farm, or business, or intellect, or strength has deteriorated. So spiritual faculties unused will lose their lustre, concealed in the earth they must deteriorate. My sinful friend, your character before God is shriveling and your moral nature is a starveling to-day, because you have neglected to employ the crowning ficulties of your being, in the blessed work of promoting the glory of the Kingdom of God among men.

Your talent will always be buried in the earth until your heart-nature has been unearthed. "One cannot serve God and mammon." If there is 'no divine life in the soul, it is because the soul is engrossed with sensuous thought and sensuous living. He who is thus engrossed has not only buried *one* of his talents in the earth, but the whole of them, himself included. The whole man is in need of a resurrecting power. Christ, like the spring, has come to quicken the dead. The Sun of Righteousness shines brightly and healingly on the world. If men would look to that light they would grow toward it, they would leave the low things of earth and reach out after the blessings of Heaven, and then their talents would be called out, men would live as the flowers do, to beautify and benefit the world; nay more, they would live as Christ did, not for themselves but for others, consecrating their gifts to the good of others they themselves would be the gainers; love would broaden their manhood, widen their sympathies, keep their talents bright, intensify their hope and deepen their joy. Oh! let us seek for this larger, this more expanding life, this life that comes of earnest work for God.

> "Earth has engrossed our love too long,
>   'Tis time to lift our eyes
> Upward, dear Father, to thy throne,
>   And to our native skies."

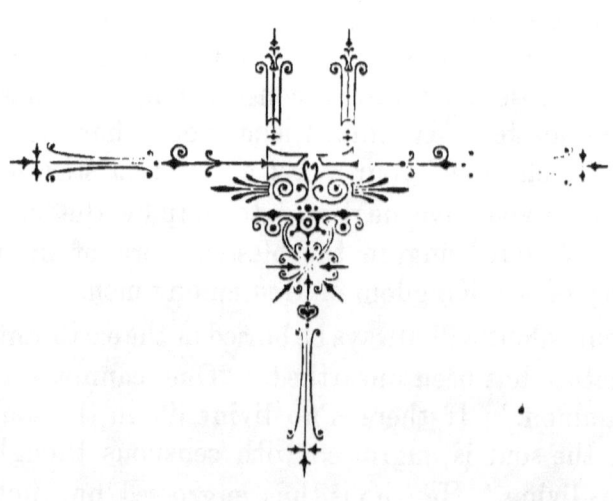

PARABLE OF THE LEAVEN.

Another parable spake he unto them; the Kingdom of Heaven is
like unto leaven, which a woman took, and hid in three measures of meal, till the whole was leavened.—*Mat.* 13, 33.

Here is what might be called a very strange mixture,
Heaven, Woman, Meal and Leaven; yet such a mixture as
is quite common in our experiences. We could not well get
along without each of them; nay, we must have them *all.*

Were it not for the thing spoken of. namely. "the
Kingdom of Heaven", which perhaps has not the appreci-
ation it deserves. Each of the other substantives mentioned
in the text might be, and indeed have been, badly interpreted. Thus: Thackery represents all women as being either
"weak or wicked", and even the Bible declares, "Adam was
not deceived, but the woman being deceived was in the
transgression." Meal, too, is suggestive of coarseness, gluttony, grinding,littleness and even deceitfulness; thus Tenny-
son speaks of those who "dabbling in the fount of 'flictive
tears, nursed by *mealy*-mouthed philanthropies, divorce the
feeling from her mate the deed." And as for leaven, that
is, yeast, what is it but bubbles of carbonic acid, transforming the starch of the meal into alcohol. which is, as the

temperance orators affirm, the very essence of corruption and death.

Leaven in the Scriptures generally means something that is bad. Paul speaks of "purging out the old leaven". Christ bade his desciples to " beware of the leaven of the Pharisees". The Jews, possibly because unleavened bread was a symbol of their bondage in .Egypt, refused to eat bread that had been leavened. They were also commanded to put every particle of leaven out of their houses during the time of their sacred feasts. Even the ancient Romans, idolators as they were, disliked the use of leaven in sacred things. because, as Plutarch said, " the leaven is born of corruption and corrupts the mass with which it is mingled."

But the leaven cannot be used in a bad sense in this parable, because that which is unquestionably good is compared to it. The parable does not teach that error, or heresy, or apostacy, or "the mystery of iniquity", or the corruptions of the world are like unto leaven. If such had been declared the figure would have been a very truthful one, for all unseen forces that are at work beneath the surface of society might properly be compared of leaven; but it is not such that Christ is speaking of; he speaks of the silent mightiness of his Gospel, and of his spiritual reign in human hearts and the world; he does not say that such is leaven, but that "the Kingdom of Heaven is like unto leaven which a woman took and hid in three measures of meal, " till the whole was leavened".

Those interpretations therefore that throw an unhopeful light on these matchless parables of Our Lord, as for instance, the theory that the mustard seed represents a deep and widespead worldliness, and the leaven an all-embracing corruption. which is to work in and gradually overcome the Church, cannot in reason be accepted, but on the

contrary, it must be concluded that, pure and precious as is
the Kingdom of Heaven, so is the noiseless but wide-work-
ing leaven, to which it is likened.

It is not to be supposed that perfection must be ascribed to the meal; the very fact that the heavenly leaven
is to be hid in the mass of meal, suggests the imperfection
of the mass, that is its *need* of transformation. It is admitted that in a sense the meal is to part with its native
characteristics, the leaven is to assimilate the mass; the
meal therefore represents something which is of itself imperfect, something that can be changed or improved by being brought into contact with the leaven of which Jesus
speaks, the warming, penetrating, transforming forces of
the Kingdom of Christ.

To make this matter still more evident, it is suggested
that there are three measures of meal, that is three parts.
The old theologians thought that the three measures of
meal stood for the three parts of the known world, Europe,
Asia and Africa, and concluded, rightfully too, that the
spiritual forces of the Kingdom will ultimately penetrate,
quicken and transform those great continents, converting
them from idolatry to Christianity, from sin to righteour-
ness, from self to God.   Others of the early fathers, Augustine for instance, taught that the three measures of meal
represented respectively Shem, Ham and Japheth, the three
sons of Noah, whose descendents embrace all the inhabitants of the earth, and that the Gospel of the Kingdom, as
it shall in its future unfoldings touch every human heart,
will turn all the children of men from darkness unto light,and
"from the power of Satan unto God," a blessed thought,
and as I believe a logical and truthful conclusion.

We shall be safe also in regarding the three measures
of meal as standing for man in his individuality and entirety

his body, his mind and his soul; nor should we exaggerate the truth if we were to declare that according as man shall allow himself to be influenced by the sanctifying spirit of the Gospel, its healthful, quickening, spiritualizing power, he will stand forth a perfect man; his body free from disease, his intellect exalted, his soul redeemed and fitted for the companionship of the glorified above.

Now, in regard to this Gospel leaven, the text suggests four facts, namely, that it is an independent power, that it is a hidden power, that it is a transforming power and that it is an all-pervading power.

1. Then the Leaven of the Gospel is an independent power. Christ taught that the Kingdom of Heaven is not a component part of this universe; it does not inherently belong in human nature; it is not the result of any intellectual or spiritual quality that man may possess; it can indeed harmonize this universe with itself; it can unify and assimilate humanity; it can touch the soul immortal with superhuman power and lift it into unearthly excellence, but is absolutely independent of man, or the world in which he lives.

If this doctrine of the independence of the Gospel, as taught by Christ, is true, what becomes of the theory of evolution? It may not affect the chronology of geology, the Gospel may belong to another world than this, yet this planet may have been rolling in its orbit a hundred million years. It may not affect the idea that life on this earth began with a few simple forms, mere cells or bubbles, out of which all existing forms of animal existences have been developed; but it does materially affect the opinion which has recently been advanced and warmly advocated, namely, that the Christian civilization of to-day is the result of the progressiveness of the human race. It does affect the idea that the Gospel is nothing but a development of the human mind. Christ does not so teach, but he does teach that the Gospel is of the Kingdom of Heaven, and as independent of earth as is the Leaven of the mass it leavens.

The Holy Scriptures recognize the great, the wonderful fact of growth, they declare that " God made every tree to grow," that "the thistle grows," that "the dust groweth into hardness," that men morally may "grow like the cedars," that "faith groweth exceedingly," and that the body of Christianity in the world shall ultimately "grow into a Holy Temple in the Lord"; but such growth is invariably preceded by proper preparation and planting. In order to a tree or a thistle, a seed must first be dropped into the soil; in order to a moral growth a moral principle must first be introduced into the mind; in order to faith the heart must receive something that it can believe, and in order to the promised Temple of Christianity, which in the future shall cover the earth and reach to the Heavens, there must first be the planting of the corner-stone and then the gradual upbuilding. It is so to-day, no people or empire become Christians by evolution; wherever the Gospel has grown into power, "a sower has first gone forth to sow"; there was no Gospel in Canaan until Christ planted it there; it grew in Asia-Minor because Paul and Silas and others sowed there the precious seed; it spread throughout the Roman empire because Christian people propagated the Heavenly truth, and it is spreading the wide-world over at the present time because certain faithful followers of the Lord Jesus are busy sowing Gospel seed " beside all waters".

If the Gospel in certain localities is not spreading with that rapidity and vigor that it ought, it is because it waits to be applied by some ready agent. Truth of any kind does not take forcible possession of the mind and heart; Gospel truth is not an exception to this rule; it is not incorporated by any energy of its own; where there are no agents or instruments, the good seed remains unsown, and the wonted harvest is not gathered; hence it is said "the Kingdom of Heaven is like unto leaven that woman *took* and *hid* in three measures of meal"; you and I are to take and hide it; the Kingdom cannot grow while we fold our hands and dream of pretty theories of evolution. Give us "sowers," faithful laborers in God's vineyard; he has already ordained the laws and decreed the conditions. Give us workmen, I say, that needeth not to be ashamed, and to-morrow you shall witness a Gospel evolution.

It might be supposed, were we to read this parable of the leaven by itself, that *men* are not the chosen agents to do this great work; but, considering all the parables in their scope, we see that man is a chosen instrument as well as woman, for not only is "the Kingdom of Heaven like leaven which a woman took," but it is also "like a grain of mustard seed that a man took". Men, as well as women, therefore, are agents, and Christ spoke as he did, not because either sex is rejected as workers, but because it is more proper to say that woman shall hide the leaven and man should sow the seed, than it would to say that man should hide the leaven and woman shall sow the seed. Yet, as nature dictates a particular sphere for each, so in the moral universe we expect to find a special service allotted to man and to woman. This difference of sphere and office is suggested in the Word of God; the parable of the mustard seed and that of the leaven almost emphasize this difference. As in the vegetable kingdom there are certain plants and trees that grow by accretions from without and certain others that grow by accretions within, so in the differing phazes of the Heavenly Kingdom there is such a two-fold development. The Gospel has both an inward force and an outward expansion. The parable of the mustard seed illustrates the growth external, while that of the leaven illustrates its inner forcefulness. Now, man finds his sphere more in public than in private, and woman hers more in private than in public. One has to do with the external propagation of the Gospel, the other with its internal life; one impresses truth on the mind, the other on the heart; one formulates systems of theology, the other forms religious character; thus there is a beautiful significance in the figures employed by Christ when he said "the Kingdom of Heaven is like to a grain of mustard seed which a *man* took and hid in his field," and again "the Kingdom of Heaven is like unto leaven which a *woman* took and hid in three measures of meal until the whole was leavened."

There is, then, a place for each, a work for each one to do, a place for the sower and reaper, a place for man and for woman, and a place for the little child; for "out of the mouths of babes hath God ordained strength." The seed waits to be sown, the leaven waits to be hid; living germs of Gospel truth wait te be planted in the human mind, and hid in the human heart. The work does not require great intellectual acumen, nor wide scientific experience; it is but to implant a principle. The leaven is ready, who will apply it to the three measures of meal that represent needy humanity? All the Kingdom of Grace, all the infinite truth of God were of no avail unless applied.

"A lady, recently converted, felt an impulse to pray for others, but her little daughter was the only one who prayed with her. " Oh, mother," she said, " let me go and tell the neighbors what the Lord hath done for our souls." "They will laugh at you, darling, and call it all delusion." " But I think they will believe me." So she ran and told the old shoemaker across the way; he was

moved to tears, he began to pray for himself. Thus the
leaven was planted, it took effect; he persuaded others.
Soon the village was aroused, and fifty found the Savior.
If, with a sincere love for souls, *we* take this Gospel leaven
and hide it in the human hearts, we shall see that it will
work out similar results.

2.   The leaven of the Gospel is a hidden power. "Like
unto leaven which a woman took and hid." There are several senses in which the truth of the Gospel is hidden. It
is hidden because not discovered by those who are unwilling
to find it. "None are so blind as those who refuse to see."
A man may close his eyes to the evidences of creatorship in
the universe, and with false blindness, say there is no God.
He may look out on nature and behold its variety, beauty,
order, a glorious empire where all things work according to
a predetermined plan, and because he does not want to believe, declare that God does not rule. He may resort to
some kind of blind metaphyisics, and try to make it appear
that the Gospel is a myth, or a perished theory, while he
counts time from its birth, lives in the midst of its monuments, and sees its results in civilization, education, hope,
and in a mighty love-power that is moving to the moral
conquest of the world. To hundreds and thousands
of our fellow-men the Gospel is nothing, because they try
to find nothing in it. As the apostle said "if our Gospel be
hid it is hid to them that are lost."

It is hidden because they who *truly* seek *surely* find.
In another parable the Savior likens the Kingdom of Heaven
"to a treasure *hid* in a field," like silver in the rock or gold
in the mine, waiting to reward the diligence of the explorer.
The field is the wisdom of God. Let a reasoning man
traverse that field, and surely as he shall discover the divine
dotency in a thousand forms, as when it lifts an oak out of

an acorn cup, or builds for the birdling a wing that can
surmount the air, or makes a chain that holds a planet in
its orbit, so he will find the law by which a sin-lost soul
may be redeemed. Need I say that millions have found it,
found it in the revealed Word, for "the commandment
therein is a lamp, and the law is a light, and the reproofs of
instruction are the way of life." Nay, finding Christ by
faith the soul finds a sanctifying power; the truth he uttered is "the power of God unto salvation, to every one that
believes." " He was in the world and the world knew him
not, but as many as received him, to them gave he power to
become the sons of God."

The leaven of the Gospel is hidden because it is itself a
power, and all power is invisible. Archimedes said "give
me a place to stand on and I can move the world." Suppose the place were found, the levers adjusted, and this old
globe began to tilt and swing, on what spot would you put
your finger and say, " here is the power?" There is power
in the torrent that leaps over Niagara; it might, if applied,
move all the machinery of the earth without loss to itself;
but the sleepless giant of the flood has never been seen by
the human eye. We see the long, moving train of cars, but
cannot see the mighty genius that pulls them. We see telegraph poles, wires, batteries, but not the subtle something
that writes your message a thousand miles away. The human will is a power, it can break away from the bondage
of sin, or leap from the embrace of omnipotent love, but
the will is invisible. There is power in pure character, it
has tranquilized excited mobs when sword and cannon could
not do it; yet character is something that is felt, not seen.
So the Kingdom of Heaven is hid, or unseen, because a
power in itself. " It cometh not by observation;" it is spiritual and has a spiritualizing power; it comes softly as
autumn blushes come upon the fruit, silently as falls the

snow upon the plain, quietly as the frost-fern upon the
window; it comes sweetly as the spring, insinuatingly as the
dawn, and all quickening as the spirit that breathed life into
inanimate creation.   Though unseen

> "It can minister to a mind diseased,
>   Pluck from the memory a rooted sorrow,
>   Raze out the written troubles of the brain,
>   And with a sweet oblivious antidote
>   Cleanse the stuffed bosom of that perilous stuff
>   That weighs upon the heart."

The leaven of the Gospel is hidden because ineffectual
until received in the heart.   Whatever of outward manifestation the Gospel may possess, it must be the result of
its hidden life; if comparable to a field of aspiring, outreaching mustard, the secret of its growth is its inward
power; or if likened to a mass of leavened meal, the expansion of the mass is due to the force that has been concealed
within.   With this fact in view Paul very properly declared that "he is a Jew who is one inwardly, and circum-
cision is that of the heart in the spirit, and not in the letter,
whose praise is not of man but of God."

Inasmuch therefore as the Kingdom is within, its power
is not to be estimated by any mere externalities, it is not in
cathedrals and churches, not in rites and ceremonies, not in
family antecedents, nor wealth, or pomp, or display, not in
high-sounding names and titles, not in orthodox professions
of religion, all this may be but a gaudy bauble, blown into
appearance by a windy arrogance, ready to burst at the moment of greatest magnificence.

If a man is a Christian it is because the Christ-life has
been made to permeate his inner nature, just as the leaven
has been incorporated in and thoroughly mixed with the
meal.   It is a truth that takes possession of the mind, a
conviction that moves the will, an inspiration that fires the

affections, a divine energy that subdues, reanimates, controls the entire man; a force working from within outwardly, as all reformation must and displaying its presence in a good life and a godly conversation. We are all *in* the Kingdom, but is the Kingdom *in us?*

A young lady of my acquaintance, who had been an invalid for years, pale, emaciated, very feeble, annoyed with a constant cough, each breath a burden, said to me when I visited her. "I am very happy in my religious experience, it is real, peace and joy are in my heart, but I cannot testify, I would like to live to do the will of my Heavenly Father, instead I give to him my life," and when I considered her patience, her faith, her cheerfulness, her interest in whatever might interest others, though there was no noise, no demonstration, I knew that the Kingdom in its power was in her heart. So when the Gospel is in us, hidden like the leaven in the meal, it is a well-spring of purity and sweetness, having leavened our moral natures it makes us a leavening power to others.

3. The figure of the leaven suggests also that the Kingdom of Heaven is a *transforming* power. The leavening process is simple and understood by all; first the leaven that is a few living cells of the yeast plant, is put into the meal, the starch or sugar of the meal is then converted into alcohol by contact with the particles of yeast, which in turn diffuses carbonic acid all through the substance, causing the dough to rise, while the alcohol passes off in the form of vapor and is lost in the air, the dough in the meanwhile having undergone a complete change in its substance. So the leaven of the Gospel coalesces with man's moral nature, permeating it with a new life, purging its corruptions, lifting it into a higher sphere, and produces not an entirely new creation but a complete transformation.

This change-working power of Christianity has made for itself a wonderful history in the world. Planted by Christ and his desciples, working from the center outwardly, by degrees it made itself felt until at length the whole Roman world was more or less leavened by its power. Nor did the leaven of the Gospel cease its operations after the downfall of Rome, but insinuating its influence into the midst of Teutonic tribes, it changed them from a barbarous to a civilized people. Take for instance that wing of the Teutonic race, that fell like an ominous thunder cloud on the semi-savage tribes of Britain, at the time of the invasion they worshipped heroes and heavenly bodies. On Sunday they worshipped the Sun. On Monday the Moon, on Tuesday a hero whom they called Tiue, on Wednesday Wodin or Odin, on Thursday Thor, his son, on Friday Freya his wife, and on Saturday Soeter, a water god. Yet idolatrous, warlike, savage though those Saxons were, scarcely had two centuries passed away before all those Saxon peoples were converted to Christianity; the leaven working in their midst made for them a peculiar national character and an independent Teutonic Church which was the brightest star in the whole ecclesiastical firmament; nay more, it put an end to civil war and greatly modified the bloody fierceness with which war had been carried on, so that, as Freeman says, "the heathen English who had been satisfied with nothing less than the extermination of their enemies, deemed it sufficient to reduce them to political subjection, when those heathen became Christian."

Thus we may trace the history of this Gospel leaven in its progress thrugh the world. and discover that it exerts its transforming power. not only on those who willingly accept it, but also on society in general. True, even in Christian countries there are many who live and die in moral ignorance, sunken to the lowest depths of vice, no better, possibly worse, than many heathen are in character; yet on the whole how marked the difference between Christian and heathen lands; the influence of the Gospel is felt throughout the land and more or less in every circle of society. It does not change *every* heart, but the general tone and character of the nation is better for having received the Gospel.

But this leavening power is most evident where it has been hid in the individual heart, for the change is not merely in dogma or opinion, but the secret springs of life, the whole character is transformed thereby; it awakens new thoughts and feelings, new hopes and desires, it reveals new grounds for trust and confidence, new sources of happiness, new motives for action. As Spurgeon said " none of the fanciful transformations of which Ovid sang, can rival these matchless workings of God."

Christian, what has this transforming power done for you? Perhaps it has swept profanity from your lips, or subdued the rising passions of your soul, or cleansed the thoughts of your heart; it has arrested your idle pursuit of earthly phantoms; it has made Christ your satisfying portion; a poor, homeless wanderer in the world, it has made you a child of God and an heir of eternal life. Perhaps you hardly understand the change, it is so sweetly mysterious, it is " like the wind that bloweth where it listeth, and we hear the sound thereof;" or you may, like the Scotch girl who was converted under the preaching of Whitfield, say "something I know is changed, it may be the world, it may be my heart; there is a great change somewhere, for everything is different from what once it was." No matter whether you understand it or not, if you have experienced such a blessed transformation, you have an argument and an evidence that no opposing philosophy can gainsay.

4. Finally, the leaven of the Gospel is an all-pervading power. "It is like unto leaven which a woman took and hid in three measures of meal until the *whole was leavened*". Men in every age since the days of Herod have endeavored to annihilate the Christian religion. Nearly two thousand years have passed away but that religion is not extinguished yet. The leaven has been at work; that it will leaven the whole earth is far more probable now than ever before. Christ was never concerned about his cause. He foresaw innumerable obstacles and oppositions, yet calmly declared that notwithstanding "fowls of the air," "tribulation and persecution," "the deceitfulness of riches," and the cunning of the "devil," his Gospel should *win*, it should secure for itself an all-pervading victory.

This thought is chief in the parable of the leaven; that of the mustard seed suggests that the Gospel of the Kingdom shall become very great in the earth; but the parable of the leaven is a prophecy and promise of the Lord Jesus Christ that the Gospel shall assimilate the whole world, and touch and sanctify the secret springs of *every* living soul. The figure of the leaven is a strong declaration of this fact. Leaven that has once been incorporated in a mass of meal *cannot* be extracted, and not only so, it leavens every particle that it touches, and in turn each touched particle becomes a leaven. So the Gospel has come to earth ever to remain; no force or philosophy can possibly eradicate it; it sanctifies everything it touches, it transforms its foes into friends. it will ultimately subdue *all things* unto itself.

This being the case, redeemed man, a world that has been leavened by the truth and spirit of the Gospel will have restored unto it *all* that has been lost by sin.

Man's original domination over fish, and fowl, cattle and creeping things must be fully restored.

Man's promised supremacy over the physical geography of the globe must be realized in redemption. What, for instance, is "a desert made to blossom as the rose"? What is the promised "new earth" of the Apocalypse? What are they all but the old earth improved and sanctified by the skill of a redeemed race?

Redeemed men will possess a perfect body also, for "Godliness is profitable unto all things, having the promise of the life that now is." Purity of heart and the possibilities of the inquiring mind must affect the physical frame of man, as the stern physiognomy of the old Roman was the result of his education and employment, as the beauty of the Greek was occasioned by Grecian culture, so a Gospelized and baptised manhood must develop a new creature in Christ Jesus, a being that shall need no death ordeal as a preparation for eternal life. "Behold I show you a mystery," says the apostle; "we shall not all sleep, but we shall all be changed in the twinkling of an eye;" that must be a perfect body that is not to be permitted to see corruption.

Man redeemed will be a thinker too. In the great apostacy man to a considerable extent lost his power to think. One of the grand objects of the Kingdom of Heaven is to renew the intelligence of the race. "Be ye transformed," says the apostle, "by the renewing of your mind that ye may prove what is that good, acceptable and perfect will of God." Indeed, it is promised that the millennial glory shall be a glory of perfect intellectualism. "The knowledge of the Lord shall cover the earth as the water covers the sea."

Mankind, leavened by the leavening power of the Gospel, will become purely and perfectly scientific. Even the

great engineers, and the rich railroad kings of this progress-
and scientific age, under the wonderful impulses which a
Gospel civilization has given to them, are, though they
know it not, helping to fulfill the glorious prophecy of
Isaiah. " Prepare ye the way of the Lord, make *straight*
in the desert a highway for our God, every valley exalt,
every mountain and hill-side make low, and make the
crooked straight and the rough places plain, and the glory
of the Lord shall be revealed." Who knows but some day
the whole scientific world will succumb to the humanitarian
purposes of the Gospel. Perhaps, in the redemption, electricity, for instance, will be sanctified to the service of God
and the blessing of man. It is possible that the ocean cable
shall, to-morrow, become the Gospel trumpet that will give
no uncertain sound. Nor is it unreasonable to suppose
that ."the angel that will fly through the midst of Heaven,
having the everlasting Gospel to preach," will be nothing
more or less than the spirit of the lightning. That new
electrical beam that is about to break upon the world and to
hang like a meteor over palace and city, plain and mountain, superseding every other artificial light, may literally
drive night away and enable some scientist to say, with the
enthusiasm of Joshua, "Sun stand thou still upon Gibeon,
and thou Moon in the valley of Ajalon." Indeed, by the
magic power of electricity and through some more delicately
constructed telephone, the songs of angels may be softly
whispered by our hearth-stones or by our beds of death. At
least it is declared in the Word of Divine Truth that the
Lord " maketh spirits his angels, a flame of fire his minister,
the winds his messengers, and the lightnings his servants;"
that he directeth the lightning unto the ends of the earth,
and " maketh a way for it." Doubtless the significance of
hese divine utterances is not yet fully understood, but each

advancing age, each new discovery in science, each new invention in art shows that the divine purpose is "ripening fast, unfolding ever hour," and that when the leaven of truth shall have leavened the whole mass, and the world has been fully redeemed, all the laws of nature will be under control of man.

But the best of all is, when the three measures of meal shall be fully leavened, sin will be done away, righteousness will dwell in Heaven and on earth, " The Tabernacle of God shall be among men. He will dwell with them; they shall be his people, and God himself shall be their God." Then every soul will be saved, every heart will be pure, every lip will be inspired, every tongue shall confess, every knee shall bow." I want to be on earth at that time. I want to shout with the angels "it is finished," " the whole is leavened," "the great redemption is accomplished," "Hallelujah the Lord God Omnipotent reigneth."

In conclusion, I feel impelled to make two or three practical suggestions.

1. The glorious period of the world's redemption may be near or distant. Each soul, by his influence, hastens or retards that day. Friend, which are you doing?

2. The truth of the Gospel presses now upon your conscience; Christ in spirit waits to work a moral transformation in your soul. Will you resist? Do you say "go thy way for this time?" Oh, brother, to-morrow you die. Now is the accepted time

3. There is only one way to be saved; the power of Grace must be hid in your heart.

4. There is only one source from which salvation comes; not philosophy, not science, but Christ. "There is no other name."

" As some rare perfume in a vase of clay,
    Pervades it with fragrance not its own,
So when he dwells in deathless souls,
    All Heavenly sweetness seems around them thrown."

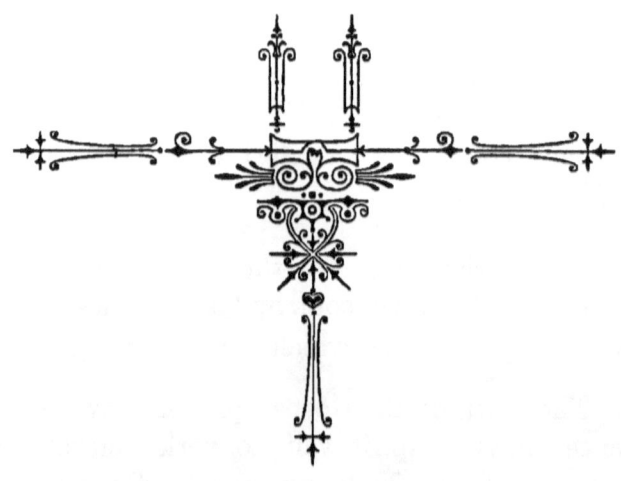

THE IRREPROACHABLE GOSPEL.

For I am not ashamed of the Gospel of Christ; for it is the
power of God unto salvation to every one that believeth: to
the Jew first, and also to the Greek.—*Romans* 1, 16.

Nature, it is said, has its limitations; things are known
by their forms, their qualities, their characteristics. It is
said that men carry their "sign-boards" with them, so that
one who is versed in human nature may, by the walk of
a man, by his laugh, by the shape of his mouth, by the
color of his eyes, the intonations of his voice, or by the
bumps on his head, read his mental and moral proba-
bilities.

Yet it is not true that such laws have no exceptions.
Nature has been known to break through her ordinary environments; great minds have been supported by feeble
bodies; coarse organisms have produced refined and susceptible natures. Men frequently contradict circumstances,
rise superior to education and prejudice, and disappoint the
expectations of friends and foes.

It was so with the Apostle Paul. Benjamitish blood,

Jewish nationality, Phariseeic prejudice, instruction under
Gamaliel and inborn predilections, instead of rendering him
narrow, exclusive. commercial, political, formal, produced a
broad-guaged, universal, cultivated, warm-hearted and devoted disciple of the lowly Nazarene.   The reason was that
another force, hitherto unrecognized, a divine force, that
which is in Christianity broke in upon the circumstances
and sanctified them all.

Think of a Jew, with all the native prejudices of his
race: a scholarly Hebrew from Tarsus disputing against the
first Christian converts at Jerusalem;a Benjamite keeping the
clothes of those who stoned the first martyr; a thoroughly
educated Phariseeic lawyer on the royal road to eminence,
" breathing out threatenings and slaughter," legally, con-
scientiously indignant against the followers of Christ and
their doctrines; think of such an one becoming a Christian;
of all possibilities such an idea seems most improba-
ble; but such a change actually took place under the transforming power of the Gospel.

Nor was Saul's conversion superficial, a mere temporary
expedient, it was deep, it was thorough. it was absolute.
Fallen from his prosessional loftiness, contemptuously
treated by those who admired him most; persecuted by his
own countrymen, poor. mingling with the indigent and
the lowly in consequence of this new following; yet he
proclaimed doctrines that he had opposed, adhered to the
Nazarene whom once he had despised, and declared that he
was "not ashamed of the Gospel of Christ, for it is the
power of God unto salvation "

What was the peculiar phase of the Gospel force that
so captivated, charmed and transformed that thoughtful,
scholarly citizen of Tarsus? Some are won by one phase
of its power, and some by another. Clement, of Rome,

was attracted by the Christian patience. sublime heroism
and unfaltering faith of an elect lady who, in the great
coliseum before twenty thousand spectators. submitted to
be devoured by a lion rather than forego her love for Christ.
Paul became a Christian through the power and glory of
the Christly voice and presence. Whether presented in the
person of its founder or in the character that it creates, the
Gospel wins the admiration and devotion of men. Looking at this Gospel let us consider some features of which
we are not ashamed.

I. WE ARE NOT ASHAMED OF THE ORIGIN OF THE GOSPEL.

1. It is objected that it had an obscure origin, in
Bethlehem of Judea, in a stable. or perhaps a cavern,
among a family of troglodytes or cave dwellers. that it
grew in the rude atmosphere of Galilee, among a turbulent
and rebellious people. and was fostered in Nazareth, an obscure village, among the barren hills that surround the
place, and it was supposed that no good thing could come
out of Nazareth.

It is extreme narrowness that rejects a man or an idea
because of surrounding poverty and obscurity. Then the
steam engine must be rejected because Watt, its inventor,
was a native of Greenock, which at the time of his birth
was nothing but a fisher's hamlet. For the same reason
electricity must be rejected, for it is not known exactly who
discovered it. Mr. Lincoln, too, must be rejected because
he grew up in the backwoods or on the river. Shakespear
must be rejected also because his father would have been
unknown were it not for the genius of his illustrious son.

. Yet we do not reject but admire the mind of a Shakespear, the honest statesmanship of Abraham Lincoln, the
wonderful genius that caught the lightning and chained it.

and the intelligence that discovered a mighty giant in the tea-kettle. We admire these men and these ideas despite the genius from whence they came. So it is nothing against the Gospel that it was first preached in Galilee, for prejudice to the contrary notwithstanding, at least one good thing has come out of Nazareth.

2. It is objected that the Gospel originated in the brain of Jesus, a Jew, whose parents were exiles, whose father was a caloused-handed carpenter, who was himself a wanderer, homeless, penniless, pillowless, whom the sects despised, who, when only thirty-three years old, was executed as a malefactor. It is fashionable in certain circles to reject him, therefore his religion is rejected also.

Still we are not ashamed of Jesus and his Gospel. We are not ashamed of any man who can rise above his obscurity, who will not be held down even by the fetters of poverty, whose character *will* shine despite all the attempts of calumny to reproach it. We are not ashamed of one whose posthumous influence, despite the brevity of life, the unfavorableness of his circumstances, and the malicious endeavors of his enemies grows more wide-spread and glorious, although pontificial courts, royal governors and imperial arms attempt to crush the uttered truth and the pure spirit of the one who has departed. We glory in such an one. We believe that the thoughts of such an one are worth immortalizing. It is so with Christ and with his Gospel. Obscurity, nor poverty, nor malice, nor crucifixion, nor nineteen hundred years of bitter opposition and persecution have been able to dim the light of the life of Jesus; that life is to-day a sun among the stars in the moral heavens. "His name is above every name." We are therefore not ashamed of him or of his Gospel.

3. But the Gospel has an origin, better than round

hills, or quiet vales, or meditative man. It claims a heavenly origin. It was evolved in the council of the Most High. The hallowed influences of the Gospel of Christ have been breathed upon the world by the eternal spirit of God; bright eyed angels sung its welcome to earth. It is a divine truth given to the world by divine methods and through human agencies. It is a truth that bears testimony to its own divine character; whatever may be said of the person of Jesus, and certainly much may be said about it, for the doctrine of the person of Christ is the central doctrine of Christianity, whatever may be said of this, the truth that he uttered is certainly from above.

For instance, the Gospel implies humiliation and condescension; this is the golden thought running through the whole plan of redemption; it is enforced by an example that is not common to earth, that could not have been born of the proud spirit of man. He who dares to stoop that he may become a stepping-stone for his brothers exaltation has in him something of the genius of Heaven. This is the way that God works; thus the rain-drop falls from the sky, sinks through the soil, kisses the roots of the trees and grasses, and by its condescension paints the green of the summer leaf, and the beauty of the flower. In such a manner God works in the Gospel, its truth strikes down through men's burdens and underneath their sins, lifting up the soul into the summer realm of spiritual life and lovliness; therefore we are not ashamed.

Again, the Gospel implies unselfishness. This, too, is supermundane; there is nothing more devouring to a human soul than selfishness; it is most belittling in its effects, and there is nothing more expanding than that spirit which prefers another before itself. Those broad-guaged ideas that embrace all mankind in a common brotherhood, not hypothetically only, but actually, are from above, not from beneath. It is human to be narrow, it is divine to be broad; there is in the Gospel an infinite breadth of benevolence and brotherliness; therefore its truth is divine and we are not ashamed of it.

Again, the Gospel is love. Love is omnipotent. As some one has said "no cord or cable can draw so forcibly, or bind so fast, as love can do with a single thread." For love a mother would die for her child; for love a child has been known to cling to a drunken and brutal parent; for love of Edward I, Eleanor sucked poison from his wounded arm at the risk of her own life; for the sake of love every burden is borne, every duty is done, every sacrifice is made. Love makes this dark world light; whoever loves is born of God. Love built this universe; love seeks the lost; love saves the fallen, and the love of God in Christ "endured the cross, despised the shame," that it might save and redeem a sin-crushed earth. The Gospel is the glad tidings of eternal love; it is pregnant of it; it has most of love therefore most of God, hence we are not ashamed of it. It may have been uttered originally by the poor man of Nazareth; it may have been proclaimed first of all on a hillside in Galilee. No matter, its truth is divine, and we can not be ashamed.

II. NOT ASHAMED OF THE HISTORY OF THE GOSPEL.

1. It is objected that in its embodied form, that is, in the Church, the history of the Gospel has not always been what the followers of Christ might be proud of. The track of its history has been marked by the rise and fall of sects, the declarations of dogmas, the contentions of factions, the hate of bigots, and the cruelty of sanguinary persecutions.

If honest, I must answer, yes, to this indictment. So far as society is concerned these things are true. Truth in this world is destined to fight its way against the false opinions of men, against organized forces of error, against the bitter antagonisms of foes, against the narrowness of bigots, against selfishness, cruelty and pride, and against the ignorance and the imprudent zeal of its friends. Therefore not at once, but ultimately, the virtues of humanity, self-sacrifice and love are displayed. It is not supposable that the Church can leap into perfection in a day. It is not possible that a heaven-given Gospel can be comprehended in a generation. The strange thing is not that the Church has been defective and deficient, but considering " the pit from which it has been digged." it is wonderful that it has been pure and prudent as it has.

2. Some have predicted and announced the failure of the Church, of Protestantism, of Christianity, of the Gospel; but they have mistaken the decay of sects, which cannot be denied, for the decline of truth. Personally, though cherishing a deep love for the Church, especially for the Church of my choice, yet historically speaking, I care as much for the sects that have been, yea for the sects that now are, as I do for shucks; they do, indeed, protect the seeds of truth for a little while; nor could the world have done without them; but, by and by, according to a divine and natural law, the ripened germs must fall out of the pods that environ them and seek new opportunities for development. We say then, let the sect go; it is the truth we want, not the pod; the decay of sects cannot affect the truth of the Gospel of Jesus Christ.

3. It has been objected that the world has been continually growing worse under the regime of Christianity. If this is true the world is without hope, for if the Gospel

—and by the Gospel we mean the ethical teachings of Christ—cannot make the world better, nothing can. It condemns murder and the hateful thought that precedes it; it does not permit one man even to call another a fool; it requires that I shall be correct myself before I criticise another; it demands meekness, mercy, forgiveness; it insists that a good man will love his fellow man whether he is loved in return or not; it condemns alike the adulterous act and the lustful look; it forbids divorce except for one cause, and pronounces re-marriage to be adultery; it demands alms, but not for the sake of the notoriety; in brief, Christ sums up his ethical instruction in regard to the duty that one man owes to another, in the immortal words of the golden rule, "whatsoever ye would that men should do to you, do ye even so to them." Nor are these principles cold moral propositions merely, but they are quickened by the declaration that there is a God that sees all, and knows all, who holds every human soul responsible, and waits to reward the righteous and to punish the wicked. If such sacred sentiments and divine sanctions as these have, in two thousand years, made the world worse, then the world will never be any better.

4. But the statement is counter to all history. The Church, with its Christian ethics, has moved a little in advance of the gradual unfoldment of virtue. The character, the spiritual life of mankind has since Christ developed in periods. In the first period of the Christian era the grace of moral steadfastness was strengthened; in another period the grace of tolerance became prevalent. Eventually the period that will witness the complete emancipation of the human mind shall have broken in upon the world; then, perhaps, the grace of universal love will become pre-eminent, and lastly, the period of sublime confidence and assurance, that which will demonstrate that death does not

destroy, will shine upon the mind like mid-day upon darkness.   Thus we are not ashamed of the Gospel, for the world
has grown better under its regime.

5.   Nor need we be ashamed of the last hundred years
of the Gospel.   It is strange that the century which has
been most abundant in predictions about the extinction of
the Christian religion should be most marked and vigorous
in its religious progressiveness.   The eighteenth century
closed with a popular form of unbelief that was open,
blatant and blasphemous in the extreme.   Even good men
feared that Christianity was sinking out of sight.   But the
nineteenth century was ushered in with a glorious revival
that swept over this country, quickening the spirituality of
the Churches, and continuing for upwards of twenty-five
years.   The second quarter of the nineteenth century was
made peculiar all over the civilized world by the prominence
of a subtle rationalism which extolled Christianity in the
letter, but endeavored with destructive criticism to stab it
to the very soul.   Once more the world looked for the Gospel to perish, but it disappointed every infidel expectation
and appeared more active and aggressive than ever.   While
the knife was piercing to the very heart, Sunday schools
started into existence. temperance organizations moved into
line, Bible societies began to give the Word of Life to the
nations, and the great modern missionary movement commenced pushing forward to the moral conquest of the world.
Thus, while it was confidently and repeatedly declared that
Christianity was declining, it was in truth expanding and
sweetly working its way into the hearts of men.   Indeed,
the Gospel has gained as much in the last eighty years as it
did gain in the eighteen hundred years that preceded. Considering therefore the history of the Gospel, a Christian has
no need to " hide a blushing face."   It has made for itself
a glorious history, we are not ashamed.

III.   NOT ASHAMED OF THE NATURE AND PURPOSE OF THE GOSPEL, " FOR IT IS THE POWER OF GOD UNTO SALVATION," TO EVERY ONE THAT BELIEVETH.

1.   Though no one has ever seen power, and no one knows what it is essentially, yet, having seen its effects, all mankind, from the child to the sage, desire to come into possession of that something, which is called power. The very infant is made angry if he cannot become a law unto himself. The savage seeks that power by which he can command the beasts of the field and the birds of the air. The husbandman wants power to subdue the earth.   The geologist is ambitious to master the mysteries of the rocks; the electrician to catch and to use the forces of the elements, and the astronomer to decipher the hieroglyphics of the stars.

What is that that lifts a majestic oak out of a little acorn cup?   What is it that keeps the ocean within bounds and rolls up its eternal flood?   What is it that on wing of flame rushes through the Heavens, piercing the bosom of the storm and smiting whatever it touches?   What is it that holds suns in their places and keeps the worlds in their orbits?   It is *power*, it is God, for power is of God and God is power.

There is a power marvelous as that which appears in nature.   What is that which has put the idea of right and wrong into human hearts?   What is it that strikes conviction into the conscience?   What is that that causes truth to win an ever widening way in the world?   What is that in the Gospel that caused it to sweep onward to destiny, though confronted by the most subtle unbelief?   What was it that impelled that same Gospel though a false church stood square in its way?   What brought it forth from

German philosophy unscathed, and French infidelity uninjured? What was it in Christianity that caused it to successfully withstand the learned unbelief of England and to go on in its work of love despite the ravings of its enemies? What was it in the Gospel which, though opposed by science and speculation, and persecution, caused it to stand like some grand old cathedral after the storm has played among its towers? It was power, "the power of God," for all power is of God, all moral as well as material power. Thus the apostle declares that the Gospel is power. Not *a* power, but *the* power. "*the power of God.*"

Whatever is capable of producing an effect is power. The Gospel has produced effect, therefore it is power. The effects of the Gospel are evident and numerous. One can see them in the beaming countenance of Stephen, in the sublime character of Paul, in the fancies that live on the canvas of a Raphael, an Angelo, a Correggio and a Rembrandt, in those glorious harmonies that broke from the lips of a Handel, a Mozart, a Haydn, and a Beethoven. One can see the effects of the Gospel in the world's grandest specimens of architecture, in the profoundest literature, in the science of a Humboldt, a Herschel and a Newton, in the philosophy of a Bacon, a Hamilton and a McCosh, and in all the march of modern civilization. One can see the effects of the Gospel in the spirit of law, in the science of government, and in the tendencies of modern diplomacy. The Gospel too has impressed the wild man with the gentleness of a child, it has dashed from the lips of the cannibal the bowl of human blood, it has snatched the immolated victim from the sacrificial altar, it has converted spears and tomahawks into implements of husbandry, it has transformed indolence into industry, it lifted Madagascar out of darkness into light, it redeemed India from idolatry and China from superstition, it was preached by

Moody and sung by Sankey among the professors and students of Oxford and Cambridge, and it caused their pulses to beat with new and spiritual vigor. The Gospel therefore is a power in itself, for that which is capable of producing such remarkable results must be a power. If then, the Gospel is power the world need not be ashamed of it, "for power belongeth unto God " and whatever is endowed with power must be one of his creatures.

2.   All power is for some purpose; that of an argument is intended for conviction; that of imagination is to create beautiful ideals;t hat of nitro-glycerine is for destruction; that of steam is for railroads, machinery and manufacturing- So the Gospel is power, a power in itself. Employed it is an irresistible force, sweeping everything before it.   But if a power it is for a particular purpose; what is that purpose? Let the apostle answer. He declares that the Gospel is the power of God unto salvation. This, then, is the divine intent in the Gospel, for this special purpose God has put his power into the glorious truth of redemption.

I have mentioned some of the accidental benefits of the Gospel.   Let us not confound these, important as they are, with the ultimate design. It is not art, it is not science it is not civilization, it is not knowledge, it is not moral force, but transcending all these it is *salvation*. By salvation we mean deliverance. preservation from peril or calamity. The Greek word is *sotheria*, which means safety. The Gospel then is the power of God unto human deliverance. unto absolute safety. Not from Egyptian but spiritual bondage; not by a human but a divine deliverer; not from the waves of the sea but from that just " indignation and wrath" which threatens to overwhelm "every soul of man that doeth evil;" not from the flames of a burning dwelling

but from the quenchless fires of a burning conscience; not
from bodily disease alone but from the moral leprosy of
a corrupt and fallen nature; not from the perils of a military invasion but from the crushing consequences of a
broken law.   The Gospel therefore comes to us, not with
the sculptor's chisel or the poet's song; not with the scientist's experiment or the pedagogue's blackboard and dia-
gram; it comes not with a life-boat or a patent fire escape;
not with the materia medica or a scalpel; not with cannon
or diplomacy, but it comes with the cross, the symbol of
eternal love. infinite condescension and magnetic power; it
comes to restore harmony to a world that had been made
discordant by sin; it comes to harmonize that world with
law divine; it comes to lift sinful souls from the horrible pit
into which they had sunk, up to the glorious possibilities
and privileges of children of God. In brief it comes to
proclaim universal pardon of the offenses of all the subjects
of the King of Kings, and regeneration and redemption, on
condition of repentance and acceptance by faith of the soul-
healing remedy of the atonement which has been provided
in Jesus Christ.   Therefore the "Son of God," after his condescension, life, suffering, death, resurrection, and when
about to ascend to the right hand of the majesty on high,
said "all power is given unto me in Heaven and in earth,"
and so it happens that the Gospel that he left us, that is the
method by which the soul may secure unto itself eternal
life and safety, is "the power of God unto salvation."

Such being the nature and the purpose of the glorious
Gospel of the Son of God, why should we be ashamed of
it? What is there in the Gospel to be ashamed of? It is
not the foe of free thought, for it enjoins "prove all
things;" it is not a monster of intolerance, for it says "him
that is weak in the faith receive ye;" it is not inspired with
a mercenary intent for it recommends " love thy neighbor

as thyself;" it cannot be a fabric of fables for the grandest, the most substantial institutions of earth are built upon it; it is not a malicious dispenser of immorality for it advises "shun the very appearance of evil;" it does not impose on humanity heavy burdens, grievous to be borne, for "its yoke is easy and its burden is light." Why then is the world ashamed of it?

The Gospel does not declare that hope dies with us; it does not teach that the grave is the end of all; it does not tell you that your vanished loved ones have sunk in a sea of death never to rise again; it does not bid you go to yonder city of marble monuments and hillocks green and weep, because in that silent mausoleum all the brightness of life went out forever; it does not say toil on, toil lovingly, sacrifice each day, each succeeding year, until life's thread is run out, and then die, die to live no more. No! No! It teaches that "your labor is not in vain," your "works shall follow" you even into the evermore; your soul shall not die; even your body shall triumph over the grave; it tells of happy meetings beyond the flood; of a nightless land where there shall be "no more death, nor sorrow, nor crying, nor pain; it tells of jasper, and emerald, and gold, and rivers of life, and thrones, and kingdoms, and crowns, and songs, and shoutings, and hallelujahs, when all the former things shall have passed away. Why then be ashamed of it?

Nor is the Gospel a provision of redemption for a select and chosen few; it comes freighted with a power of salvation for all the world of love-needy humanity. Sin, the one impediment, it proposes to remove; it is the power of God unto salvation to every one that believeth; to the Jew first, that is to the Deist, and not to the Jew or the Deist only, but also to the Gentile, that is the Pagan, and not to the Jew and Gentile, the Deist and the Pagan only, but to all who believe it, that is all who are willing to live by its moral rule.

Men may talk about the mistakes of Moses, or the mistakes of Usher; they may talk about things in the Old Testament that they do not understand; they may boast of apes being their patriarchal grandfathers, and polliwogs as being their royal ancestors; men may talk about theology or science, or about the latest born of the philosophies; but as for me, considering the origin of the Gospel, considering its history, considering its power and purpose, and what it has done for human souls, for one I am not ashamed of the Gospel of Christ. So long as it can animate a human heart with glorious hope it shall be my consolation, and adopting the language of the psalmist I would say, "if I forget thee, let my right hand forget its cunning, let my tongue cleave to the roof of my mouth, if I prefer thee not above my chief joy."

But on the other hand, one might well be ashamed of infidelity; it has changed its face at least fifty times during the last eighteen hundred years; and to-day it goes forth, not with love beaming in its eye, not with charity on its lips, not with benevolence on its palm, but it is a monster going forth to destroy. We are ashamed of that which has never thrown one flash of light on human ignorance; never comforted one sorrowing soul; never healed one broken heart; never wiped away one falling tear. We are ashamed of that which is nothing but a negation, that which means no faith, no Church, no Bible, no Christ, no future, no God, no responsibility, nothing but blackness, darkness and despair. We are ashamed of infidelity, but not of the Gospel which is the power of God unto salvation to every one that believeth. And, dear friend, if you would not be ashamed of yourself; if you would crown yourself with a glory of manhood, character and destiny, abandon your infidelity and become a Christian, not in creed merely, not in profession only, but in life and in work.

If, then, there is no reason why we should be ashamed of the Gospel let us cease to oppose it; and as there is every reason why deathless responsible beings should glory in it, let us heartily accept its saving truth, let us make its precepts the rule of our lives, and its eternal hope the joy and confidence of our souls. We need not wait, every eternal interest prompts us to make the avowal now. We need not hesitate for all things are ready. Whosoever will may come and take of the water ot life freely. Should all the ends of the earth look by faith unto the Son of God, they might be saved this moment. Sufficient authority and infinite power are in his hand. "He is able to save unto the uttermost all that come unto God by him."

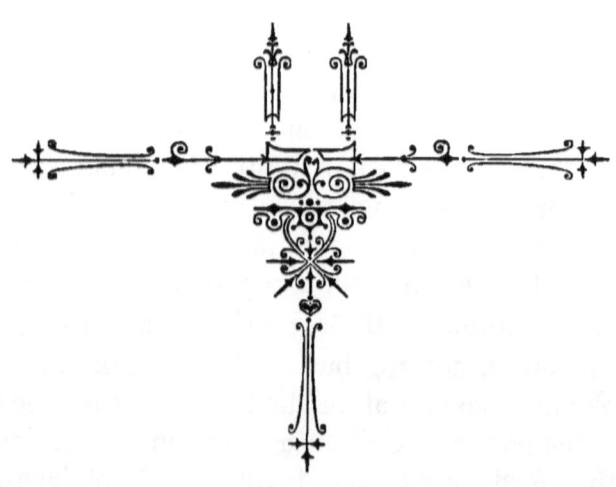

THE PILLARS OF OUR FAITH.

But ye, beloved, building up yourselves on your most holy faith,
praying in the Holy Ghost.

Keep yourselves in the love of God, looking for the mercy of
our Lord Jesus Christ unto eternal life.—*Jude* 20, 21.

The present religious outlook is, to many excellent
people, anything but encouraging. Influenced by a prevalent skepticism, they are willing to admit that, after all, the
Gospel may be a failure. So, indeed, it may be; it is not
impossible that the world may reject it, although its truth
may remain unchanged, its inspiration unaffected.

A conflict of ideas is expected; every moral assertion
and question, every school and sect give evidence to the fact
that the battle has been raging, and that it cannot cease
until truth is absolutely triumphant. Christianity commenced in a conflict. The epistle of Jude, a short epistle
of one chapter, with only twenty-five verses, complains of
antichrist in the Church, and is occupied in describing false
teachers and seducers, and in dictating the method of
evading their influence and avoiding their errors. If, then,
the children are being tried in the crucible of criticism,

they are but acquiring the experiences of their fathers; nor should they seek to shun the ordeal, for in the end, the world will have a stronger faith and a sturdier religion, because Christianity has been compelled to fight its way along the line of the world's opposing opinions. We expect, therefore, the clash of arms. Though Christianity may not to-day be doomed to do battle with the wild beasts of the amphitheater, it is destined to confront the lions of the forum.

In an age when a variety of religious opinions, and opinions that are not remarkably religious, are in conflict, and it is supposed that Christianity is being pushed to the wall in the battle, it is well to ask what is Christianity? And having assured ourselves as to what it really is, then to inquire is that system of religious truths that is known as Christianity defeated, or is it triumphant in the fight?

There can be no doubt that much that is supposed by some people to be the Gospel, at least essential to it, and against which a score of knightly lances are aimed, is nothing more than some vain conceit of an uninspired brain, a rude relic of a barbarous age, or the fungus growth of some deteriorated theology. We must not imagine when these fall that the citadel of the Gospel has fallen.

There has been for instance, of late, considerable fighting over ritualistic forms and ceremonies; but so little has ritualism to do with the genius of the Gospel that, whether ritualism were unhorsed, or rode the field a victorious cavalier, it would make no difference with the essential truth of Christianity.

Though the present age should witness the annihilation of Calvinism, Arminianism, Methodism, Baptism and every other ism, it would not necessarily follow that

Christianity had perished, but the Gospel might shine with brighter radiance because all the overshadowing isms had faded away.

To the same effect are the recent utterances of a certain popular lecturer, who boldly and poetically says that "advancement depends on intelligence; whoever quits growing is orthodox; heresy is what grows, orthodoxy rots," and that " there is nothing in theology worth speaking of but the devil." If that lecturer chooses he may believe in the "eternal divorce of the Church and the State;" or in the good effects of a " baptism of soap." It may be true as he said that some Christians have been slaveholders; they may have been guilty of falsely interpreting Scripture; they may have deduced strange and even dangerous opinions from the Bible; they may have been poor logicians; they may have persecuted those who differed from them, and the lecturer himself may make fortunes out of the unbelief of multitudes, and be greeted everywhere with loud cheers and enthusiastic applause; but, having made all his points and finished all his arguments, what does it amount to as an attack on Christianity? It happens simply that the mountain has travailed in birth and brought forth nothing but a mouse. The great central truths of the Gospel still stand unshaken and untouched.

What then is 'Christianity? The text suggests its distinguishments. It wondrously lifts the Gospel into the clear light of a self-witnessing character; led by its thought I should speak of the Gospel as distinguished by the purity and potency of its doctrine, by the spirit and inspiration of its worship, by the sweep and sublimity of its devotion, and by the ground and scope of its assurance. This would make too vast a field for us to traverse in one discourse; we therefore narrow our inquiries down to the doctrinal

peculiarities of Christianity. Do you ask what are its doctrines? The answer certainly must be, those forms of religious truths which were taught by Christ and his apostles.
Let us then examine some of the salient points of the Gospel, so that we may learn whether or not the infidel icono-
clasts of to-day are hurling their lances at a man of straw
or a mountain of adamant. What then are the doctrinal
pillars of our faith?

I. THE DOCTRINE OF THE UNITY OF GOD.

The thought of God lies latently in every human soul,
and waits the working of those forces that can quicken it
into evidence; hence the philosophy of the ages has generally steered clear of an absolute denial of God. Indeed the
denial of the divine existence is not an original suggestion.
Man must cut loose from his inborn conviction before he
can lay the foundation for even a plausible negation, consequently the scarcest class of people and the most unpopular is the atheistic, that class that boldly declares there is
no God.

Prone to evil, evil prevalent in the world and potent in
the human heart, men, while they could not root out from
their minds the thought of God, "changed the glory of the
incorruptible into an image made like to corruptible man,
and to birds, and four-footed beasts and creeping things;"
they revelled in poetry and deified it; they gave free vent to
passion and worshipped it; they sought pleasure and drank
wine, and declared that Bacchus should represent the
voluptuousness of their natures; they were enamored of
beauty and enthroned it as a divinity; they exalted all kinds
of imaginary gods and goddesses over fields and floods and
stars; they decreed that Jupiter should be god of the clouds,
Neptune of the sea and Pluto of the dark domain of

death. Thus they "changed the truth of God into a lie, and worshipped and served the creature more than the Creator."

When Christ came the world was a vast augean stable. Idolatry had made it so. Christianity undertook the herculean task of cleaning it out. In the midst of the polytheism of the nations Christ lifted up his voice and said, "Hear, O Israel, the Lord our God is one Lord;" the same had been uttered by the law of Moses. The psalmist too had declared "thou art God alone." The great apostle also laconically announced "God is one," and again "there is one God and Father of all," and also "there is none other God but one." In fact, Israel was the only nation of the apostolic age, unless the Druids of Britain were an exception, that was not polytheistic. Kings, tribes, cities families, individuals, chose some deity from the pantheon and worshipped it. Like Egypt, Babylon, Assyria, Greece and all the nations that preceded, Rome had its chosen divinities. At one time thirty thousand different gods were enthroned in the city of the Cæsars. So with all the barbarous people of northern Europe, and so it was with all the nations of the Orient.

When Christ and his apostles went about declaring in the name of the new religion that "the Lord our God is one Lord," the idols and divinities of earth were made to tremble in their sanctuaries. It meant that Vulcan, Pan, Neptune and Jupiter, Buddha, Brahma, Vishnu and Siva, Woden, Thor and Tiue should be relegated to the mythical region whence they had come. It meant that polytheism should disappear, and with it should vanish the accumulated filthiness of centuries; and vanish it did. The spreading light of Christianity scattered the darkness and purified and

sweetened the earth. So that there can be no question
about it, the world is a good deal cleaner to-day than it was
two thousand years ago.

Does the infidelity of to-day attack this doctrine of the
unity of God? Does it direct its guns toward this tower of
strength in Christianity? Then, what part of the army
of unbelief is marching directly against this citadel? Not
agnosticism, it is unconcerned whether there is a God or
not; not rationalism, it simply asserts that reason shall be
pure and its syllogisms solid; not spiritualism, for it is only
an etherialized form of deism; not materialism, at least in-
tentionally, for it asserts the eternity of matter, and is
willing to accept the idea that possibly God may be behind
it. Atheism alone attacks this doctrine, but it has only a
small following, for what man of thought will fellowship
a class of idiots who profess to know what they cannot
know anything about? How can any man know that there
is no God? Evidently, therefore, when men professedly
antagonize Christianity they do not attack this pillar of its
truth. They may war against some unreasonable notion of
deity, but not so much as one missile have they to fling at
this rock, this abstract idea of the unity of God. The pig-
mies might as well try to beat down Gibraltar with pellets
of mud.

This doctrine is the sweetest, the most comforting, the
most assuring, the most reasonable doctrine that is possible
to the minds of men. It is a thought that the world cannot destroy if it would. What the world would be without
God, no language can tell, and what is the power of that
thought upon the conduct of humanity no arithmetic can
compute. It is a sublime conception. Intelligence cannot
reach beyond it. The divine ideal may be inborn, but the
fulness of the thought must have been revealed. That

there is one God, supreme above all, a necessary being, absolute in his existence, one infinitely wise, good and just, the omnipotent, the immutable, the eternal one, the Father of all, cannot be discoverable by reason alone, but once having been revealed, the mind grasps the thought and keeps it. and all opposing fancies vanish away like morning mists before advancing light. But this is one of the pillars of our faith, a fundamental doctrine: the first of all the commandments is "the Lord our God is one Lord." Let not the enemy imagine that Christianity has fallen so long as this pillar stands.

II. THE SECOND PILLAR OF OUR FAITH IS THE DOCTRINE OF THE DIVINE PROVIDENCE.

Providence is God exercising his wisdom and power in the government of this world and this universe, for those particular purposes that he regards as necessary to be accomplished. As a doctrine, it is Christ's affirmation of the goodness of creation, and his contradiction of that prevalent, hurtful fancy, the essential evilness of nature. The doctrine of providence is the broadest, the fullest, the most comprehensive doctrine of Christianity. It signifies that God is good, all his works are good, all his laws are good, and that he is at work always and everywhere for the good of his children.

Scripture is full of the idea that creation is good; it is the first doctrine on record therein; it teaches that God created light and called it good; he saw that the earth was good: he pronounced the earth's products to be good; he set the stars in their places and they were good; the things that have life that came forth of the waters were also good: and finally. having made man out of the dust of the earth, "God saw everything that he had made and behold it was very good."

It is strange that this self-evident truth should have been compelled to fight its way against an opposite doctrine, the doctrine of the essential evilness of matter, a doctrine which became wide-spread, almost general, asserting itself at the very altars of the Church, and to some extent flourishing to the present day. Blind to every evidence of providence, it taught that all matter from mountain to molecule is haunted with a living principle of evil, that man's contact with matter is his greatest misfortune, that for his sin he should torture his body, and that the shortest way out of sin is the shortest way out of the flesh.

This idea explains the anchoretic tendencies of the Hindoo and the disgusting mendicacy of the Fakir; it affords a reason for the aceticism of the Buddhist, and the abstemiousness of the Pharisee: it gives significance to celibacy, and makes evident the underlying meaning of monasticism; in brief, it blocks the wheels of progress and smites the world with moral death. But more, in a sense it dethroned the Supreme Being, at least robbed him of all his material domain, for if matter is evil, how can a pure and holy God include matter in his government? The ante-Christian world therefore declared when it beheld the destructive sweep of the tornado, the scathing flash of the lightning,and felt the bewildering reel of the earthquake,that there must be a malignant God as well as a good one, that the good reigns in the realm of soul and the bad in the realm of sense, and that a fierce and uncertain conflict is perpetually proceeding between them. But such ideas could not obtain did the world truly believe in a divine providence.

Christ came and proclaimed that providence: he showed that a spiritual power shapes and controls the whole material mass; that the two kingdoms of sense and spirit are really one and in harmony; that over both one God reigns supreme; that under the perfect action of divine law even the harsher aspects of nature are fraught with benedictions for humanity, or that as the apostle said, "all things work together for good to them that love God."

When Christ taught that matter is impressible and controllable by a superior mind, he laid down the foundation thought upon which the wondrous temple of modern science has been built; that belief, now so popular and inspiring that, ultimately intelligence shall subdue force, for, if one mind is all-controlling, other minds may attain sometime to such power and dignity also.

This doctrine of providence, or that the universe is the Lord's, was the very doctrine that the world most needed. Such a thought had long been a disideratum in the human mind. When Philip said "show us the Father and it sufficeth us," he gave utterance to one of the deepest longings of the heart-nature of man. Humanity groaned to see and know that above nature and commanding it is God. Until such providence is manifest the soul is uncertain whether it is orphan or not.

The Book of Nature, though it had been studied for four thousand years, gave no testimony to the fact that matter and God are one. Christ came and proclaimed a providence; he taught that yonder vast out-lying universe with all its beauty and variety is the creature of God, that it is his, its laws and forces and elements are all his, that he clothes the grass of the field, he adorns the lily, he feeds the fowls of the air, all are his, his to command, his to promote his glory, his to work out the greatest good of his children. This thought too involves faith, reasonable faith; who can hesitate to trust infinite wisdom and omnipotence to manage all the affairs of this universe, great and small?

As far as that hurtful theory of the essential evilness of matter is concerned, Christ, by the sweet sociability of his example, by the simple beauty in which he spoke of beasts and birds and flowers, by the tact with which he wove into his matchless discourse, fields and vineyards and all the suggestive symbolisms of nature, most effectually contradicted the doctrine. He not only said annoint thy head and wash thy face; not only did he strike away the mask from the disfigured face of hypocrisy; not only did he bless a marriage feast with his presence and sanctify the joyous wine by his miracle, but he promised that the earth should be the inheritance of the blessed meek, and under the influence of his spirit the great apostle could say "every creature of God is good, and nothing to be refused, if it be received with thanksgiving."

But there are two divine ideals which, as they appear prominently in the holy faith of the Gospel, with a majesty incomparably sublime, rebuke this false philosophy that the material universe is inherently malignant. Those ideals are the Incarnation and the Resurrection. These teach the whole world of humanity that matter is good enough for infinite goodness, and that the glory of the Heavenly is not too good even for bodies like ours, bodies that have sprung up out of the dust.

The significance of the Incarnation and the Resurrection, in one word of Redemption, is not that God, on account of human apostacy, found himself in a difficult strait, and was compelled to call his omnipotence into requisition that he might work himself out; that infinite thought was not an after-thought; but Redemption is the expression of a great, all-pervading, all-penetrating and eternal law of providence, the crowning evidence that God, the universe and humanity are bound together in the bonds of a glorious and inseparable trinity; that God is "above all, through all, and in you all;" in short. that if you will only accept them "all things are yours, ye are Christ's and Christ is God's." Down through universes, and laws, and atoms, the Father extends his arms to reach, embrace and lift up his fallen child, up above atoms, and laws, and universes to the very bosom of his infinite love.

Since Jesus Christ made proclamation of his great doctrine of providence, crowned with the glory of Redemption the world has moved onward; this holy faith has built it up; when men began to see that matter is good, not bad, they looked into it, they employed its forces and its elements for their convenience, comfort and development. Society is enriched and home is made sweet according as the crude notion of the malignity of matter passes away. So it happens that men on whose brows have shined the light of a Christian civilization do not shrink away from material things as if they were possessed of a devil, but making stepping-stones of them they rise continually into a better life. Redemption, therefore, that is providence in its completeness, is the force that touches the secret springs of man's loftiest ambitions, and leads him out into the field of his infinite opportunities.

Thus we have examined the second pillar of our faith; having seen it standing forth in the amplitude and strength of its divine glory, may we not say, in the words of Marcus Antoninus, " what would it concern me to live in a world void of God, and without a providence?" This idea of an universal providence, which of course implies a particular, that is a divine influence thrown around every individual soul, the soft touches of the divine finger on the harpstrings of the human heart, is to man's moral sense, as self-evident as the light to his eye, or the law of gravitation to his reason. Whatever, therefore, may be the variety of

human conjecture, or the conflicts of theological speculations, there can be no disposition in the heart of man to
antagonize or repudiate this fundamental truth. Sweep it
away and you have dethroned the Almighty, you have divested him of his glorious attributes, you have plucked law
and harmony from the universe, you have destroyed your
hope of eternal life, and you are left in utter helplessness
and weakness while there is no strong hand reaching down
into your "slough of despond" to lift you out.

But this doctrine, unentangled and simple, is not to-
day and never has been very furiously assailed; the world
generally accepts it; in so far therefore the world generally
accepts Christianity, for providence is a fundamental truth
of the Gospel. Mankind does not greatly enjoy antagoniz-
ing a principle so apparent to moral sense, and so pregnant
with high-born possibilities for the race. In their disputations and desperation, men have struck off from this doctrine this fanciful appendage and that; one generation
threw about this pillar of faith a net-work which was torn
away by another; this theologian endeavored to stick on a
lily, and that one tried to adorn it with a pomegranate, but
when all the pomegranates, and the lilies, and reticulations
of human ingenuity have been swept away with the besom
of destruction, this pillar of our faith, just as Jesus displayed it, still stands, with its base on the earth and its
capital in the clouds of the eternal habitation, secure as the
throne of God; around it the world's populations gather, and
in the integrity of their heart-natures confess "the Lord
reigneth, he preserveth the souls of his saints, light is given
or the righteous and gladness for the upright in heart."

III. THE THIRD PILLAR OF OUR FAITH IS THE DOCTRINE OF
THE REMISSION OF SINS.

The world, at the time of Christ, needed to have pointed
out to it an effectual remedy for sin, which should harmonize with the highest dictate of reason. the moral methods of
the universe and the righteousness of God. That need was
wide-spread as humanity, for wherever man breathed the
breath of life there was sin. and wherever sin appeared there
was the demand more or less earnest for the sovereign
cure.

Whatever its cause. sin is the most appalling fact in
the universe. Sin lurked in the subtle question of the first
deceiver. in the credulous curiosity of the first woman, in
the craven cowardice of the first man. and in the very devotions of the first brother. Scarcely had fifteen centuries of
the world's history passed away when sin merited and received a rebuke, severe, sweeping and overwhelming. The
Egyptians were sensible of sin when they paid large reven-
ues to numerous colleges of priests. Sin was the great
plague of the Hebrews during their pilgrimage of forty
years in the wilderness. Sin confronted them in all the
peoples by whose territorial borders they passed. Sin was
the rock that struck and broke into pieces the Babylonian
empire, and sin is everywhere doing its work of destruction
to-day.

But what is sin? And what is salvation? A variety
of answers might be given. Sin is perversity of choice, a
force in man that deflects him from the true course, a
wrong aim by which he misses the mark of destiny, a bias
within that twists, wrenches and deforms man's moral
nature, and brings spiritual ruin on his soul. But Paul said
"sin is transgression of the law;" in accordance with this

definition I should say that sin is an attempt to break the links by which God, the universe and humanity are bound in one sweet and blessed trinity.

Punishment of sin in its primary sense is the natural consequence of such an attempt. In other words, it is that "tribulation and anguish" which must come on every soul of man that seeks to disengage itself from the all-encompassing arms of divine law and love.

Repentance is the act by which a prodigal son returns to the embrace of his Heavenly Father.

Prayer is the soul in struggle to climb up into the higher possibilities of being.

Faith is the power that takes hold of the approved method, and Salvation is the grace of divine love, made manifest in Christ Jesus and applied to the soul's hurt for its eternal healing.

Christ came to proclaim the law and pronounce the remedy; it was unique; except in foreshadowing ceremonies the world had never dreamed of such a method before. A remedy for sin had been sought in altars, shrines, tithes, temples, sacrifices, scourges. Men had consulted priests, oracles, philosophers, physicians; they had performed penance, lavished wealth, accomplished good works and sought cleansing from sin in numerous ablutions and baptisms; but these could only blunt the edge of conscience, they could not cover, lift, take away or blot out guilt.

Christ, perceiving that men "loved darkness rather than light, because their deeds were evil," that "all like sheep had gone astray," or, as I have expressed myself, that they were breaking away from the embraces and providences of God, and thus doing violence to nature and to destiny declared that, in order to reinstatement and reunion with the Father, a radical work must first be done; the affections and desires must be bent backward; the nature that had been wrenched and warped by sin must be made straight again; the wrong bias taken out; the roots of bitterness extracted, and the soul placed in its true position; in short, there must be a new moral birth into which Christ himself is the door, the way, the truth. Therefore Christ gave utterance to a self-evident truth in the great scheme of divine providence when he said "God sent not his Son into the world to condemn the world, but that the world through him might be saved." And he spoke philosophically when he said "He that believeth on (that is liveth by) the Son hath everlasting life, and he that believeth not (or liveth not by) the Son shall not see life."

Thus there is a remedy for sin, it is in grace. God has made provision for such an emergency in his eternal law and counsel. If there is an all-superintending providence there must be such a remedy. Salvation from sin must be a potent law in God's universe, invariable as any other law. As relief from hunger is a potency in the law of vegetation, or as life is a potency in the co-operating methods of the material universe, so forgiveness, remission of sin and salvation from its guilt and consequences is a potency in the perfect law of divine love. The love of God could not have been perfect had it been unable to make all just and necessary provision for every poor fallen soul that stands in need of redeeming power. Admitting then that there is a God, that he rules in this universe, that he has a Father's compassion for all his children, we should be smitten with astonishment if there were nowhere to be found a way out of our moral undoing.

Christ is the expression and manifestation of that law and that power; he is the hand of omnipotence reached out

to an erratic world to lead it from hoplessness to hope, from
sin to God. He taketh away the sin of the world. He is
the sin-remitting power in Heaven and in earth. He is able
to put back sin, just as health puts back disease, He can
move "our sins from us as far as the East is from the
West." "To him gave all the prophets witness that
through his name all who believe on him shall receive remission of sins."

Remission being a divine law, we find that its effects
are the same everywhere, its operation is invariable, it is
known by its fruits. Wherever a sinner finds the law and
uses it, whether he recognizes the hand that offers it or the
voice that commends it or not, it accomplishes the same
work. The most brilliant, the most benighted, the civilized
and the barbarian are saved under the influence of that law,
not alone from a future hell that one might fear, not from
a future Heaven that one might desire, but saved in the
present time, saved from the sinful act, saved from the corrupting power of sin, saved from the guilt and stain of sin,
saved to holiness, and love, and God. Saved, if like Saul of
Tarsus, knowing the source from whence the salvation
comes, and saved, though like some ignorant heathen, we
have never heard of Christ, "for when the Gentiles, which
have not the law, (written), do by nature the things contained in the law, these having not the law, are a law unto
themselves." So then, men are not saved by believing in
the person of Christ, but by living by the principles, and
under the influence of the life of Christ. The law is the
same therefore the wide-world over, and when in eternity
the building of Redemption, fitly framed together, shall
have grown into a holy temple in the Lord, all who have
been redeemed, Jew and Gentile, bond and free, learned and
unlearned will discover, though some of them may not know

it now, that Jesus Christ is the foundation and the chief corner stone.

This then is the doctrine, that God in his providence has provided a means by which his children, though fallen and sinful, need not be forever banished from him. By the side of this truth there may be a score of glosses and theological fancies, glosses and fancies that thoughtful men must criticise and oppose but who would fight against this law of pardon? Who is willing to declare that God in his fatherhood will not receive and redeem a poor, penitent soul, who out of the depths cries "Lord save or I perish?"

Ever since the proclamation of this divine law of remission, humanity has been looking up, for sin degrades, but when sin has been cancelled, courage comes to the soul and hope to the heart. Let a man drop his sin, come into harmony with God and God's universe, let him feel in his conscience the healing power of divine love, and realize that he has thus come into that state where he is " heir of all things" and he must grow; then he will walk and faint not, he will run and not be weary, he will mount as on wings of eagles. Let us then thank God for the possibility of pardon.

IV.   THE FOURTH PILLAR OF OUR FAITH IS THE DOCTRINE OF
THE UNIVERSAL BROTHERHOOD OF MAN.

Christ taught this doctrine when he said "Love your enemies;" also when he associated with publicans and sinners; also in his remarks to the woman at Jacob's well; also in the parable of the Good Samaritan; but particularly when he declared "God so loved the world that he gave his only begotten Son that whosoever believeth in him should not perish, but have everlasting life." And in the fullness of time one of the apostles was delegated to make clear and unmistakable announcement of this great truth; nor did he timidly undertake his work. Emboldened with the spirit of his Master he declared, "of a truth, I perceive that God is no respecter of persons, but in every nation he that feareth him and worketh righteousness is accepted of him."

This was an announcement world-wide in its scope, and universal in its significance; it contained not a grain of fatalism, election or bigotry; it recognized no outward condition or creed as a standard of measurement; the sole requirement for affiliation with Almighty God, to say nothing of affinity with man, is, according to this distinguishing doctrine of the Gospel, reverence and righteousness, in one word it is character.

This idea, in the age in which it was uttered, was entirely new, it was revolutionizing, it was disloyalty to the sentiment that had been prevalent for centuries, it contradicted the custom of the Jew who refused even to recognize an unproselyted Gentile; it struck at the philosophy of Greece which taught that "an inferior race is born to be the slaves of the superior;" it menaced the practice of a world-conquering empire, for that empire trampled under its feet everything that was not Roman; it was a shaft aimed at China, that stagnant nation which, for thousands of years sat isolated with walls of exclusiveness built solidly around her; it was a golden apple, thrown into the midst of India, that empire of caste and social petrifactions; yes, and that doctrine of the universal brotherhood of man is falling to-day with tremendous force on the sectarian narrowness and the pious bigotry of all classes of exclusive Christians who stand in the way of the moral progress of the world.

That divine doctrine is also most significant, it means that every binding fetter shall ultimately be broken; it meant that Nero's slaves were as good as their royal master; that princes are no better than peasants; that all men in the sight of God are free and equal; that Russian serfdom should pass away; that 1776 should resound with the thunder of the Declaration of Independence; it meant that the clanging chains of American slavery should be heard no more, and that the time will come when white, black, high, low, rich, poor, shall be conscious of the God-given dignity which belongs to them, and all shall confess that "we have all one Father, and one God hath created us." The world is gradually approaching that era, and when it shall come the sweet spirit of the Gospel having touched every human heart, all enmity will be done away, caste will be known no more, and humanity will be one blessed and unbroken brotherhood.

It cannot be that there is a man anywhere on the globe, if he has one spark of moral sense glowing in his breast, who would throw himself into antagonism with this distinguishing doctrine of Christianity. Opposition to this divine truth means the perpetuity of pride and the continuance of oppression; it means that injustice shall reign and extortion rule; it means that tyranny shall once more strike its smarting thongs into the lashed and bleeding backs of men; but on the contrary the doctrine of the universal brotherhood of man having free course, running and being glorified means the universality of peace and the reign of love.

Having walked round about Zion and considered her bulworks, and discovered what are the pillars that support the temple of Christian truth, we may well inquire is the Gospel in danger? Must these pillars fall? Amid the conflicts that are raging and the general confusion of antiquated faiths, can it be said that the unity of God, his Universal Providence, God's Power to Pardon, and the Brotherhood of Man, are going down in the turmoil and the strife? Every conscience, believing and unbelieving, Christian and unchristian, answers this question with an enthusiastic No! But these, in their breadth, constitute the whole of the Gospel. Christianity is supported by these eternal pillars, how then can it be said that the Christian Religion is fading out, and that the time will come when it will be a defunct theory ot a well-nigh forgotten age?

The fact is these self-evident truths stand unchallenged; the unbelieving multitude who proclaim war on the Gospel waste their words and fight the air. Nor will it pay to attack these pillars of truth. Nero and Domitan, Decius and Galerius, Celsus and Porphyry, and Julian the apostate, and all the adversaries who succeeded them, down to Hume and Voltaire, and Paine set themselves in array against the Gospel, but they are all dead. Every enemy of Christ, who appeared and raged in the first eighteen hundred years of the Christian era are dead now, and their philosophies have perished with them; but the Gospel, declaring one God, one universe, one humanity, one Lord, one Law-giver, one salvation, still lives and grows and magnifies while it lives. In fifty years Ingersoll and Bradlaugh and all the men of their ilk will be dust; and when they shall be forgotten, when their threats and denunciations have whispered their last echo in the minds of men, the Gospel will continue its good work of winning heart to heart, humanity to law, the universe to God and God to all.

But when faith is assailed by some moral cyclone that is sweeping over the world, or by some upspringing skepticism of my own heart, what is the best method of resistance? It was to answer this question that Jude wrote his epistle; he advises "contend *earnestly* for the faith once de-livered to the saints." But how? Not by force of arms, not by heated and excited discussion, but " by self upbuild-ing in the faith of the Gospel, by prayer in the Holy Ghost, by keeping self in the love of God, and by looking for the mercy of our Lord Jesus Christ unto eternal life."

Thus each seeking, growing, praying, loving soul has the promise of a certain but bloodless victory. Thrusting self on the love of the Savior; loving God with all the heart, mind, soul and strength; enriched and baptized with the Holy Spirit; praying in the Holy Ghost, the mind and soul expanding by growing in the knowledge of the truth, one need not trouble himself about opposing forms and systems of doctrine; he will grow into the certainty of the truth himself, and his daily life will be the evidence of the truth and beauty of his Religion to others.

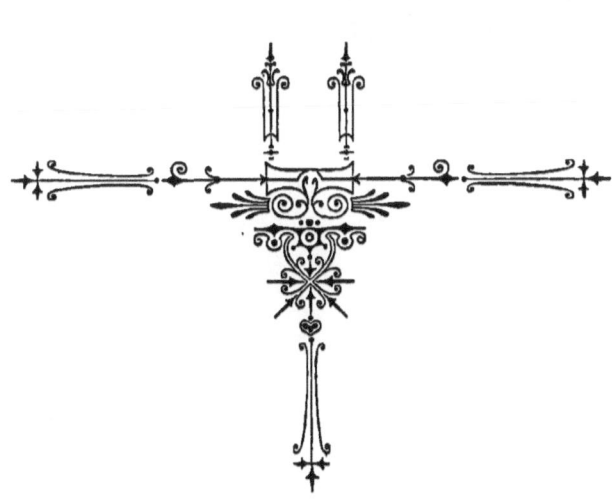

THE STANDARD OF RIGHT.

And when he was departed thence, he lighted on Jehonadab the son of Rechab coming to meet him; and he saluted him, and said to him, is thine heart right, as my heart is with thy heart! And Jehonadab answered, it is. If it be, give me thine hand. And he gave him his hand; and he took him up to him into the chariot.—*II Kings,* 10, 15.

The two characters mentioned in this text are Jehu and Jehonadab; the first a tempestuous, cruel and crafty king, and the second an austere and decided Bedouin Arab. Each were great in their way. Jehu was a great charioteer, a great soldier, a great politician, a great iconoclast, and Jehonadab was great in independence, great in purpose, great in self-denial, and great in his influence with his clan and over his family, an influence that was felt and recognized for several generations, for, adopting his sentiments, his descendents drank no wine, planted no vineyards, built no houses and sowed no seed.

The crafty Jehu desired to secure the service and influence of Jehonadab, therefore he met him with a royal salutation, took him up into his chariot, professed to be very zealous for the Lord, pretended that he believed as Jehonadab did. "My heart is with thy heart," said the prince. " Is thy heart right? If it is give me thy hand," and he gave him his hand.

This question, is thy heart right? means a great deal more than Jehu meant, and a great deal more than Jehonadab would be willing to answer in the affirmative. The abstemious Arab did not declare that his heart was right in the full meaning of that word, and the diplomatic Jehu did not ask that searching question to himself. It is one of the most important questions that can be propounded, and deserves our most serious attention. The language is so simple that we readily catch its meaning, though its depth may not be so easily sounded.

The inquiry is not in regard to creed, whether you believe in Apostolic Succession, Free Will, or Election; these may be important in theological discussion, but practically they are of no account. It is not a question of denominations, whether you be a Baptist, or a Methodist, a Presbyterian, or a Quaker, an Episcopalian, or a Catholic. Each of these may be good in their places, and every man ought belong to one church or another, but by the question in consideration all dividing lines are obliterated; it is of vastly greater moment than any ecclesiastical distinctions; for no doctrine, or ceremony, or polity can make right the hidden affections of the human heart.

Nor has the question anything to do with social position. Listening Senates may sit enwrapt at your feet; a nation may wreathe its laurels for your brow; armies may wait your word of command; you may be a merchant prince, or an adept among artists, and society may make you its king, or you may walk in the more humble walks of life, to literature and greatness a stranger; it matters not; social position cannot answer the fearful question that waits to be decided. Is thy heart right? Oh! what a question; let us be careful to regard it prayerfully and properly. We may observe then, that

I. THE OPINIONS WHICH WE FORM OF OURSELVES MAY BE ERRONEOUS.

Human nature is prominent at least in one respect, prominent in its selfishness. We mention this not to suggest that selfishness is an unlawful element in character; on the contrary, we believe that it is a good and essential element in all true character. Properly limited, controlled, directed, self-love is an exponent of moral power; from self love springs to a great extent love for others. Not appreciating the value of shelter, raiment, food, knowledge, salvation for your own comfort and development you will not be likely to appreciate it for the sake of others. What would it matter to you that some are homeless, naked, hungry, ignorant, lost, if you had no regard for these things yourself? Then you would eat your crust as cattle crunch their corn, heedless of a dying world around you.

But the probability is that self-love is usually too largely developed; there is danger that it will become all-covering. producing extravagant views of personal needs and personal merit; rendering us greedy and grasping, until we have become a sort of Dead Sea, receiving but imparting not. It is said in classic fable that Narcissus was so handsome that all the nymphs fell in love with him, but no feminine accomplishment, no grace or beauty of the gentler sex could make the least impression on him, he was proof

against all their blandishments, but coming one day to a
fountain, and stooping to drink its pure, sweet water, Lo, a
beautiful image was reflected from the pellucid wave; for
the first time Narcissus was smitten, those locks how fine,
those cheeks how fair, those lips how tempting, those eyes
how bright and winsom; he woed, he whispered, but there
was no response, and there by the fountain he stood pining
away and died at last of a passionate love of himself. This
may be an exaggerated picture, yet how many there are
whose world consists of the little circle in which their own
self-hood moves, and who are charmed of nothing save by
what pertains to their own individual importance.

Even among true men there is general complaint that
self is larger than the circle that it fills. Who is willing to
allow that he is in exactly the right place, and receives absolutely all that belongs to him? Poor men believe it
would be better for them were they rich, and rich men are
always nervous to get richer. Politicians seek after place,
prominence and promotion. and even ministers complain
that they have not the position that belongs to them, that
they are competent to fill a larger place, that they ought to
push others aside in order to make more room for themselves. With such tendencies in ourselves, how can we
correctly judge in regard to the rightness of our hearts?
We shall be apt to over estimate our moral worth.

Then again our chances for self deception are numerous, inadequate knowledge, insufficient education, natural
inability to discover the difference between differences, in-
experience, and many other things may possibly mislead
our judgment and cause us to form an erroneous opinion.
Child-like, we may be deceived with trifles. Jehonadab-like
we may be ensnared by fair professions and promises. Riche-
lieu-like we may be moved by flattery. The castle we build
to-day to-morrow we may see in ruins. The philosophy

that seems so reasonable now, may the next time the wind changes lose all its force.   Thus we are living in a mirage. Life is all a delusion. We are daily being duped by some deception.   Under such circumstances how unreliable must be the opinions that we form even of ourselves. How can we imagine that we are competent to discover and hold forth to the world, of our own strength, an absolutely reliable law of right?

Robert Burns, the most practical of all poets of human nature, expressed a good deal of truth in that oft repeated stanza:

> " O, wad some Pow'r the giftie gie us
>   To see oursels as ithers see us!
>   It wad frae monie a blunder free us,
>   And foolish notion;
>   What airs in dress an' gait wad lea'e us,
>   And ev'n in devotion!"

So, frequently the people are better judges of personal merit than is the individual. But even the multitude measures a man according as he reaches up to or falls beneath their particular standard; the South Sea Islanders measure men according to one rule, the Esquimaux according to another, and the civilized nations of Europe according to another; therefore, though we could see ourselves as others see us, the case in question would not be changed; we could not even then decide upon what is right, for the public standard is not necessarily correct. Often the good are ignored and the unworthy are honored in the public regard; vox populi is not vox dei; the multitude clamored that there should be a king in Israel, but that was not according to the will divine; the mob demanded the release of Barabbas and the rejection of Jesus, but their cry "away with him," was not the voice of God. No! it is as Sumner said "the sacred rules of right are not to be found in the foot-prints of a trampling multitude." We cannot, therefore, look to ourselves, nor to our fellow-men for a standard of right, for the opinions both of the individual and the multitude may be erroneous. We may inquire then

II. WHAT IS THE STANDARD OF RIGHT?

Certainly, the question of the text, is thy heart right? is unanswerable until that standard is discovered. Let us then, by careful inquiry and cautious moving look until we find the standard, or conclude that there is not and there cannot be an infallible rule of right.

1. The standard rule of right and wrong cannot be our knowledge. If knowledge made right, then the greater our knowledge the greater would be our righteousness. To make a rule there must be a consummation, a perfection; but we cannot describe a circle around human knowledge and say this is all, our capacity is always increasing, and our facilities are always multiplying. Each generation knows more than the preceding; what we think we know to-day we shall probably find that we are ignorant of to-morrow. "I know," says the poet, "my soul has power to know all things, yet she is blind and ignorant of all." How, then, can we take such an indefinable, illimitable, changeable thing as human knowledge and out of it con-construct a rule of right? Right or wrong for man cannot depend on what he knows.

The principle that knowledge is the parent of goodness utterly fails when applied to practice. Voltaire was a knowing man, but it is declared that his character passed at considerable discount; Hume was a scholar, but an "advocate of licentiousness and suicide;" Rosseau was eloquent

and largely learned in the classics, but "guilty of the basest
performances which,denying not, he only tried to palliate."
One may go to school for two score years, graduate from
all the colleges in the country, be possessed of the most
studious habits, know more than Franklin or Newton, or
the ripest scholar in the country, yet remain morally un-
improved and be altogether incapable of making a rule of
right, for, as Paul said, "professing themselves to be wise,"
philosphers may "become fools" and be "given up to uncleanness." Even moral instruction does not make men
moral, for if the commandment came from man, why
should the teachings of one be any more authoritative than
another? And certainly æsthetical culture has not made
men pure, else Greece might have been proud of the purity
of its peoples; with all her culture Athens was a cesspool
of licentiousness and lust, of cruelty and crime. In brief,
the conclusion is inevitable, an infallible moral rule cannot
be found in human knowledge as a necessary element in it.

2. This much desired standard is not to be discovered
in the state of our feelings. Men are so constituted that
they cannot all feel alike even under the same circumstances. Some people are more susceptible of feeling than
others; some are cold as ice, others are warm as the glowing
coal; the emotions of some men are all on the surface,
others lie deep as the pearls in the Persian Gulf, and it requires no little effort to find them. The masses move from
the sanctuary untouched by the love of Jesus, only the few
are subdued; of the crowd that pass by the little barefoot
beggar on the corner, only a few drop the wanted penny
into her hand, the busy throng hurries on its way; to declare therefore that feeling is a rule of conduct, is to render
moral action uncertain as the wind; build up a code of
morals on human feelings and you would have an incoherent
confused, meaningless mass of statutes that would be fickle

as quicksilver, striking this man's mood to-day, and that man's fancy to-morrow. according to the particular temperature that touched it.

3.   Nor is the standard of right and wrong to be found in our original theories. If theory were the rule there would be as many rules as theories; there would also be a perpetual conflict.   What some nations consider to be right others regard as wrong. Christian peoples are taught to respect the aged, that grey hairs are honorable, that when parents are enfeebled by age their children shall care for them; we set apart for them the best room in the house, we devote to their use the couch of honor, we welcome them at our table, when sick we minister to their necessities, when they die we follow them mournfully to the grave, we erect marble tablets to their memory, we strew flowers on the sod that covers them, we enshrine them in the truest affections of our hearts, and with joyous anticipation look forward to the time when we shall grasp their hands again on the golden shore. But there are peoples who believe and practice differently, and think and feel the very opposite of what we do; people who believe that when their parents become helpless under the burdens and infirmities of years, it is right to kill them. Here, then is a great difference in moral theory; our opinion is that it is wrong to murder the aged, theirs that it is wrong to detain them in their infirmities when they are burdens to themselves and their children. Who shall decide when nations disagree?

If, then, right and wrong is a mere matter of theory, there can be no methods by which moral merit and demerit can be gauged. As we have seen the icicle clinging with unyielding grasp to the cornice of our dwelling, so long as the frost continued its congealing work, and softly melting away when the sun threw out its beams, so we have seen man cling most rigidly to his opinions until brighter rays of truth began to pour upon them, and then those opinions have disappeared. Many thoughts which we called our best are

> "Like the snow-flake on the river,
> A moment seen, then gone forever."

Shall we then accept such melting nothings as the standard of right and wrong? Can we accept a human theory or opinion as a rule of right and yet be true to common sense?

4. If then, neither theory, nor feeling, nor knowledge are just criteria of right and wrong, what is the standard? Where shall we find an infallible rule that will aid us in correctly answering the question of the text, is thy heart right? We reply that it can be found nowhere but in the will of God; that must be the standard, for we cannot go beyond it; it alone is all-covering; there is consummation and perfection in it. If that rule can be found, and our hearts are in unison with it, it being absolute, we cannot be wrong, we must be right; or out of harmony with that rule, we shall at least see in what direction our duty lies. But where shall we go to find God's fixed and unchangeable standard of right? Not to nature, for moral things. cannot be measured by a material rule; not to sprinkling priest, or failing patriarch; not to the philosophy of the schools or the ethics of the moralist; these have been tried and too frequently have been found wanting; but we may go to the faithful page, if indeed it is a revelation from God, and find that infallible rule therein made plain.

5. A field now opens up to view which has been traversed time and time again, yet at each new exploration new discoveries are made in evidence of the fact that the Bible

contains the revealed will of God, and is a sufficient rule of
faith and practice. It is a field too vast to be entered now,
but passing, it may be observed that our Heavenly Father
has not left his Will and Testament to us unsupported, but
rather he has thrown about it the most convincing evidence. That the Bible is something more than the product
of a human brain is proved by the perfect harmony of
every part of the record; by the hallowed precepts it proposes, and the pure life it enjoins; by those revelations of
God and those disclosures of the future that characterize
it; by an array of miracles performed in attestation of its
own truth; by its long list of fulfilled and perpetually
fulfilling prophecies. Its truth is proved also by the great
plan of Redemption which the Bible unfolds and which
could not have been the thought of uninspired and earth-
groveling men, and also by a thousand external evidences
that confirm its statements; thus bodies of embalmed
kings, fallen monuments of past ages, rocks written all
over with a pen of iron, are to-day rising from the graves
where they have reposed for thousands of years, and coming into court testify to the truth of the inspired page. All
these facts, and others too numerous to mention, point to
the Holy Scriptures as the record of the divine will, the
great unalterable, God-given standard of right and wrong.
We observe that

III. COMPARING THE HEART WITH GOD'S RULE OF RIGHT,
" NONE IS GOOD, NO, NOT ONE."

Weighed in this balance we are each found wanting,
according to this measurement our hearts are not right, by
this rule applied the best man abhors himself. It declares
" the wickedness of man is very great, and every imagination of his heart is evil continually;" that is man as a

whole. not an individual here and there, is under the ban of unrighteousness.

Compare your heart, for instance. with the ten commandments of the decalogue. Is there not something which, as it were an idol. holds a higher place in your thought than God? Is it true that he is in all your thoughts? Then your heart is not right. Are you not frequently found bowed down before an idol, a golden calf perhaps, not literally as Israel did. but in such a sense as that to get rich seems to be your sole occupation? Then your heart is not right. Is your language always chaste, never profane, never speaking the name divine thoughtlessly, uselessly, irreverently? If not the heart is not right. That blessed Sabbath, do you love to rest on that day, in body, mind, soul, in the sense of self-devotion to God, entering the sanctuary, restful in worship, meditation and prayer? If not your heart is not right. Have you in every respect obeyed the divine mandate, to honor father and mother, not casting them off to shift for themselves, nor making them feel humbled by the dependence of their condition? If not thy heart is not right. Have you never endangered human life by your neglect, nor without a cause hated your brother. thus fostering the spirit of murder in your heart? Have you never trespassed upon those sacred boundaries with which God has defined society, and defended the family, nor under the inflammation of passion cast a lustful eye beyond the line? If you have your heart is not right. Has all the property ever gotten by yourself been honestly obtained, so that not one cent's worth can in Christian justice be claimed by another? If not your heart is not right. Have you never tried to injure your neighbor by an ungenerous remark, by a word intended to put him in a bad light before the people? Have you never desired the possessions of another, nor resolved that by loaning him money that you knew he could not pay, those possessions you would some day secure? If you have done such things your heart was not right. Or if each one of those commandments has been observed and kept, not because you really wanted to observe them inviolate, but simply because they were law, then, certainly, the heart was wrong, radically wrong. It is not enough to serve God from compulsion, or from fear; the righteous heart elects to serve him from principle, because it is in blissful harmony with the divine will. Nay more, Christ puts the moral requirements of God's law on the ground of love, so that if God is not loved with fulness of heart, mind, soul and strength, then, according to the spirit of this rule it is impossible to answer affirmatively the question, is thy heart right?

That there is in these questions a fearful pertinency must be admitted I ask them because I desire to be pertinent; how can I be faithful and yet forbear to present the truth with searching plainness? But those interrogatories embody the rules according to which heart righteousness is to be measured; they indicate what shall be the decision of the judgment; they proclaim the solemn truth that we are all wrong; the whole world is guilty; why this is so may not be a practical question, but that it is so is a solemn fact. Why did Christ taste death for every man if every man were deserving of life without it? And why should there be a light to light every man that cometh into the world if every man that cometh into the world were not born in darkness?

I have read, somewhere, of a Hindoo robber who, while waiting in prison, to be executed according to the mandate of the law, informed the jailor that he was the custodian of a certain important secret which he desired to

communicate to the king. Admitted into the royal presence the culprit declared that trees could be made to bear
fruit of gold if a coin were planted by a hand that had
never been guilty of a dishonest deed; but robber, nor
prince, nor prime minister, nor priest dared to plant the
coin. I think, observed the thief, we ought all be hung, for
there is not an honest man among us. So, though we are
not all robbers or assassins, yet if our lives depended on
clean hands and pure hearts, there would be some spot or
stain demanding our execution.

But suppose there were no Gospel to win the soul to a
better life; no word divine uttering its terrible denunciations against sin; no law asserting its power and pronounc-
ing its penalty; no spirit striving, no conscience reproving,
and no church to call the world from darkness to light,
could there be any thought of sin? Certainly, for everywhere the heart whispers its own guiltiness to an accusing
conscience. In Pagan lands, among heathenism and idolatry, philosophers like Plato have regarded man as one who
has been stripped of his moral glory; and scholars like
Marcus Antoninus have declared that " men are born mere
slaves to their appetites and passions," indeed every pleading votary at an idol shrine gives evidence to the fact that
"all have sinned."

But the question might be asked are we right with
ourselves? Is the heart true to its own convictions? Do
men live as well as they know? And the answer must be
given that an unrighteous heart is not excusable on the
ground of its ignorance; if men sin at all they sin in broad
daylight; they sin because they trample on their supreme
convictions; the Chinaman knows he ought not to eat
opium; the Indian knows he ought not get drunk; thus according to their own thought men are wrong; they know

very well that there is often a conflict between the will and the desire, between the thought and the action; we are not right with ourselves; even independent of the Book and the Gospel, most men, before the tribunal of their own moral sense, would stand convicted and condemned. They weigh themselves in the balances and are found wanting.

The fact is we are all wrong, naturally wrong; we go astray from our birth; untrained and unrestrained we are more likely to grow crooked than straight; we are radically wrong; the virus of sin lies at the very roots of our natures; our hearts are touched with a hereditary taint as well as our bodies; the slug of sin is within us as sure as the worm is in the butterfly; but moral possibility is also within us certainly as there are wings folded up in the nature of the caterpillar; give us favorable opportunity and a willingness to mount upward and we shall leave the groveling grub behind us; until that better being is called out our tastes, our desires, our feelings are downward, depravity takes hold of us, " the whole head is sick, the whole heart is faint;" we are morally corrupt and need a physician; the cry of every serious soul is "is there no balm in Gilead, is there no physician there?"

Christ came to make this crooked world straight; Christ came to make corrupt hearts clean. "He is the propitiation for our sins, and not for ours only, but for the sins of the whole world." His remedy is efficacious, ask the dying thief, ask a thousand living witnesses, ask all the glorified. Oh! friend, is thy heart right? If it is not right surely it ought to be righted. You have failed many times in your most earnest endeavors to make your heart right. Your best attempt resulted in nothing more than a breaking away from some bad habit, which perhaps overcame

you at last, and the malady of sin, like an eating cancer,
still remained in your moral nature. But what you have
failed to do for yourself Christ can succeed in doing for
you. Wilt thou be made whole? Behold "all power is
given unto him in heaven and in earth."

When Israel had defiled the land by their doings, and
were cast out like an unclean thing, and scattered abroad
among the heathen, the Lord promised that when he should
become sanctified in them "a new heart also will I give,
and a new spirit will I put within you." That new heart,
that new spirit is what the sin-smitten world most needs.
God is no respecter of persons: he will do as well for us as
for Israel. He says "I will take away the stony heart and
give you a heart of flesh."

What a difference there is between the old heart and
the new; the old was hard, stubborn, cold, dead, like a
stone, nothing moved it, eternal things, nor deathless love,
nor all the agony of him who died on Calvary could stir its
emotion; but made new under the power of the Holy Spirit
the truest passions, the deepest feeling, the livliest interest
in Heavenly things are aroused. Again the old heart was
proud, lofty, self-righteous, but the new is made humble, it
bows at the feet of the man of sorrows, it chooses suffering
and affliction, and the lowliest place rather than the enjoyment of the pleasures of sin for a season. The old heart
was earthly, groveling, sensuous, the perishing present was
all-sufficient for its highest ambitions; but the new is Heavenly, the spirit of Christ has touched it, its hopes tower up
into the eternities, the light of the Golden City bathes its
thoughts, desires, affections, it is full of the music and melody of celestial song, and

> " They who carry this music in their heart,
> Through dusky lane and wrangling mart,
> Ply their daily task with busier feet,
> Because their secret souls a holier strain repeat."

But we must drop this great and important question; it is a sermon in itself; it is a question that each must decide for himself and not for another; it is a question that we shall confront some day at the Judgment Seat of Christ. If thine heart is right, or if there is a desire and purpose in your soul to get right, then whatever your education, or your social position, or your peculiar opinions, whether you be rich as Crœsus or poor as Paul the eremite, give me thy hand as my heart is with thy heart.

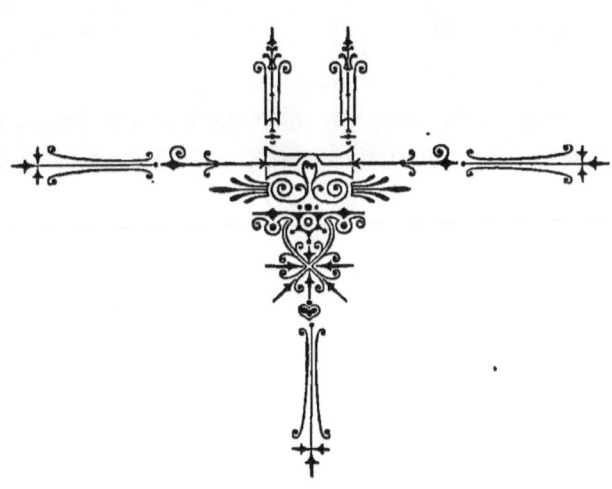

PROFIT OF GODLINESS.

For bodily exercise profiteth little; but godliness is profitable unto all things, having promise of the life that now is, and of that which is to come.—1 *Tim.*, 4-8.

Paul left Timothy in Ephesus in charge of the Ephesian Church, and wrote to him a letter of advice and instruction, which was the more necessary because Timothy was a youth and the Ephesian congregation was in trouble. Some of its members were departing from the faith, and giving heed to seducing spirits and doctrines of devils, and others were formal and hypocritical, pretending to great spiritual attainment because they abstained from meats and marriage, and sought merit in bodily mortification and penance. Paul therefore advised Timothy, in the language of my text, "exercise thyself rather unto godliness, for bodily exercise profiteth little, but godliness is profitable unto all things, having promise of the life that now is and of that which is to come."

Discussing this question in regard to the profit of godliness, it will be necessary to seek in the onset a correct definition of the term. What then are we to understand by godliness? Literally godliness is God-like-ness; but it cannot be that in order to peace, prosperity and happiness in the present world, or in the world to come, the human must become divine, like God. God is inimitable, any attempt at aping him would be blasphemously absurd; the finite cannot imitate the infinite; man and God are so unlike as to be incomparable, yet godliness is a quality that pertains to man; hence the injunction "add to your patience godliness," "follow after godliness," " lead a quiet, peaceable life in all godliness;" but, as it is impossible to be godly in the literal sense, what may be understood by godliness when applied to man?

The apostle declares "great is the mystery of godliness," "God was manifest in the flesh;" in this passage the apostle, by implication, teaches that Christ was the godlike man; "on him" it is said "the spirit was poured without measure." So we judge that a godly man is one who like Christ has received on his heart the baptism of the Holy Ghost, not in that fulness in which Jesus received it, but according as he is able to receive it.

Perhaps the meaning will be made more clear by considering the meaning of the term God. The word God is an Anglo-Saxon word and means good. A godly man therefore is one who is good. " The fruit of the spirit is goodness." Godliness then, or goodness, pertains to fallen man under certain operations of the divine spirit. In short, godliness is reverence and love for God; conformity to the divine will, assimilation into the divine likeness and character; it is Religion in the heart; it is the Gospel in practice; it is holiness; it is purity of life; in two words it is Christian character. Now the apostle declares that this "godliness is profitable unto all things, having promise of the life that now is, and of that which is to come."

We desire at this time to consider the profitableness of such a life, and invite attention to

I. THE DIRECT STATEMENT OF THE TEXT, "GODLINESS IS PROFITABLE UNTO ALL THINGS."

This is the language of a wiser man than I. This declaration fell from the lips of the great Apostle Paul; his talents were as brilliant, his opportunities as good, his experiences as broad as those of any opponent that Christianity ever had. Endowed with natural gifts of the very highest order, inspired from above, standing at the fountainhead of all the philosophy that has tinctured modern thought, he proposed that "godliness is profitable unto all things," and challenged the world to dispute it. Where is the logician who has proved the statement to be untrue? And where is the argument by which its fallacy is demonstrated?

The unscrupulous Rousseau, nor the speculative Renan, nor the mythical Strauss, nor even the poetic Ingersoll has been able to prove that that "godliness which has the promise of the life that now is. and of that which is to come," is not "profitable unto all things." Indeed the proposition has never been seriously questioned; and the gist of the apostolic thought has been crystalized into that old saw, adopted alike by Christians and infidels, "honesty is the best policy;" and it will obtain in human hearts so long as the moral sense retains its place, for godliness is the superlative degree of right. But let us look at the apostle's declarations concering godliness.

" It has the promise of the life that now is." There is not an important want in our natures for which there cannot be found in the Scriptures a specific promise. The psalmist covered the whole ground when he said " the Lord is my Shepherd, I shall not want." We want bread, yes, and it is promised "your bread shall be given, and water shall be sure." We need raiment, yes, "if God so clothe the grass of the field shall he not much more clothe you, O ye of little faith?" We need defense against slander and calumny, yes, and the promise is "trust in the Lord and he shall bring forth thy righteousness as the light, and thy judgment as the noon-day." We need support in sorrow, yes, so it is declared " the eternal God is thy refuge, and underneath are the everlasting arms." We shall need superhuman aid in the hour of death, very true, and therefore the prophet tells us, " though passing through the waters they shall not overflow thee, and through the valley and shadow of Death, thou shalt fear no evil, for his rod and staff shall comfort thee." These are all exceeding precious promises; they show that "godliness has the promise of the life that now is."

The promise is all-covering, but is it true? Is there any evidence of its fulfillment? We need to look at the thought from the standpoint of its practicability, as well as from the fulness of its promise. From such a standpoint we can at least say that generally speaking a good man has the best chance in this world.

Godliness promotes good health. It is declared that "the wicked shall not live out half his days." Statistics show that one quarter, of all who are born die before they are seven years old, and one half die before they are seventeen, a principal cause being the infirmity and corruption inherited from their ancestors. Had the fathers been virtuous and temperate the children would have enjoyed a greater longevity. Among those who survive seventeen, it can be clearly shown that the average life of temperate exceeds that of intemperate people, that the virtuous live longer than the vicious, the just live longer than the dishonest, and the godly than the sinful. For instance, the average length of human life is twenty-five years, but that of the Friends, a devout Christian sect of Great Britain and Ireland, is fifty-six years; that the average of life among them is more than double that among other people, is a strong argument in favor of the health-promoting and life-protecting power of godliness.

Nor is this strange; the fact is a natural one; the world expects that godliness will promote the health of one who possesses it, for it forbids all excess, it panders to no passion, it prevents wrong, it requires temperance, industry, frugality, cleanliness, and provides for soul and body the sweet recuperating rest of a Sabbath every week; and sure as the world shall become Christian in practice as well as theory, all filthiness will be destroyed, all epidemics will be prevented and the longevity of the patriarchs may eventually come back to the world. Not until the people become godly will a rejuvinated earth be able to sing with full significance,

> " O death where is thy sting,
> O grave where is thy victory?"

Godliness makes a clear mind. The health of the mind depends largely on the health of the body; the stomach and the brain are intimately related; pure, sublime thought cannot be evolved from a brain that has been fed by a stomach that is a gas retort, or emits an oder of nitrogen, or flushes the blood with fumes of alcohol. As godliness therefore promotes health it must also lend its aid in strengthening the brain and clearing the mind.

But godliness works out its favorable results in still another way; it affords the mind a character whereby it is linked to the eternal; it lifts thought from the gross and the sensuous into a divine sphere, and occupies the mental powers with the grandest themes and the most glorious ideals, not sectarian and narrow, but broad and lofty as the thought of the divine soul of Jesus of Nazareth.

Godliness secures worldly prosperity. It could not with fairness be stated that all who are prosperou are godly, and all who are godly are prosperous. Christians are poor sometimes. and wicked men are often wealthy; yet it can be said that godliness in its amplitude, as it enters into character and develops a perfect manhood, must endow its possessor with a power that will help him on the way to success and prosperity. A godly man will be prudent. forethoughtful. not rash in business, for he will take time to pray over it; he will be considerate, seeking to adapt certain means to certain ends: he will be sober, neither a voluptuary nor a spendthrft, not wasting his substance in riotous living. but economical and careful, and will add industry to his sobriety; thus grasping, sanctifying and employing his own powers and opportunities he will successfully direct them along the varied lines of honorable business.

Besides a godly man, because honest in all his deal, true in all his transactions, wins for himself a good reputation, and this is worth everything in prosperity. True, such men as Tweed get rich, yet there is a sense in which they are the poorest, the most unsuccessful men on earth. They are poor in peace. poor in self-respect, poor in friends, poor in character, and poor in everything that goes to make a man. Gold and city lots and marble fronts do not make such people rich. Better be a poor fisherman, little and unknown, living on the sand in a hut, content with a hard biscuit. rich in the conscienceness of ones own integrity, rich in the good-will of ones indigent neighbors, rich in faith toward God, than the most affluent rogue that ever reposed on the soft cushions of a palace.

But these are exceptional cases. We are not to judge by them. The question is are the chances for a good man ordinarily better than the chances of an ungodly man? And it seems to me that even the casual observer must see that if men "obey God they spend their years in prosperity and their days in pleasure;" "but the hypocrites in heart heap up wrath, they die in youth and their life is among the unclean."

But there is one more thought that I must notice; it is that the godly man will be likely to succeed because he follows the leadings of Providence and seeks to be installed in that particular profession or trade that is best adapted to his nature and circumstances; there is such a thing as divine guidance for man, we can get our proper places by asking God for them. The divine spirit will lead us to consult our tastes, tempers, capacities; and when there is a suitableness between ourselves and our positions we shall be most apt to succeed. Now if godliness will help render a man prudent, sober, industrious, honest, and adapt him to his place. why should he not prosper? What is to hinder him? Is it not true that godliness is profitable unto all things having promise of the life that now is?

Godliness is profitable in death.

Who can die like the Christian? If you reply Socrates did, I answer, not with such triumph; besides Socrates was in spirit a Christian. Infidels are not so hopeful and happy in that hour. "Hold on to your principles," said a scoffer to his dying friend; "but what have I to hold on to," said he. Enmity to Christ is not an agreeable thing to live with. but it is a dreadful thing to be haunted with in the hour of death.

> "The last end of the good man is peace,
>   How calm his exit;
>   Night dews fall not more lightly to the ground,
>   Nor weary, worn-out winds expire so soft."

Godliness also has promise of the life that is to come.
It sweeps beyond the present and commands the eternal future, lifting the everlasting doors, revealing joy in the presence of God, crowns that fade not away, and glories incorruptible; in short, godliness comprehends time and eternity and therefore is "profitable unto all things." We can say this at least, that Christianity gives man some hope, but infidelity gives him nothing. Vice promises pleasure in this world, although it bitterly disappoints its votaries, sometimes bringing pain while the soul is looking for sweetness, but it promises nothing, absolutely nothing, for the eternal future, unless it is despair. Beauty cannot command the gates that open into the Jasper City. Affluence, though it tower into fabulous dimensions, cannot bribe death, nor extort from the grave the mystery of immortality. Yea, I may gain the whole world and lose my soul; I may be monarch of all I survey, yet find the portal of glory closed against me; but faith upspringing from pure character lifts the veil. Religion sweeps away the mists from the evermore, and a godly life sweetly promises to the soul a Heavenly destiny. If there is any promise of eternal bliss, it is not to the vicious or the sensuous, but for men like Paul, who have fought the good fight, finished the course, and kept the faith; it is for those whose lives have been radiant with the light of the throne of God. Let us consider

II. THE UNREASONING RASHNESS WITH WHICH THE RELIGION OF GODLINESS IS OPPOSED.

Some people can believe almost everything but the Bible, even that a man is a lineal descendent of an oyster, and have faith in in everybody but Christ. It is said that priests have been degraded for dropping their miters, and that dictators have been humiliated becouse a rat squeaked.

So there are men who reject Christ because a Christian has stumbled, and discard the Gospel because of some pious idiosyncrasy in its adherents. Let men show that godliness is unnecessary before they abandon it; let them prove that Christians are false before they condemn them.

It is unjust to condemn all for the sake of a few; might as well judge of the skill of Phidias by the marble bits his chisel has chipped from the block, or the masterpiece of an Angelo by the priming on his canvas, as judge of the beauty of the Gospel by a half dozen of its indifferent adherents.

It is equally unfair to dismiss the claims of Christianity without considering them; for it is possible that by ignoring them the most desirable boon and blessing capable of being possessed by man in the present life is thereby rejected. Wise men will not tear down the Gospel until something better has been found to take its place, for it may be detrimental to the world's best interests to destroy it. It is possible that the Church may be too much like the statue of the pope in prayer, its devotion artificial, its lips marble, its heart stone; yet, after all, it may perpetuate, in monument at least, the purest principles, the divinest doctrines, and the noblest impulses and inspirations that ever stirred the depths of the human soul. Let us not then rashly run upon the Gospel, axe in hand, and attempt to hew it down.

An oriental monarch demanded to know of his ministers how he might make his subjects happy. Many suggestions were made, numerous rules were proposed; one came with his speech, another with written documents, but the last who presented his opinion simply said "love God." Now it may be that this last was the best statesman of them all; perhaps it were better for all peoples of all lands and nations, if their rulers were God-fearing and God-loving men. It may be that the kingdoms of the earth would be greatly benefitted if kings, princes, presidents, senators, ministers possessed so much love for God that they would admire, love and practice his moral law. Personally, I would prefer to live under the iron rule of a Cromwell, with the banner of Christ waving over me, than under the regime of a Robespierre, drinking of the spirit of a Christless commune. I say, perhaps it might be a good thing if every ruler were possessed of a Christian conscince so tender that when the Eternal thunders "thou shalt not steal," their love for God and right would compel them to respond Lord, I will not!

There is in the human mind such a disrelish for political, diplomatic and governmental injustice, that we should be very shy of controverting that religious system which, having the prestige of antiquity and the power of a deep, wide and exalted influence declares that its sole and constant intent is to recast individuals and empires in the mould of godliness, and according to the patterns of truth and right; but such is the Gospel, reject it therefore and we may reject its highest good.

Then again, there may be some good in the bare idea that Christianity is in the world. Though the Christ of the Gospels were unreal, a beautiful myth only, an imaginary life, a mere picture thrown upon the moral canvas of the world, still it is possible that that ideal affects humanity for its good; at least it gives us something to think about; it presents a perfect man to our thought, and a perfect man, though only an ideal, has not been so much as idealized outside of the Gospel; we see the picture and are moved to measure up to its excellence; without the ideal we could not

reach out after something better than we are; the coming of
that thought into the minds of men, was, as Renan said,
"a capital event in the history of the world."

Or, suppose it were contended that the moral character of the Gospel is simply a sublime notion, too lofty to be
reached, or to be practical, still it must be productive of
something.   Philosophies are nothing but fancies, yet those
philosophies produce peculiar types of thinkers; so the
Christian notion of a higher moral life, as it spreads from
empire to empire, extends from century to century is creating
its peculiar type of character, a character so marked indeed
that the thought and civilization of this era cannot be transmuted into the thought and civilization of the world before
the flood, nor of that which preceded the Apostolic age;
nor is there a man of sense, anywhere on the globe, who
would be glad to see the change were it possible.

So it is in regard to the Gospel declaration of a continuance of existence after death; even on the supposition that
this too is but an ideal, the world is better for that thought
than it could be without it. It touches our hearts and
whispers " be ready"; it softens our sorrows; it puts a divine
significance into life; and invests godliness and virtue with
a winning power; the thought of a future life takes the
thorn from the pillar of death; transforms the grave into
a restful couch for sleep, and it fills the universe with deathless, bright-eyed beings, in whose invisible circles our loved
ones are waiting. We say then, although all these are
nothing more than beautiful ideals, ideals that never will be
realized, the world is better for them; but if they are real
as we are confident they must be, if there is an all powerful Christ, a perfect salvation, a pure and spotless character,
an immortal life, a reward and a retribution, who can tell
the mighty influences of those world-redeeming truths?
Let us try to show that

III. ANY POSSIBLE OPPOSITION TO THE GOSPEL OF GODLI-
NESS IS PUERILE AND FOOLISH, BECAUSE IT CAN NOTPOS-
SIBLY DO THE WORLD ANY HARM. '

That wickedness in the world is an indisputable fact; a great and important problem is. How can the world be lifted into a higher moral plane? Many reformatory meas- ures, each having its own peculiarity, have been proposed, adopted, and have failed; the wrecks of human efforts in this direction lie strewn along the track of the ages. But now, after every other plan has proved deficient, the Gospel is declared to be a panacea for human ill, and we are told that it is profitable unto all things in this world and the next.

Every thoughtful person must have observed that shrewd opponents never attack the moral principles of the Gospel. They bend every effort to destroy the evidences of Christianity, but make the most touching confessions in re- gard to its moral sublimity. If the world may retain the ethics of the Bible, ethics that develop a spiritual life, and a moral character, the loss would not be absolute though compelled to cast away its scientific evidence. So far as these moralties are concerned the controversey between Christianity and its opponents is nothing but a war of words; the bitterest opposition can raise no possible ob- jection to goodness of heart, purity of life and sweetness and heavenliness of spirit; it has at least one marked and essential quality, that is. harmlessness.

Godliness implies conformity to divine law; there can be nothing injurious in this, though every man, woman, and child were to keep sacred and inviolate each and every commandment of the Decalogue, the world of humanity would recieve no harm. Tell us what injury could come to body, mind or soul, if Polytheism were to be superseded by

Monotheism, and the world were to worship one God instead of a million? The universe could suffer no harm though all idolatry were prohibited and all image worship and superstition were done away; human nature would remain unharmed, even if swearing were no more, if profanity were never heard on the streets, and if every lip that is now profane were to become chaste and pure. No laboring, toiling child of earth could suffer hurt because, for every six days of hard work he should permit himself to enjoy one sweet, recuperating day of rest, the Christian Sabbath has done the world no wrong. Though filial love should swell in every human breast, the family, nor society, nor the world could be harmed thereby; surely it were harmless to defend human life against every unholy effort to abridge it; and to protect and fortify the sanctity of the marriage vow; to prohibit political, social, and private injustice of all kinds; to destroy perjury, whispering, slander and calumny; to annihilate covetousness and put down every unlawful and sinful desire; to instill love into human hearts in a degree so great that every man shall love his neighbor as himself, and his God with all his heart, mind, soul and strength, could not possibly bring harm upon what is now a selfish and sinful race. Yet, this is precisely what the Gospel proposes to do, when is given to it uninterrupted sway. We affirm, therefore, that immorality would be no more abundant; pauperism and ignorance no more general; and pain and sorrow no more severe, if every sinner should become godly, and all the world were to become Christian; the Gospel universally obtaining and forever supereminent could not do the world any harm.

It has been said that Religion has made men crazy; but the authorities on this phase of unfortunate humanity do not recognize pure and undefiled Religion, as a cause, immediate or remote, of insanity. Morel, for instance, makes immorality the starting point, not Religion. He traces the developments and the results of mania, melancholia, dementia, through four generations; in the first he finds alcoholic excess and brutual degradation; in the second hereditary drunkenness, maniacal attacks and general paralysis; in the third, silly, sentimental sobriety, goodishness coming from sheer inability to be anything else, hypo, lympermania or fright, systematic insanity and tendency to murder; in the fourth he finds feeble-mindedness, stupidity, gradual transition to complete idiocy and the probable extinction of the family name and blood; Thus God in his providence at last wipes out immorality.

Insanity, therefore, is deprivation of health, it arises from a corrupting virus in the blood, it does not proceed from Religion; Godliness is not responsible for the world's vast stock of diseased brains and cantankerous livers. Insanity is the result af sin; men get crazy for the want of Religion, never from the swe t and peaceful enjoyment of it. " The fruit of the Spirit is love, joy, peace, long-suffering, gentleness, goodness, faith, meekness, temperance." They that are Christ's have crucified the flesh with the affections and lusts. How can such graces and virtues make men mad? They who have peace and joy in the Holy Ghost cannot be melancholic; they who make the best of this life and seek to be furnished for a world to come are not demented.

I do not pretend to say that Christians never lose their reason; when one thinks ot the stock from which we have come, and the experiences through which we have passed, the savagery of our Saxon sires,the gluttony of our fathers and the fearful flood of intemperance and licentiousness that Niagara-like has been pouring into our viens, we are surprised that the world is not one vast Bedlam and that the human race is not an army of lunatics a billion strong. It must be that some other force has counteracted the inherited tendencies of our natures; that force, for all I know, may be the soft, sanctifying spell of the Gospel of Jesus Christ, for there is no balm for a troubled heart or an agitated mind that is more potent than purity, more pacifying than a well grounded hope. There is not a maniac among men whose insanity could not be mitigated if the Gospel could exert its power upon him, nor a human soul on this broad footstool of God that could possibly be harmed if somehow the spirit of Jesus could captivate and mould him.

It is urged that Paul received harm for having been a Christian, for he was "in perils of water, in perils of robbers, in perils among his own countrymen," perils which could not have come upon him had it not been for his religion. This is true. But it was Paul who said "godliness is profitable unto all things;" it would seem that he made at least as much as he lost, for though "troubled on every side, he was not distressed; perplexed, yet he was not in despair; persecuted, but he was not forsaken." There was something in his Religion that caused him to glory in infirmity and to enable him to count not his life dear so that he might win Christ. The gain therefore counterbalanced every loss, and there was no harm.

His religion was always gain to Paul. At one time he enumerated some of the evils that come upon the children of sin, surmisings, disputings, pride, ignorance, envy, raillery, strife: then, looking on the other side to those who have put on Christ, he said, " BUT godliness with contentment is great gain." Again he considered all his earthly promise, his birth, his blood, his nationality, his prospects as a lawyer, his importance as a Pharisee, and "all things" else, his education, influence, talents, worldly possibilities. as wealth, fame, honor, position and dignity all of which if pursued might have brought him gain, but all these he counted loss; they were straws, they were dross, compared to Christ. "Yea, doubtless," he said, " I count all things loss for the excellency of the knowledge of Christ Jesus my Lord." Coming down to the last hour did Paul regret the consecration he had made? Did he think that he might have made a better choice? Did he believe that harm had come to him for having been a Christian? Far from it. The retrospect of the past was a comfort and an nspiration, as he meditated upon it, he said, " I have fought a good fight, I have finished the the course, I have kept the faith; and now the time of my departure is at hand, I am ready, ready to be offered, henceforth there is laid up for me a crown." "for me to die is gain.'

But suppose that the Apostle had thought of his sufferings. would not that have dampened his ardor? Ah ! but he did think of them; he added them all up, a fearful sum, troubles, distresses, perplexities, desparings, persecutions, toils, sufferings, strifes, shipwrecks, perils. weariness, painfulness, hunger, thirst, cold, nakedness; afflictions, deaths, and, when he had compassed the sum of them he reckoned along a different line, with different, factors, and a different result, here is the column: hope, love, liberty, things prepared, glory, honor, peace, sonship, heirship, crowns incorruptible, immortality, eternal life and, a far more exceeding and eternal weight of glory, and now he subtracts this from that and tells the difference. What is the difference? "I reckon," he says, " that the sufferings of the present time, are not worthy to be compared with the glory that shall be revealed in us." So, then, Paul's religion did not hurt him; and, it would not hurt us, even, though we had much as he.

Thus we have seen that godliness is profitable unto all things, not only theoretically, but practically profitable, profitable as a fact, profitable as an ideal. We have seen that it covers time and eternity and therefore it must be in itself everything. Whoever is wanting in godliness, really has nothing, and is in need of everything; he is pursuing phantoms, they will all vanish from his vision soon; and then his soul before God will be naked, and poor, and mean, he will feel like crying on the rocks and mountains to hide him from the presence of him who sitteth upon the throne. Oh! that I could impress the young people with the importance of this truth. Young man, young woman, you have nothing in all this universe of God unless you have this godliness that promises all the present and all the future. It alone gives value to time and eternity, and of all that charms you now, and brightens to-morrow with their dazzling glory, nothing will remain by and by but character. Godliness is the state of being Godly. It is character. Have you it? Have you that character that shall be able to stand the scrutiny of the judgment?

I have tried to disclose to you the reasonableness and the beauty of godliness; you doubtless see and believe it remains for you to act. Oh! accept Christ as the standard of character, seek him, measure yourself by his rule. Friends may point the finger at you, but remember you decide and act for eternity. Others may try to persuade you to accept their notions, but remember it is character you want, not dogma. "Refuse profane and old wives' fables and exercise thyself rather unto godliness, for bodily exercise profiteth little, but godliness is profitable unto all things, having promise of the life that now is, and of that which is to come."

STRENGTH.

Finally, my brethren, be strong in the Lord, and in the power of his might.—*Eph.*, 6, 10.

The design of the apostle in the epistle to the Ephesians seems to have been to manifest the superiority of Christianity by comparing it with the religion of the guardian goddess of Ephesus.

By bringing this epistle into review we shall not only learn something of the manners and customs of the people, but also that the Dianian system of faith was fustian, while that of the Gospel is a great moral power in the world.

The first element essential in a system of religious faith is the idea of God. All religions must be measured according to the perfectness in which this first truth is perceived. The Ephesians bowed before the image of Diana, and said " great is Diana," " whom all Asia and the world worshipeth." And who was Diana? An idol, a mere symbol of time, empire, strength, and plenty. From such a concept of God there would grow a religion no greater than the conceit itself. Where the parent is gross we expect to find grossness in the offspring.

Without throwing himself into antagonism with the prevalent opinion with regard to the greatness of Diana. Paul, who desired to correct and elevate the Ephesian thought of God, taught the new religion to the Ephesians, by an allusion to the greatness of Jehovah. Who is he? Not a mere symbol, not an idol, but "The One God," "Our Father," "Manifold in Wisdom," "Rich in Mercy," "Great in Love," who planned for the good of his children before they were born, before the earth's foundations were laid, and hath "blessed us with all spiritual blessing," "in the riches of the grace of Jesus Christ." Thus if Diana was great, God is infinitely great. According as this Christian theology towered above the theology of the Ephesians, it produced a purer worship, a better character, a truer manhood.

The worship, the religious experiences naturally belonging to these two systems of faith, Paul alludes to, for the sake of comparison. as being "mystery," a term at once understood by the Ephesians. In the first chapter, ninth verse, he speaks of God "having made known to us the mystery of his will;" in the fourth verse of the third chapter he speaks of "knowledge in the mystery of Christ;" in the ninth verse of the same chapter. he speaks of making men "see what is the mystery."

The Dianian "mysteries" consisted of two parts, the lesser and the greater; the first was merely a preparation for the second. On the first day of the greater mystery the novitiate was instructed; on the second day he was commanded to bathe in the sea; on the third, sacrifices and

oblations were offered; on the fourth a procession was formed in honor of the Goddess Ceres; on the fifth he went with
Ceres in search of Persephone, the lost daughter of the
goddess,descending with her into Hades,and returning with
her to the realm of light; then, having experienced her sorrows and realized her joys, he was rewarded with the privilege of spending two nights in the temple, the first in the
sanctum and the second in the sanctum sanctorum, secretly
closeted with the fair goddess, who taught him myths and
held high orgies which, on pain of death, he might not di-
vulge. Such was, in outline, the religious experience that
pertained to the votaries of Diana. It may have been impressive in its ceremonies, a sort of ancient Free Masonry;
it may have been instructive as a science, and it may have
been world-wide in its reputation; but that it greatly "subdued the passions" or enhanced the morals of the people is
seriously questioned. Pindar says "it taught the end and
the origin of life;" but more, it inspired Pindar to compose
triumphal odes, peans for processions, songs for the girls,
dance songs, drink songs, and dirges. Nor did the mystery
of the Dianian faith prevent its votaries from being dupa-
ble, untruthful, fickle, profane, proud, arrogant, resentful,
sensuous, lustful, licentious; "for it is a shame," says Paul,
"even to speak of those things which are done of them in
secret."

Paul does not mention those mysteries particularly,
but the word "mysterion," called them all up; he does, however, offset these experiences with that which is far better;
one can readily discover the paralels and comparisons which
the apostle employed, in order to set forth the greater excellence, of the glorious truths of the Gospel. Thus he off-
sets instruction, with "the mystery of the divine will that
has been made known"; over against the bath in the sea he
puts "Redemption in the blood of Christ"; he covers the

old sacrifices and oblations with the idea of being reconciled by the cross. Better than heathen processions is the walk, so frequently mentioned, the walk which is "not according to the course of this world, but worthy of the vocation with which we are called, and whereby we endeavor to keep the unity of the spirit in the bond of peace."

The search after Persephone is offset by the fact that Jesus Christ has come, come to "preach peace, to bring us near, to break down the middle wall of partition, therefore, we are no more strangers. Christ dwells in our hearts by faith"; And the secret interview in the Temple and behind the most sacred veil is, in christianity completely overshadowed by the sweeter, purer thought of being made to sit together in heavenly places in Christ Jesus, and through him, finding access by one spirit to the Father, that we might know the exceeding greatness of his power, when he raised Christ from the dead and set him at his own right hand in the heavenly places.

Now, therefore, knowledge of God, redemption from the act and the result of sin, reconciliation with the Father, propriety and circumspection of conduct, and heart-intimacy with Jesus Christ being the mysteries of godliness, that is, the experiences of the Christian: what kind of a character should we expect from such holy living and meditation? Not the same as characterized the worshipers of Diana; not the spirit that worketh in the children of disobedience; not darkened understanding; nor alienation from the life of God; nor that moral character that is past feeling, given over to lasciviousness, and working uncleanliness with greediness; not such, but a character comporting with the blessedness of salvation, and built on faith in God, therefore, it will be meek, lowly, truthful, loving, strengthened in the inner man, tender-hearted, kind, forgiving, crowned with spiritual blessings and sealed with the Holy Ghost.

The ruinous effects of a false faith, has, among no people, a more suggestive example, than that afforded by the Ephesians; not only the softness of their climate, but their refinements in religion, their very faith in Diana, educated them into luxurious living, and love of pleasure, and made them a soft, unmanly and effeminate people. The Lydians made an easy prey of the Ephesians. The Persians, three years later, swept them with the bosom of retribution. After the battle of Mycale they were tossed like a shuttlecock into the hands of Athens. The Romans literally gave them away to the king of Pergamum; Paul therefore suggested to that effeminate people that while Dianian voluptuousness was seducing all their manliness, Christianity could transform them into heroes, for he who has in him the Spirit of Christ would dare even at the sacrifice of his life, to vindicate his principles, and, with such an heroic element, active within him, he would die if need be for his native country; Paul therefore exhorts the Ephesians to put on the whole armor of God, that they might be able to stand, *stand*, having their loins girt about with truth; *stand*, having on the breast-plate of righteousness; *stand*, with their feet shod with the preparation of the Gospel of peace; *stand*, with the shield of faith beating back the fiery darts of the evil one; *stand*, flourishing the sword of the spirit which is the Word of God, and having done *all*, *stand*.

Thus we see the trend of the whole epistle to the Ephesians; it is an exhortation for weak men to become strong; an argument setting forth the feebleness of heathenism and the mightiness of the Gospel; a picture presenting the futility of the mysteries of Diana, and the glorious experiences of the Christian; it is an index finger pointing to the weakness of moral character produced by ungodly ideals, and the beauty and excellence of that life that is quickened into activity by the power of the Holy Ghost; in brief the epistle to the Ephesians teaches me that, to cherish a heaven-born ambition, to perform a holy mission, to break the shackles from a false faith, to extricate a human heart from all grossness and wrong, to build the Race up into a divine brotherhood, to make this world better, requires a Religion and a Faith that has the strength of God in it; the Ephesians needed such a Religion, so do we; there is no hope for this world in any other; we must be "strong in the Lord and in the power of his might.

The world's great desideratum is strength; it has at least no more than it needs. Some things the world has in abundance, wealth, for instance. True, many a man is poor, life is a constant struggle with poverty; men are poor not because there is not enough in the world to supply every need, but because it is not in all men to get rich, and some are greedily grasping that which belongs to their brothers. Again, there are many whose affluence is a curse to them, it would do them good to give a part away; at least, the world is rich, there are cattle on the hills, there is fuel in the forest, there is gold, in the rock, gold in the ocean, gold in the air; if the world were more richly endowed than it is, it could not use its riches.

The world also has trouble enough, at least enough for all practical purposes; we are born unto it; it comes to us in tender life; it clings to us when the hair grows gray; it pales our cheeks, it wrinkles our brows, it breaks our hearts, it bows down our proud spirits, it increases with our years, none are exempt; and, it seems that some have a great deal more trouble than they can bear; there can be no doubt, the world is rich in trouble.

I say *rich* because though it may not seem so, yet trouble may be a blessing in disguise; it is as much of a blessing as is night. When trouble or sorrow comes we say, night has settled down upon our souls. We think sometimes that night is not good, yet it is certain that night is a blessing; it is even glorious; we can see a great deal farther in the night than we can in the day; if the earth had never known a night; if noon had perpetually poured on the earth a flood of glory, the blue sky would have been nothing more than a canopy; but night came, and with it came the stars, the invisible worlds on high, and all the infinite distances of space; thus we can see farther in the night than we can in the day; so it is in the night of our trouble; it comes to us full of spiritual revelations, and visions of the city out of sight, such as could not come in the gala day. Stars of hope shine on our night of trouble; vision is clearer in the midnight of sorrow than in the noon of joy. I say then the world is rich in trouble; we have an abundance of it.

Besides abundance of wealth, and abundance of trouble everybody must confess that sin is abundant enough in the world. We have heard it spoken of as being one of the ills that flesh is heir to, or, as being a mere misdemeanor, and even as being a force helping man to secure his highest dignity and destiny. If it is this, only this, and nothing more, then the way to destiny is not up, but down, down through the lowest degradation, down through the nethermost filth and corruption; it is a misdemeanor that smites the world with moral death; it is an inherited ill that can change this world into a hell, and human hearts into the very pandemonium of perdition. It strikes a thoughtful soul with terror to see the world of humanity plunged into the appalling catastrophe of sin, swept in its fearful whirl, and sucked down into its vortex of woe. If you want to know why the world is poor, why its crushed and broken heart is always bleeding, why humanity is wasting under the withering wing of disease; if you want to know why great empires have been hurled from their course of glorious destiny; and, tyranny, despotism, selfishness, misery, war and ruin have always and everywhere prevailed, the answer to your question is embodied in that one word, sin. He is no friend of his race who would add one feather's weight to this awful incubus of accumulated and concentrated damnation that is resting down upon the souls of men; the world were better by far if somehow this blighting avalanche might melt away; the world does not need sin, but it does need strength to resist its destructive power.

True, the world needs a great many things that it has not got, or it needs to appropriate those essential things that have been providentially provided; it needs more wisdom, wisdom to husband its forces, wisdom to utilize its powers; it needs a wisdom that will prevent the throwing away of golden opportunities, and a wisdom that will fix its eye on the deathless interests of the eternal future. It needs more Religion, a Religion that will render it more honest, more generous and brotherly. It needs also more faith, a faith more reasonable and heavenly, but the worlds greatest desideratum, that which it needs most is strength. Give us strength and we can wrestle with poverty; give us strength and we can carry our burdens and bear our troubles, give us strength and we can overcome sin and the evil passions and tendencies of our hearts; yes, give us strength and we can pull the sting from death, and throw wide open the everlasting gates of gold; we need nothing quite so earnestly as we need strength.

In childhood strength is needed; in mature life when responsibilities multiply, strength is needed; and in old age when sun, moon and stars are darkened, strength is needed. But man is naturally weak, no creature is so helpless as he, matter is in his way, often he is unable to overcome it, nay, it bears him down: the little lark leaps upward from the sod, and soars above the cloud, singing its song of triumph amid the blaze of morning light, while man is dragged down by a clod and chained to this dusty earth. Even his mind, great as it is, is unequal to his emergencies; there comes a time when thought must pause, the greatest created intelligence has its horizon, and that horizon everywhere touches the unknown; a few in thought sweep beyond the ken of the multitude. but the masses are perpetually confronted with mysteries that they cannot ravel, and riddles that they cannot solve.

Particularly in moral matters does man display his feebleness. The inebriate would break away from his habits if he could, sober, he resolves for the sake of that poor wife whose heart is broken, and for the sake of those dear children whose happiness is destroyed, to dash the wine cup to the ground; but his trembling hand cannot obey his wish, and his moral power, more futile than his arm offers no resistance; therefore the waves of inebriacy roll over him again; so it is with the best men. so with ministers, so with churches, often their desires are greater than their strength; they would save this world all at once if they could, but moral power fails them just when they need it most.

The church on the whole has shown itself to be weak; almost two thousand years have passed and the world is not redeemed yet. There are places on the earth to-day where the foot-stepping of the children of God are never heard; even beneath the shadows of its edifices wickedness thrives; in no community is the church what it ought to be; sin like a flood is pouring over the souls of men and all denominations combined are too weak to hold it back. Thus from the right hand and the left, from front and rear, from hell beneath, from the heavens above' there come voices that taunt us with our weakness. Is it not true then that the world's great desideratum is strength.

But the text comes to us in our need, sweetly anssuring that the world's needed strength is in God. " My bretheren, be strong in the Lord and in the power of his might." As the oak has no strength in itself, but through its roots draws it up from the elements of the soil, and through its leaves woos it from air, and cloud, and sunshine; as the cannon, though it be a Krupp gun, is feeble in itself; as the powder too is harmless until touched with fire; and as the great projectile which might force its way through the iron mail of a man of war, is useless without an impelling power behind it. So man, if he has any strength at all, must find it, not in himself, but without him, his strength is from the Lord.

As evident as is human weakness, so evident is the power divine; God, from the vials of his omnipotence has poured strength upon his universe; it is the strength of the Almighty that leaps into the soft kernel of the acorn grows into an oak, multiplies into a forest, and transforms into a fleet of great ships that sweep pirates from the seas, and carry the commerce of the world. It is the strength of God that enters into those iron bands which form the hot ribs and sinews of the locomotive; it appears also in the wire strands which, twisted into cables, support the suspended bridges of East River and Niagara. The very hills and mountains are fractions of omnipotence. Behemoth is strong, " his bones are like pieces of iron;" the war-horse "rejoiceth in his strength and góeth forth to meet the armed men;" and "the heart of Leviathan is firm as a stone, hard as a piece of the nether mill-stone;" but whence comes the strength of the horse, Behemoth and Leviathan? It is grazed from the grasses, it is drunk from the rivers, it is drawn from the billows of the sea, it grows on the breasts of the mountains, it is poured from the bosom of the storm, and dispensed and provided by the mighty hand of God. Yes, it is the Lord who balances the worlds upon nothing and sends them spinning through space in the journey of ages.

But come with me and I will show you the embodiment of all strength, not as it is distributed throughout the material universe, but as it appears in concentrated form; it is in Christ. He said "and I, if I be lifted up, will draw all men unto me:" what is this but a declaration of the infinite magnetism of the cross? The apostle said "in him dwelleth all the fulness of the God-head bodily." What does this mean if not that Almightiness is embodied in Jesus? Again, Christ said, "all power is given unto me, in Heaven and in earth." But what is this if not the concentration of omnipotence in the Lord Jesus? The mightiest forces in this universe are moral forces, and all moral force centers in the cross; it were easier to snap the bands of gravitation than for human power to stir a stubborn will, but the strength of the Lord and the power of his might has done it many a time. It was the mere preaching of Christ, and him crucified, that on the day of Pentecost melted the hearts of three thousand people. And there is power in that name to-day to rescue the inebriate, to lift the world's most crushing burdens, to scatter darkness, to destroy sin, to bring to light immortality and Heaven.

Here, then, is reserve power, here is omnipotence waiting to be utilized, nay to be appropriated. Is it for man? Is it for me? Will the Lord help me in my extremity? Can I somehow link my weakness to omnipotence? Paul seemed to think so, so he said to those Ephesians, and he says to us, be strong in the Lord and in the power of his might. I know there is power somewhere. I know it has been working, it sustains this world of ours. It has been pushing the Church onward to victory. It has led her safely through persecutions and inquisitions. I know too there is latent power in the Church power which has never yet been called into exercise; if she were to rise in her strength she could sweep darkness from human hearts, and drive the demon of transgression from the world. Some day, by some means, those latent energies will be quickened, and of a truth "one shall chase a thousand, and two put ten thousand to flight."

The trouble is that the individuals who compose the Church, are, with a few exceptions, disposed to let some great work lie undone, unless some one else shall do it. We are disposed to leave everything to the Chruch, forgetting that without our effort the Church is nothing. We fancy that the church is a great locomotive, steam always up, that it is going to pull this world to redemption, and we as individuals are nothing but passengers; we pay our fare and show our tickets and that is all that is expected of us; but what a mistake! The fact is we are all parts, and important parts of this great locomotive, and it cannot work unless we ourselves are in working trim. The prayer meeting is the fire box, the class is the combustion chamber, each member is a flue in the boiler, the officiary are the steam chests and cylinders, the treasury is the sand box, the Gospel is the driving wheel, the pulpit is the cab and the minister is the alarm bell. Give us divine fire in the furnace, water of life in the boiler, Christ for an engineer, then, moving on the track of duty, the locomotive will soon pull the world out of the mire of sin, and up to the city that is out of sight.

But I repeat it, the Church is weak, and Christians are weak individually, because so many aspire to be passive,

uninterested passengers, or because we depend too much
on earthly forces. Each Christian receives all the power
he lives for. My nearness to God, my fidelity to duty, my
purity of character, is the gauge of my strength and the
measure of my influence. The consecrated soul is strong.
Even the stammering tongue may speak, the palsied hand
may work, and the fearful heart may be strong, for success
in life's moral endeavors depends not on this one's might
and that one's power, but my spirit saith the Lord.

There have been in this world of ours, and there are
now, true hearts and brave, hearts touched by divine power.
Abraham, strong in faith, abandoned Fatherland looking
for the fulfillment of divine promise. Moses, touched as it
were by divine power, chose to suffer affliction with the
people of God rather than enjoy the pleasures of sin for a
season. Paul and Silas, strong in the strength which God
supplies, praised him in the Philippian prison. And the
early Christian Church was aroused by unearthly forces
when it conceived the plan and endeavored to carry it out
of preaching the Gospel throughout Asia minor. So well
was that work done that eleven out of thirteen of the prov-
inces of Asia minor received the Gospel during the life time
of the apostles. The whole peninsular indeed was perme-
ated with the spirit of the truth as it is in Christ. and it
stood forth before the thought of men as a fair illustration
of what even a feeble Church can do if it be strong in the
Lord and in the power of his might. Paul too was inspired
by the same power when he resolved to capture for Christ
the illustrious city of Ephesus; for this purpose he visited
it, secured a few converts, appointed teachers, labored there
most earnestly for three years, appointed a pastor, instructed the elders and wrote epistles: nor was he disappointed;
he was strong enough to win despite opposition, and by and
by that royal city, the city of arched aqueducts and tunelled

hills, the city of castles, theaters and monuments, the city of the Dianian grove, and of the most splendid temple became the seat of a Christian sanctuary in which worshipped a people who kneeled down and prayed, and wept sore and fell on Paul's neck and kissed him, sorrowing most of all for the words which he spake that they should see his face no more, "and they accompanied him unto the ship."

Nor are Scriptural characters the only ones who have been strong in the Lord. Every man who dares to do right is in some degree under control of that power. Every heroic soul who is ready to stand by what his conscience approves, and to die rather than violate a principle. Every noble spirit that can say:

> " So close to glory is our dust,
> .So near to God is man,
> When duty whispers low 'thou must,'
> Replies, I can."

is strong in the Lord and the power of his might. The sense of duty is divine. There is something superhuman in the man who is prompted by that sense. It was that which inspired the soul of John Brown when he "thanked God for the privilege of dying for a cause." It is that that touches the courage of the fireman and makes him prompt in the most perilous places to sacrifice himself with the hope of rescuing another.

The universe is a vast reservoir of power that has been provided by omnipotence himself and all that any true heart has to do is to go to the well and draw, it is just as much for your need and mine as for a Paul or an Elijah; yea as much for you as for the Lord Jesus Christ if only you are moved by as holy and as lofty a purpose; Paul caught the inspiration of this glorious truth and therefore told the Philippians, "My God shall supply all your need, according

to his riches in glory in Christ Jesus." Whatever task
duty may call you to perform in the Lord is your strength,
and the facilities that shall enable you to perform it. If
you want to fill your barns with plenty, the Lord will supply the rain, the dew, the sunshine, and the strength for
your laboring arms; if you desire to build a palace that shall
rival the Golden House of Nero, you must come to Almighty God for all the material and the appliances; if you
you want a factory for the making of fabrics of cotton or
of silk, come to the Lord's treasure house and appropriate
whatever of law or of force, or wondrous natural elaboration, your craving soul may need. If you want a beauty of
moral character, with every sin spot washed away, come to
the Lord and find whatever wisdom, law or grace shall be
needful to accomplish the work. If great duties are pressing
you, if noble resolves are breaking into being in the depths
of your soul, or if fearful conflicts are confronting you,
come to the Lord and recieve from his hand that strength
that will render duty, resolution, and battle a success; there
is no task too difficult, there is no attainment too great, if
only the heart is "strong in the Lord and in the power of
his might."

.   But, Alas! There are many failures; fields have
been worked that yielded no harvest; the other day there
were sold in Washington, for a song or a six-pence, hundreds of rejected models. that represented the fruitless toils,
and the blasted hopes, of many years and many studious
inventors. Many have gone in search of the golden fleece
and found nothing but a wild waste of waters; many have
heartlessly led some forlorn hope; and many have sought
to enter in at the straight gate and have not been able, but
why? Why is it that men fail? Why do our best laid
schemes come to naught, and our fairest prospects fade

away? There can be but one answer to this question, we have not always been strong in the Lord and in the power of his might; in our ignorance or our wilfulness we have pursued some other plan than God's, or we have not followed the trend of eternal law, consequently failure and disaster came like a flood upon us. If the time shall ever come, that men will learn to acknowledge God in all their ways, then he will direct their paths, and they shall never be confounded.

There is nothing in which a sinning world is more apt to fail than the manner in which it appropriates divine strength for moral ends; the tendency is to depend on self, or on some natural means; and because inadequate forces are started into the work, the result is not what was anticipated. There is in this universe, only one thorough and radical remedy for sin, that is Christ, he " whom God hath set forth to be a propitation, through faith in his blood, to declare his righteousness for the remission of sins that are past, through the forbearance of God," " there is no other name given among men whereby we must be saved."

If any other remedy is employed, there may be partial success or there may be absolute failure. A man by the power of his own will may break away from some or all of' his bad habits; by force of culture he may develop a suavity dignity and charm of manner; by dint of civil authority and power the evil natures of great multitudes may be restrained. Still the evil may exist; under the outside polish there may be coarseness and brutality; and though every habit that refined society refuses to tolerate should be cast away; yet the past is unforgotten, it still stands sadly defaced by transgressions of divine law, for which the trangressor must be brought to account; and even though you are heartily sorry for your misdeeds the stain and the guilt of them

remains, you need not only forgiving grace but cleansing
power; and this is accomplished not by any virtue in yourself, not by any law of nature but only through that means
that God has set forth. So, that, in the salvation of your
soul, you need to be strong, not only in yourself, but in
the strength of the Lord and the power of his might.

A similar mistake is made when we attempt to persuade men to become Christians, we do it in our own
strength, we fancy that it can be accomplished by the convincing power of our argument, or by the vivid beauty of
our description, or by administering to sin-sick souls heroic
doses of human theology; this man is choking with a bone
of Calvanism in his throat and some Methodist doctor gives
him a dose of Arminianism; that one has stumbled and
hurt himself over Universalism and we try to heal the
wound by applying the pungent ointment of God's unchangeable justice, and thus we depend on ourselves or on
human agencies. Oh! when shall we learn that it is not
by might or by power but by the spirit of the Lord, the
work can be accomplished, if at all, by a living Gospel that
has a living Christ in it. We may be good artists and
draw the most charming pictures, but there is no moving
cloud, stirring breeze, fluttering leaf, or flowing stream unless God touches it with his life. We may carve statues
of men, we may say this is a saint and that a sinner, and
they may stand forth cold as the marble in their beauty unless the breath of life has been breathed into them. Argument may be good, reason may be pure, imagination may
be lofty, and eloquence may be worthy of admiration, but
"it is the spirit that quickeneth." Therefore less proud
and trustful of self, let us seek God more; less vainglorious
because of our own importance; let us be strong in the
Lord and the power of his might.

THE WONDERFUL WORKS OF GOD.

Many, O Lord, My God, *are* thy wonderful works *which* thou hast done, and thy thoughts *which are* to us-ward: they can not be reckoned up in order unto thee: *if* I would declare and speak *of them*, they are more than can be numbered.—*Psalm* 40, 5.

This Psalm was composed by David and dedicated to the Chief Musician. The first half is a thanksgiving song, wherein the author acknowledges the divine goodness in deliverance from some great calamity, either personal, national, or both, the King being the nations representative, and the last half is an expressed resolution of consecration to God.

The king and the people had good reasons for thanksgiving and dedication. God had listened to a nation's prayer; out of a horrible pit had he rescued them; their feet had he placed on a rock and established their goings; and so wrought up to ecstacy was the national enthusiasm that a new song fell from its lips, even praise to God.

Similar expressions of gratitude have been common to nearly all nations. The Egyptians had their "annual feast of the inundation," a period of general praise and rejoicing for the overflowing Nile. The Persian law suffered no man to confine the motives of his sacrifices to any private or domestic interests; so that when from gratitude for favors bestowed, any man would dedicate his gifts to the sun god, the voice of the empire went up in thanksgiving also. The Greeks in celebrating their annual Eleusis, offering prayer and gifts to Ceres and Proserpine, simply anticipated us in an annual thanksgiving for the ingathered harvest, and the Roman Floralia, however it may have been abused had its origin in a sense of gratitude for the return of Spring with its blossoms and flowers. The Chinese also have their "Ying Chun," or yearly vernal festival, when with singular demonstrations, they render praise to the god of agriculture. The annual jubilee at Peterhoff, is the Russian Thanksgiving for the birth and life of the sovereign, which means, in other words, a day of praise for the national existence. In most Roman Catholic countries the national idea is almost lost in that of the church, the proclamation for worship arising from that source rather than from any parliamentary enactment. The English have no annual Thanksgiving; but on special occasions, as in case of recovery from sickness in the royal family, or at the cessation of war, or after a signal victory, the nation in some form gives expression to its gratitude; but whether the mint, or parish bells, or parks of artilery be used to express the emotions of a grateful people, all would by them be considered empty, unless the sanctuary resounded with praise.

Dr. Franklin says, that "in a time of great despondency among the first settlers of New England, it was proposed in one of their assemblies to proclaim a fast; an old farmer

arose, accused them of provoking Heaven with their com-
plaints, reviewed God's mercies, showed that they had much
to be thankful for, and moved that instead of appointing a
fast they appoint a thanksgiving, which was done, and the
custom has been continued ever since."

There is no other great nation on earth wherein one
day in each year is sacredly set apart for thanksgiving by
the government, in the sense that this republic celebrates
its annual feast. Independence day is not so emphatically
a national holiday as this; therefore with inexpressible
emotion each Christian patriot recognizes this, his country,
as the most Christian country on the globe.

This is a Christian country because its laws are founded on scripture; its judicial oaths are administered on the
Holy Bible; it legislates in favor of the Christian Sabbath;
it reckons time from the birth of the Christian Savior, and
in a sense, places every legal document in the custody of
Christ; thus in conformity with the common practice President Arthur concludes his thanksgiving proclamation with
the words, " Done at the city of Washington, this 25th day
of October, in the year of our Lord, 1882."

More, the Christianity of this nation is Protestant. All
over this broad land to-day, from the Atlantic to the Pacific, from the lakes to the gulf, on the mountain and in
the glen; in the forest and on the prairie; to a hundred
thousand sanctuaries, whether in private dwelling, school
house, church, or cathedral, or in God's grander temple, outside, shall go forth twenty-five million protestants, with
songs of praise on every lip, in loyal submission to a Protestant President's proclamation, which will be utterly ignored
by at least three million Roman Catholics; and, they shall
go forth chanting as they go, " Many, O Lord God, are thy
wonderful works which thou hast done, and thy thoughts

which are to us-ward, they cannot be reckoned up in order unto thee, if I would declare and speak of them they are more than can be numbered."

The text suggests as a theme suitable for consideration the wonderful works of God as manifest in this republic. We may therefore meditate on God's favors in the past, his purposes in regard to the future, and our responsibility in the premises.

Two hundred and sixty-two years ago, when mad November lashed the fickle Atlantic into fury; a frail bark, freighted with a precious burden, might have been seen struggling through the fog and tempest, scarcely able to live in the swelling sea, but preserved by prayer, directed by faith, sustained by omnipotence. It contained a hundred Puritan passengers and their melancholy effects, yes it contained more, stowed away where human eye could not see them, were germs, principles, which for five thousand years had been carefully watched and protected by a divine providence; that had been wrested from the revolutions of thought, and saved amid the crash and desolations of empires; principles they were which in their unfolding shall witness the future glory of this Republic.

Dr. Foster suggests that European, and, of course, American civilization, originated in Egypt. I think earlier, the cradle of our civilization was rocked by patriarchal Abraham, beneath a Chaldean sky and amid the vine clad hills of Canaan. We inherit from him our conceptions of God; that faith which shall live as long as the world lasts; that integrity which would not take from another a thread, even to a sandal thong, lest it might be said another has made us rich; and that sublime science, which more than any other, unfolds to the thinking mind the works of omnipotence in all their wondrous beauty.

Pressed onward as by a divine impulse this prototype American found himself at length in Egypt, and subsequently his family were all there, a nation in the bosom of a nation, evolving a civilization whose type shall change with the changing centuries until gloriously consummated. There, amid broad-based pyramids that dipped their apices into Heaven, marble Pharaohs that kept silent sentinel huge Sphinxes that guarded the dead, temples and statues that towered along the plain, and catacombs that were filled with decayless corpses, the principles of that evolving civilization were crowned with the quality of solidity and permanence. From thence came those broad-gauged views which to-day characterize the genius of the American republic.

But this developing civilization must pass into other hands; it would have been incomplete had it avoided those indented peninsulas which lie between the Adriatic and the Ægean. Greece must place her polished hand upon it; Egyptian angularities must soften into graceful curves; from prosaic plains it must rise to revel in the poetry of a varied landscape, where hills melt into valleys, valleys swell into mountains, and mountains again leap abruptly into peaks, where fountains sport, streams shimmer and dance, lakes reflect the blue of Heaven, and seas charm with their ever varying tints Thus the gentle and more poetic side of our civilization is directly traceable to Greece. She has bequeathed all that elevates and embellishes human life. except the inspiring influences of the Gospel, and even for that she gave her wondrous language. As another has said, " whatever there is of heroic action in human conduct; whatever there is of intensity expressed in the passions; whatever there is of poetic diction or oral discourse; whatever there is that relates to the beauty of the human

form, or the just proportion of human structures as mani-
fested in sculpture or architecture, we have inherited from
those Hellenic tribes."

It has been said, and nothing is more evident, that
"Westward the star of empire takes its way," therefore,
from Greece this civilization of which I speak crossed the
Adriatic, and in the most ambitious empire the world ever
knew, and amid the uninterrupted din of arms and shouts
of victory, where Licinius and Justinian legislated, and the
Cæsars reigned, there the civilization which has given birth
to our peculiar institutions was run into a new mould to
come forth with new characteristics. The Roman sword
was unsheathed for a divine purpose; it sent a life current
through the veins of the generations. The victories of
Hannibal, Scipio, Pompey, Cæsar. The fall of Carthage,
Greece, Gaul and Briton in resurrected form live to-day in
the genius of the American people. Latin poets, Roman
orators and legislators preside to-day in our schools. The
Latin tongue has bequeathed all its beauty to the Saxon
that we speak. The heroic deeds of Roman legions make
patriots of us all. Justinian compiled his codes and wrote
his digests and institutes for our use; and more than all
Rome waded through bloody seas, humbling mighty nations in her march, and spread her conquests over the then
known world, that the world being merged into one empire, and ruled by one spirit might be the better prepared
to receive the Gospel and confer its benedictions on nations
yet to live; that Gospel also is ours.

But Rome met its dissolution. Luxury at last made
the Roman warrior a prey for the barbarian. Just across
the Alps there lived several semi-savage Teutonic tribes;
these were divinely chosen to be the almoners to the new
world of the God-given civilization which had been developing for thousands of years. Side by side with these had

been the Celts, but the Teutons had driven them westward
or held them in submission in southern Europe.   The Celt
is ceremonious, and readily submits to a supposed superior,
and was never cut out to be a Yankee.   On the contrary,
the Teuton is independent, thinks for and governs himself,
and is much better suited for the temperate than the torrid
zone.   To those two races God gave the subjugation of a
hemisphere.   Was it chance or was it Providence that
caused Pinzon in 1492 to follow a flock of parrots, which resulted in turning the tide of Celtic emigration to the West
Indes and South America, and left North America to be
settled by the Teutons?   I believe it was divinely ordained,
at any rate the unwavering industry, the sharp intelligence,
the rugged independence of the Teuton has built up in the
North the best political system ever devised, and given to
the world the best government the sun ever shown upon.

Thus our North American civilization has been a plant
of slow but solid growth.   Gathered up from so many
sources, through so many centuries, cradled among the
eternal pyramids, schooled amid æsthectic culture, trained
in Roman senates, developed into a mastery of manhood,
breathed upon by the spirit of Puritan devotion, cemented
by Christian love and overshadowed by the wings of the
Almighty.   Is it not evident that the hand of God has been
in its glorious unfolding?   Surely every Christian patriot
can say, " many, O Lord God, are the wonderful works that
thou hast done."

Guarded thus amid the conflicts and changes of centuries, we should expect that the same Providence would
clear the way and defend it in the strange land whither it
had been brought.   Indeed, in nothing is the divine approbation of this republic more clearly seen than in its
history.   Through a series of difficulties apparently insup-
erable has the new world civilization pressed its way.   Nor

could those difficulties have been overcome had not Jehovah, who declared "I will bring the blind by a way they know not, I will lead them in paths they have not known, I will make darkness light before them and crooked things straight, these things will I do unto them and not forsake them," exerted his omnipotence to move or moderate every obstruction and render the national progress possible.

This Providence was manifest in the very outset. Thus at the time of the European occupation of that part of North America now known as the United States, there was a population of three hundred thousand aborigines, about the same number as to-day dwell on the slopes of the great Mississippi. They were a race of savages, every man of which required a whole empire for a hunting ground, and the liberty of a continent to accomodate his roving fancy; their smile was a growl, their laughter the screaming war-hoop, their delight the reeking scalp, their scepter the barbarous tomahawk. There is scarcely a State or a territory where the blood of the white man has not been shed by those barbarians. Money enough has been spent by Indian wars and treaties to cancel the national debt. With our abundant wealth, our teeming population, unquestioned prowess, heroic soldiery, military science and superior genius, we have not been able fully to subdue the red man. Fifty million Europeans barely manage to keep three hundred thousand aborigines at bay. What then could the American colonies have done in their weakness, their poverty, their lowly and despised condition, with odds so fearfully against them, had not super · human power interposed in their behalf? I claim therefore a Providence in the constant feuds that existed among the aboriginal tribes; in the jealousies that divided into helpless factions a formidable host of barbarians, and rendered them more deserving of the sympathy than the sword of the colonists. I claim that Providence too in the yellow plague, which before the landing of the Pilgrims, had swept away, as with the besom of destruction, at least nine-tenths of the savages who lived where the white man's dwelling was destined to be. This is not harsh or ungenerous, it is but the outworking of that now generally recognized law "the survival of the fittest." It simply teaches that God will push his purposes through avenues the most appropriate to reach the greatest good to the greatest number. There is no alternative, savagery and sin must give way before civilization and righteousness. If our civilization is the fittest it will survive. God will clear the way. We need not be in haste to exterminate our opponents.

But again, if the hand of Providence restrained the savage, that hand was equally as evident in the circumstances which rendered possible the early independence of the nation. Let us not be too vainglorious, the liberty of law, the excellence of republican institutions, the glory of a great empire which we now enjoy were not gotten altogether by the valor of our arms. It may be humiliating, it is true nevertheless, the paw of the lion could have crushed out the life of the thirteen struggling colonies had not God himself interposed. He "covered our defenseless heads with the shadow of his wing," and the lion withdrew to more inviting resorts. While we were throwing off the yoke of England, England was subduing the world. The eighteenth century opened with a war between England, Germany and Holland on one side, and France and Spain on the other. It was a fearful war of races in which the Teuton from Bleinhim, Gibraltar, Ramillies, Oudenarde and Malplaquet came forth as the conquerer of the Celt. In

the middle of the century England assumed the quarrel of
Maria Theressa, and having pushed her conquest into
South America, returned with thirty-two wagon loads of
gold. On the heels of this followed the seven-years' war,
which involved the whole of Europe, but from which England came forth with Canada added to her domain.

Already British power in India had commenced; but
when the war of independence raged, it required more than
common sagacity to secure that which her valor had won.
This, then, was the opportune moment "to proclaim liberty throughout all the land, unto all the inhabitants
thereof." When the British shield hung over Canada, her
sword lay on the head of France, her guns on the bosom
of Spain; when with one hand she held the scepter of Scot-
land, and with the other petted the passions of Russia;
when the great heart of the English people, whatever may
have been the ambition of her lords, beat in sincerest sympathy for the oppressed colonists in America, and when
British eyes were fastened on India's mountains, glittering
with gems, and her rivers rolling over sands of gold; then
was the time to strike, and strike we did; but God gave the
opportunity. God gave the courage and the strength for the
blow, and God gave the victory.

Now, the smoke of the battle having cleared away,
each antagonist can well afford to be magnanimous. There
was providence for England in her defeat, as much as for
us in our triumph. We fought and from fields of blood
came forth bearing the laurels of a nation's liberties. England fought but lost one empire to win another. We
turned westward to subdue a hemisphere and spread a Christian civilization; England eastward, peradventure to subju-
gate the other hemisphere, and certainly to redeem the
Orient for Christ. We shall meet again by and by, both
battle-flags shall blend their colors in the breeze, and when

the circuit of the world has been made, when the smoke of battle has rolled away, and the knowledge of the Lord covers the earth as the waters the sea, we shall meet and embrace each other.

"Above all pain, all passion and all pride;
Above the reach of flattery's baleful breath,
The lust of lucre and the dread of death,"

and confess, "the Lord God omnipotent reigneth,"

But again, God has so overruled events as at length to break every fetter and liberate every bondman. The greatest question that ever agitated American politics was proposed in 1620 when the Dutch landed a cargo of negroes in Jamestown, in Virginia, and which was not finally answered until that period between 1861 and 1865, and answered by an appeal to arms. It was the question which created the Missouri compromise, the question that provoked a contest between the slaveholders and their opponents at the time of the annexation of Texas; the question which passed the fugitive slave act, the question that inaugurated civil war when Nebraska and Kansas were admitted, that fearful question which inflamed secession, bathed the nation in blood, and cost a billion of dollars. It was a question of no small importance that could command in its support the prestige of centuries, the precedents of nations; a million and a half bales of cotton every year, half the money and half the brain and muscle of this great republic. It was a fearful question which could command a million armed men to the field, repair for years the waste of battle and of pestilence, send to sea an iron-clad navy unmatched in history, unknown in the world's wildest dreams before, and mark out a track of grim desolation, where avenging deities might pass, thousands of miles in length. Yet the destiny of this vexed question, of slavery, was settled years before the civil war broke out. Manassas,

Fredricksburg. Murfreesboro. Chancelorville, Corinth, Chickamauga, Petersburg, Richmond, nor all the sanguinary scenes of the South decided this question; these were but the death throes of a gigantic enemy which had received its mortal thrust six decades before. God himself answered this question when he proposed to enthrone a nation on this continent that should in all future time be an asylum for the oppressed of all peoples, for, as the lamented Sumner said. "Aloft on the throne of God, and not below, in the footprints of a trampling multitude are the sacred rules of right, which no majorities can displace or overthrow."

On the eleventh day of July, 1787. according to Dr. Foster, when congress passed an ordinance for the government of that territory which lies to the north and west of the Ohio river, God himself interposed to erase the foul blot of slavery from our fair escutcheon. By that act that territory was devoted to freedom; but it was an unclaimed wilderness, unknown by the white man, inhabited only by savages. Then Ohio, Indiana, Illinois, Michigan and Wisconsin, which are embraced in that territory, had not been created into States. The unbroken sod, the tall pine shivering in the storm, the copper and the silver undisturbed and unseen, the breeze seldom apprehended by a sail, made no prophesy whatever of the future. Old Dominion, genial Kentucky, the rich pastures of Tennessee, and all the Sunny South presented to the emigrant more alluring promises. The astute statesmen of the South were perfectly willing that the Northwest should be free, if they might only enjoy the sweet privilege of propagating undisturbed their darling doctrine south of the Ohio. Soon, however, a God-directed torrent of emigration began pouring into this vast region. Since 1787 the immigration hither has been two fold greater than

any other section except the Pacific slope. The sentiment
of those hardy peoples in the log cabins turned the tide of
political controversy; that sentiment ever deepening, expanding, prevented slavery from infringing on the given
boundary; that territory rapidly developed into five sturdy
States, populated by seven million free and independent
people; they were all educated to believe that industry is
honorable, and that all men are free and equal born. and
when the appeal to arms was made, true to Union and to
liberty, Ohio, Indiana, Michigan, Illinois and Wisconsin
contributed the force which, in the providence of God,
broke the power of the rebellion, and bequeathed to us a
free country, where the clanking chains of slavery and the
groans of the bondman are heard no more. Thus God
waits the evolutions of centuries, wins by the might of
principle, and causes the wrath of men to praise him. And
when we think of that unseen power which has preserved
principle, despite the press of centuries, the crush of empires, the swell of seas, the tumults of savages. the envy
of kings, the jealousies of factions, and gave it to us
crowned with the diadem of freedom, we are ready to exclaim, " many. O Lord, are thy wonderful works and thy
thoughts to us-ward, they are more than can be numbered.'.

So proud was the old psalmist that he said " Walk
about Zion, and go round about her, tell the towers thereof,
mark ye well her bulwarks, consider her palaces, that ye
may tell it to the generations following." So for the glory
of God let us consider our country, go round about her,
mark well her greatness and her grandeur. let us see what
kind of an asylum God has provided for republicanism and
freedom.

Ancient Greece had a sea-coast of about fifteen hundred miles. This made Greece and tempted her populations to maritime pursuits, but God has given to the United States an indented shore of five thousand miles, where two mighty oceans roll up their perpetual surge. If the Ægean and the Ionian seas made the Hellenes, the Atlantic and the Pacific oceans must create for us three times the glory of the renowned people of Hellas. The area of the Roman empire at the period of her greatest glory was probably less than 3,000,000 square miles. She had then been fighting for nearly a thousand years. Not including Alaska the area of our country is about 3,000,000, and as yet as a nation we have seen only a little more than the first century of existence. Our mountains are among the tallest, our lakes are the greatest, our rivers are the longest in the world; and as Douglas Gerald said, "the richness of our soil is such as to need but to be tickled with a hoe in order to make it laugh with a harvest." We have always grain enough on hand to fill the nation's mouths for a full decade, despite chinchbug and grasshopper. There is beef enough on the plains which any man can have for the getting, and there is cotton enough in the South to keep a constant humming in the gin, and fuel enough in the forest and the mine for a thousand years to come.

Follow the sun as he rises fresh from his Atlantic bed to run his swift race of three thousand miles, and his beam will flash upon thickly populated states and rapidly developing territories, each great enough to be an empire of itself; and as he advances westward from Maine to California, penetrating deep valleys, spanning a hundred rivers, climbing everlasting hills, reflecting from eternal snows, flashing over impenetrable forests, expanding the beauty of a floral empire, ripening the grain of a million harvest fields, painting the blush of unnumbered orchards, tasseling the cornfields of Indiana, Illinois and Iowa, smiling on the sloping plains of Nebraska, beaming on the minerals of Colorado, playing in the garden of Utah, discovering the gold of Nevada and California, and awakening the gigantic industries of 50,000,000 free and independent people, and you have some idea of what God is doing every day for this great and happy land.

Or commencing, if you please, where the Aurora Borealis, behind pyramids of ice, suspends its gorgeous drapery, and crossing the country from north to south, pursue your way to where the little coral is busy annexing Cuba to the United States, and you will surely confess "the lines are fallen unto us in pleasant places, yea we have a goodly heritage." Leaving frost-made palaces where mosses seem to be placed for fairy feet, you will press your way through long zones of fir and forests of pine; through terraces of climbing ivy and parks of royal oak, and graceful chestnut avenues to where, in evergreen woods flourish the myrtle and the orange. Your heart will swell with inspiration amid the picturesque hills of the Hudson, tremble in amazement beneath Niagara's thundering flood; wonder at the towering monarchs of Marripos a, go into ecstacy over the beauties of Yosemite, and find refreshment in a luscious bunch of grapes that weigh a dozen pounds. But mark you, these magnificent boundaries, this lavishment of wealth, this abundance of beauty, belong to our country, they are parts of God's great gift to the American people. Surely we have cause for thanksgiving.

There are to be sure many special reasons for thanksgiving besides those general ones to which attention has been called. One might, for instance, enlarge on the fact that no invader has landed on our shores during the past year; that civil war has not disturbed our domestic tranquility; pestilences have not terrified us; that the nation has grown stronger while sharing with the whole world its immunities and privileges; that our industries have been prospered, our harvests abundant; that our schools still thrive, and our religion is still a quickening force in the conscience of the nation. Blessings have also come to this particular community to which reference might be made, as our new railroad facilities, our improved streets, our increased industries, each of which tell of the general prosperity of our beautiful city. And certainly each individual, as he looks over the past year, though trials may have come to him and sorrow may have swept over his soul, can see in a thousand instances that his Heavenly Father has protected and blessed him, even making "bridges of his broken hopes, and rainbows of his tears." But I have preferred to take a broader view, showing that we possess these minor blessings because of the greater; the all-covering ones of country, God and Christ.

It is said that disintegrating elements are already in our midst; that foreign drift floating in upon us from every quarter will produce heterogeneity; that constant tendencies to centralization will transform at length the republic into a monarchy; that this nation must be crushed at last by its own weight, and that a variety of climate, such as we have will eventually divide the country into conflicting sections. Now we have nothing to fear from immigration, immigration has made us, we are a nation of foreigners; Europeans and Asiatics come here to build our railroads and develop our resources; it is imperative, however, that they be confronted, not with that fawning, craven spirit which for the sake of a vote would surrender a principle, but with that sterling public virtue which demands the continuance and defends the honor of those peculiar institutions for which our fathers fought and died.

The greatest danger threatening the nation to-day is its monopolies, those powerful combinations which make laws for their own interests, and having no conscience, knowing no government, ignore every statute that does not pour the public funds into their own treasuries. Individual and corporate enterprises must be encouraged, but woe betide the day when the iron heel of monopoly is on the neck of the nation. American liberty will not be properly guarded until Uncle Sam himself becomes a rival to every powerful monopoly.

It is estimated that at the close of the present century there will be in this country a population of a hundred million souls. It is a favorite question with statesmen, "how can so many be kept peaceful and happy under one form of government?" China has solved the problem by putting a premium on education. But China, with her 300,000,000 could better afford to be ignorant than can America with her fifty million. Monarchies may venture to repose learning in the custody of a chosen few, but republics must educate the masses, for the ballot in the hands of an illiterate multitude who are controlled by a corrupt and educated few, is as some one has said, the torch of the political incendiary, but with intelligence it is the bulwark of liberty.

Climate may indeed have something to do with the formation of an opinion, and particular zones may give force to conflicting ideas; but it is evident destiny is shaped by other forces than local surroundings. The Nile did not make Egypt, Italy did not make the ancient Roman, or there would be an Egypt and a Rome to-day. The problem of national history is a problem of right and wrong. God is in it, that survives which is most in harmony with divine will, therefore the greatest responsibility resting upon this republic is that which rises from a worshipful recognition of God.

Brothers, as we love our country and would bequeath its principles to generations yet unborn, I protest the recognized freedom of the press may never be infringed. The public schools shall never be surrendered. Every child must have the best legacy his country can give, a good education. Then, given an intelligent, independent, honest, God-confiding people, with a government built on eternal justice, and no invader shall intimidate, no despot rule, no weight can crush them, the problem of self-government shall have been solved, and democratic principles radiating from a nation sanctified by the cross, it shall come to pass the world will recognize no king but God, and the Church no bishop but Christ.

The future of this republic, as foreshadowed by the past, is pregnant with unequaled glory. No other nation has impearled in its foundations such precious and imperishable principles. No other is so magnanimous. No other people possess so many potent elements in one grand combination. The very blood mixture so common in this country is prophetic of a superior type of physical and intellectual manhood. By ties of consanguinity the whole world is ours. Whatever is good or great in the blood of other people flows in our veins. We have the valor of the Briton, the brilliancy of the French, the solidity of the German, the breadth of the Russian, the beauty of the Italian. Indeed we have more good in our institutions than ever was in any other nation; the good is always more persistent than the evil, so we believe that in the providence of God, the good of our civilization must outlast the bosoms and the centuries that cherish it. On this continent God's purpose in regard to humanity must be consummated.

Let us live worthy of so great a country and so promising a future. Particularly let us live to the honor of that

divine one whose wonderful thoughts are continually toward us. From this place of worship where we, have
united in thanksgiving, let us repair to our several hearth-
stones, enjoy the festivities that may be provided, and with
hearts full of gratitude to Almighty God, let us do as the
President suggests. " make this day a special occasion for
deeds of kindness and charity to the suffering and the
needy," so that under the sunshine of your Christian sympathy "all who dwell in the land may rejoice in this season
of thanksgiving."

NOTE—The above sermon was first preached in Geneva,
Wis., Thanksgiving day 1876, and has been repeated with little
alteration on several similar occasions since. Each time it was
preached its publication was invited. It is the author's contribution to the first centennial of American independence. The
author also desires to acknowledge his indebtedness to Dr. Foster for certain facts and suggestions.

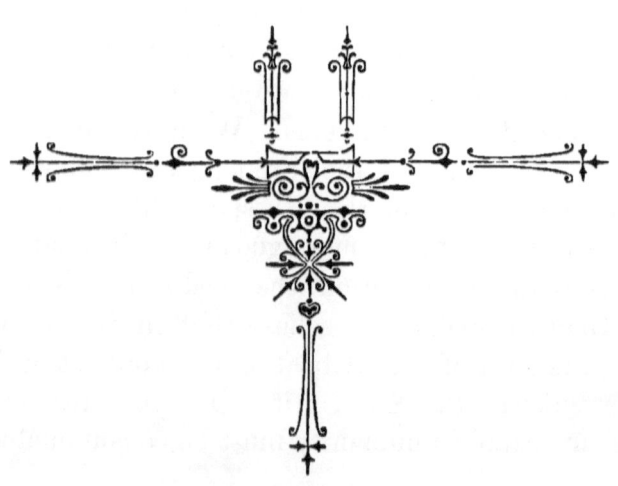

SHORT BEDS AND NARROW COVERLETS.

For the bed is shorter than that a man can stretch himself on it; and the covering narrower than that he can wrap himself in it. *—Isaiah* 28, 20.

Isaiah, a Judean prophet, began with this chapter a new section of his prophecy, and aimed his shaft at the Ten Tribes, proclaiming a prediction that had reference to the invasion of Samaria by Shalmanezer.

The Samaritans prided themselves in the beauty of their country and the strength of their citadel. They deemed themselves able to resist the invader whenever he should appear.

The prophet however faithfully declared to Israel that Shalmanezer would surely come, and be divinely commissioned to perform his work; that he should be strong as a tempest of hail, fierce as a destroying storm, that he should spread over the land like a flood of mighty waters, and sweep away every refuge of lies, dashing the crown of pride to earth, trampling the Ephraimite under foot, and

plucking the citadel of Samaria, eagerly as a man might
pluck and eat the first ripe fig of summer. Thus their
very strength was insufficient, like a bed too short or a covering too narrow.

The Samaritans were as immoral and superstitious as
they were haughty and self-confident; iniquity prevailed,
and even the priest and the prophet were sensuous and
vulgar; their vices made them willing to embrace foolish
fancies. They believed that they had made a covenant
with death; that is they imagined that by their sorceries
and divinations they could charm death away, and declared
that they had made, probably by offering sacrifices to
demons, an agreement with Hell, or Hades, the place of
disembodied spirits.

Again, the prophet rebukes this Ephraimitish magic
and witchcraft; he declares that the covenant should be
disannulled and the agreement should not stand; that despite their fancied alliance with death and Hell. Shalmanezer should come and smite them with a fearful slaughter,
and this should be God's answer to their wickedness and
blasphemous superstitions. Their vain conceits and idle
credulousness were a bed that is shorter than a man can
stretch himself on it, and a covering narrower than a man
can wrap himself in it.

The prophet however did not neglect to declare on
what conditions the Samaritan people might be secure; the
conditions were that they should accept no earthly thing,
but the Lord of hosts as their crown of glory; that they
should look to him, not to themselves, for judgment in
government, and for succor in trial, and that they should
build character not on superstition, but on Christ, whom
God hath set in Zion for a corner stone.

This paragraph in the history of Israel might easily be inserted in the record of our own time. Multitudes are to-day engrossed in the things of sense; hundreds and thousands err through strong drink; many have turned away from Zion and Christ; strong delusions are embraced under the sounding name of science, and men live, indifferent of the eternal future, as though they had compromised with death and Hell; but as in the old time so in this. There is no promise for the people who forget God; the world's surest refuge is Jesus Christ,

Taking for our theme short beds and narrow coverlets, let us look at the insufficiency of human devices in supplying the needs of immortal souls. We may observe then that

I. THE SOUL REQUIRES A PERFECT REFUGE.

A variety of opinions have obtained in regard to what is the essence or substance of the soul. What is it? has been a favorite question among speculative philosophers. One answers, the soul is potential life; another that it is subtle air. The stoics maintained that the soul is a flame of Heavenly light; another declares that soul is thought. It is something in me, said Fichte. The soul, says another is the focus in which flow the movements of bodily life.

It matters not what name may be given to the substance of the soul, or how its nature may be defined; it is enough that there is such an existence, that every man is possessed of a soul. Whatever else it may be, your soul is your inner, your superior self. It is the essence of life. It is the whole of man. It is man crowned with his eternal possibility.

According to the declaration of Scripture, the soul came from God, not as the body came from the hand of the skilful Creator, but in a more intimate sense, even as the breath comes from the seat of life; the soul is a respiration from the bosom of eternal being. God breathed and man became a living soul.

The pre-existence of the soul therefore does not consist in its having lived in the body of a beast, bird, fish, or reptile; there is nothing more degrading to human dignity, than this last born of scientific speculation; but it consists in its having been in the bosom of the Father. Each human soul is a drop of life from the fountain of infinite being; it has something of the infinite in it, and with its individuality, gotten in the present world, when the body shall return to its mother dust, " the spirit shall return to God who gave it."

Because your soul is divine in its essence it is quick with Heavenly aspirations. It causes the mind to look outwardly toward realms that are yet undiscovered. It makes men eager for excellence. It causes human nature to shudder at the thought of annihilation. It incites all men to inquire if a man die shall he live again? And when this feverish life is over shall we bathe our weary souls in the crystal river that flows from the throne of God?

Each human soul is the architect of its own destiny. Destiny did not come with creation. The soul was not put on top of its possibilities, like a statue on a column, but at the base, and required to win for itself an upward way. We each work out our own salvation, the facilities are in our hands, we cherish in ourselves an upward or a downward tendency, we win for ourselves crowns of glory or chains of darkness; from the moral self-hood of the present will grow the moral character of the future; the experiences of each new day add new features to destiny; it doth not yet appear what we shall be; to what we achieve to-day may be added the glory of another achieving to-morrow, or the neglect of the present hour may deepen the degradation of the next.   It is indeed a fearful responsibility, but such is that which God has put upon each deathless soul.

It is an important question, how can the soul's eternal interests best be secured?   Surely it were not enough simply to live, the beast lives, the basest reptile lives, the insignificant insect lives.   It is not enough to stand in statu quo, to be forever what you are.   Your inner self-hood must be in a condition of advancement, growing better, nobler, grander, each day, each year, forever.   It is not enough to hope, hope is sometimes a fruitless and blossomless exotic, it is groundless and delusive unless rooted in the expanding powers of your own moral being.   What will secure this growth, this approach to the infinite life of Infinite One?   This question demands and deserves the candid consideration of every thoughtful person.   One would desire to entrust the cultivation of the mind of his child to the best teacher; he would seek, in sickness, the most skilful physician; he would not purchase a policy of insurance on his house from a company of whose reliability he was uncertain; he would not feed his horse with substance that might do him harm; ordinarily, men are careful of their children, of their houses, of their horses; can they be careless about their souls?   Dare they leave the unfolding of spiritual destiny to influences that might degrade and damn forever?   Is any one so foolish as to attempt to rock it to sleep in a bed that is too short or hide it with coverings that are far too narrow? Rather would not every wise man adopt the language of the poet and say:

> " Build thee more stately mansions, oh my soul,
>   As the swift seasons roll!
>   Leave thy low-vaulted past,
> Let each new temple nobler than the last,
> Shut thee from Heaven with a dome more vast,
>   Till thou at length art free;
> Leaving thy out-grown shell by life's unresting sea."

II. HUMAN EXPEDIENTS ARE INSUFFICIENT TO MEET THE NECESSITIES OF AN IMMORTAL SOUL.

1. *Atheism is insufficient.* The idea of God is the birthright of humanity; it is co-eval with the race. Men have endeavored to persuade themselves that if they could only believe there is no God, then, free from moral restraint and responsibility, they would be happy, but the heart of man refuses to believe it.

God is a necessary thought in the mind. The soul rises instinctively from things to the cause and crown of things. Thus, we see beauty, and ascend intuitively to the supremely beautiful, perceive thought and rise to the absolutely thoughtful; observe goodness and think at once of perfect goodness; or discover personality and are made to meditate on the Supreme one. We see a universe in which beauty, thought. goodness, being are manifest, and ascend by faith, or by intuition, to an absolute, an Infinite Being in whom all these qualities exist, as belonging to him and complete in him, and this being we call God.

It is impossible to obliterate this thought of God. The mind cannot rest short of the perfect, the absolute, the Infinite Unit. The fool may say in his heart there is no

God. But this very profession is the proof that he is a simpleton, because he asserts a contradiction; he has the idea of God in him, an idea that has been the common inheritance of the race, yet he denies the subject to which his highest inborn ideal applies. He must blot out his thought of God before he can declare there is no God; but this he cannot do, hence his negation is absurd, and his atheism is a wild chimera in the brain of a fool.

But suppose you demonstrate that there is no God; that all the arguments that set forth his existence are nothing but the meaningless harrangues of so many popinjays; that the universe is the product of chance; that there is no moral law because there is no moral government, and that there is no restraint because there is no amenability, and then you try to put yourself to bed with that idea, could you rest?

With moral principle dead and buried, with intuition and reason utterly confounded, with deity the sole source of inspiration and hope swept forever away, with the foundations fallen out of things, with your soul plunged into fearful and eternal orphanhood without defense or dependence, though responsibility were gone, you could not rest, for anxiety and perplexity would be multiplied a thousand fold. The soul is immeasurably greater than this bewildering negation of God. The bed is shorter than a man can stretch himself on it.

2. *Materialism is insufficient.* What is materialism? It is the philosophy of dirt; that which attempts to reduce man to the condition of a mere animal, and would make his thought, his emotion, his will, nothing but the result of his material organization, a mere "dust heap" that the first breath of mortality will sweep away. Such a philosophy is utterly insufficient for the wants of a human soul. If I

am the descendent of a zoophite, the great grandson of an
orangoutang, the latest development of evolution, how mean
are all my antecedents and what assurance have I that
evolution will not cease and involution begin?   Who
knows but man, having reached the end of his possibility,
will shrink away from his attainments, the light fade from
his intellect, the facial angle become more and more acute,
his smile transform into a chattering grin, his body turn
into the body of a fish, and finally dissolve into a bowlful
of protoplasmic jelly?   Then, how hopeless are my prospects! Nor is this an idle fancy, there is just as much
probability that men will degenerate into fish as that fish
have developed into men.   Can such philosophy make humanity any less gross, or the world any more moral?   Can
it afford courage to a broken heart, or nerve the soul to
stand for the right?   On the contrary, does it not give free
scope to passion, and make men believe that they are mere
puppets, the results of their organization, doing only what
nature dictates shall be done.   Atheism is bad enough, it
sweeps from human hope the Infinite; but materialism robs
being of God and dignity also; it degrades man to the
baseness of the brute, and the littleness of an atom.

I think it is generally conceded that however much of
thought and fancy, and perhaps of curious fact, there may
be in the isms and philosophies of to-day, there is but little
moral life. A materialist, however anchored to his opinions
he may be, would look beyond his ism or his philosophy to
find for his son the vital essence of character. There is
nothing in a doctrine of dirt that teaches man what is
right and what is wrong.

Materialism, for aught I know, may be the base of
modern science; possibly it has discovered for the world
many important facts; those facts may be most helpful to

men; but with all the discoveries of science, from the wonders of chemistry to the marvelous harmonies of the stars, materialism is a bed too short for a human soul to stretch itself upon, if, after all, it makes man a mere dissolving atom in the universe, his love and reverence a simple thing of sense, and moral principle nothing but an accident in the evolutions of the cosmos. There is not a soul however degraded or exalted, but longs for something infinitely better than materialism can afford it.

3. *The dogma of destruction is insufficient.* There is a philosophy extant to-day which would excide from human thought all promise of a future state. It consigns to the grave all your capacity for knowledge, all your busy brain has wrought, all your ardent heart has wished, and all your generous hand has done. It answers your anxious inquiry if a man die shall he live again, with a cold and cruel, no! and leaves body, brain, mind, love and soul to rot in the foetid arms of death. Is this the stake to which a soul can fasten itself and be satisfied, that soul which like an anchored ship is restless to break its chain and plow the waters of unknown seas?

There is not a native instinct in the human heart but declares that life must conquer death. Even justice is given a voice and proclaims that a future life is imperative. The soul shudders at the bare thought of destruction. The present is undesirable if there is no hereafter. Every undeveloped power of the mind cries for a continuance of being. To what purpose is all this battling for the right if there is nothing beyond? Man is an enigma to himself if this fleeting life is the whole of existence. No future! the thought is too mean for a man to entertain for a moment. The soul cannot stretch itself on the procrustean bedstead of annihilation. It refuses to lie down and be chopped off just to accommodate a dogma that is at war with every possibility and assurance of being. A man must first ignore his own dignity before he can crawl through this little knot-hole of destruction.

4. *Rationalism is insufficient.* Rationalism is the attempt of reason to be religious without the aid of Christianity.

Its religiousness is manifest in that it advocates equality, fraternity, peace, benevolence, freedom, and the worldwide dissemination of moral principle. Rationalism however teaches that whatever cannot be understood must be rejected; the supernatural in the Holy Scriptures, it is claimed, cannot be understood, therefore inspiration, prophecy, miracles must be rejected and nothing of the Bible accepted save the plainest historic statements and the simplest moral declarations.

Rationalism therefore is an effort of the mind to assert the inutility of the Bible as a God-given and inspired book. It fancies that it is possible to make good and complete eternal destiny without a revelation, a providence, a prayer, a Christ or a creed; but for this very reason it is insufficient, it disallows the very things that the soul needs.

The soul needs a system of fundamental doctrines so evidently true that it commends itself to man's inner consciousness, and is adopted by all mankind whenever presented, for when left unguided by some fixed principle of truth, the mind is a compassless craft at sea, the sport of every tossing wave and changing breeze. The soul needs a creed.

The soul needs also a Christ, just such a Christ as the Scripture reveals; the embodiment and representation of all humanity, and all providence, and all wisdom, and all love, who can be apprehended by each heart, who reaches down to every need and lifts up the world to the helpfulness of Almighty God, a mediator between God and man. The soul needs Christ.

The soul needs to come into communion with the Father of Spirits. There come experiences into every human life that make prayer imperative. In the moments of our purest, most exalted thought we commune with God.

The soul needs to discover behind nature an intelligence that can control its forces for the good of those who live under them; an intelligent, moral being, who can present to this waiting world a standard of righteousness, absolute and authoritative, that wears no mark, considers no philosophy, wants no argument, but bides its time and commands the submission of all mankind.

Not only does the Bible supply these deep and awful longings of the soul, but the equality, the fraternity, the peace, the benevolence, the freedom and the world-wide diffusion of moral principle that constitute the boast of rationalism, have never been practical except where the religious life that springs from the Holy Scriptures have endowed them with vitality and power. Nay, they have scarcely been possible even to theory without the Bible. There was no equality. no fraternity, no peace, no largeness of benevolence and no aggressiveness in morality, until the scroll of Scripture was unrolled and the human heart caught some of the inspiration that inspired its precepts and promises.

Rationalism therefore is too narrow to satisfy the demands of reason, and altogether too narrow to supply the needs of deathless souls. It may be good as far as it goes. It has helped to emancipate the mind from the thrall of superstition. It has started into life a vigorous Biblical criticism. It has compelled the Church to defend the authenticity of the sacred canon. It has called out substantial proof of the genuineness of the Gospel records. It has aroused an enthusiastic search after external evidence of the fulfillment of prophecy, and it has caused Christians to put the argument in favor of miracle on a scientific basis. Thus it is good as far as it goes; but for other than these indirect influences, the dogmas of rationalism are dry crumbs for undying souls. It may have been a good check to formalism; sometimes I think that rationalism is formality and superstition gone to seed, but a weary world needs some other breeze to fill its sails of hope, and when the heartnature once takes hold of the love of God in Christ, and makes that love a part of itself, as thousands and millions of our race have done, then the muttering thunder of rationalism dies away like the echo that in the distance is sobbing to its death.

Exalt therefore and applaud rationalism to the very highest degree possible to it; still it will be a bed too short for a full grown man with unfolding hopes and expanding spiritual powers to stretch himself upon. Hide moral responsibility behind this as a covering, and the soul will appear as one morally naked and groaning after God, revelation and Christ.

5. *Spiritualism is insufficient.* Spiritualism and rationalism are perfect antipodes, one of the other. Rationalism is reason without faith, and spiritualism is faith without reason. To serve the soul faith and reason must go hand in hand.

If salvation were the reward of abstract faith, then spiritualists would be the most saved because they believe most. They believe in the supernatural, in inspiration, in vision, they believe in the Delphic oracles, raps, the march

and countermarch of chairs and tables, in luminous hands, •
planchette, phantom forms; they believe that Christ was an
ideal, not a real person; that his death was not real, only
ideal; they believe that the Gospel is a revelation of ideals
that become valuable according to the spiritual mould
through which they may be run in man-soul; and they believe the universe is but a dream, an ideal; that our senses
delude us, everything is a vision, a hallucination.

The soul cannot be satisfied with a refuge of shadows;
there may be some truth in spiritualism, but of itself it is
incomplete.   Faith is good if well-founded.   Faith without
a bottom-rock of common sense is folly.   Belief does indeed ennoble man, but to be ennobling it must be reasonable.   My faith is unreasonable and childish if quickened by
the spiritual insight of another.   The faith that ennobles
grows out of the sweet reasonableness of one's own inferences and experiences; it cannot come through a medium;
it must proceed from a fact, not an ideal.   Ideals are phantoms that vanish in my grasp.   Might as well trust the
vanishing images of an opium sleep as the hazy spectres
that are supposed to appear before a medium in a clairvoy-
ant trance.   The soul cannot build its eternal destiny on
such aerial bubbles as these.

That philosophy or ism which, with its enchanting
rod, smites the universe into a mere ideal, is altogether too
fine for intellectual men to trust in.   Cobwebs may catch
flies, but men sweep them away and tread on the spiders
that built them; they want something more substantial
than gossamer; they know themselves and the world they
live in to be real, despite the philosophical impressions of
Berkeley; it is too full of hard turns to be a dream; life is
real; everything is real, and nothing can satisfy a human
soul if it be not real; for a real life there must be a real
love, for a real soul there is a real future; for a real sinner

there is a real Savior, and from the real Gospel of a real
Christ to real man may come a real character and a real
destiny. Your ample soul cannot rest in the gossamer
folds of a fanciful spiritualism. The soul needs both the
natural and the supernatural, the evolutions of reason and
the sweep of faith, but not the faith of fancy. it must be
the faith of substance, "for faith is the substance of things
hoped for, the evidence of things not seen."

6. *Formalism is insufficient* I can imagine some one
to say there is a God, the Heavens declare his glory, and
the firmament showeth forth his handiwork; he is a Spirit,
the Father of Spirits, and I am his offspring; I love the
trees, the flowers, the singing of the birds and the bright
stars; but all these beautiful things do not satisfy me; in
my heart is an aching void that the world in all its lovliness
cannot fill. I am dissatisfied because there is a divine nature in my breast, there is a divine spirit in me that wants
God and Heaven. Death cannot harm me, I shall live forever. I need a guide to the city out of sight; my Heavenly
Father has furnished that guide in the Holy Scriptures;
they are a lamp to my feet and a light to my path; they can
direct me in the highway of holiness; I will walk therein;
the interests of my soul shall be my chief concern; I will
worship God, I will look above the perishing things that
surround me.

Then, I can imagine such an one undertaking, with
good intentions, to work out his own salvation; he gets the
form of godliness, catechism and confirmation entitle him
to a place among the members of the Church. The Holy
Communion is the evidence of his penitence, baptism is
the testimony of his regeneration. He is regularly at
Church, before the altar in due form, mouth and eyes engage in worship; he keeps inviolate every form and method-
ically attends to every prescribed rule. The minister says

the Lord is in his Holy Temple; let all the earth keep
silence, and silence reigns.   He repeats every part of the
confession.   The minister says O Lord open thou our lips,
he responds, and our mouth shall show forth thy praise,
and the mouth begins to sing, we praise thee of God.   Yet
somehow the worshipper is dissatisfied; he grasps divine
truths, he utters glorious things, he meditates on symbols
that are pregnant with sublime significance, and partici-
pates in rites and ceremonies that are wonderfully suggestive and inspiring.   Yet there is an emptiness in his heart.
He knows that his moral nature transcends his ritual.   He
feels that the cradle in which he rocks ceremoniously to
and fro, is too small for his immortal soul, and realizes that
the elegant patch-work of prescribed forms, that is laid
first on one spot and then on another, just to suit the case,
is too narrow for a soul that chills in any other refuge than
the living bosom of the eternal God.

It is conceded that some kind of form is important,
for all life has some external manifestation.   The flower
life, for instance, expresses itself in stems, leaves, petals,
seeds.   Insect life expresses itself in an ovary, a catterpillar
and a pair of powdered wings, and the canary life expresses
itself in a germinal dot, yellow plumage and joyous song.
So a potent spiritual life must express itself in altars, temples, forms of worship, due attitude, ritual, choirs, and discourses.   The very fact that these things are is evidence
that there was somewhere a spiritual power to produce
them.

It is not enough that we have inherited these spacious
sanctuaries, inspiring songs and suggestive ceremonies.   We
belittle ourselves if simply living in them and appropriating
them, just as the martin does some church steeple, or the
owl the ivy covered tower of some castle.   It is puerile to

be carried to church by a mere force of habit, and sit all of
a row like so many flower-pots in a green house, and wait
to see if perchance the gardener will drop a rose already
blown upon our mold. We need to have a life in ourselves,
bursting outwardly and expressing itself, just as the flower
bursts out from the seed. If this life is wanting, our songs,
our ceremonies, our sanctuaries are nothing better than
last-year's birds nests, they are like the shells that the birdling discarded yesterday, we can find no satisfaction in
them.

The soul refuses to be buried in a coffin of formality,
no matter how exquisite it may be. Every man who looks
into his own conscience despises himself for having in frigid
formalism endeavored to palm himself off for what he is
not. It is a bed too short and a cover too narrow for a
soul.

III.   CHRISTIANITY IS A SUFFICIENT REFUGE,

There are two or three things that ought to be said in
regard to this idea of the sufficiency of the Gospel.

1.   Whatever else may be said of the Gospel, it cannot
be said that it is dwarfish or narrow.

The great cry of the nineteenth century is "more
room." Our fathers were content to live in log cabins, but
we have an eye on largeness, we want houses, mansions,
palaces; the youth of the last generation were satified with
district schools, but now the college is on every lip and in
every heart. We are spreading out, aspiring upward; we
want more room. Nor is this want objectionable; as the
race becomes more god-like, each individual will need more
room; houses large and elegant, breadth, breadth of view,

breadth of culture, are all right; but particularly do we need abundance of room for our religion, and this is right also.

This universal longing for a religion that has breadth to it is one of the favorable signs of the times; it is the very thought that will bring the world to Christ some day. for his religion is the religion of breadth; thus the deity of Christianity is infinite; the Scriptures of Christianity are of universal adaptation; the salvation of Christianity is for all the world. and the character of Christianity towers to the very height of moral sublimity. It is the roomiest religion. There is room in it for the employment of every good and perfect gift; for every noble purpose. for every loving sacrifice. and for every lofty ideal, and there is room in the Gospel for every son and daughter of Adam.

While the fundamental truths of the Gospel are firm as the eternal hills, its spirit is fluent, sweeping on through ages, deepening, widening, sloughing off an excrescence here. breaking out into new beauty there, and so comprehensive is its future hope that it promises to every redeemed soul a glorious progressiveness throughout eternity; it doth not yet appear what we shall be.

The breadth and greatness of the Gospel, as it shall be when it has accomplished its work, and unfolded all its hidden truths and divine power is, in the apocalypse, presented in symbols of marvelous beauty and significance. Its breadth is therein displayed under the figure of a city that lieth four square. I am aware that it is supposed to be a description of Heaven. but what is Heaven but the Gospel in its glorious consummation? That city is a perfect cube, its length, and breadth, and height are equal; that is it is absolutely complete; it is a truth to which nothing can be added. and from which nothing can be taken away.

It represents the Gospel in its consummation as being so ample that there is no danger of being crowded; there could have been no narrowness about the surveyor who planned and laid out so great a city. It is inconceivably immense; compared with this outlook everything else sinks into pigmy insignificance. It is large as this world, nay more, it has been reckoned that within its walls of twelve thousand furlongs it could furnish a room 19 feet square and 16 feet high for each inhabitant of five million worlds as large as this. Surely this is broad enough. Men talk about the Gospel as being narrow and insufficient, too small for their broad ideas, but they know not what they say, for no human thought ever took in the full measure of this god-given truth.

2.   Not only is Christianity thus complete, and infinitely outreaching the broadest views of the broadest liberalism, but it covers the deficiencies of every human expedient.

We have spoken of some of those expedients. Atheism, materialism, spiritualism, formalism, and have seen how inadequate they all are to supply the needs of a human soul; but just where these things fail the Gospel shows itself to be all-sufficient. It softly touches with its wand the anxious heart of man and says, child, thou art not alone, there is a God, he is thy Father, the Father of all, he numbers the very hairs of your head, he counts each tear that trickles down your cheek.

> " And in his home, though pæans swept the hall,
>   And glory domed the universal light;
> If over one poor soul hell spread its pall,
>   There would be night, and wailing in the night."

The Gospel, voiced with sweet assurance, whispers to the soul something of its value; it tells that human life is better than a bubble, better than the aggregation of dissolving atoms; it is a drop from the fountain of life, it is a bright beam from the light of God; and that it would profit a man nothing though he should gain the whole world, the whole material universe, if he were to lose his soul.

The Gospel also crowns the soul with immortality; it bids every mournful expectation away; its voices echo through the centuries declaring not only that Christ hath plucked out the sting, but that he hath abolished death, and brought life and immortality to light; down through the grave flashes its Heavenly ray, burning out its corruption, and up to Heaven darts its revealing beam making manifest the truth that "there shall be no more death, neither sorrow, nor crying, neither shall there be any more pain," but

> " We shall flourish in immortal youth,
> Unhurt amid the war of elements,
> The wreck of matter and the crash of worlds.

The Gospel also brings the supernatural down to the natural; it puts a divine feather in the wing of reason; it renders spiritual existence rational and evident; and shows that the pass-word at the everlasting doors will not be "ceremony," but "character," that character that comes from a heart that has been made pure by washing in the blood of the lamb.

Thus the Gospel covers the deficiencies of every human expedient. With an everlasting Father, with a being transcending in value the material universe, with a life that nothing can destroy, with a reason that takes in the infinite, with a spirituality founded on solid fact, with a character that outshines the stars, all guaranteed in the Gospel, what can the soul ask for more? Trusting in the glorious

Gospel of the Son of God, the soul is sensible of its sufficiency; it knows that the religion of Christianity is not a bed too short, nor a covering too narrow.

3. But it would have been too small as a refuge for an immortal soul, if it had ignored the fearful fact of sin; that little word sin is a word of fearful magnitude; the want that springs up in our natures because of sin is an awful want; its poisoned roots strike deep into the recesses of our moral being. O do not laugh when the thought of guiltiness before God lies like a dead weight of conviction on the conscience. When the whole world is corrupting under its power, do not say it is nothing but a little irregularity. Do not call him demented who, when he discovers his own moral deformity, cries with all the earnestness of the blind man, Son of David have mercy on me. When my soul is sick because of sin do not send me to the apothecaries for a dose. Do not administer to me Andrew Jackson Davis' prescription for a sin-convicted soul:—
" Bruised Cinnamon bark, 1 tablespoonful; bruised nutmeg 1 tablespoonful; cardamon seed, horse radish, ginger root, mandrakes, Turkey rhubarb, powdered, each 2 tablespoonfuls." Do not tell me that such a dose as this can cure my sin-sick soul. Do not tell me there is no remedy. The Gospel is the remedy; it is adapted to my need; there is balm in the blood; it is efficacious; how the remedy works to cure my moral malady I cannot tell; but it is the testimony of thousands, millions, from the apostolic age to this, that the blood of Jesus Christ cleanses from all sin. It makes the profane lip chaste, it speaks peace to the infuriated passion, it stirs the soul with the forces of divine life, it fills the hateful heart with the softening influences of love, it turns our Hell into Heaven, and so softly strikes the harp-strings of the human soul that they vibrate with

celestial music, and notes of praise leap upward from them to the throne of God. Thus the religion of Jesus has the power to make sinful men holy.

In conclusion, we have no time for review, and the application must be brief; would that I could make it in one burning sentence, but I cannot; this only can I say to my fellow man: Your soul needs a refuge, an all-sufficient refuge, one that can save you, for you have a great soul, a soul full of deep and awful longings; you want God, you want eternal life, you want salvation; let me then assure you in the language of St. Paul that " my God shall supply all your needs, according to his riches in glory, by Christ Jesus." Come to him.

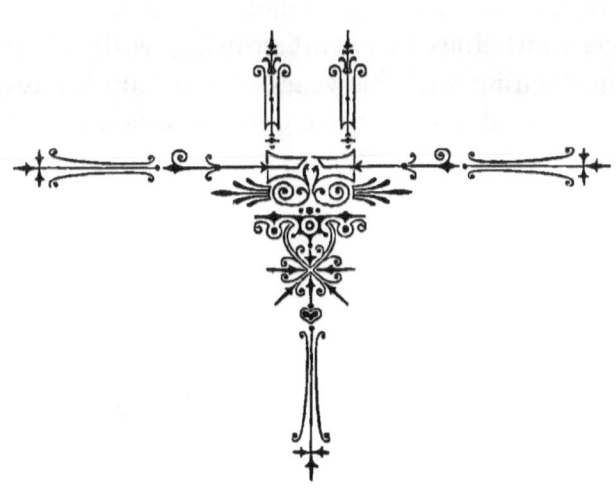

THE BREAD OF LIFE.

I am the living bread which came down from Heaven; if any
man eat of this bread he shall live forever; and the bread that
I will give is my flesh, which I will give for the life of the
world.—*John* 6, 51.

Man is a complex being, living two lives at once, a
life physical and a life spiritual, therefore requiring bread
for his body and bread for his soul.

Christ recognized these respective imperative demands
by miraculously satisfying the material hunger of thousands and, in the opportune hour, recommending living
bread for deathless souls.

Man, in each and every stage of his existence, is a
creature of the most imperative longings; he comes into
world, passes through it, and dies in want. The infant
seeks impatiently to satisfy this want; restless childhood
is in constant search after something that will satisfy;
ambitious youth finds this want growing with his growth
and strengthening with his years. In mature life responsibility is increased and new demands are awakened; and in

old age this want is rendered even more intense, because then the captive spirit looks out into eternity and longs to be free.

Though books are multiplied, knowledge is increased, earth and ocean pour out their treasures, though the elements have been brought under control, though barbarism and tyranny are disappearing, and the Gospel, like a strange sweet spell, is in the world; yet the world is not quiet, it never had more nor greater wants and longings; the race is calling and toiling for bread, that is, for something that can satisfy its yearnings, as much to-day as ever.

It is a very important question, what can the nearest satisfy? The text contains the only plausible answer. It is the answer which he gave who spoke as man never spoke, he upon whose lips was poured the spirit without measure. " I am the living bread which came down from Heaven, if any man eat of this bread he shall live forever, and the bread that I will give is my flesh, which I will give for the life of the world.' Let us inquire therefore in regard to

I. THE ORIGIN OF THIS BREAD.

It is " the bread which came down from Heaven." We are not at a loss to know to what the term bread refers; we know it is a term by which Christ is described; indeed Jesus is the them · of the book of John, particularly of this chapter, the name Jesus occurs more than twenty times herein, and there are over a hundred indirect references to him in those fifty-three short verses; nay, more, it is Jesus' own declaration, " I am the living bread which came down from Heaven."

If Christ came then he was before he came; if he came down in the sense of descending from above, then he must have been above before he came; or if coming down signifies some moral condescension, then he must have enjoyed a certain moral eminence prior to his condescension.

Christ said " I am the living bread which came down from Heaven," which means, as I take it, that he actually came down from Heaven: that he condescended to this world of sin; that he came down, not from the upper air, not from starry space, but from Heaven, the place of supreme dignity, glory, authority and power; he declared that he came thence to this world.

There is a three-fold world beyond us: this three-fold world is in the Scripture called Heaven; there is the atmospheric Heaven, hence the Bible speaks of the birds, the dew, the clouds, the frosts, the winds, the rain, the lightning of Heaven; there is also the astronomic heaven, and in Scripture frequent allusion is made to the lights, stars, hosts, of Heaven, while Venus, the morning star, Arcturus, Orion and the Pleiades move in the midst of and are commanded by him who spreadeth out the Heavens. Finally there is the Heaven of Heavens, the place where God's honor dwelleth, the Scripture speaks of it as the habitation of angels, Cherubim, Seraphim, and of spiritual principalities and powers; thus in the most glorious sense Heaven is the sovereign assembly of rulers, the seat of supreme and universal government, the place of the power of infinite dignity and authority. Now Christ said " I came down from Heaven, all power is given unto me in Heaven and in earth," I control the forces of this world, the elements, and the prince of the power of the air are in my hand; I command the stars, the universe is subject to me; if there are souls to be redeemed in other worlds than this I must redeem them, and I shall ascend whence I came, far above all principality, and power, and might, and dominion, and every name that is named, not only in this world but that which is to come; I am come to this world on an errand of love, my mission is a mission of salvation; I come that the world might have spiritual life and have it more abundantly.

We should expect from such a character as Christ was just such a life as that which he lived. It is not strange that his presence and power were felt in every kingdom from the lowest to the highest; that nature's forces should obey his law; that sorrow should be subdued and trouble softened; that he should beat back sin and pardon the sinner, and that he should command the gates of death and the portals of eternity, for it is declared "in him all things consist."

Men talk learnedly about the impossibility of miracles, because they do not study Christ; his admitted personality is a guarantee that the greatest marvel would have been had he not worked a miracle.

To declare that the control of nature is impossible, when the Creator himself commands its control is as absurd as it is false.   To declare that in such a presence the regular order of things cannot be set aside is certainly a wild declaration.   Man himself frequently sets aside the regular order of things; he often produces results in nature that would not have been brought about by any invariable sequence of natural causes, left to their independent action: If man should move a pebble from the place where nature put it, if he throw a stone into the air, or catch a falling body before it reaches the ground, he interferes with the regular arrangement of things; it is a part of the plan that he should interfere; when he hurls a cannon ball five miles, when he apprentices a light-beam to an artist, when he sails in the heavens with a balloon, or when without horses or beasts of burden he causes a train of cars to ascend a mountain, or when chloroform or electricity is made to do his bidding, he disturbs the natural order of things, the regular course of law.

Even so natural a man as Tyndall, had he with that scientist's present knowledge stepped into Jerusalem, during the reign of Augustus, would have caused sound, light, heat, electricity to become his credentials; but a greater than Tyndall was there, and therefore matter and men, and human hearts gave testimony to his power. The miracle was the credential of messiahship; thus when Christ was asked "art thou he that should come, or do we look for another?" he answered, "the blind receive their sight and the lame walk, the lepers are cleansed and the deaf hear, the dead are raised up and the poor have the Gospel preached unto them."

But the miraculous is the ordinary aspect of the universe; creation is a miracle; the supernatural is everywhere the most natural; each thoughtful man has stood in awe of the mysterious miracle of nature that is perpetually performing; the incarnation is no more mysterious than any other expression of divine power and wisdom; no more than the divine expression of a flower; the marvel is not that such a character as Christ should perform a miracle, but the marvel is that there ever was a Christ, that God should love us lost sinners so much as to put on our humiliation and our dust, on purpose to redeem us. O this is the mystery! this is the thing that angels desire to look into. every interference with natural law pales before the superior brightness of God's great plan of redeeming love. O hear it all ye worlds, shout it to each other ye sons of light, God has come down from Heaven to earth to save lost men.

The socinians say that Christ came down from Heaven though not in the sense of ever having been there, but in the sense that every good and perfect gift is said to come from above. They deny therefore the divinity of Christ, assert that he was nothing but a man. They say that the divine attributes ascribed to him in Scripture, are nothing but deputed titles. And they declare that Christ simply preached the truth to men, set them an example of moral heroism, and sealed his doctrines with his blood.

But the multitudes did not understand Jesus' declarations concerning himself in this socinian sense; they murmured because he said, "I am the bread which came down from Heaven." The questions which they proposed were, is not this Jesus the son of Joseph, whose father and mother we know? How is it then that he saith " I am come down from Heaven?"

If the people had misinterpreted Christ's declarations certainly he would have corrected them; but he did not; on the contrary he allowed them to believe that he really came down from Heaven. If they were mistaken he was willing that they should be, and he added bewilderment to their surprise by saying " doth this offend you? What and if ye shall see the son of man ascend up wheree he was before?"

If the words of Christ were nothing but lofty figures of speech, and high-sounding symbols, they were misleading, they made mischief, they embarassed the cause, and they were wicked, for, for a born man to talk of condesending to the world, for a creature to aspire to be equal to the Creator is blasphemous in the extreme.

Though Christ himself had indulged in such hyperbole honest men like Peter and learned men like Paul, would regard such speech as unworthy of panegyric, yet Peter, Paul

and the other apostles proclaimed Christ Lord in terms no
less strong, and described his glory in language no less
sublime.

John explains that Jesus Christ had a beginning, even
when the Word was made flesh, that he was a substance,
that he was a divine man, that as such he dwelt among
men, he was a light shining in darkness, and he was called
the only begotten, in him was life, the life of the Word,
and that the Word was made flesh, the Word was God;
thus although in the earthly sense, there never was a Jesus
Christ until the incarnation, yet the Word was in the beginning, and to manifest itself in the flesh the Word came
down from Heaven.

The Apostle Paul still father explains that the divine
being, in the person of Christ was rich, he was in the form
of God, and thought it not robbery to be equal with God,
and he took upon himself the form of a servant, and was
found in fashion as a man, and in him dwewlt all the fulness of the god-head bodily.

The god-head, in some sense dwells in all men, it
dwells in all men in the sense of imparting life, and per-
petuating existence; it dwells to awaken heroism, to inspire
to noble deeds and self-sacrifice; it dwells to lead out into
the undiscovered fields of knowledge, and it dwells in human hearts to make men wise unto salvation; but in every
sense in which God can dwell in humanity he dwells in
Jesus Christ, and dwells fully, absolutely; therefore Christ
Jesus is the focus of all glory; he is the synonym for infi-
itely glorious possibilities. He is the living bread which
came down from Heaven.

Thus the pre-existence of Christ is proved by his own
declarations and confirmed by the teachings of the inspired
apostles. This fact explains many other facts, and renders

possible the posthumous ministry and the perpetual spiritual influence of Christ. It makes true the assertion, and
renders veritable the proposition, "if any man eat of this bread
he shall live for ever," for, in revealing an infinite source it
pledges an infinite supply for every love-needy, life-needy
soul; the metaphor could have had no meaning had not
Christ come down from heaven. This brings us to consider

II. NATURE OF THIS BREAD.

Christ is presented to us under a variety of symbols.
the variety is so great that one can scarce look upon anything in nature but some feature of his character is suggested; the little flower by the wayside, the very road on
which you travel, the waters that go playing through the
meadow, the land, the sheep, the shepherd, the tree that
offers you shelter and bids you eat of its fruit, the sun in
the heavens, the rock, and the very robe you wear, all have
a voice and speak of Christ. In the text Christ introduces
still another symbol of himself, " I am the living bread."

Of each, and of all the matchless figures of speech used
by Christ. it can be said, that they were not far-fetched,
but were suggested by the circumstances and by association.
This symbol of bread is not an exception to the rule. Attracted by his miracles, knowing that he could supply their
every need great multitudes followed the Lord Jesus
Christ. The multitude was unusually great at the particular time referred to in the context, because it was the time
of the Passover. Then the people of Palestine were all
astir and in transit toward Jerusalem,

The Passover occurred just before harvest, at that time
if any, bread was scarce and commanded a high price.
Christ performed a notable miracle, feeding five thousand
men with five barley loaves and two small fishes. So

pleased were the people that in a short time after the miracle, probably as soon as they became hungry again, they
pursued Christ over the sea, for they were aware that the
Disciples had carried away with them twelve baskets full
of the miracle made bread.

The Jews had been frequently pinched by famine; they
had toiled hard for bread which often had been denied them
but with Christ as their king they thought that, a temporal
evil could not assail them, therefore fostering in their
hearts revolt against the rule of Rome, they followed the
baskets and fragments crying bread! bread! bread! Moses
in the wilderness had given their Fathers bread, it had
fallen like the dew or the rain; O! what if Christ could
command its descent in a perpetual shower, then labor
might cease and anxious hearts could rest, and then they
could accept the miracle as the credential of messiahship
and crown Jesus as their King.

Many to-day seek Christ from similar motives; they
take only a sensuous view of Christianity; they are mercenary, seeking Christ, not for character, not for the divine
life that he imparts, but for self and pelf, for loaves and
fishes. Christ would turn human hearts away from such
low intentions; he would not have them toil exclusively
for the meat that perisheth, but for that which endureth,
for that which the Son of God came to supply.

Bread, whether baked in the oven or rained from the
sky, can serve, at best, only a temporary purpose, it is not
the bread of life, it is only a type of it. While the body is
an essential part of being, and its health, maintainance,
and the education of the mind, are among the important
demands of life, the training and development of the moral
nature transcends them all in importance.

Man is only partially and poorly satisfied when his bodily hunger is appeased. Soul-hunger is deeper, more fearful, and far more worthy of consideration, therefore Christ said "I am the living bread," I can supply your spiritual need, I can nourish your moral life. so that he who cometh to me shall not again be tortured with that hunger of spirit that all the world cannot satisfy; he that cometh to me shall know what it is to be satisfied. and the bread which I will give is not that perishable substance that is baked in an oven; not that which descended on the desert of which the fathers ate and are dead, but the bread which I give is my flesh, which I give for the life of the world. Your motives are low and gross when you labor exclusively for the other, they are exalted unto the highest when you earnestly seek for the bread that can bring life unto the soul.

There seems to be an abrupt transition in the words of Jesus from bread to flesh. It is said if the Master had continued the simple, beautiful figure of bread, the doctrine would seem less harsh. It is objected that the change of figure puts a sort of cannibalism into it, and that the idea of eating flesh and drinking blood, especially the flesh and blood of Christ, is most revolting.

But in reality Christ did not change the figure. but completed it in the use of the term flesh   Man shall not live by bread alone; vegetable diet, though good, is not sufficient of itself for the support of the physical and the mental man; the nutriment of all living bodies must contain the constituents of those bodies; bread does not contain all the constituents of the living bodies of men: an animal diet is as necessary as vegetable besides, the Hebrews believed that the very life of the flesh was in the blood. Christ, therefore, when he said my flesh is meat, my blood is drink indeed, simply carried out to its fullness, the beautiful idea that he came to give life unto the world.

The language of course is not to be literally interpreted. Christ uses the figure of eating and drinking because such was the topic of discourse. The simple thought is as flesh is an essential aliment for man, so the grace and salvation of Christ; secured by the sacrifice of himself is necessary for the moral strengthening and development of the soul; it is more than bread, it is the very elixir of spiritual life, "meat indeed." An outpouring of the life of Jesus brought life to the world, and he who by faith receives that bread divine in assimilated into the likeness of Christ. So that the precious life that went out on Calvary springs up again in every redeemed soul. As it is received it is sweeter than honey to the moral taste. He who has once tasted that the Lord is gracious will say evermore give me this bread.

Thus the doctrine is taught as that by some condescension to earth, as when the wheat is cast upon the furrow, by some strange manifestation of an unseen life, as when the stalk springs upward from the seed; by some providential display, as when fields wave with golden grain; by some inexplainable law of death, as when the grain is crushed and prepared for the oven; by some process of spiritual assimilation, as when the essence of bread becomes an essential part of the body; so Christ, the Word, has condescended to earth and given himself to us, and by some sacrifice, some devotion of his body, and blood, and life, that we cannot fully understand, the world is benefitted and the moral nature of man shall not die. Let us consider

III. THE PURPOSE FOR WHICH THIS BREAD IS GIVEN TO THE WORLD.

All food is the gift of God. Man may plant, and sow, and reap, and raise sheep and cattle; he can cook and present food in a great variety of forms; only furnish the material and he can fix it up to suit himself, but he cannot manufacture an atom of any substance that enters into his daily food. Every atom is the gift of God. So the Bread of Life is the gift of God. "Blessed be God for his unspeakable gift." Now, if given it was given for a purpose. For what purpose then, according to what plan or law was Christ given to the world?

According to the text and many other Scriptures Christ was given "for" or in place of the world. "He gave himself a ransom for many." "His flesh is given for the life of the world." He tasted death for every man. That word "for," that idea of substitution. or in the place of, is scouted as unscientific, unphilosophical and impossible. Yet, I am bold to say that, scouted though this idea may be, it is nevertheless in harmony with a prevalent law of being.

Look on a vegetable; what is it but God in that particular form revealing himself to you? Consider its mission, it is to regale your sense. it is to perpetuate your life. it must pass away, it must die, but it will die for you, it is possessed of a life that is not its own, but an imparted life, a life that has been bestowed by God. but for what? For you.

The whole vegetable kingdom, with its infinite variety and beauty, the grasses, the flowers, the plants. the trees, in ways unnumbered do good service for man; the entire vegetable kingdom lives and dies that man may live; on oak and pine, on seed and flower, on leaf·and stalk, and root, the law of sacrifice and substitution is plainly writ; go where you may, from zone to zone, and that law will always and everywhere confront you.

Rising into the animal kingdom, we find that a similar death and substitution prevail; here is suffering and death for my need; I am nourished by the death of many living creatures who die for me; but the life of those animals is not their own, it is given, it is but a drop from the fountain of all life which is God, and is given to them for me; therefore it is. as is the death of vegetation, only a little higher type, a feature of a divinely appointed vicarious system, a sort of substitutional arrangement. There may be a superabundance. God sometimes shows his munificence by waste; but the life of flying bird, lowing kine, bleating lamb is for the great world of humanity. The whole animal kingdom surrenders its life or goes down to death that man may live.

The intellectual is the next higher grade of life; it is supported by thought that has truth in it. The past has been busy providing thought-food for the present. There is a sense in which we are all thinking for each other: those who think truth and those who think untruth. Many a philosopher has found himself indebted to the erroneous thought of another for the deathless truth that impearled his own thinking. Indeed, we all bring our intellections and offer them on the sacred altar of Truth. Multitudes of thoughts perish at the birth of every truth. Thus the law of substitution prevails in the world of mind as it does in the world of matter. The human mind is at work; ultimately the absolute truth will obtain; when it shall obtain, and the world shall sweetly rest in it, the completed work will be recognized as having been done by vicarious means.

The highest sphere of life is the moral. Is there sacrifice or substitution here? By no law of nature must men die for each other; they do sometime, it is true, but it is the exception, not the rule, and even the exception is accidental, it does not enter into the divine plan.

But according to Scriptural philosophy, a man is the center of universal consideration; earth rises, Heaven stoops to serve him, because, perhaps, the earthly and the Heavenly meet in his nature. In so far as earth can subserve a human interest earth is for man; "all things are for your sakes," and to satisfy any want that earth cannot fill Heaven, God himself stands in waiting. Ten thousand fields might fade, an universe of flocks might perish, but they could not supply the needs of a deathless soul. A soul-want is deep as eternity, only the eternal can fill it. If, therefore, the soul-life is nourished and all its needs are supplied; if God works in his moral as he does in his material realm, there must be sacrifice, there must be subtitution for the soul. God in some sense must condescend to the spiritual necessities of men; his life must somehow stoop, and become the substitute and the sacrifice for the moral life of the world.

To that one who is conscious of his need of God, and finds in his moral nature a vacuum that only the moral life of the divine one can fill. To one who has tried every man-made remedy and still finds that his heart is empty, how sweet to look Calvary-ward and to hear that voice with celestial sweetness saying " I am the living bread which came down from Heaven, if any man eat of this bread he shall live forever, and the bread that I will give is my flesh, which I will give for the life of the world." But the fullness of that sweetness is to experience it. There are many all over the world that can say " now I live, yet not I, but Christ liveth in me."

It is a reasonable and inspiring thought that, as omniscience has for man devoted the vegetable kingdom with all its beauteous life and all its nourishing properties; and he animal kingdom with all its variety of existence; and thought also, with all its sweep of power, so for the immortal soul he has consecrated himself, in the person of the incarnate Word and for the aspirations of the deathless spirit he has devoted the life and joy of eternity.

Bread, food, is a natural provision for a natural want. The vegetable and the animal kingdoms are in substitution for the race in the sense of supplying its need. So, the condescension and sacrifice of Christ are a divine provision for a moral need; they are God with his infinite resources of love, wisdom, and fatherhood adapting himself to the wants and spiritual necessities of every human soul; this provision is as needful as bread, it is bread of a divine type.

The sacrifice of the cross therefore affects man, not for the same purpose, but according to the same philosophy, as does every other God-ordained sacrifice. The mission of Christ to the world was not to banish pain, or prevent suffering, or relieve of responsibility, or even to avert physical death, for we are all the children of curruption, "the worm is our mother and sister," and even in a moral sense each soul must die for his own sin, but Christ came to open up to man's waiting, wanting heart the kingdom of spiritual supply.

There is something more therefore in the sacrifice of Christ than in the idea of a substitute, or an equivalent; something more than is conveyed in the thought that if he had not died the world must have died. For, if Christ was God incarnate, he was of more worth than the world; one infinite life is of infinitely greater value than any number of finite lives. The atonement therefore, as the death of Christ is sometimes called, was nothing more or less than the entire kingdom of divine grace brought within the reach of every love-needy heart.

All moral providence inheres in Christ Jesus, he is the focal point, the universal moral center. Indifference to the overtures of his kingdom is moral insanity; inallegiance and wilful rejection is spiritual suicide. Might as well war with the laws of vegetation and refuse the merciful provisions of the material universe as to lead sedition in the kingdom of God's moral rule, or what is the same, refuse the Bread of Life. "Except ye eat the flesh and drink the blood of the Son of man ye have no life in you." There is, there can be no sterling, perfect moral character and pure spiritual life outside of the provisions of the cross.

The purpose for which this bread is given to the world is fully explained in the text. This living bread, this bread from Heaven is given, not for the life of angels, but for the life of the world, this world of men, this world of sinful men, and for the whole world; if any man will eat this bread he shall live forever. It is Heaven contributing itself to earth; it is God giving himself to man, to each man who will accept, the poor and the rich, the black and the white, the great and the lowly; it is for the life of the whole world.

It is not given that the world may exist simply, but that the race may live in the truest, the highest sense, not as the rock lives, or the flower, or the brute, nor simply as the philosopher lives, but that the souls of men may be healthy and vigorous with the life of God; for to carry out the figures when the Bread of Life is received as the food of the soul, the divine life is imparted to the human and in a sense the human is made divine; both are made one. O sweet experience when our life is hid with Christ in God, and he is formed in our hearts the hope of glory, controlling all our aims and creating all our joy.

The importance of this spiritual life suggests that it should be earnestly sought and eagerly accepted; that nothing on earth is, comparatively speaking, worth a thought beside. It should receive the most serious attention, and the unwearying effort of every reasonable man; but alas! most are pursuing the meat that perisheth; dazzled with the tinsel of time they forget or reject the gold of eternity; excited in the greedy grasp and scuffle for loaves and fishes, they allow their moral natures to famish and die; engrossed in the things of sense their roots have become coarse, the juices of spiritual life cannot flow, their leaf has paled and their bloom is blasted.

With such a contracted existence, such base experiences, no wonder that men are unbelieving and immoral, and lose faith in the future and confidence in the spiritual possibilities of the present. Would I could remove these false impressions. God is not unjust. Having furnished every needed temporal good, the soul has not been forgotten, there is an infinite supply for its moral need; living bread has come down from Heaven; it has pleased God that in Christ all fullness should dwell. Let us look up to him, moral reaching out toward him with all our longings, all our powers, then we shall be undeceived and smiling sunbeam and distilling dew will quicken our moral natures, render earth more yielding, our leaf green, our bloom imperishable.

Dear friend, have you an appetite for this Heavenly bread? Without it the moral nature perishes; eat or die is a law of the spirit as well as a law in physics: but if any man eat of this bread he shall live forever. Labor not therefore for the meat that perisheth, but for that which endureth unto everlasting life.

It is said in classic fable that the Muses of Knowledge, Art, Intellect and Fame had their charmed and beautiful abode on the brow of a lofty hill, that there flowed a crystal spring, there towered a temple of gold, and whoever would wear the crown of success must climb the hill, drink of the spring and worship at the holy shrine. So, the way of the Christian is ever up, up toward sweeter and more enchanting heights, up to a purer spring than classic poet ever dreamed, up to a fairer temple than ever crowned the acropolis of Athens, up into the life of God. Christ is the gate of that ascent, and the bread of that life, he is the hand divine, reaching down to help us up, he is our crown of life. Let us climb the hill, let us drink of the waters, let us clothe character with the mantle of the righteousness of Christ.

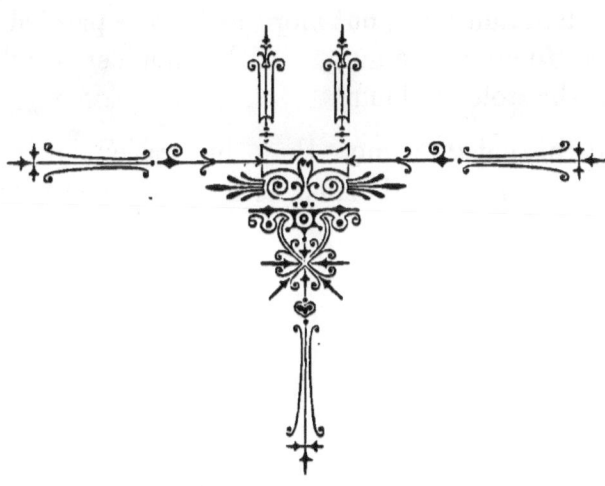

THE CHRISTLESS WORLD.

That at that time ye were without Christ, being aliens from the
commonwealth of Israel, and strangers from the covenants of
promise, having no hope, and without God in the world.

But now, in Christ Jesus, ye who sometime were far off are
made nigh by the blood of Christ.—*Eph.* 2, 12 and 13.

Considered as a literary production, the epistle to the
Ephesians may be regarded as a funeral oration, pronounced
by Paul over the grave of all ancient, and particularly of
Grecian philosophy, civilization and religion.

In his oration the speaker pays a well deserved tribute
to Christianity by representing it, not as a new
born thing of time, but as the offspring of eternity; not
as a product of matter but with all matter beneath it; not
as a philosophy but a life; and, as appearing not as when
the avenger of Julius Cæsar is supposed to have appeared
in snow, hail and flood, but more as Horace painted the de-
fender of Rome as coming " with shoulder brightening
through the stole of cloud."

But this epistle is more than an oration; it is also a
repertory of facts; it begins with a statement of facts,

namely, that Paul, the writer, was an apostle of Jesus Christ by the will of God, and that the apostle was commissioned to bear to the Ephesians peace from God our Father. In the course of the epistle a number of other facts are stated, all of which when put into one fact means that Christ, who is far above all principality, and power, and might, and dominion, and every name that is named, not only in this world, but also in that which is to come is the sole fountain of spiritual blessing, the only cynosure of the world's redemption.

The text also is a comprehensive statement of historic facts. In language the deep significance of which should alarm those who are in their sins and arouse every Christian to seek the salvation of the lost, it declares the unhappy condition of those who are in the flesh and out of Christ. The declaration is made that such are alien to the commonwealth of Israel, strangers to the covenants of promise, hopeless, and without God in the world. It is of these fearful facts that I wish to speak to-day. Let us consider

I. THE MEANING OF THE TERMS.

1. What are we to understand by alienation from the commonwealth of Israel? Is it to be supposed that a Jew, in a political sense, enjoyed great and exalted privileges? Certainly not, because the Davidic empire was never very great or important. In its palmiest days it extended only from the Mediterranean to the Euphrates, and from the Red Sea to Lebanon. The present sultan of Turkey rules over a territory containing 675,920 square miles more than that over which Solomon reigned. There was some honor belonging to a Roman citizen, honor which was often purchased at a great price. But in a political sense it was

more disgraceful than honorable to be recognized as a citizen of the crumbled Jewish commonwealth. When. therefore, the apostle declared that Christless Ephesians were aliens to the commonwealth of Israel he did not refer to any political dignity or immunity.

But Israel was a holy nation, a spiritual commonwealth, which unlike the temporal kingdom of David is destined to continue forever; it was not actually holy, but representatively so. It represented "the Heavenly Jerusalem, an innumerable company of angels, the general assembly and Church of the first born, which are written in Heaven, and the spirits of just men made perfect." It was from this representative spiritual empire that the carnal and Christless Ephesians were excluded. Thus the inspired Paul virtually taught that all Ephesians. living and dead, who were out of Christ were also out of Heaven.

Not that as much is required of an ignorant heathen to account him in Christ, as is required of one who is enlightened. Perhaps obedience to the light that is in him is sufficient to regard him as in Christ; but that the heathen sinner has no better chance than any other sinner; "as many as have sinned without law shall perish without law." Salvation is for those only who are in the circle of the spiritual commonwealth. And of course the opportunities of salvation greatly increase as men take on themselves the yoke of Christ and learn of him

2. What are we to understand by "strangers to the covenants of promise?" The covenants must have reference to some distinguishment pertaining to the commonwealth.

Each ancient empire bequeathed something to the ages that followed. Babylon gave the ultimate grandeur of a barbarous civilization. Egypt with other good gave agriculture. Greece gave poetry, philosophy and architecture, and Rome gave jurisprudence. But what did the spiritual Israel leave to the world? It left nothing if it did not leave the covenants of promise, that is the Holy Scriptures. In answering the question, "what advantage then hath a Jew?" the apostle said "much every way, chiefly because unto them were committed the oracles of God."

Nebuchadnezar's palaces have fallen into inextinguishable ruin; the pyramids are but monuments of fallen greatness. Grecian philosophy is no more. Rome has halted and gone down to dust, and the scepter has departed from Judah and a law-giver from between his feet; but the Jewish oracle, divinely given, still speaks to man, revealing God, disclosing eternity, assuring redemption and radiant with the glory of an everlasting covenant and promise.

To this covenant the Ephesians were strangers, not because they had never heard of it, the apostle does not rest the case on such ground, but because they were out of Christ, and because they were disobedient to the divine voice that spoke within them. They were not included in the pale of the promises of Holy Writ. They could lay no claim to the blessings temporal and spiritual which are assured to the pious, nor the blessings that are pledged in Messiah. There was no antidote for their despair. It is a fearful thought, but out of Christ a soul is without the limits of the conditions of the covenant. The universe has not a word of promise to whisper to a Christless heart.

3. What are we to understand by having no hope? We are certainly to understand that the moral state of the unchristian Ephesians was that of utter hopelessness.

They had no well-grounded hope of a future life. The Ephesians in thought were Greeks. The Greeks gave their philosophy to the Romans. The Roman Cicero called the hope of immortality "a surmise of future ages." Seneca speaks of it as "that which wise men promise but do not prove," and Pliny declared that neither soul nor body hath any more sense after death than before birth." Most of the Grecian poets agree that "the dead are sensible of nothing." Aristotle held that "death puts an end to all things," and Plutarch speaks of "the fabulous hope of immortality." So far as concerned a future life, therefore, the Ephesians were wanting a well grounded hope; indeed it might be said that they had no hope at all.

They had no hope of empire. Those conquering phalanxes that had defied the world, that had swept the sea, and Grecian culture which poets had sung had all vanished away. Every hope of empire, every promise of glory had whirled in the vortex and sunk into oblivion. Not a star of hope shone from their political midnight.

Nor did the Christless Ephesians have any hope in thought. The thoughts of Grecian thinkers, the declarations of scholars had not been realized. One school had always been in conflict with another, and reason itself had at last lost its very foundations. So completely had every proof failed and every promise perished that darkest doubt enveloped the Grecian mind. It had settled into stoicism or universal skepticism, and to avoid every positive assertion the Greek scholar availed himself of some doubtful mode of expression, as "it is possible," "it may be so," or that darkest and doubtfulest of all utterances " I assert nothing not even that I assert nothing." A condition of mind more hopeless than this is inconceivable; but such was that of the cultured Ephesian out of Christ. A people alienated from Heaven, a people estranged from the divine covenant, must be without hope.

4. What are we to understand by being without God in the world? Not that the Ephesians had no God. They worshipped the goddess of rivers, she who wore on her brow a turret, a nimbus behind her head, the signs of the Zodiac on her neck, a lion on each arm, and bees, deer, and oxen on her skirt. She was worshipped with pomp and expense, with mirth and games, with song and sorcery, and her votaries shouted under the marble arches of her sanctuary "great is Diana of the Ephesians." Yet they were without God in the world. They enjoyed no grateful assurance of love divine, no thought of Providence and Fatherhood. In heart and soul, in the deeper longings of their spiritual natures they were Godless.

In this world of limited knowledge, this world of fear and questioning, this world of weeping eyes and broken hearts, this world where burdens press, sin smites and death pursues us, it were dreadful to be without God.

Thus the portrait of the unchristian Ephesians is drawn by the master hand of the apostle: it were impossible to throw upon it a deeper shading. It is the picture of a sunless sky, a starless midnight, and an orphaned soul in the midst, Godless, helpless, promiseless, and an outcast from Heaven, because out of Christ.

The apostle does not declare that the Ephesians could not be saved until the Gospel was preached to them. It is possible that many were saved before they heard of the Gospel. Heathens have been converted and lived Christian lives who never heard of Christ; but he does wish to impress us with the thought that men will not be likely to be obedient to the light that is in them until the Gospel has been preached to them. Let us consider that

II. THE TERMS OF THE TEXT DESCRIBE THE MORAL CONDITION OF ALL THAT PART OF MANKIND WHO ARE UNCHRISTIAN.

1. The world out of Christ is Godless.

In a tract published by the Free Religious Association, a writer, who confesses "it paralizes my whole spiritual nature if I doubt whether Jesus was a man," teaches that the god of Maximus Tyrius, who was a god without thought or will; the god of Aristotle, who was the divinity of nature only; the sovereign of Cleanthes, who was simply an executive of law; the First Nature of Seneca, which was Fate; the Bacchus of the Stoics, which was Indifference; the Mercury of the Ancients, which was Reason; Ceres, a teacher of husbandry; Diana, a huntress; Minerva, a warrior, and the god whom Saint Augustine worshipped were all one. To say, says that writer, "that different races worshipped different gods is like saying that they are warmed by different suns." Having read that tract I could not resist the conclusion that practically the author himself was an atheist; for he who is willing to put deity side by side with Saturn, Jupiter, or Phœbus Apolos, and declare they all are one, must be distinguished for his irreverence, and an irreverent man is practically without God in the world,

I need not stop to argue the fact that Fetichism has no God; Shamanism has no God; and that Dualism is without a God, at least, in this world; that Pantheism is Atheistic; and that Polytheism also is Godless. But Mohamedanism is also without God, for, though the name of diety is

on every lip, yet, of a loving Father, of a Creator conde-
scending to his creatures, of a God, regarding those creatures not as as servants, but as sons, and of a God in man
making man one with God a Moslem is entirely ignorant.
Mohammedan deism is stolid fatalism.

Deism, that which is commonly so called. may concede the existence of a Supreme First Cause, but ignoring
the only revelation that God has ever made of himself, the
Deistic conception of Deity is contracted, the Deist's trust
is superficial, and his belief soon gives way before the as-
saults of Pantheism and Atheism.

Naturalism too is Godless. If all organizations are
nothing but potent dust. If human souls are simply sublimated substances. If. Deity is nothing but the ultimate
development of all things, then. there is no God in this
world, there is no God in Heaven, there is no God anywhere. and there never can be a God for the poor; longing
heart of man, for nothing has reached. and probably never
will reach an ultimate development.

Nay, more. there are those all around us who profess to
believe in God; who argue his existence with all the convincing evidences of theology. yet are without God in the
world. They hypothecate a Deity whom they do not worship, and get eloquent over a piety that they do not possess·
God is indeed a thought in their mind. but not a living,
saving, sanctifying power in their souls. Not knowing
Christ they know not God; not having seen the Son by the
faith of the Gospel. they do not see the Father.

Thus go where you will on this green earth, among
the palms of the Indies, or the thronging populations of
China, or the civilizations of Europe, or the Cathedrals of
Christian England, or the colleges of free America, and
practically if not theoretically, you shall find that mankind
out of Christ is without God in the world.

2. The unchristian world to-day is hopeless.

Hope is a sentiment born in the human soul, but it is a sentiment merely unless enthused with the power of a living truth. God, according to his abundant mercy, hath begotten those who are in Christ Jesus unto a lively hope; they, therefore, who are without Christ have not this lively hope. Outside of the Gospel what the world calls hope is nothing but desire; for instance, the so-called hope, cherished by the people of Ningpo, that by paying liberal fees to spectral ferrymen, and great bribes to spirit offices of justice, a disembodied soul may secure some immunity in the world to come, scarcely deserves the name of desire much less of hope; and the Budhistic hope that in the life to come women will be transformed into men, and men shall be absorbed into the unconscious being of their favorite idol, is but one step above absolute desperation.

The Chinaman throws the sable pall of his hopelessness even over the sunny things of the present life. Perhaps this is what makes him look so sad. I never yet saw a Chinaman with a smiling face. It may be that this fact of an empires hopelessness explains the reason why so many woo an hour's repose in an opium dream. According to a popular Chinese tract, "the floating multitude, earth and Heaven. wife and children are nothing but vanity, we exchange them all for a lonely mound; friends seldom meet in the winding roads of the yellow streamed Tartarus, and the passing shadow leaves no trace behind it." What China needs is Christ, Christ to teach the unending personality of the human soul. Christ to save from sin and from the tormenting fear of Tartarus. When China shall have been redeemed, and shall become Christian. then in that good time which is surely coming, Heaven, earth, wife, children will be vanity no longer; then the whole vast empire will possess a hope, which, like an anchor to the soul, shall be sure and steadfast, cast within the vail.

Look at Japan, can the Sintooism which is prevalent in those islands, that which deifies the feudal chiefs, teaches that creation started without a creator, prescribes a morality the stimulus to which is fear, and directs to scriptures that contain no promise of the future; can this afford to the people of Japan a reasonable hope even for the world that now is, to say nothing of that which is to come?

Look at Africa; on that dark continent there are at least 100,000,000 people who live without an aim, and who will die hopelessly as dies the brute.

Look at India; that great peninsula which Bishop Thompson characterized as "a babel of devils." Can the Islamism of India that knows no propitiation, can Budhism, which declares that punishment must follow transgression as sure as the cart-wheel follows the ox, can Brahmanism, with its caste. slavery, suttee, thugee—can any or all of these give hope to the teeming millions of India? Hitherto they have not, but they have filled the orient with misery and woe, and having brought blindness and gross darkness upon the souls of the Hindoos, those old isms are to-day, like great constellations that slowly fades away.

But we need not travel through oriental lands in order to discover that the world without Christ is hopeless; the same fearful fact confronts us even in Christian lands, and under the shadow of every Christian Church and cathedral. Who are the hopeless ones? Who among us are withering in their despair? Those who believe in and trust a God of infinite perfection? Those who find that Infinite One by their sides, as it were, in the person of the Beloved, forgiving their sins, flooding earthly gloom with Heavenly radiance, arching the troubled Heavens with the bow of promise and fringing the future with eternal glory; are these the hopeless, the unhappy ones? By no means; on the contrary, these rejoice and are exceeding glad; but those who are wanting in hope, and are smitten with despair are doubters and skeptics, those who have cut the cables of their faith, and are like rudderless ships at sea, the mere playthings of the storm whirled about by every breeze that blows.

All around us are skeptics, agnostics and pessimists; men who according to their unbelief have sunken into the depths of despair. One doubts whether the Bible is a revelation from God, therefore whether God ever did, ever will, or can, though with softest utterances whisper to the hearts of his waiting, listening, longing children. O how much of hope is cast out of the human soul when man in his unbelief sinks into the slough of skepticism.

The agnostic does not know, he says, that there is a God, or a future life, therefore all hope with him is buried in indifference; he sinks into the mire a little farther than the skeptic. Ask him, brother, you do not think you are fatherless and an orphan in the midst of this universal magnificence, do you? I do not know; there is some kind and helpful hand reached out to help you in your trouble? I do not know; beyond this life of death and darkness there surely is sunshine and immortality? I do not know. O, you can lift yourself out of this mire of unbelief if you try? I do not know; and thus he sinks farther and father into the hopelessness of his utter indifference.

What unbelief may bring ultimately on the human soul it is impossible to tell; but the philosophical unfaith of the present time has landed in the dire mud of pessimism. This latest boon of all the philosophies is sure that the conditions of human existence are the most unhappy that can possibly be conceived; it sees not a ray of light; it declares that life is not worth living, and advises that the best thing for us all to do is to commit suicide at once. Thus unbelief has at length struck from the temple of being its foundation and its dome, leaving nothing but a solitary pillar that is tottering to its fall, and is ready to crumble away.

The Greeks who said " I assert nothing, not even that I assert nothing," were no more unhopeful than is the christless world to-day.

3. As were the Ephesians of old, so the unchristian peoples of to-day are strangers to the covenants of promise.

In regard to the condition on which the divine promises are assured, there can be no difference as to the Jew and the Gentile. If God has promised certain blessings and privileges, he of course has pledged them to one man on exactly the same terms as he has pledged them to another. "Of a truth," said Peter, " I perceive that God is no res_pecter of persons, but in every nation he that feareth him and worketh righteousness is accepted with him." The nations therefore that fear God and work righteousness are the people of God, but the nations who do not fear him and do not work righteousness are not his people; they are strangers to his covenants and promises; they have no part in the promise given to Abraham, and no part in the covenant made with Israel at Horeb.

There are two forms of promise, in "the Book of the Covenant," the temporal and the spiritual. Is the promise made that "blessed shalt thou be in the city, and blessed shalt thou be in the field, blessed shall be the fruit of thy body and the fruit of thy ground, and rhe fruit of thy cattle, the increase of thy kine and the flocks of thy sheep, blessed shall be thy basket and thy store, blessed shalt thou be when thou comest in, and blessed shalt thou be when thou goest out?" it is on condition that thou hearken diligently unto the voice of the Lord thy God to observe and do.

Or does God promise spiritual blessings, such as were promised to Abraham and to all nations through him, namely, pardon of sin, peace with God, the spirit of adoption, sonship with God, assurance of sonship, spiritual life, and eternal glory. The promise is assured to us on the condition of our faith, our faith in the promised Messiah; and on the condition that we manifest our faith by becoming the seed of Abraham, not his natural but his spiritual seed, like him believing the promise, like him keeping inviolate the manward side of the covenant, which is in one word, obedience to God; hence the blessings of Abraham come on the Gentiles through Christ, that we might receive the promise of the spirit through faith. "If therefore we be Christ's we are Abraham's seed and heirs according to the promise.

In the Old Testament, there is not so far as I know, one promise, that is given in such a manner as that one who is a stranger to the covenant, or does not heed its terms, can claim it with any degree of assurance; and in the New Testament, so far as I am able to understand it, every precious promise therein pertains to those who are in Christ Jesus, or have entered into that spiritual life that Christ came to bestow. Outside of obedience to God and faith in Christ there is no promise. Look to nature for that which can produce spiritual life and fearful disappointment will confront you. There is no assurance of pardon, there is no peace for a troubled soul, there is no evidence of sonship with God, there is no comforting testimony of a future life; where God has not spoken by a special revelation. Therefore it is by proclaiming the promises that men will be induced to comply with the conditions. The engrafted word is indeed able to save the souls of men, but it must first of all be engrafted. When once a man, deep down in his soul, has been made to feel that the Bible was designed and written expressly for him, that it is exactly suited to his needs, that it is the voice of his Heavenly Father calling him away from sin to a nobler and better life, he is in the highway of salvation, but continuing to ignore it in his heart, however much he may know of it in his head, he continues to be a stranger to the covenant's promise.

This covenant of promise, this Holy Bible, is the foundation fact of Christianity, outside of its pale there is no Christianity and no Christ, and it is an incontrovertible truth that a world without a Bible or a Christ has no spiritual life in it, no assurance of salvation, no Heaven; a Christless world is estranged from the covenant.

4. As the Ephesians out of Christ were excluded from the Heavenly Jerusalem, the spiritual commonwealth, so the world unchristian is to-day alien from the household of faith, and the general assembly and the Church of the First Born which are written in Heaven. In short out of Christ the world is in Hell; not the Hell that shall be, but a Hell that now is, the perdition of unbelief, the distraction and misery of unpardoned sin.

Part of the Christless world is plunged into a Hell of poverty. Look for instance at the poor laborer of Japan

performing work that in Christian countries is performed
by the brute; or look at Turkey filled with beggars; and
India with hermits gaunt, and hungry, and improvident.
It has come to pass as the prophet declared, that under the
degrading effects of sin, man has become a beast of burden,
drawing iniquity with cords of vanity and sin as it were a
cart rope.

The world out of Christ is, part of it, in a Hell of superstition; such, for instance, as torments every Celestial,
lest he should choose an unlucky spot to build on, or to be
buried in, and makes him imagine that in August and
September all the disembodied ghosts of Hades are let loose
for a raid on the world; or such as drove the Hindoo devo-
tee to throw himself under the crushing wheels of Jugger-
naut, and the Hindoo mother to cast her child into the
greedy waters of the Ganges; and such as terrifies the
African with the thought that star and cloud, mountain
and plain, lake and river, beast and insect, are all haunted
with evil and hurtful influences that must be charmed
away.

Nay, right here, under our own eyes, out of Christ is a
Hell of misery, crime and shame. Everywhere the courts
are in session, and the Judge is on the bench; everywhere
the criminal is being led to his dungeon or his doom;
everywhere are the sons and daughters of guilt who are
living in infamy, and who will die in despair.

The world out of Christ is in a Hell that continually
waxes worse and worse. The tendency of sin is always
downward. Anciently those who turned away from God
became idolaters. The Vedas degenerated into the institutes of Menu, and these into an oriental literature that is now
defiling everything it touches. Greece degenerated and

speedily vanished. Rome became more and more vuluptu-
ous and perished. The broad way ends in destruction.
Indeed the Scripture declares that evil men and seducers
will wax worse and worse. In the present century Sabbath
breakers are bolder than ever. Among certain classes legal
recognition of the marriage bond is entirely ignored, and
divorces have become proportionately more numerous; bad
books were never so abundant as now, robberies and forge-
ries were never committed on such gigantic scale as during
the last fifty years. Christianity is indeed marching on,
but the Hell of sin grows deeper and blacker about the
lives of evil men and seducers day by day. Where this
burning Hell will end God only knows; it may be but the
kindling of that fiercer fire that shall burn in the world to
come.

I admit that I have drawn a most melancholy picture;
and you, dear reader, may call me a pessimist if you please,
but such is the moral condition of the world out of Christ.
It is godless, hopeless, promiseless, heavenless; it is wandering in starless midnight; it is plunged in moral darkness;
it is as it were swamped with polar seas; it is torn by sin's
tornadoes; it is scathed with wrathful lightnings, and it
grows worse and worse.

I have no censure to fling at the honest efforts of
statesmen. I admit that education is a reformatory agent.
It is true that religions of human invention have
in them some sublime ideals; and I admit there is something in material nature that is capable to some extent of
lifting the soul upward; but the world may be sure that despite government; and education, and human ethics, and
the religion of nature, history is pregnant with the truth
that ignoring Christ it grows no better, it waxes worse and
worse. This brings us to consider that

III.　THE UNCHRISTIAN WORLD CAN BE REDEEMED BY PREACH-
ING CHRIST AND HIM CRUCIFIED.

Ephesus was redeemed; they who were sometimes afar
off were made nigh, so that they were no more strangers
and foreigners. but fellow citizens with the saints and of
the household of God. And not only the Ephesians but
the Jews and Greeks in all Asia were quickened. the eyes of
their understanding were enlightened,and they were renewed
in the spirit of their minds.

That which promoted Ephesian redemption is sufficient
to save the whole race of men. We know very well what
the redemptive agent was, the glorious Gospel of the Son of
God; that which was proclaimed at Pentecost; that which
Paul declared during three months, amid disputations, in
the Jewish synagogue at Ephesus; that which he preached
for two years from the teacher's desk in the school of Tyranus:
that which the apostle taught the people from house to
house; that blessed Gospel, that sovereign balm which has
saved its millions out of every kindred, and tongue, and
people and nation.

True, the Ephesian Church at length lost its first love;
splendid Christian temples were in the course of time transformed into Mohammedan mosques; the crescent glittered
where the cross had shone; a pestilential morass succeeded
to the place from whence the sea retired, and to-day the
melancholy old site of Ephesus is a suggestive picture of a
people who have rejected Christ. Yet the Ephesians once
dead in trespasses and sins were quickened, they who were
sometime afar off were made nigh by the blood of Christ;
he became their peace, broke down the middle wall of partition, and having slain the enmity reconciled them to God
by his cross, and for five hundred years the shout of redeeming love resounded throughout Ionia.

Concerning the fullness of the joy of all those saints in light who went up from Asia Minor during that five hundred years, we are not informed, but what we know not now we shall know hereafter.

We are told how the blessed work was done; in temptation, with many tears, just as the work is done now on our charges at home, and in the broad, slow yielding fields of missionary labor; in all humility of mind; not as "menpleasers, not as self-seekers, but serving the Lord by keeping back nothing profitable, but by preaching the whole Gospel, the love of it, and the justice of it, whether men will hear or forbear, by teaching publicly and from house to house, by preaching repentance toward God and faith in our Lord Jesus Christ. Such kind of work patiently and prayerfully performed will witness the salvation of men.

This Gospel may be a stumbling-block to free religionists, but so has been free religion to many 'who have embraced it It may be to the philosopher foolishness, but so is all philosophy that is in conflict with his own. Certain doctors may declare that the Gospel is a failure, yet somehow the Gospel fills an immeasurably large place in the human heart. It is not a science, science cannot stir the soul as the Gospel stirs it. It is not morality, for morality is but a law and knows no salvation. It is Christ crucified, Christ the wisdom and the power of God. It was this that whet the sword of Luther, magnified the influence of Wesley and gave success to the Moravian missionaries among the Esquimaux, and not until in India was preached the Savior who died, not as a martyr, nor as the hero of some exciting tragedy, but as a sacrafice for the sins of the whole world did the idolater begin to abandon his idolatry, or the Brahmin his caste. It has the same sin-destroying and hope-inspiring charm everywhere; indeed, the world's

brightest hope is Christ; Christ crucified, glorified, Christ
the sovereign inspiration in the conscience of a redeemed
race.

That Christ has conquered is no longer an open question. In 1872 a thoughtful traveler declared "the whole
heathen world is in a transition state." In 1873 a prominent American statesman declared that the labor performed
by American and British missionaries fully justifies the
Christian charity that sent them out, and the other day
Keshub Chunder Sen declared that Christian ideas and institutions are taking root on all sides in the soil of India.
Read the various missionary reports, their accounts of successful work now doing are sufficient to fire every human
heart with unearthly inspiration. The latest missionary
report of the Methodist Episcopal Church assures us that
Japan is asking for Christian teachers, and the children on
the streets are singing Jesus loves me. It says that in the
city of Titian, where Confucius wrote and labored, Christ is
victor. In Africa the Gospel is winning its way. India is
quickening into life, the valley of dry bones is in commo-
tion; Christianity is favorably impressing the better classes
in the land of Montezuma; as for Italy the Gospel is surely
revolutionizing that land of song, and its spiritual future is
brighter than its smiling sky. Indeed Europe is brightening into a flame of Christian zeal; Scandinavia demands to
know the doctrine of the mighty Savior; Germany is gathering her forces, and the mountains of Switzerland are
echoing with the song of full salvation. The question is
no longer what of the night? but what of the day? How
long ere the risen sun shall have reached its zenith? Christ
has conquered.

But the world is not all saved yet, nor will it be until Christendom shall be ablaze with heavenly zeal. The millennium to-morrow, means full consecration to-day;indifference to-day means indefinite postponement of the worlds redemption. The world's salvation is in the hands of the church; neglect is failure; nay, wilful neglect is crime; the blood of 700,000,000 will God require at our hands.

Can I think of a world without Christ without feeling my soul stirred to its very depths with anxious pity? Can I look into the sorrowful face of him who trod the wine-press alone and not feel my purest sympathies awakened? Can I love my Divine Master of the tearful eye, the liberal hand and the self-sacrificing spirit, and not be a missionary? It were impossible, I would go to the ends of the earth for his sake, and in tears and prayers consecrate the last penny of my property, yea surrender life itself, gladly, if I might thereby promote the honor of his kingdom in the world. When we shall have succeeded in lifting up the everlasting doors of this broad earth, when the king of glory, like the light of a day, that can know no evening, shall have come in and taken possession, then shall we see the travail of our souls and be satisfied.

May the time be hastened when there shall be no more strangers and foreigners, but all the peoples of earth shall be fellow citizens with the saints, and of the household of God, and built upon the foundation of the apostle and prophets, Jesus Christ himself, being the chief corner stone shall become a habitation of God through the spirit.

THE MOUTH OF THE WICKED.

By the blessing of the upright the city is exalted; but it is over-thrown by the mouth of the wicked.—*Prov.* XI, 11.

It is natural to love the place of our birth; with regret-fulness and pain one tears himself from his native soil. Wild, and to many uninviting, may be the region where first he drew the breath of life, yet it is the dearest spot on earth to him; softer gales may smile, fairer flowers may bloom and a richer landscape spread about him, yet it will not be home.

But we cannot all and always linger about the place of our birth. It would have been a poor thing for the world and for humanity, if the race had remained in Eden. The sword that drove out our first parents from those rosy bowers of rest was a merciful one; it is still driving us; by the stern law of necessity, or that stranger one of greed, mankind are migratory like the birds. It is thus that the world is discovered and the earth subdued, uninhabited re-gions are filled with people, the wilderness is made to blos-som, cities are built and man triumphs, and thus, by the law of self-interest we become attached to new localities.

The rapidly increasing population of this continent affords a fine illustration of this truth. Americans are a heterogeneous people, but with all their heterogeneity they are gradually melting into a homogeneous nation. We are English, Celtic, German, Slavic, Hindoo, Indian and yet American. The newly arrived emigrant soon learns to sing,

> " I love thy rocks and rills.
> Thy woods and templed hills."

Wherever men congregate society necessarily exists. Each person in a community is "endowed by his Creator with certain inalienable rights," and accompanying these rights are certain corresponding obligations; hence the question of individual responsibility to society, and of society to the individual is an ever expanding one. It is a question that grows with the experiences of years, and continues growing, not only until it involves the question of the greatest good to the greatest number, but until by a perfect solution of every problem in government there shall have been secured the greatest possible happiness for the entire mass of the governed.

Local politics are sometimes sneered at, but to the parties immediately concerned, the doings of a county board, or a common council may be of more importance than all the plans and plots of foreign courts or diplomats. Yet there are those who know all about the charge on Tel el Kebir, or the last quarrel in the French chambers, and are happy, professedly, to be ignorant of what their own aldermen are doing officially. They make a distinction by saying one is news, the other is politics; it is news they want, not politics.

Indeed, it has come to be supposed that moral or religious principles have nothing to do with politics. It is said that religion is for the Church, the minister, the women, the children, and morals are for the family, the school. the teacher, but politics is only for parties. So it has come to pass that religious men quietly suffer a political wrong, and endure political lying and thieving because, forsooth, the science of politics is excused from the sphere of morals and religion. For one, I abominate the doctrine, and believe that morality and religion are the only forces that can purify the public, or the officiary of the public. Those forces should touch and control the home. society. business. parliaments, county boards, and common councils. Until righteousness shall thus control and mould politics, politics local and national, will always be a mud puddle of filth and corruption; for "by the blessing of the upright the city is exalted, but it is overthrown by the mouth of the wicked."

Fortune has smiled on us and cast our lot in one of the most charming and promising little cities of the great commonwealth of Wisconsin. The surrounding country is rich and fertile; the streets are well shaded and graded; our homes are cozy. convenient, and many of them elegant; the stores are numerous and do a thriving business; the factories cause the blood of industry to leap in the veins of the people; the schools are filled with as healthy and hopeful a brood of boys and girls as ever stirred the din and tumult of a playground; the people are social and intelligent; indeed, we are righteously proud of our little municipality.

It is a vital question what may secure, and what will prevent our prosperity? The first part of this question is easily answered. We know that industry, commerce, intelligence and morality are potent factors in the exaltation of any community; but the things that prevent our weal and welfare we are inclined to forget or ignore. I desire, therefore, to refer to some 'of those things which, in the mouth of the wicked overthrow the city.

I.   THE MOUTH OF INFIDELITY WORKS DAMAGE TO THE CITY.

Infidels say throw away the Old Testament, for the geology of Genesis does not correspond with the last born of scientific opinion; it does not teach that men have been developed from apes; the Mosaic code is not perfect; many of the characters mentioned in the Bible were bad men; it tells of wars sanguinary and cruel; some of its poetry is hyperbole; away with it! it is not fit to be read by our children.

But that Old Testament is the oldest book of antiquity; it truthfully sets forth the Mosaic theory of the order of creation; it teaches the dignity of man; its laws were happily suited to the peoples of that age; it tells of good men as well as bad; it tells of patriotism, courage and self-sacrifices; its inspired songs outlast the muse of Greece; its history is connected with the present by the golden bands of a common hope and a common nature; and its oracle has outlived the Delphic and flashed its truth over the ever changing centuries. Why then destroy the Old Testament? It is at least as worthy of continuance as any other good book.

Ingersoll frankly declared that he "hates" that old Book; he is one of those who think that its influence is demoralizing; yet he insists that the race has progressed intellectually and morally, or as he expresses it from a dugout to a monitor; from a bit of carved bark to an Astor library; from a ye'low daub to the masterpiece of a Rembrandt; from a notched stick to the sculptured marble of a Praxiteles; from the bushman's skull to the skull of a modern philosopher, and the world admits this fact of progression; but this old Bible has been opened on millions of altars while the world has been moving on: progression has been greatest where the hallowed influences of the Holy Scriptures have been the greatest felt.

Infidels also say down with the New Testament, for it contains nothing that is really new, every moral precept therein, they say, was written long before a disciple wrote it. But would you therefore destroy that Book? Would you annihilate each new book that contains an old truth? But that New Testament tells of a better life, suggests a moral preparation, requires purity of heart, shows a perfect man as an example, a teacher who taught not pride but meekness, not revenge but forgiveness, not friendship merely but philanthropy: he taught that to do a good deed for a needy soul is the same as to do it for God; he taught repentance not sin, law not anarchy.

Infidelity says away with the Book! away with Christ! away with Christianity! But to do away with these is to do away with the moral forces that underlie them. Infidelity means nihilism, it means selfishness, it means haughtiness, it means hopelessness, it means the despair of annihilation. Property, law, life would be worth nothing, even in this beautiful city, if the moral restraints of Christianity were driven out and unbelief were to be regnant in individual hearts.

He therefore is an enemy to the moral well-being of the place who slyly broadcasts the poison of his infidelity; he blinds men to the truth of their amenability and robs them of moral restraint; he helps to make monsters of his neighbors; he diligently sets to work influences in the minds of the masses which ultimately must work out their moral ruin; and with his mouth he overthroweth the city.

II.   THE MOUTH OF SLANG HAS A DEMORALIZING POWER.

By slang I mean the language of vulgar wit, the jargon of billingsgate, that which is called peddlar's French or St. Giles' Greek; we hear it every day and are made the unwilling pupils of its low humor; its genius consists in calling things by their wrong names thus, it calls a face a mug; it calls a head a nob, an accomplice it calls a pal, a carousal it designates as a spree, a master it calls a boss, to move is to vamose, to be drunken is to be slewed, to pay money is to bleed, to vaunt or boast is to blow, to run away is to skip; some of the newspapers are flooded with this "bosh" of the streets; they would not pander to such "clap-trap" if it were not popular; its popularity indicates the baseness into which many of the masses are sunken.

Now, such slaug cannot do a community any good; it is not only an illegitimate use of words, but it is the language of deceit, the cant of hypocrisy, the flash of falseness, the mark of bad breeding and the index of moral indifference Let your child, uncorrected, pick up and use such billingsgate, and he will soon learn to swear. Slang is the first degree of profanity; given over to slang he will steadily advance along the line of lawlessness; indifferent to the laws of men, soon he will scorn the law divine; he will decieve you indeed with mock solemnity as readily as he showers you with his gutter gibberish; and his flippant use of a low and vulgar vocabulary will be the flood that shall sweep away all his moral seriousness; then look out, for he has already graduated into that class which is called dangerous.

What is seriousness? Seriousness is not solemnity, but it is that thoughtful, manly spirit which will not give way to incessant jesting or false pretense, but that which intends all it says, and finding that life is full of earnest meaning, and not a thin film of soapsuds, refuses to be light and empty as the bubble that dances in the air.

The man of slang is not only coarse and vulgar, but he is an infidel of the rankest kind; he throws an atmosphere of levity around things that are in themselves the most solemn and sacred; thus he talks unfeelingly of the dead as having passed in their check; unmoved by the beauties of moral principle he takes a sort of pride in being what is commonly called a tough; having done the deed that makes him a criminal before the law, his greatest ambition is "to die game," and fearless of the consequences of sin, heedless of the promise of future punishment for the sinner he speaks of perdition as being a "hot-house," and of God as being "the boss."

People who are wanting in seriousness are a dangerous element in society; they cover truth with slang; they reject and antagonize the most sacred claims of religion; they mock and slander morality; with their evil communications they corrupt the good manners of many who would like to be decent; there ought to be, in my judgment, a law declaring that slang, as well as profanity and slander, is an offense in society.

The city that is made up of a population of slang-slingers is already morally overthrown. If ever it should grow and prosper it will be because these have stepped aside and made room for a more serious and reliable class. Your successful manufacturers and merchants are serious, though social and pleasant men; your industrious yeomanry are serious-minded, thoughtful and contented men; your most respectable classes are made up of serious, earnest, contemplative people who feel that responsibility is resting upon them; but your hilarious, harum-scarum, irresponsible people are your prison peers and vagabonds, your peddlars of slang and princes of levity. The age, society, needs more seriousness and less slang. The mouth of the wicked is overthrowing the city.

III. THE MOUTH OF INEBRIACY IS A MENACE AND A DES-
TRUCTION TO ANY COMMUNITY.

It is an important question are we Americans a happy
people? Certainly we ought to be. With a country so
vast and varied, so rich in agricultural possibilities, so abundant in mineral wealth, so busy and prosperous in commerce and manufacture. With part of our abundance going to bless the people of other lands; with a population
increasing at the rate of a million a year, with railroads
stretching in all directions, with free schools and great colleges, with free speech and free franchise, with a glorious
history and a brave people we ought to be very happy, but
we are not.

Tens of thousands of our fellow citizens are in want of
food, clothes and shelter; tens of thousands can neither read or
write; the country is overrun with criminals; the peoples
hard earned money is wasted; tens of thousands are insane
or idiotic; thousands upon thousands are each year dropped
into premature graves; the heart is full of sorrow; in every
house there is a skeleton; the cause of humanity and Religion is impeded. The Americans are not really a happy
people.

What is the cause of this unhappiness? I will tell you,
STRONG DRINK. We swallow about a hundred million gal-
lons of distilled spirits. and eight million barrels of beer
every year, which costs $800,000,000. We pour this deluge
of damnation into our stomachs, and throw away every
year more than the value of the meat we eat, and the cost
of all our manufactures, and the value of all our forest pro-
ductions. and the value of all our market gardens, and the
value of all our orchards, and reap a harvest of ignorance,
pauperism, crime and sorrow.

The habit of strong drink is a fearful incubus on the resources of this nation; we could better afford once each decade to reduce all our fields to ashes and burn up all our granaries than keep up year after year the damning desolation of intemperance.

It is said that during the war this nation lost a million of its citizens, and that eight billion dollars were expended or invested .Every fifteen years strong drink kills a million of the children of Columbia, and every ten years costs enough to cancel every dollar of the war debt, general, State and county. If we could give up Alcohol, and instead engage in civil war once every fifteen years we should make something by the change.

The demon that is doing such devastating work in the nation generally is busy in the commonwealth of Wisconsin. In 1881 there were 7300 prisoners in the county jails, and 8250 in the police stations and lock-ups of the State. We are burdened with 1800 paupers and 1800 insane people. The State pays annually hundreds of thousands of dollars for their support. Four fifths at least of the crime, pauperism and insanity of the State are produced directly or indirectly by intemperance. It is estimated that in 1900 we shall have at least 3200 insane persons to provide for; the buildings to accomodate them will cost $3,000,-000, and the charge to the public for their support will be $640,000 annually, a burden which the State will find most difficult to bear, and then it will go on, ever deepening and increasing. What can be done to arrest this onflowing avalanche of burden? I answer, prohibit the use of strong drink within the bounds of the commonwealth of Wisconsin, and in twenty years two thirds of the burden will be scattered.

The war has been carried into this little municipality. There are in this city twenty-one saloons, three drug stores, and one bottling establishment besides breweries, where intoxicating drink is sold. The twenty-one saloons at least are doing a thriving business, for they can afford to pay rent, government license, and a local license of two hundred dollars. A larger congregation could be found in those saloons than could be found in all the churches on a Sunday evening. I wish I had local statistics, but this city is much the same as the rest of the world—well, in 1870 the wages paid for labor in all the manufacturing industries of the country were $775,584,313 and that same year there was expended for intoxicating liquors $619,588,371. I have no doubt that the sum paid for labor—and the sum paid for liquor in this city will bear about the same proportion. I do not mean to say that 6-7 of the entire earnings of the laboring classes are spent for alcoholic beverages, but that if the money expended for all kinds of industry is represented by seven, then the money spent by all classes rich and poor, for drink would be represented by six.

Thus one can easily see that under the damning discipline of drink, business and industry are threatened and must eventually go under. What then shall we do? Let the devil have his way unresisted? Be content while our young men are wasting under the spell of intemperance? Bid for a population from other places? Must others come to supersede those already here? I say no! While we welcome each newcomer, particularly if he comes as the sworn enemy of rum, let us shut the saloons, let us save our brothers if we can. No boy is safe, no family is safe, no business is safe, so long as intemperance reigns. Each saloon is a school of slang, a hot-bed of infidelity, a nursery of crime, a rendezvous of idlers; there ignorance is encouraged, intellect is blasted, hopes are ruined, homes are desolated, youth is debauched, law is violated, and life is endangered. Shut them up! We must overthrow them or they will overthrow us. Whisky, in the long run, is too much for any man or any community.

IV.   THE MOUTH THAT USES TOBACCO EXERTS NO GOOD INFLUENCE UPON A CITY.

Tobacco is a plant the botanical name of which is " nicotiana tobacum." a species of night shade. It is not generally distributed by nature, but man works heroically to make it cosmopolitan, a plant for all zones, a solace for all classes and all sorrows. Nature, however, seems to be in perpetual conflict with man in his endeavors; for instance, the seed changes but man selects; weeds in the surface soil choke it, but man burns the surface; drouth or dryness kills but he waters; cold destroys but he covers the plant with straw; caterpillars three inches long are sent to devour it, but man madly pinches the worm between his fingers; nature endeavors to kill the leaf by developing a flower, but man resorts to topping; nature tries again to destroy the leaf by means of suckers, but man maliciously plucks them off; again she attacks the plant with her moist vapors, but man builds expensive dry-houses; once more she attempts to pole-burn the weed, but man resorts to ventilation. Nature endowed tobacco with an exceeding unpleasant taste, as if by this means she would foil man, but he dips it into molasses, or a licorice paste, or a decoction of figs. or glycerine; finally, ready for use, and used as man commonly uses it, man's own nature rebels, the brain says I am dizzy, throw it away! the stomach says I am faint, cast it out! She throws off the poison, and the yellow steaming vomit on the floor seems to say, O you nasty fellow! then nature is convulsed, and cold and clammy, and seems to say never impose on me again in that way or I will kill you!

But man is born to be a conqueror, he will conquer to-bacco or die in the attempt. I fear, however, that he will die in the attempt. To-day nicotiana tobacum is the victor. We have read of the triumphant march of the American army into Mexico, and of the German march into Paris, but these are nothing compared with the grand march of the tobacco plant into the mouths of the people, it is moving in by battalions, by regiments, by divisions, by hundreds of thousands of hogsheads and acres. England (I learn from an article in report of State Board of Health for the year 1881) in 1857, consumed 32,856, 913 pounds, but in 1880 she got rid of 50,000.000 pounds. In 1870 the United States disposed of 262.735,341 pounds, and in 1880 she opened her mouth while 473,107,573 pounds of tobacco marched into it, Just think of it, 1,300,000,000 cigars are stuck between the teeth of Uncle Sam's children every year. We conquer tobacco by holding it with our teeth or rolling it in sweet morsels under our tongues, and pay an enormous tax for the privilege.

But think of the enemy that we have to contend with with our mouth; it is a rank poison. The same article declares that tobacco is composed of three ingrediants. an alkaloid called nicotiana, one drop of which will kill a dog; tobacco camphor. the properties of which are not fully understood, and an oil, so pungent that one drop on the tongue of a cat will throw her into convulsions and cause death in ten minutes. It produces a functional disturbance of the heart, lungs and brain; it produces feebleness of mind, apoplexy; it causes cancer; those who use short pipes or cigars are liable to a cancerous affection of the lips. I honestly believe that a glass of beer is less objectionable than a quid or a smoke.

This insidious foe is in our midst; it has unfurled its banners in thirty-two different places in this fair city; it has taken possession of store and saloon, factory and church; it throttles the illiterate and the scholar, the poor and the rich, the aged and the young; the breath of our boys is fœtid with the fume of tobacco, and sometimes the pulpit has been desecrated with the quid. In the form of snuff, and shag, and plug, and pigtail, and cigar, and cigaret it confronts us, invading our nerves, corrupting our blood, cankering our lungs, irritating our hearts, disturbing our brains, creating a thirst for strong drink, wasting our wages or our fortune, and deranging the morals of our citizens generally. The board of health ought to declare it a nuisance; the legislature should pronounce it a thief.

These four foes, infidelity, slang, inebriacy and tobacco are in our midst. The pulpit fights the first; the free schools wrestle with the second, temperance societies antagonize the third, and all ought combine to annihilate the fourth.

By the blessing of the upright, it is said, the city is exalted. If a community is fortunate enough to possess among its citizens a few sterling, upright men and women, they, by all means, should be its leading spirits.

When Alexander the Great was marching through Persia, his discouraged soldiers resolved to proceed no farther, because their way was blocked with ice and snow, but Alexander put spirit into his army by leaping from his horse and going forward, axe in hand, to break for himself a path through the ice; his army soon followed him. So society catches the spirit of its leaders. Such is the power of example that people of influence aid greatly both in making the sentiment and in creating the character of communities.

Because the leaders of Tarsus aspired to crown that city with metropolitan honors, exerting their personal influence to win for it a good reputation, encouraged within its bounds schools of science and art and general culture, and endeavored to render its residents loyal to Rome, peculiar privileges were conferred upon it, and even Paul was proud to be one of its citizens; he said "I am a man which am a Jew of Tarsus, a city in Cilicia, a citizen of no mean city."

One of the most solemn duties of a free country or community is that of choosing its officers and creating its leaders; it involves the exaltation or degradation of the whole, and it tells sooner or later on the destiny of society. A little printed ballot in the hands of a freeman is wonderfully suggestive, it not only tells the names of certain candidates for office, but it also tells the moral character of the man who deposits it. One cannot vote for narrowness and not be narrow himself, or for corruption and not be corrupt, or for wickedness and not himself be unrighteous. Your ballot is the expression of your feelings and desires, it is the profile of your moral self, by that little act of voting you exalt the city and help to add dignity to citizenship, or you surrender society to be overthrown by barbarians and vandals.

When the people shall be so well instructed in moral principle as that, they will choose men of good morals and good sense to represent them in council and in Congress, the evils that are now afflicting society will begin to fly away before the benediction of their noble endeavors, but until society is willing to vote for good men it must pay the price of its folly.

The reformation of society, therefore, implies first of all the reformation of the individual. But how shall this be done? Not by talk altogether; lectures and sermons may be good in their place, but of themselves they are inadequate; when duty is made evident we need something more potent than theory or argument; it is then that we need the heroism of an indomitable purpose.

The fact is, we are infidel, we crawl crab-like in the mud of slang, we are drunken and are addicted to filthy habits, because unwilling to break away; with truth on every hand, with culturing influences pressing upon us from every quarter, unbelief and uncleanness are not necessary, they are moral conditions that are preferred by indocile minds. We all know better than we do; what we need is a little individual heroism mixed with moral resolution.

Righteousness is indeed the only power that can exalt a nation or an individual; but righteousness is not attained at once, it does not grow over the soul like Jonah's gourd in a single night, it is the result of an effort of a life time. If therefore, young friend, you have any respect for yourself, or desire to bless the generation in which you live, then take the first step toward moral excellence, though you should never be able to attain unto its fullness; throw away that cigaret, expel that filthy quid from your mouth, dash the intoxicating cup from your lips, drop that slang, cease that profanity and turn away from that unbelief which each day is helping to degrade you more and more, and, no doubt, the first step will make you more confident to take the second. Let the text be your motto—"By the blessing of the upright, the city is exalted; but it is overthrown by the mouth of the wicked."

THE RESURRECTION BODY.

But some man will say, how are the dead raised up? and with
what body do they come?—*I Cor.* 15, 35.

Every man, woman and child is linked, by nearly two
hundred generations, to eternity. We have descended from
an uncountable ancestry, only two of whom have evaded
death; and pressed by a thousand forces we are each of us
hastening toward that dreadful termination.

In a century we shall have been swept utterly from
the stage; in fifty years scarcely a remembrance of us will
be left; in twenty-five years our generation will be superan-
uated; even so short a period as a decade will witness sad
havoc in this congregation; yes, in five years many will
have done their last work, and of some of us it is probably
true that this year we die. With such a destiny confronting us, how pertinent the question, if a man die shall he
live again?

Man cannot be stoical when mortality is before him,
he may postpone the answer to this question but the
question gathering force from every funeral dissolution,

sorrow, pain and fleeting hour comes back with over-whelming intensity, refusing to be crowded out by any philosophy of annihilation and demanding an affirmative reply.

To this important inquiry the soul answers, yes! although reason may reply, no! Man therefore is in perpetual agitation until the claims of immortality are fully satfied; not until then is it possible that meditation on death can be painless. We are unhappy until this decision is reached, and the soul is furnished for a world to come.

The revealed sublime truth of a resurrection is one of the many evidences of a continuance of existence after death. We propose, therefore, to consider this doctrine, and also the body in which the ressurrected will appear, "for some men will say, how are the dead raised up, and with what body do they come? Notice then

I. THERE WILL BE A RESURRECTION.

1. *It is inferred.* Stand on the sea shore, gather a handful of sand, the small grains fall through your fingers, a moment more and the inrolling tide buries them beneath its foaming bosom, there is no life, no beauty, yet, yonder perfect mirror that hangs on the palace wall, reflecting every form of life, every shade of color was made from those lifeless sands, the change seems incredible, it is true nevertheless; who knows therefore but the few grains composing our dust may, under the hand of a divine artisan, or by some mysterious elaboration of nature's forces, reflect the image of immortality in the eternal world?

A servant, it is said, received from his appreciative master a present of a silver cup; accidentally it fell into a large vessel of aquafortis, or nitric acid; it soon disappeared, of course; every trace was gone, and the servant sorrowed

over his misfortune; but at last the master came and pre-
cipitated the silver from the solution, and the silversmith
fashioned it into a cup more chaste and beautiful than the
original. So is it not impossible, after we have fallen into
our graves, and death has obliterated every remembrance on
earth of us, after surviving friends have sorrowed for our
departure, that omnipotence shall touch the forms that contain our dust, and command into his presence our bodies,
more perfect and beautiful, honored, spiritualized, immortalized, glorified?

It is said that the mummies that come from the Egyptian necropolis have not all been preserved according to the
same method, for the vitals of some have been removed-
while in other cases the vitals remain entire. It has been
supposed by certain chemists that the latter are bodies of
criminals, upon whom was performed a suspension of life,
with the intention of restoring them at some future time;
but that the method by which the suspension and revivis-
cence were produced is now a lost art. If the ancient
Egyptians could thus kill and make alive again, shall we
suppose that the possibility so to do is beyond the reach of
modern science? But if science can accomplish so much,
why should it be thought a thing incredible with you that
God can raise the dead?

That eminent Sweedish chemist, Dr. Grusselbach, spent
years in an endeavor to recover the lost art of resuscitation,
and was successful, so it is said, at least so far as to benumb
a snake, rendering it hard as a stone and brittle as glass, and
after preserving it in this state for several years he restored
it to life; indeed for fifteen years this animal underwent
through the experiments of the chemist a series of deaths
and resurrections. Now, if a man can accomplish
such wonders, even calling life into a petrifaction, is it impossible that omnipotence shall rebuild the dissolved man-
sion of a departed soul?

The question is, does God in nature ever work according to such a plan? Not only does the naturalist assure us that such is the case, but such a modus operandi has come under our own observations. For instance, take the common but beautiful illustration of the silk-worm. It envelopes itself in a silky web, simultaneously its form and its nature undergo a marvelous change, from a busy caterpillar it is transformed into an inactive unconscious chrysalis, requiring neither nutriment nor sunshine, and encoffined in its little cocoon it continues in this unconscious state from two weeks to two months, but at length supplied with wings, it bursts through its self-made sepulchre and soars forth a new creature, into the experiences of a new existence, and amid the scenes of a new creation.

Such analogies do not, it is true, intimate that man is immortal, but they show that an insect passes from one state of existence to another, and they suggest that a transformation and a translation need not be impossible to man, but that he may sometime come from the coffin and the grave to enter in triumph another sphere, and to pursue a nobler destiny.

But an objector may say that such comparisons are not parallels; they are but suspensions of animation, while death seems to be an actual termination; well. then, let us consider the vegetable; "that which thou sowest is not quickened except it die." Each seed sown, unless it lose its external contour and see corruption, is inadequate to future development and fruition; the decaying acorn is the embryo of the future forest, and the dying corn is the germ of the well-filled granary; this decay is but the removal of the obstructions that are in the way of the upspringing life. A beautiful vase, closely sealed, was found in a mummy pit in Egypt; it contained peas which had been coffined in the vase and entombed in the pit probably for

three thousand years; on the 4th day of June, 1844 they
were planted, and at the end of thirty days showed signs of
life; they grew; though buried for centuries they had lost
none of their vital power. If the life principle of a simple
pea remains thus undestroyed, what shall we hope for a
human being who has gathered all his living force from the
deathless forces of the universe?

Thus when we consider those transformations that appear in art, in science, and in nature, it is reasonable to in-
fer for man a ressurrection.

2. *It is revealed.* Notwithstanding the suggestive
analogies to which allusion has been made, the doctrine of a cor
poreal ressurrection, among ancient and modern theologians
and philosophers, has found many antagonists. It scarcely
entered into the polemics of the ante-christian world. While
the Pharisees silently accepted the doctrine the Saducees
openly denied it. Even at the time of Christ, while some
believed "many doubted." For teaching this new doctrine
as it was said to be, the apostles were arraigned before
courts of examination. By the learned literati of Athens
it was supposed that Paul recommended to the Pantheon a
new divinity when he spoke of this doctrine, so ignorant
were they of the idea of a resurrection. Pliny says it is
an impossible thing to call back the dead. Celsus calls the
hope of a resurrection the hope of worms. The Shasters do
not contain it; Confucius never grasped the thought; philosophy never discovered it in all its wanderings; science
never dictated its laws; poetry never found it in any of its
flights, and to the Koran it would have been unknown were
it not for the Cross. It is a truth peculiar to the Christian
revelation. With this light shining through the damp,
death-darkness, reason discovers in the grave an avenue to
eternity.

Let us then look into this revelation; first, in so far as it appears in the Old Testament; there we learn that Job, though through a mist of tears, could see the dim outline of the resurrection body, for he said, "in my flesh shall I see God." Isaiah, whose thought was in perpetual revolution about Jesus Christ said, "He will swallow up death in victory, thy dead men shall live, together with my dead body shall they arise; awake and sing ye that dwell in the dust, for thy dew is as the dew of herbs, and the earth shall cast out her dead." Hosea, concerning God in his power and goodness, declared, "I will ransom them from the power of the grave, I will redeem them from death. O death I will be thy plagues! O grave I will be thy destruction!"

But it is in the New Testament that this doctrine is most lucid; in the Old we see through a glass darkly, in the New face to face Unlettered fishermen like Peter proclaimed Christ and the resurrection, and well versed philosophers like Paul declared "the dead shall be raised incorruptible." To enumerate the texts were unnecessary. it is sufficient to remark that they teach a resurrection of the just and the unjust, and that Hymeneus and Philetus, who taught that the resurrection has already passed, are declared to be in error. Thus the Bible, if indeed it be a revelation from God, proves most forcibly the truth of a resurrection; it shows that the shattered pillar may be rebuilt, that the lost ship may be recovered from the billow, that the broken harp may be retuned to sweeter melodies, that though the flower is crushed its fragrance may be preserved, and that death is not an eternal sleep but the gateway to everlasting life.

We have seen that a resurrection may be inferred from the facts that are about us, and that it has been revealed in the Holy Scriptures; nor ought we fail to notice that

3. *It has been demonstrated.* If but one person has been raised from the dead, the truth of the resurrection is demonstrated. There is abundant evidence that at least one person, namely, the Lord Jesus Christ, did actually come forth from the grave and carry away the gates of death forever, for Christ died for our sins, was buried and rose again the third day, according to the Scriptures; he was seen of Cephas, then of the twelve, after that of above five hundred brethren at once, then of James, then of all the apostles, and finally of Paul as of one born out of due time. Christ therefore is risen from the dead and become the first fruits of them that slept. Nor can the testimony of these witnesses be refuted, for they spoke of what they knew, they had the testimony of their senses, they were not a credulous class, they did not believe nor even venture a statement until they had seen nor had they any reason for imposition, but on the contrary, every motive of self-interest required that they should tell the truth. If therefore we can believe the testimony of any witness we must believe the statements, of these apostles in regard to the fact that Christ arose from the dead.

But more, the testimony of the disciples was corroborated by the testimonies of their contemporaries. thus: Ignatius said " I know that after the resurrection Christ was in the flesh, and I believe him to be so still." Polycarp, an intimate friend of Ignatius, exhorted the people of Philippi to "believe in Christ whom God did certainly raise from the dead." Tertulian also declared that Pontius Pilate wrote to the Emperor Tiberius saying "because of his resurrection Christ is believed to be a God."

Five hundred persons and more, who had seen the risen Lord, must have uttered a most convincing testimony in favor of the resurrection. These testimonies added to the fear and the sophistries of the rulers, and to the sublime courage of the apostles worked their winning way into the convictions and the consciences of men. So convincing was the evidence that Christianity spread most amazingly during the apostolic age. Pliny the younger, who was consul and governor of Pontus, wrote A. D., 107, to the Emperor Trajan saying "many of all ages and every rank and of both sexes are accused (of being Christians), nor has the contagion seized the cities only, but the lesser towns, and the open country." Tertulian said "if the laws against Christians were enforced Carthage would be desolate." It could have been no weak or futile testimony that convinced the pagan and the philosopher, and which morally compelled people to believe despite the bloody hand of persecution that pursued them.

When any great event occurs, that event is usually immortalized by a monument of some kind, it may be a figure of bronze, a granite column, a triumphal arch, or a temples, for instance. Bunker Hill monument bears testimony to the fact that on the 17th of June, 1774, a battle was fought on that spot between the Americans and the British. So there are monuments that perpetuate in the minds and the memories of men the truth of the resurrection of Jesus Christ; not of stone, or of marble, not of silver or of gold, but that which is more suggestive and significant than architecture or sculpture could be; they are the Christian Church and the Christian Sabbath.

The Christian Church is a monument of the resurrection, it is built on this great and glorious truth. Ever since that first day of the week when, early in the morning loving women, with spices that they had prepared, went to the tomb for the purpose of embalming the body of Jesus, but instead found the stone rolled away, the sepulcher empty, and that two shining ones declared the Lord is risen. Ever since that memorable day the

Church has been propagating the truth of the resurrection and thousands and millions have been saved by its power.

The Christian Sabbath is also a monument of the resurrection. How came the Christian Sabbath if Christ is not risen? Ever since that resurrection morning the Sabbath has not been Saturday but Sunday; that great miracle was the hinge on which the day was turned; thus Ignatius said "let every one that loves Christ keep holy the Lord's day, the Queen of days, the resurrection day;" and Theophilis, sixty years after the death of John, said "reason challenges us to honor the Lord's day, thereby glorifying the resurrection of our Lord." That Christian Sabbath still lives; there may be those who profane it, but it will not die, and as long as time continues whenever six days have passed the soft, sweet, restful, holy Sabbath will come back again to tell the world that Christ is risen.

Thus there is abundant proof of the resurrection, it is inferred, it is revealed, it is demonstrated; the world is full of it, our hearts are touched with its inspiration. The resurrection of Jesus is the promise of ours, because he lives we shall live also. The rays of this hope-star shine down among the shadows of our Gethsemane, and up to the flashing brow of our Olivet. As Christ came up from the darkness of death, and arose from the Mount of Olives to the Father's House, so shall we come up from the gloomy vale, and, in the glory of the resurrection morning ascend to the mansions on high. Having shown that there will be a re surrection, we remark

II. THE RESURRECTION BODY WILL NOT BE A NATURAL ONE.

If the resurrection body is to be identical with that which is buried then the resurrection is not to me, a boon to be desired; the reinstatement of a disembodied soul in the old house of clay is not so pleasing a thought as that uttered by Paul, "God giveth it a body as it hath pleased him."

When the young, the beautiful, the vigorous, are suddenly cut down, we may long for the flashing eye and the protecting arm once more; but when dotage has plowed its furrows on the brow, or lengthened sorrow and protracted pain have robbed the human form of all its beauty, our finer feelings repel the thought that in such a form, with every earth-mark and defect prominent shall reappear the spirits of those we loved.

Against this doctrine of a literal lifting up of the old body, unchanged, into another life, science offers its decided protest. It assures us that these fleshly bodies so necessary to us now may be compounded with other substances; nature may replenish its wasted energies with them; storms and material convulsions may carry our mortal dust to the uttermost corners of earth, it may enter into the substance of some giant pine that flourishes on the mountain or some willow that laves its boughs in an undiscovered stream; indeed future generations may feed on the essence of our ashes. Science also declares these bodies are continually undergoing changes, that they are completely renewed every seven years, so that to gather up the fragments would necessitate the unforming of many natural formations, and man himself must crumble before his brother man. The testimony of science, therefore, while it may not controvert the abstract idea of a resurrection, raises its voice against that forbidding doctrine that the self-same body that was buried shall be resurrected in the self-same form.

It may be possible that there are individuals who, on their own responsibility, teach such a resurrection; but such teaching does not obtain in any system of theology with which I am acquainted. It is not, at least, taught in Methodist standards of theology. Raymond says of the feature body "it is both the same and another; the same in every essential to identity;" another in the sense of having been "changed so as to be qualified for the employments and enjoyments of the Heavenly state." Luther Lee taught that it will be a resurrection of the same body though greatly changed, spiritualized and glorified, and enters into an argument to show that great changes are consistent with sameness. Watson, who for many years has been the standard theologian of Methodism declares that in the resurrection the body will "experience great general changes as from corruption to incorruption, from mortality to immortality; great changes also of a particular kind will take place, as its being freed from deformities and defects, and the accidental varieties produced by climate, aliment, labor and hereditary disease." So far, therefore, as the philosophy of theology is concerned the objections and the remonstrances of science are hurled against the doctrine of the resurrection without any force or significance whatever. We do no believe in such strange things as some scientists suppose; but we teach that the resurrected body will be dispossessed of everything that rendered it gross and earthly; it will not be a natural body, and nature may do what it lists with the material that is cast away.

The phase "the resurrection of the body" jingles very prettily in the apostle's creed, but it is not the language of the apostles, it is true in a modified sense, but it is not exact and therefore it may be misleading; such an expression is not found anywhere within the covers of the Bible; in the Holy Scriptures the doctrine is presented, not as a ressurrection of the body, but a resurrection of or from the dead. It does indeed teach a certain corporiety, but the language is in harmony with good sense and sound philosophy, such as implies or asserts a particular, necessary, and wonderful change.

In the 15th chapter, first Corinthians, for instance, where Paul makes an argument specially on this subject, the apostle suggests that the body ensepulchered will bear the same relation to the body resurrected as does the seed sown to the grain that is harvested; or in the eloquent words of Dean Trench that "the decaying of the insignificant and unsightly seed in the earth, and the rising up out of that decay and death the graceful stalk and the fruitful ear, contains evermore the prophecy of the resurrection, even as this is in itself a resurrection, the same process at a lower stage, the same power putting itself forth on meaner things."

The apostle, still farther, proceeds to show by his reasoning, not that the product of the resurrection will not be a real body, but that it will not be the same precisely that sorrowing survivors consigned to its narrow home. Thus, he argues that there are differences even among terrestrial things; all flesh is not the same: there is one kind of flesh of man, another of beasts, another of fishes, another of birds; so the glory of the terrestrial is one, and the glory of the celestial is another; and we who have borne the image of the earthly, that is the terrestrial, must also bear the image of the Heavenly, that is the celestial, and the reason is because flesh and blood cannot inherit the Kingdom of God. So important is this putting away of the earthly and this putting on of the heavenly, that those who on the last day shall not have slept in death must nevertheless be "changed in the twinkling of an eye." The apostle indeed announces in the most unambiguous manner that the body sown is natural, impotent, unhonored, corrupt, while the ressurrection body is incorruptible, glorious, powerful, spiritual. It might therefore be safely concluded that the immortal soul, subsequent to physical dissolution, will never be rehabilimented with the gross and fleshly garments which once it cast aside.

But the Lord Jesus Christ also teaches that the resurrection body will not be a natural body. To a thoughtful mind the words of Our Lord are pregnant with suggestion. He declares that in the resurrection they neither marry nor are they given in marriage, but are like the angels of God, this implies a considerable change of structure.

The New Testament also represents, though the stomach is now adapted to meats and meats to the stomach, yet "God will destroy both it and them." This declaration too is suggestive, it signifies that the animal appetite for food will be done away, and that the organ adapted to that appetite shall have no place in the resurrection.

Now, if the resurrected body is to be immortal not mortal, incorruptible not corruptible; if the resurrected are not to marry or to be given in marriage, if they are not to eat and drink, if the demand for material food is to be destroyed, if we are to be like the angels of God, nay, if our bodies are to be likened unto Christ's most glorious body, then it cannot be natural, it cannot be precisely the same as that mass of decay and corruption that was consigned to dust and ashes.

We mistake if we fancy that those simple elements of which the human body is composed are sufficient for a residence in a world of spirits. Certain proportions of potash, lime and iron cannot produce a body like unto the most glorious body of Christ. In the grave we shall drop mortality; with mortality will go materiality, its wearying burdens, its diseases, its pains. its infirmities, its weaknesses, its defects; the grossness of our decaying natures will dissolve away: from the lifeless sands will flow the bright mirror of immortality; out of the flesh destroying tomb will come the burnished chalice: and from the hand of death will spring the fadeless bloom of spiritual beauty.

We shall come forth immortal from the grave; we shall have a building of God not made with hands; we shall be satisfied when we awake in his likeness.

III. THE RESURRECTED BODY WILL BE SPIRITUAL.

Let us inquire what a spiritual body may be. Revelation contains no description, but enough is said to enable us to adduce a fair inference.

The word spirit is a term by which we designate whatever is unnatural, superhuman or supermundane. Literally the word spirit means wind, breath, or air in motion, and is applied to the vapory, the volatile, and the etherial. It is a term that is sometimes made to stand for the higher intellectual and moral endowments of man. All disembodied beings, and all intelligencies who have never been possessed of a body of matter are called spirits, and, it is the only word we have with which to express our idea of the nature of God,—"God is a spirit. Derived from the word spirit is the word spiritual, by which we mean that this or that consists of spirit, or pertains to spirit.

These terms are used with the same significance in the Scriptures as in the Lexicon: and the Hebrew and Greek words which are translated spirit mean literally wind or breath, and refers, in a wide sense, to whatever is not grossly material, the higher refinements of matter, and that which is absolutely independent of matter. The word spiritual occurs once in the Old Testament and perhaps twenty times in the New. Thus the Bible speaks of the spiritual as opposed to the carnal and the natural; it speaks of spiritual things, that is doctrines, truths, experiences; spiritual bread, that is bread supernaturally provided; spiritual men, men who have grown above all grossness and have received the blessing divine: it speaks also of a spiritual house, that is the whole family of God's redeemed children; it speaks also of spiritual wickedness, or fallen angels, and it announces the fact of a spiritual body or a body pertaining to the spirit-life and the spirit world.

The most potent force in the universe is not matter but spirit. The microscope may disclose happy communities of insects on the petals of a rose, but it has never discovered the vital force, the spirit that inheres in a flower. The physiologist may discover the tiny sack enclosing a fluid in which floats a few granules or animated atoms, and declare that he has found the life substance, and perhaps he has, but the power, or spirit by which it is endowed with vitality he cannot find. Newton discovered the law that binds this universe together and keeps the starry host in revolution, but the power itself has never been disclosed even under the lens of the strongest telescope. We can discover nothing but results. the appropriating arranging spirit is invisible.

Now Scripture suggests that man is a three in one; that he is possessed of a living soul which is the result of the divine inbreathing; also of a body which has been formed from the dust of the earth; and besides he is possessed of a spirit, an appropriating and arranging power, a vital something that holds soul and body together. This vital principle may lie dormant for awhile. but when the trumpet shall sound it will arouse to immediate activity and produce for the soul a new tabernacle such as will be suited to a spiritual life and a spiritual world.

What then is a spiritual body? Let me answer this question by noticing what it is not, and what it is. It is not an extraction, some bone, some germ, taken out of the old frame, but it is rather an expansion of an essence already existing, it is an addition or something put on, for the apostle declared that "this corruption must put on incorruption, and this mortal must put on immortality.', The natural body is not a descension, something that is to come down from above, no new creature will descend from the creative hand to meet the ascending spirit. This dissolving tabernacle spoken of by the apostle is the present world, not the human body, and when the world shall dissolve and pass away, God's immortal children will live in another world or house, a house not made with hands eternal in the heavens. No new tabernacle will descend from Heaven to receive the resurrected spirit, for the resurrection is not a descension but a bona fide resurrection, the body will be "raised in incorruption, raised in glory, raised in power."

Nor will the spiritual body be a growth, for the body buried though sown in dishonor, is not a seed, and the body raised, though raised in power, is not a plant. The spiritual body therefore is not a result of law, nor a product of time, nature's forces have nothing to do with it, but it shall come forth suddenly, in a moment, responsive to the fiat of God. When Jehovah shall say to the North give up, and to the South keep not back, when the sea shall give up its dead and Death and Hell shall deliver up the dead that are therein, then "we shall all be changed in a moment, in the twinkling of an eye, at the last trump, for the trumpet shall sound, and the dead shall be raised incorruptible, and we shall be changed."

Nor will the spiritual body be a shadow, a nonenity, it will be real, substantial, it will be possessed of form, contour individuality, it will be a body, like unto the one that was buried save that it will have been rebuilt on a spiritual basis. Nor will this rebuilding interfere with identity or recognition; it will be a finer substance stamped with the same unchangeable seal; the individual soul will impress itself on the new form, therefore there will, there must be personal recognition in the resurection.

As we have seen, the resurected body will not be a natural body. It will not be produced by natural law, nor organized according to the plan of nature. It will not be made up of dissolving atoms, it will not be supported by natural products, nor will it be liable to disease or accident, nor will it serve the same purposes as a natural body. It will not live in the same conditions of existence, it will be immortal.

Relieved of all grossness, like the pure atmosphere of mountain altitudes,and imponderable as a beam of light,it will be purely spiritual; it will not be a burden as now it is but helpful like the wings to a bird, in service it will renew its strength; it will be capable of surmounting gravitation as did Christ when he ascended the skies; it will run to and fro like a spark or a fire, it will mount up with wings as of eagles; it will be transparent so that the soul will shine through as it did in the case of Christ when his face became glorious as the sun, or effulgent as when the Son of Man appeared to the dreamer of Patmos; with feet of flame it will speed lightning-like over immeasurable distances; it will partake of all the powers and possibilities of the spirit; it will live in immortal youth; and it will bear forever the glorious image of its glorified Lord; for "as we have borne the image of the earthly we shall also bear the image of the Heavenly."

In conclusion, how sublime is the truth we have contemplated! Can it be possible that man feels no interest? True the next world can take care of itself, and present duty demands present attention, yet the hereafter has a bearing on the now, and present responsibility has altogether a different meaning because life is to continue forever to what it could have if being must be blotted out in a little while.

Considering the fact that each of us is possessed of a soul that time cannot destroy; that even our bodies having slept in the grave a little while will survive the shock of death; that there is a judgment coming, and that the verdicts of that day will fix us in weal or in woe forever, is it not strange that we blind our eyes and harden our hearts, unwilling to think, refusing to feel; is it not most singular that we persistently cling to sin and trample on offered mercy though heaven woos and the tribunal trumpet thunders? Oh sinner, you are immortal! Should you not by moral culture prepare yourself for the highest possible destiny? You are a steward of the Almighty, the present is your work-day. "much of your time has run to waste", you are not ready to meet the responsibilities of that great day. Oh repent! Are you willing upon soul and body that should outshine the sun, to have writ, recreant, base, doomed.

THE END.

EATON AND HEMPEL,

WILLIAMS' BLOCK,

BEAVER DAM, WIS.

COLLECTIONS

IN THE UNITED STATES OR CANADA

PROMPTLY MADE.

D. D. BATHRICK,

DEALER IN

SHELF AND HEAVY HARDWARE

BEAVER DAM, WISCONSIN.

——o——

A tin shop in connection in charge of Mr. J. E. Flanders. Country jobs receive prompt attention at reasonable prices.
——A full assortment of——

COOK AND HEATING STOVES

always in stock. Call and see the

ADAMS AND WESTLAKE OIL STOVE.

Three-Burner.

Monarch A.

The oven is made of tin and lined with sheet-iron. Heat passes first under the vessels then into the oven. The heating chamber is made of cast iron. No other oil stove is made in which such a variety of cooking can be done at the same time. Will do as much work in the same time as any six-burner.

For Sale by D. D. BATHRICK.

J. M^CKINSTRY,

UNDERTAKER

AND DEALER IN

FURNITURE

——AND——

UPHOLSTERY.

The Undertaking department is complete, having a large stock of the finest

COFFINS AND CASKETS,

A SPLENDID HEARSE AND EVERYTHING

REQUISITE IN THE BURIAL

OF THE DEAD.

Opposite National Bank.   BEAVER DAM, WIS.

DEALER IN

GROCERIES,

PROVISIONS,

BOOTS AND SHOES.

SECOND DOOR WEST OF NATIONAL BANK.

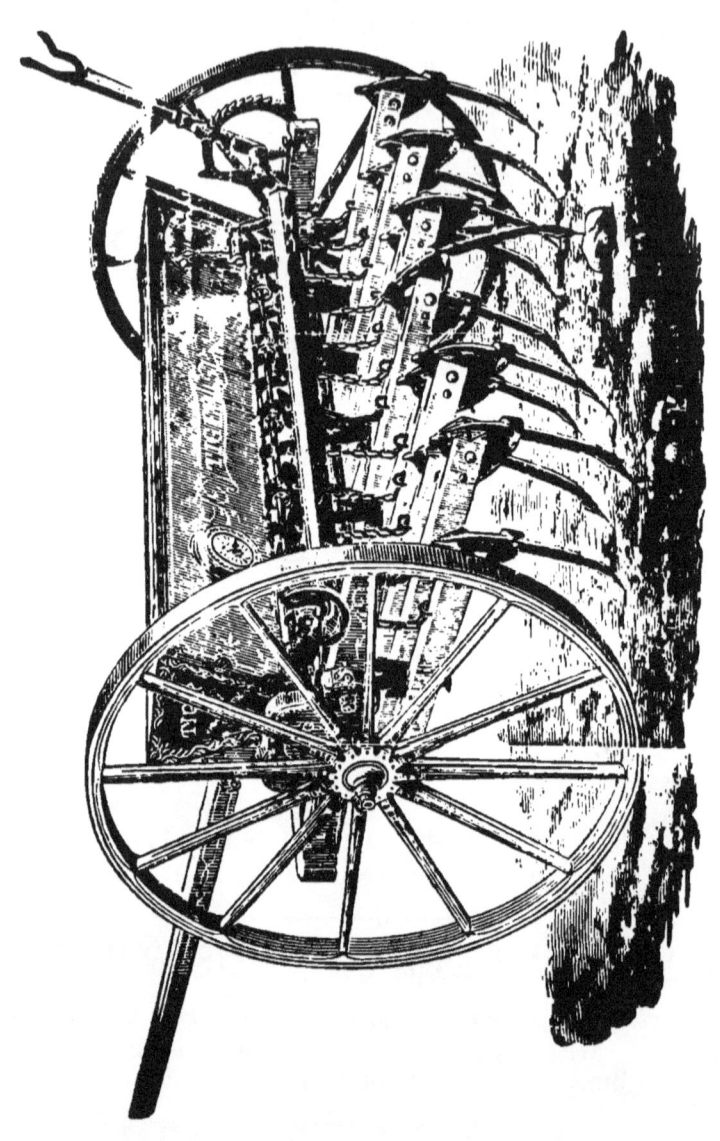

IMPROVED TIGER SEEDER With Drag Bars of Wood or Iron.

J. S. ROWELL, SONS & CO.,

BEAVER DAM, - WISCONSIN,

Manufacturers of the

First Practical Seeder Used

——In the United States.——

W. E CALLEN,

(Formerly of Milwaukee,)

PAINTER,

PAPEP HANGER

AND

DECORATOR

OF

DRAWING ROOMS

AND

CHURCHES.

Will furnish original designs. attend to all calls in City or Country promptly, and warrant satisfaction in his work.
Address Box 217, Beaver Dam, Wis.

MR. CALLEN Decorated the Audience Room of First M. E. Church, tastefully, beautifully and to the entire satisfaction of all concerned. J. L. HEWITT.

DEALER IN

FANCY GROCERIES,

CROCKERY,

GLASSWARE,

MENS' AND BOYS' HATS,

GENT'S FURNISHING GOODS,

NOTIONS, ETC.,

WOULD BE PLEASED TO SHOW HIS GOODS

AND INVITES ALL VISITORS TO

EXAMINE THEM.

FRONT STREET. - - MUSIC HALL BLOCK.

BEAVER DAM, WISCONSIN.

DEALER IN

BIRD CAGES,

BIRD SEED. GOLD FISH.

AQUARIUMS,

WIRE GOODS,

RUSTIC WORK, FLOWER POTS

A First-class Christian School, for the higher education of young women, under the control of the leading Religious Denominations.

SCIENTIFIC, CLASSICAL AND MORAL DEPARTMENTS

Massive buildings, comfortable rooms; newly painted and refitted throughout.

Do not send your girls to the Convent or District school when they can have such a safe and delightful home, with unequalled advantages in Music, Science, and Art.

Please write for circulars and catalogue to

MISS HELEN A. PEPOON,

FOX LAKE. WISCONSIN.